ALSO BY BRUCE OLDS

Raising Holy Hell

BUCKING THE TIGER

FARRAR, STRAUS AND GIROUX

NEW YORK

Bucking the Tiger

A NOVEL BY

BRUCE OLDS

FARRAR, STRAUS AND GIROUX
19 Union Square West, New York 10003

Grateful acknowledgment is made for permission to reproduce the following:

"Concession": Copyright © 1992 by N. Scott Momaday, from *In the Presence of the Sun* by N. Scott Momaday, reprinted by permission of St. Martin's Press, LLC.

"T.B. Sheets": Words and music by Van Morrison. Copyright © 1967 by Universal Music Publishing International Limited. Administered by Universal–Polygram International Publishing, Inc. (ASCAP). International Copyright secured. All rights reserved.

Library of Congress Cataloging-in-Publication Data
Olds, Bruce.
    Bucking the tiger / Bruce Olds.—1st ed.
      p.   cm.
    ISBN 0-374-11727-6 (alk. paper)
     1. Holliday, John Henry, 1851–1887—Fiction.   2. Gamblers—Fiction.
  3. Dentists—Fiction.   4. Outlaws—Fiction.   I. Title.

PS3565.L336 B84 2001
813'.54—dc21

                                           00-068172

Designed by Gretchen Achilles

To Allen Peacock,
and to Bryce, old pard—

and for Paul Metcalf (1917–1999), in memoriam

analect n. The select part, the choice essence; the "cream" or marrow.

analects n. pl. 1. Crumbs that fall from the table; pickings-up, gleanings. 2. Literary gleanings; collections of fragments or extracts.

bricolage n. *Fr. phr.* Construction or creation from whatever is immediately available for use; something constructed or created in this way; an assemblage of incongruous elements.

catena n. 1. A chain, a connected series. a. (More fully *catena patrum*): A string or series of extracts from the holy writings (the writings of the fathers) forming a commentary; also, a chronological series of extracts to prove the existence of a continuous tradition on some point of doctrinal debate. b. Generally, "chain, string."

contemperation n. 1. A blending together or commingling of elements of different character; blended condition; the product of such commingling. 2. The action of tempering, moderating or qualifying by mixture; a qualifying admixture. 3. Adaptation, adjustment, accommodation. 4. Accommodation to opposite courses of action by blending both.

disjecta membra n. *Lat. phr.* An alteration of Horace's *disjecti membra poetae*: "limbs of a dismembered poet"; used = Scattered Remains.

The way you sought death out, savored its taste.
The sadness just beneath your joyous valor.

—GARCÍA LORCA

I go on pursuing through the hours another tiger,
the beast not found in verse.

—JORGE LUIS BORGES

PART

One

DOWNBAR THROUGH THE sawdust, back here in the backmost backroom, four men—three of them carp-eyed, shaggy and increasingly deep in their drams—are draped over armless chairs, armless, wingbacked, split-bottomed chairs irregularly intervaled around an octagonal table inlaid with baize, derrydown green.

The back of the fourth, as stems from his wont, is squared to the wall half hunched to the table, right shoulder hefted, high-cocked. A plait of polycolored rawhide spills insouciantly from the back of his hat brim tigertailing the nape of a neck white and sleek as a swan's. (The rest of him too; thin as a whim, no more than a slat of beached driftwood inside a hollow gray suit.) He wears the hat, an immaculate black, on a raffish cant slung so low to the brow that while one can discern beneath the eave of its awning both the manicured batwing of a silver-blond moustache and the chevron of a recently raised imperial, the eyes remain largely a rumor. His pallor is the color of caulk.

Outside the rain's bent ragged, slanting down in scars. Mile off, less maybe, lightning trims the bark off a tree. Thunder jaws some, shirrs. Wind sharks. It's one of those nights again, eighth this week (seems like)—boding, broody, black as hornblende, like the sky clewed up all the good light, each lick, then lit out with it hellbent for home.

Smoke yeasts nicotine yellow, scrums sallow above the heads of the four players, patches there, sags some, then rankles up in quills through saloon saffron lamplight inside Nuttall & Mann's No. 10, Deadwood, Dakota Territory, another jungled, jagged, endless 4 a.m. The smoke lends a measure of grain to the light; the light is possessed of some burl. This Hour, as the professionals call it, of the Meridian.

Wild Bill cashed it in around here someplace, rumor has it, while back, August last; old news, though they've yet to bestir themselves to tack up the plaque in tribute—to his memory, or the brass of its myth.

Room's a humidor, close as a hairshirt, sodden with stench: spittoon, cuspidor and gaboon, long-staled cigar, spilt beer, sloshed whiskey, skittish men's sweat; keg pickle, Scotch egg, Limburger cheese; cowhide and soaped leather, buckskin and brine, fester, funk, fresh blood and kerosene. And fear. Rank, rancid airlessness of it. That clabbered mortality.

His face sweats down his shirtfront, soaks its pastel, blue-through. (His weskit, a cinch-waist, fleur-de-lis, silver-and-black brocade, is flocked with hawks-aloft, turquoise-and-teal, raised velvet weltings, the gold stickpin in his left lapel inset with a diamond the size of a drupe.) Atop the table upon which the cards lie before him one down and four up, an uncorked, near-empty bottle of Gideon's Brown butlers a shotglass two fingers full. With his left hand, a hand kid-gloved so tight-to it appears painted on flesh, he slips a splint of long-nine black cheroot from the clench of his teeth; with his right, hooks the shotglass, raising it to his lips, then glutches back its contents before sliding it drained, croupier-like back to its place beside the bottle. Crisp as a salute. He feels the familiar scald of its descent in advance of the searing suffusion; fume surf.

This, he thinks, this right here and right now, this alone matters. The rest—once upon a time? happily ever after?—all that's so much stemyanking.

He stacks his chips in impeccable chimneys, seldom worrying them the way his opponents intermittently do, drumming the ones on top against those below or letting them draggle absently through the channels of his fingers: whites, blues, reds, yellows; 25 cents, $1, $10, $50. At the moment he is down some, sucking wind and running light, light enough to be flirting with bust. Indeed he is but a single misstep from being cleaned out to the quick by his foes—Bill Massie, Carl Mann and Charley Rich, the latter most flush by far. It's reckon a way to jigsaw this hand, *now*, or duck shit-out-of-luck for the door.

When he coughs, ructioned and roughshod, as at protracted length, it is deep, wet, pleural and bronking, a braying from the belly of both lungs—rake across washboard, gravel out a grate, barbed wire drug through a pipe. The others, those seated at the table as likewise the mopes, gawks and railbirds slouched along the walls, visibly wince, flinch and shrink back as if in expectation of his bones bolting as free of their sockets as loose change spilled from a pocket.

Hackling something more lotion than not—membrane, morsel, red thread of thorax—into the flag of silk that he fishes unfurled from his breast pocket, after a moment's scrutiny he folds it back on itself before rearranging the geometry of its corners and returning it fluffled like a flower, boutonniered in place. His moustache is glistered, a smutch of cerise, and it is only with the utmost effort that he ignores the impulse to harrow his hand through the broken bread of his body as a raft one might wrest over reef. His lungs feel as if they are being flensed, or their ticking filed at with fleam teeth; he is coughing himself fraught to fractions—curd, clot, each necrotic clod through the cud—a decimal at a time.

Recovering just enough of himself—the sight of his own blood, the rouge of its livery, while one with which he is intimately acquainted, never fails to appall him—the words tilt out from beneath the hat, spindrift and spume: You need pardon me, boys, but I fear you find me mired in a slump and upon the steep decline, the old *élan* gone forfeit, its *vital* but fuel to the Void. The thing about dying is, after a while it drains all the sand from a

5

man. Hourglass empties, if you catch my meaning. Might I suggest, I have seen much my better days.

The rain is a prod at the window; when it beckons him on he pushes away from the table, lags over and, a sidelong eye still fixed on the competition, leans his forehead flat to the smooth cool of its pane. Trying the sash he discovers it will not budge. The rain is a taunt. He requires the grim monotony of its air, longs to cleanse the rhythm of his breathing in the solvent of its clarity, to take the storm inside his head, but when he pounds his fist against the glass, it will neither star nor shatter.

An inch or two shy of six feet, no more than 130 pounds, he appears a man at low wick, as one possessed of having nothing worth losing to lose. Something about his life, and then again his having to live it, to keep breathing, the way the two seem hourly to cleave closer and closer apart; he cannot help thinking that something inevitably must happen to distract him, to oblige him to cease paying heed, forget himself, glance aft, lose track of the tide of his lungs, if only for an instant, and by the time he slews round again—pfffft!—he will have disappeared. He knows that impunity is a lie, perhaps the greatest lie of all, knows that no one walks away from it without having been punished for the privilege, that no one escapes unthrashed or unthwarted, he knows that none of us, not a one of us, thrives.

You in, Holliday, or you got it in mind to stare out that window 'til you catch sight of Wild Bill's ghost?

Guffaws all around.

Only at some length does he lift his forehead from the glass. His brow is naturally waffled and it bequeaths its imprint, sheet music to the pane. Delaying his resumption at the table until it's become a positive dodge, he waits to reclaim his seat before easing the remark from its scabbard: Gents, a thought. You can tell a lot about a man from the way he goes about killing himself, would you not agree?

His eyes roundelay the table, snake eyes laughing, but no one sees it, how they're being made sport of and boshed, how they're being guyed. They just shift vaguely, one by one, null-eyed in their chairs.

So doubles back, tries again: Care to know why I loathe it so, this life? Yes? No? Fine then—it's because it's a killer, that's why. Nought but a motherless tyrant. The hateful part about living is, it insists that each day you wake up . . . you're alive.

Which at least, at last, stirs a response. Viz: Come on, Doc, you scarecrowed, morbid sumbitch, knock it off. Give the macabre shit a rest for once. Christ on the fucking cross, there's got to be ten thousand dollars potted there. Goddamn ghoul, play the hand, Doc, or pay the devil his due.

The remark, recited by the three, as it seems to him, in perfect unison, bites through a round of briary looks bunching hard upon the boil.

What was it? he thinks. A year ago? Less? Right here someplace. This very table, could have been, this very chair. Aces and eights. Caught him holding, aces and eights. Deadman's hand. Deadman's hand dead in its deathclutch. Back of his head blown clean out its fore. Skullchip, brain, grume-spattered floor. What was it Ben Thompson had once told him? Every time a man sits down to a card game to gamble he takes his life in his hands and lays it between himself and his adversary. Well, Bill knew that better than most, Wild Bill did, and all it got him—however pickled at the time on pink gin—was bushwhacked.

But tonight? Tonight it's all the unkindness of the cards. Discard, deadwood, rubbish, refuse, trash not fit for a scow. Famine and drought, loss after loss, hand after hand, not a break to be bought. Cold and colder still, cold as a corpse content in its crypt.

Until . . . now. This hands-down winner. Cinch hand. Nut hand. *Monster* hand. Full house, jack high in the hole, jacks and sevens showing, and the pot the splashiest one of the evening, richest one all week, a corker he's bet up after his rule, "always wager a winning hand to the hilt for not a thin dime less than it's worth." And just the single hand to beat, Massie and Mann since having folded, the one to his immediate left, the queens, Charley Rich's. Those three cunts showing.

Peels off his gloves, slowly, de-li-ber-ate-ly, m-e-t-h-o-d-i-c-a-l-l-y, left first, then right, laying them out, smoothing them down, ironing them flat across the table, buying time. All the time in the world. A bluff, but why not? Savoring it.

Then flexes his fingers, bloodless as icicles; they snick like aged kindling. (Years hence the Aspen *Daily Times* will write: "They are such—clipped, filed, shaped, buffed, and apparently lustrously lacquered—as one seldom encounters save upon the most dextrous [*sic*] of surgeons. Long, lithe, supple as harpstrings, expressive as swan's wings, his fingers are decidedly those of a concert pianist's. Or professional pistoleer's.")

He has been having this nightmare lately. Three, sometimes four times a week. His fingers are made of wire. Telegraph wire. There is no feeling in them, no sensation, no song, nothing but the numbness of copper and copperjacketing, and no matter how much he has at them with the sandpaper, nothing. And then someone—just whom he could not say; he has yet to delineate a face—steals into his room while he is sleeping and snips them off at the bottom knuckle with a shears, clean as scalpel. In the morning he awakens to his fingers strewn across the floor like cuticle.

Inside its bone pouch his brain is maniac.

And then . . .

It happened so quickly, extraordinarily quickly, quick as miracle, that's the one thing everyone would agree upon later. True story, and you were there.

(There are times when the mind is so perfectly aligned to the uncoiling of the moment, the moment of thought so immaculate, taut and unleavened, so clean with acuity, that only the poise of physical madness remains.)

The call is made, he is called, and as he thumbs over his hole card—the jack of hearts—with his right hand, he abruptly spins in his chair, the sheer swiftness of this unprovoked gesture, its suddenness, blank surprise, butt swiveling torquing towards Rich smooth as churned butter, pivot of pirouette, at the same time same motion the same hand flowing inside the flap of his coat jerking the knife from his armpit glancing 7-inch veer of steel one second inside then outside the frock, hare jacked from a hat, his left hand meanwhile having tackled Rich's left wrist locking it up shackling it down staking it flat upon the table where . . . pitch of poured metal stab, bladestrike to plungepoint, no spray outsplay no bump of blood but dull stun of wood stemming clean through corsage.

Through butterfly, pinned palm down to tabletop. Trumped.

Nor a sound save the wind and the rain, their strafe through his drawl: My dear Sir, if the queen of hearts, as you but a moment ago thought to fob it sight unseen from your vest, is not just there impaled beneath your hand, as I know it upon the memory of my sainted mother to be, I fear I do owe you an apology.

Sun's up hard. Outspread and splashy. Dayfall strewn like scree. Against its orange chafe, through the lungburn, hefts Kate off her feet, hoisting her into the sling of his arms as he punts the hotel room door open with a bootpoint; crosses its threshold like a groom.

Where for the next two hours, engulfed, the love of your life, this woman—the having come home to the hasp of her. The high hinge of her hips your horizon.

Strange...

How, however briefly, bedraggled
history
        focuses
            —MICHAEL ONDAATJE

Yet does it all come miraculously to life?
Or is it the solitary crank who's right,
The unofficial historian?
            —JOHN ASHBERY

So start over,
begin again,
try it (hovering?) from another a

         n

          g

           l

            e

i.   doc was born out of health but in those days they still called him john henry. (by the way this is the true history, the one true one, the authentic one, the only one, his history squared, the history that ghosts above history, the more-than-history, not the other one, that other one, the untrue one, the one that's hash that's been rehashed before.)

ii.   doc was born not doc but john henry and the moment he learned he was dying that was the end of john henry and the beginning of doc. they called him doc because by then he had his PhD and it took less time to say and time was the one thing doc did not have. that was and remains doc's true history. he lived his life on the clock, at the end of a rope, each tick, every tock, dangling. he lived less his life than his death. lived fast. the irony is he did not die that way. not right away. he died in due time. and that is his true history too. would he have lived and died differently if he had not caught a losing hand from the start? who knows? to cheat death you need to bluff life and though the deck was stacked squarely against him he played the cards he'd been dealt for all they were worth. they weren't worth much. he played them anyway. that is both the beginning and the end of his history.

iii.   there is history, his/stories, and they say that doc was a killer and murderer. the truth is he killed a few but not many and those mainly of necessity. the truth is he didn't have much use for killing or histories or stories, most of all his own. those were just words and he was too busy dying to pay them much heed. the irony is he never did, die. not really. he's still alive, and that is his true history too.

iv. doc saved wyatt earp's bacon in dodge and if it wasn't for that some say what would have become of him, who'd have noticed, who cared, just another lunger, another cardsharp and sot, just another gunhand for hire. wyatt earp never said such things because wyatt earp knew better. wyatt earp knew that doc was fast, so fast that come to a throwdown between them there'd be nothing but a dead wyatt to show for it. so that's the true history of how and why they became friends. wyatt in his fashion feared doc and doc in his fashion loved wyatt. this is how they made true authentic history together.

v. finally doc died which had been the plan from the start though not in the way that he'd planned it. he'd planned to be dead long before and now that he wasn't the thought of immortality so ate at him he became delirious in his lungs and committed suicide. or rather his lungs did which amounts to the same thing. the point is that though it took a while he finally succeeded in doing himself in. the true history is that it could only have been doc who killed doc because scores had tried their hand at it while he was alive and never come close and it could not have been the devil because everyone knew that if doc was faster than wyatt then he must be faster than the devil and so doc was left as he always was to do the dirty work himself. so he rented a cheap hotel room in a remote and rotten climate, bought a tin of fine cheroots, several cases of even finer mescal, burned every stitch of his clothing, threw all the windows open onto the elements, willed himself insomniac, and for months on end smoked and drank and went without sleep the whole while breathing himself in until what he was breathing was the humor of death itself. the true history is that doc breathed himself to death, inhaled and inhaled until each cell in his body had inverted to nothing but vapor. people said as well they might that they had never seen anything like it. when the time came to bury the remains the only part left was a pair of purulent lungs. they called it consumption which it surely was because something had consumed him all right. but it wasn't death, not for a minute. what did doc in at last was his life.

vi. so there you have it, the whole true authentic history of doc holliday. he entered the world ailing, perfected the art of going downhill from there, had himself a few laughs, captured an imagination or two, stayed the course as long as he could and having gone half the distance and failing to find anyone else up to the job, cashed himself in ahead of time infinitely worse off for the wear—this life of decomposition. there are other details of course, there always are, but those are for the devil to sort. what's here is the truth. every word of it. and all the ones that aren't.

THE END

———•••••———

He had to be wild or he was nothing in particular.
He had to go fast, like an American.

—CHARLES OLSON

There are the riches that await those intent upon their going
for the sake of nothing more
than someday being

gone

I BECAME DOC'S friend because once, in Dodge, he saved me from being killed by desperadoes. I remained his friend because he made me laugh, and because he was as loyal to me as blood. For several years he watched my back, and in those years, while he stood fast, my back suffered not a scratch. That alone ought tell you everything you need to know about him.

He was a dentist, but preferred to be a gambler.

He was a Southerner, but preferred to roam the West.

He had been bred a stiffnecked Presbyterian, but preferred to play the prodigal.

He was a poet, but preferred to act the wag.

He was a ladies' man, yet sought the solace of but a solitary woman's bed.

He was highly educated, yet chose to travel in untutored, shiftless, largely brutish circles.

He was by natural temperament a philosopher and fatalist whom life had made a dark and caustic wit, and that death had turned outlandishly dangerous. And while his nerve was stainless steel, his heart was purest gold, though as far as the world in general was concerned, there was nought but iron in his soul.

I never knew him when he was not bent upon dying, though that was scarce his fault. At one time or another I had doings with them all—Wes Hardin, Clay Allison, James-Younger boys, Dave Rudabaugh, Ben Thompson, Dalton-Doolin gang, Billy Bonney himself—and he was by far the most desperately minacious character I ever spent time around. If he's come down through history as what we used to call a gun-thrower and a Bad Man generally, well, it's hardly the first time history's pegged a man awry. Oh, he'd fight if he had to, fight like Attila himself—he was game to the endmost last ditch—but it wasn't natural to his grain. For one thing he was weak, weak and sickly and failing and each day failing further, and if on occasion there were those, as on occasion there were, who sought to gain his bulge, to call him out, back him up, face him down—well, no, he would not have it. He felt cornered enough by his life, I suppose, and did not take kindly to the crowding.

That said, it serves no purpose to pretend that trouble did not follow him about like a tag-along. He was prone to it, like an allergy, the way some are lent to nightmares over dreams. There's individuals in this world just seem to walk through it a bull's-eye on their back, and Doc was one of 'em—he attracted the lightning.

Overfavored by nature, he was remarkably handsome, or would have been had so much of what makes a man that way not got chamfered out and wasted. His chin was firm, his mouth more slender than a sash, but his eyes—huge and hugely blue, and buried deep in their beds as blue glyphs—were more alive than any ten men. I never saw a human soul look so haunted by the best that might have been. He spilled breeding and intelligence all over the place, but what you remembered most, what I remember to this day, is how dwindled and bone haggard and pale he looked in every tuck of himself.

As he was disposed to permit it, I would from time to time guy him upon the subject. "How goes it, Doc?" I'd say. "Appears you're all pluck, rising sap, and about as pink as pink can be. Looking more like death than ever."

"A corpse, Sir," he would invariably reply. "You address but the warmed-over remains of a corpse."

"A corpse, is it?" I'd say. "Then you *are* the miracle. A corpse that walks and talks."

"Oh, but nothing like a miracle, Sir," he'd say. "A mirage. Smokescreens and mirrors. Nothing but an illusionist's cheap trick." And fob the watch from the pocket of his vest. "But check back with me in an hour or two, and perhaps you'll find it shattered."

His code, as he once confided it to me, was simple: that no man is so contemptible, so vile or so base, as he who would flee from his demons. That Doc did his fleeing from time to time, too often at the bottom of a bottle, he would not have quarreled. Indeed his outstanding peculiarity was the amount of whiskey he could punish in a day. But whether he was running from death hellbent on some higher freedom, or rather hurtling towards it that he might feel more finely the fullness of its embrace, I would not care to say.

He lived half his life waiting to die, and the other half outlasting the dawn. Always had a hunch it was the tension between the two, the stress, that human geology that wrought of him so much the maverick, the roué and rogue, so much the singular solitaire. Moment to moment his existence was purely a balancing act, and if he seldom faced less than a tough sled, he never rode it down with less than brass balls. All his life, a matter of losing ground, until so little remained underfoot, he'd plumb lost track of the lot. Like a fog, way it struck me, some mist that's slowly lifting and taking its futility with it 'til nothing's left behind but the outline of its absence and the fragrance of its thought. That there were those who thought him self-consumed, well, they were closer to the literal truth than they ever could have presumed. Hell, I reckon there's something amiss in us all, and what was half-cocked about Doc was nothing I couldn't let pass or stand for.

They say that what you can't fix you better learn to live with, and if Doc never quite managed just how, or managed the how of it poorly, in a way some thought akiltered or crazy, well, he never lost his try. No, try Doc Holliday had down to most of a gambler's low art. If anyone in this life had the right to fold his hand, it was Doc. That he chose not to do so, but bucked the tiger until the end, says more about the sort of man he was than any thousand words of mine.

I am no raconteur. I've none of that knack atall. Don't even know how to tell a proper joke or conjure up a prayer, and each of the yarns I know by heart are too tidy to be trusted for the truth. There is this, though, for what it may be worth: I miss him, every day.

(WYATT EARP)

You didn't know that death is beautiful
And it was made in your body

—CLAUDIO RODRÍGUEZ

There is little we can do without breath,
without spirit . . . All that transpires
requires respiration

—PAUL METCALF

Life's about going the lung distance

—bp NICHOL

THE GODS WERE never to favor him.

Consumption racked, ransacked, then shagged off his mama, Alice Jane, at the close of the war. When it happened he was barely 15 and it was the central, all-consuming fact of his life. (It would not long remain so, but the sense of abandonment, much as the absence itself, never ceased to inform him. "The day she died," he would later remark, "was the day I knew—there was something terrible loose in the world, and it was no respecter of human character. You could play by all the rules—love, honor, respect, obey—and it didn't matter a lick. It'd come for you as it chose, and then nothing on earth might avail. On earth, or anyplace else.")

They had been uncommonly—some dared whisper inappropriately—close, so it was a blow redoubled when three months later his daddy, the Major, Henry Burroughs, wed a neighbor girl half his age, occasioning father and son to fall out for the rest of their days. Thereafter the Sabbaths he could be prevailed upon to suffer inside the First Presbyterian Church were scant, but he continued to honor the avowal he had made his mama that he remain at Varnedoe's Valdosta Institute to acquire the lineaments of the gentleman's education including a smattering of Latin and Greek. (The French, the pidgin Spanish, those he would appropriate later, catch as catch can.) There, four years running, he made all A's.

Soon he was roundly rumored to have emptied his pistol over the heads of a gang of nigras at the whites-only swimming hole outside of town, and he did in fact rig a nest of blackpowder kegs intending to blow the Freedmen's Bureau at the county courthouse skyhigh, relenting only at the eleventh hour being unable to bring himself to it. (If he was highstrung he was not headstrong, hotheaded or reckless; neither was he heedless or headlong, nor, as a child, was he stout or robust, especially for a boy. Callow, some, but seldom feckless.)

He began carrying a trimmed but otherways unmarked deck of Bicycle cards shoved down in a pants pocket, which on a wager he could cut to any named ace.

At the first opportunity he took to raising a moustache and cultivating an affinity for what he then still was unaware was called the bon vivant, boulevardier school of clothing; he possessed a tailor's eye. (Gray quickly became his color of preference. A son of the chopfallen South, it likeways suited his temperament; to elicit elegance from drabness much as one stills John Barley from corn.)

He rode as is said born to the saddle and knew enough about the problematic bloodlines of horses not to loiter at racetracks.

The adolescent years drawn to a close, the Major, largely on account of the Freedmen's incident, orchestrated his removal to a college up North to become a dentist, a D.D.S., Doctor of Dental Surgery. His dissertation was entitled "Diseases of the Teeth" and he graduated first in his class, the 16th Annual Session of the class of '72, from the Pennsylvania College of Dental Surgery in Philadelphia, shortly to become part of the University of Pennsylvania in the Ivy League.

Setting up practice in Atlanta, he was invited to partner with the "prominent" Dr. Arthur C. Ford at 26 Whitehall Street near the Western & Atlantic Railroad. And it was there, the world arrayed at his feet all his for the having, that he took poorly, same as his ma. The coughing began. He ignored it, or tried to, but noticed each morning how his lungs felt more jaded and chafed and in time how embrittled. The coughing continued, increased, became chronic. The night sweats began. His ribs grabbed like drillbits. As often as not, when he awoke, it was buckled over, unharnessed and gasping. (Had she infected him? His own mother? The thought, even later, never occurred to him. Why would it? Consumption, so it was thought, was not contagious, not yet, not in those days. Had she infected him? Possibly. Probably. Why not? Of course she had. This is not irony. It is tragedy or fate or chance or far worse. It is destiny, perhaps, insofar as destiny is capricious and caprice insofar as caprice may order character. It was his misfortune to inhabit a house wherein something mortal was loose on the air—lethal microbe, fatal pathogen—and he inhaled it and it appropriated him for its host and, so, that is biology not irony. If not his mother, then perhaps someone else; we are what we breathe.)

He tried everything. Mineral salts, the snakebite remedy, decoctions of sulphur and clove, inunctions of iodine and creosote, tablets of strychnine and arsenic cut with iron and phosphorus, a variety of Native homeopathic cure-alls and folk notions, assorted Old Country caudles, alegars and possets; mare's milk, ground lamb's tongue and boiled rye; whiskey in catnip and mullein tea; spirits of camphor and ammonia. Any number of cuppings and clysterings, poultices and vesicants, fly blisters and mustard plasters, those of croton oil, tartar and liniment. He suffered through the flannel sweats, sponge baths, steam tents, ice immersions; body rubs with duck canvas toweling. Wearing blue-lensed spectacles. Sleeping with a black cord X'd about his chest like bandoliers. In time he even resorted to the patent medicinals and medicaments, the analeptics and restoratives, balsams and nostrums, elixirs and elevators, esters and enhancers: Stafford's Olive Tar, Hale's Horehound of Honey, Hood's Heat-treated Sarsaparilla, Ayer's Tonic Pills, Atkinson's Black Drop, Dr. Sweet's Infallible Liniment, Limerick's Great Southern Liniment, Duffy's Oriental Pure Original Malt, Chickasaw Plantation Chill Syrup, Dr. Pierce's Golden Medical Discovery, Mrs. Winslow's Soothing Salvant Serum, Cheatham's Reduction of Coke, Dover's Black Mountain Root Powder, Mother Jones's Vaso Chest Lanolin, Godfrey's Camphorated Cordial, Dr. J. Collis Browne's Chlorodyne, Globe's Flower Buttonbush Cough Syrup, Cuticura Blood Purifier & Resolvent, Dromgoole's Amagdlin Pectoral. And once, if once only, a mail-order supply of domesticated leeches applied to his chest after the arcane arrangement illustrated in the enclosed literature. Naturally none of them worked; he worsened.

It was his Uncle John, the physician, the same who had righted his cleft palate as an infant, who diagnosed what by then both had for some time been dreading, suggesting he consider, if only as last resort, the still experimental if increasingly fashionable "Come West and Live" cure, this new invention in "invalid living": the spa, or sanatorium, the Health Resort. His mother was seven years dead, but he carried her wasting raw, fresh-laid on his heart, all the ways she had suffered it, and so such talk did not overmuch impress him, but he consented to go out there, content to orphan himself to the moment as he might encounter it or it accrue to him, such being the myth or metaphor he had read about, or perhaps—as he sometimes believed—he had dreamed it. No matter. In time he took it for his credo, believing a man has as exigent a need of one as does a sailor a sextant.

He went out there then, seeping his wet cough, his lungs a silt of blue bacilli, clutched with febricula, gripped by its algors, the while seeking a cure he was not hopeful of nor kindly disposed to, the single place it latterly was rumored to reside, in the high elevations, crisp dry air and high cool sun of its mountainsides and deserts.

The one everyone knew and talked about was the Manitou in Colorado Springs: 300 homes, four churches (all Protestant), two schools, six grocers, one hardware store, two tailors, several bowling alleys, a roller-skating rink, three croquet grounds, a tennis court, numerous hiking trails, open-air concerts, guided hunting excursions, a campground and a photography studio. Handy to the recently laid Denver & Rio Grande railspur, the resident physician there was the internationally known Dr. Samuel Edwin Solly, himself a consumptive. The literature authored by its owner, General William Jackson Palmer, solicited "consumptives of good moral character."

He fled straightaway to Dallas.

He was 22 years old and already could measure the rage of it, what had befallen him, the affront of it crusting over to a callus, this hardness like horn that appalled nearly as much as it bewildered him, but he went out there to rummage what he might of assuasion and replenishment. And because he recognized he had need of its purchase, he sought the succor of a newfound self, the one he knew or presumed was there if only he reached far enough dug deep enough looked long enough into each moment that remained to him, faced up to the finality of each finite moment and did not blink or flinch or shy away from savoring whatever indemnity or sorrow might lurk there. Because one moment you are never going to die, never in this world, one moment you are invincible untouchable immortal pure deity—you are 22; so *young*—and the next you are cordwood. Or chum.

All the fallen angels, stricken gods, all the unending deletions.

Perishable lives. A reality so unreal it can leave its impression upon a person, as it surely did upon him, that is both the most lost and liberating feeling imaginable: to forget or die, whichever came first. He was learning—it is not merely the bad times that do a man in.

And if to others it did not appear to matter to him which came first, which during the bleaker moments surely it did not, still there were others, those of a more—what?—mentholated clarity, when not every breath was a pattern of poison sound and every night this perfect   reeking   blackout.

In Dallas he quickly went partners with Dr. John A. Seegar, also a native Georgian, at 56 Elm Street above Cochrane's Apothecary between Market and Austin. The sign painter, Pink Thomas, added his name and title to the shingle—J. H. HOLLIDAY, D.D.S.—all in caps. But it didn't last long. A few months. He could not reconcile himself to what was respectable. The contradiction was too enormous, time too short, life and its shrift, the damn skimp of it, and it baffled and bewildered him, crowding out everything else.

It was the time when one thing was ending and another had yet to begin, so that balance eluded him. Its equilibrium. The equanimity of an equipoise. He was still to discover that it was less his aspirations than his obsessions that would impel him towards inclining provinces of ruin, that moment when one falls into one's true self, true nature, the exiting towards that entrance, everything a function of appetite. And so, having yet to arrive there, he could not have said what he expected, save that the expectations he once had entertained for himself, thrilled to and nursed, the potential and prospects, such *ambition* no longer made right sense. All the drunken 3 a.m.'s wrestling with the pointlessness to which the only conceivable response, the only honorable response, is whimsy.

So he went ahead. Purchased a sideiron. A handgun. A self-cocking, nickel-plated Colt .38, sawed down its barrel and began packing it in a shoulder harness beneath his dental gown. Purchased, next, a handmirror, one of uncommon clarity in which he practiced putting on his poker face for hours on end from a confluxion of aspects and angles. When the air in his room grew too gamey, he sought the silence and solitude of cemeteries. The violent anonymity of boot hills and potter's fields settled him. He enjoyed the company; he had never been around such rapt listeners.

"Birds of a feather," he thought to himself, fancyfree among the headstones, or pacing their bones like a map. "This is what it must be like, eating memory."

Often he sat up through the night for the ease and lift it afforded his lungs, counting cards, acquainting himself with the specter of their idiosyncrasies, rehearsing the repertoire of "trickwork," the subtle cheats, sleights and stratagems, deceptions and deceits, each of the digital manipulations. For when nothing else remained and the little that did had crumbled to corrosion, still there were the cards and the rough science of their inconstancy. The hazard of the cards was the only steadfastness he had ever known, and the sole continuity.

The South had instructed him in how to drink, how a man's brain can train itself, clear enough of itself to lower gates, trip relays, to draw lines and circuits, conduits, seal off corridors and compartments where the alcohol drift might be diverted, its fumes locked down, stayed behind doors trapped beneath lids steered inside chambers and vents, shunts, all the ways you could facet and deflect them, siphon and filter. Already he was drinking in pints, addicted less to the physical relief than the emotional salve, the quality of its assuagement, and soon he equipped himself with a hipflask that he arranged to have inscribed with the Undertaker's Refrain:

So who'll be next, who'll be next
as this bright new year rolls 'round,
to be laid out in a gorgeous shroud
in his casket 'neath the ground?

Atrocities go on and life goes on and there is a quality to the moment that never changes never deforms an arrest of identity until all that remains is to adventure like a feather down this throat of ruptured sky.

———•◦•———

HE WAS BORN (*inter faeces et urinas*) at home, an only child (a baby sister, Martha Eleanora, had died but the year previous), on Thursday, August 14, 1851, in Griffin, Spalding County, Georgia, some 40 miles south of Atlanta.

Not a great deal to report weatherwise. That day the skies were uncommonly high and cloudless, summery, sultry and still. The skies that day were unruffled by southerly breezes. The heavens did not heave with sheet lightning or divest themselves of their black weight. No comet sped east to west across the firmament. No cyclone convolved beyond the door. No pit viper coiled itself about his wrist as he lay quiet in his cradle. Nor did Time stop, God speak, statues bleed, or what once had been water revert abruptly to wine.

The labor was protracted, but while the birth was not a breech, it was apparent at once that he was afflicted with the family stigmata—the cleft palate, deviated septum, the partial harelip that did not permit him, save in vain, to suckle. That he not choke to death or fall victim to the pneumonia that—as it had with his sister—inevitably arose owing to the introduction of fluids into the lungs during ingestion, his mother nursed him with an eye-dropper and a small teaspoon, and later with a shotglass, an irony of the sort that—when the time came—was scarce to be lost on him.

At eight weeks, his paternal uncle, John Stiles Holliday, a surgeon graduated of the Georgia Medical College, was summoned from nearby Fayetteville to perform the operation that corrected the defect to the extent that it could be corrected. Scarring was minimal—that which remained he later would camouflage beneath the wing of moustache he wore throughout his life—but it did saddle him with a significant speech impediment which Alice labored diligently to help him overcome and which the sorghum of his Dixie-deep drawl later mainly concealed.

He was a fine-boned baby, a fact no one appreciated more than she, and however much the angels had disfigured him, she took pride in what God had decreed.

On September 16, 1866, at the age of 36—the same age at which, 21 years later, he would follow in like fashion—his mother died, leaving to him both her locket and her precious volume of Poe's *Collected Poems*. A gentle, generous, genteel woman given to admonitions of a pithy, if mildly arcane sort—"You make suhtain, now, to keep out the wind inside that wood when you fetch it, y'hear?"—she had by then been sick for more than two years with the consumption that by the end had eroded the marrows of her body to the substance of stardust and shadow.

Even so, the asperities of the war had not affected her son. She had seen to that, convincing the Major in advance of the conflict to remove the family south to Valdosta, near the Florida border. He was 10 years old at the advent of the war and while it lasted she succeeded in perpetuating the fiction that he lived a charmed and immaculate life. He wanted for nothing, never went hungry, never saw a soldier nor heard a shot fired in anger. The carnage remained for him a rumor. He lived during those years the text of a storybook, palmy days, jasmine and honeysuckle, day after day this insulated, everlasting summer; all the blue, wisteria evenings that she arpeggioed him off to bed to tunes of her own composition. The music of Spanish moss.

Thus did he emerge from his childhood undaunted, self-sure in the conviction that as the world could not touch him, neither might life deal him a losing hand. There would remain about him always the aura of it—the sense of providence, provenance, pedigree, privilege; it shone through galvy as zinc. Bred of the beloved child, the extravagant man; he never comprised less than the center of his own universe, nor to that universe less than its sun.

And then she had died, and in her death evinced a deathly glow, as if in the act of her dying some alchemy had occurred burnishing the base metals of her body until they had become as gold—ingot, ore, solar within her soul. And yet it was not the glow that her son would later remember, but the shadow. It was the receding whiteness of her shadow, whiter than mothwing on mollusk, that he never would fail to recall.

———

THERE HAD BEEN a time when like everyone else he had endeavored to maintain his health—watched what he ate, exercised regularly, taken his proper rest, been moderate in each of his habits. This phase of his life lasted, at the outside, two years (while he was living in Atlanta, and later, briefly, in Dallas), until he grew so weary of the regimen that there arrived the moment, not that he could have named it, when he decided he would resign himself— tempt the fates, push his luck, defy the odds, force the envelope, dice at last with death. He knew that for him, it was all of it, here on, a matter of roulette. So he decided that he liked being sick, that he enjoyed the physical challenge, and it would leave him crestfallen when thinking that he had taken a turn for the worse it proved little more than a minor setback.

However impaired or stricken, he refused to live like an invalid, rebelled against the shut-in's existence, could not feature himself one of "that vile fraternity," the *poitrinaires*, those proscribed and prostrate. There was no romance in it, no adventure, no honor and no . . . style. Beyond a certain point it was pointless to require of him that he do what was required of him, for he held his health in loathsomely low regard and would conceive of himself as it pleased him, not as others might perceive him or the unleavened facts of his condition allow.

"In all things henceforth, moderation abound," had been the wisdom of his uncle's admonition, and now—drawn innately to ledges and brinks, their margins and rim-most peripheries—he proceeded to do precisely as he pleased: all, in excess. It was with him a first principle, to live as one might, well or less well, but by his own lights, always his own lights alone. (What was he thinking? That the curse of the cure, the cure and its convalescence, must be worse than the disease? That he was ill-meant to suffer such self-abnegation? His mother had refused him nothing. "So what else might a self be for," he considered, "if not to indulge with abandon? To have at, partake, delight in? To plunge on." He knew with the poet—without knowing the poet—that those marked to disappear early race ahead outpacing their own laughter, engaged in perilous journeys, flown to stars so far-flung that few, indeed, can follow.)

It wasn't denial, though it may well have been its opposite, for he knew how flawed the flesh, how unfailingly it fails; biology/his destiny. Seismically attuned to each of its daily deteriorations, he was more intimate with the ways a body can blaspheme against itself—all the insults and indignities, defaults and defamations, all the *petits maux*, annulments, the bluntless traumas, mutinies and minor deaths, the disintegrating beauty than are most women. And so he considered the facade of the corpus contemptible: a hank of hair, a shank of bone, a puddle of blood, a subcutaneous arrangement of meats; the mortalness of these mortal remains. The contours of his lungs would censor and constrain him all his life, nor would there be a moment—drunk, drugged or sober—that he would not suffer the anguish bred of their constriction, but he would not die taken to his bed, the wreck to its rack resigned to its ruin, confined, self-ridden, rotting. It was so impossibly Southern—vainglory in all things, valor in most, and death before defeat.

To embrace the fact of a diminishing existence, live between the lines of a lie made a legend, to go where one is going yet never arrive, to gather to ground on sunless days or find refuge 40 fathoms down—the crafting of one's gradual disappearance, where a deliberate performance wrought of self-conscious grace is not uninteresting. This inexorable narrowing, as he sometimes thought of it, like melting away through a mirror, say, or down the hatch of a hollow black hole. To become one, in a way, with the room where one stays, the flesh of one's body stretched so thin it becomes the tissue of one's ceiling, one's floor, each of these four walls. Walls that pitch inward, ceilings that sag, corners too sharp by three-quarters. Where there is the clearance to accommodate neither a complex emotion nor an original thought and the sky reels down like the retraction of a celestial fist smothering you beneath the brocaded pillow of heaven as your shadow looks on seating itself like soot in its chair slumping there like an exhausted courtier or crawls misshapenly along floorboards, shinnies fruited wallpaper, shimmies creepily across voluted ceiling curling like parchment held to candleflame into a kitten of smoke in the cove of its corner, unbundled, abandoned, abused and maligned, disguised by the shift of its wayward disfigurement. Become pure inscape—frangible, defunct, increasingly fragile, until you are left with nothing but to think to yourself, "Never to have been born. My God! What a luxury!"

Diagnosed consumptive: September 10, 1873. Now raise high a glass before lowering the shingle; then pack the valise before gathering to the platform: the 8:27 Western & Atlantic, outbound, West. Backclap cousin Robert, embrace Auntie Permelia, bearhug Uncle John, a peck upon the forehead of the tearful Sophie Walton.

A lingersome last glance downtrack for the self-absented Major.

(He had taken formal leave of his favorite cousin, Mattie, his Uncle Robert and Aunt Mary's firstborn, some several days before. They had embraced, after which he had kissed her long and hard upon the forehead, and before he had turned to go, she had remarked, "You will come back, won't you, John?" He might have said anything; he chose to say nothing, letting the silence suffice. "Well," she had continued, "then you must promise that you shall write, a line or two, from time to time, to let me know where you are and what you are doing, how it is you fare. You will write, won't you, John?" And so he had allowed as how he would, he would try, only half meaning it, if that half in deadly earnest. His intentions were unclear. He could not risk the clarity, not yet. He could not see his way past the cost of the moment.)

"There there, but why all so glumsome? 'Tis only for the while. I shall write as I am able. You mustn't fret, but trust, as do I, that I am for a better place." And bravely grins. "Rumor has it the adventure there's a peach. How barbarous could it be when it is only orchards that I'm bound for?"

And like the aerialist bent to his tightrope, boards his perfect margin of altitude, reckoning the arc of the slippage in the one improvised move of a cavalier gesture. This is how history is written: incandescent across the sky in the shift of a single isobar.

That temblor.

Those crosswinds.

Twenty-two years old, nailed to a scaffold of pain.

Don't look down. There are no nets.

SOPHIE WALTON. MY nurse, my childhood, Old Mam, sable Nanna, the almost-mother who taught me cards and how much more they are than games.

My tears that day were all for her: silver coins, coffers full to flowing, this loot, bullion and doubloons upon going away forever, for that much, even then, I knew: no photo later, letter, no word or rumor, just this remembrance, of our tears and of her face, each feature gone to ghost.

Down that traintrack, I might have plunged oceanfloors, and never, not once, drowned.

SOPHIE: There was the terrible knowledge, blunt and unmuffled, that his body had betrayed him, his beautiful body, diseased now and dismantling, unmasted, unmastered, unmoored; that he was going to die soon.

Eventually life finds most of us out, but he was still a boy, my motherless boy but barely begun, and it was too soon, and there was nothing to be done, and because there was nothing he could do to alter the fact or smooth away its truth he bore its shadow coiled fast inside him, aching carbon animal, pestilent wherever he went.

And so what, then, was the right way to proceed in light of it? Upon learning that one's life is lost before it has rightly begun, how does one move forward then? Go the next step? The next? What is the name of that direction? How sift such a loss for its light?

It was a thing done to him, unto him, visited upon him, this abduction, its banishment, the divestiture and the leasehold it granted him, to compose his life instead of living it, to make of it a poem, and of its hole, a hate sonnet. He must learn to live bruised, in stanzas, his world/laid waste.

He was humiliated by it, the violence done him, that vandalism, the beshatting of his soul. It was only later, much later, that he would come to understand what is perhaps most difficult for any of us to understand—how humiliation is the first step towards liberation.

———◦•◦•◦———

ADVENTURE. ESCAPE AND exploit, escapade, odyssey, he was embarking upon an odyssey, nothing spiritual or holy, not a pilgrimage, quest or vision, nothing so metaphysical, lofty, so epic or elegiac. He wasn't walking consecrated or knightly ground. Would have scoffed at the suggestion. But survival, experience, its gathering, vagrancy and vagabondage, seeking, acquiring, accumulating, acquitting himself, doing aright by it. To better fill the finding of himself, persist in its fastening, sink a footing, a furthering, to feel it the more deeply, or devise a body wherein might more hospitably dwell the diaphanated rags of his lungs; like dragging breath through seaweed.

Because damned if he'd permit the facts, the wretched facts of his scuttled existence beach him like a boat or wring the wind from his lungs like a sail. He was outbound and glad of it, giddy to be rid of the rest, knowing in his bones that he wasn't coming back, not at all, not ever, save bleached, too, as those very bones.

He had an education, a profession, something of a nestegg

(his mother had bequeathed him property in Griffin from the sale of which he pocketed $1,800). All he wanted for now was time, time enough to reckon a single reason to go on living.

Life may be a lesson, but it is not one apt to be learned until after one is long dead.

The way every odyssey drifts West
inchmeal
towards its Iliad.

———————

Whatever his health before, whatever his prospects as a man . . . from now on his life was posthumous. And he knew it. By a slow, nearly measured declension, he began to divest himself . . . Whether in friendship or passion, the true, underlying issue was always good-bye.

—STANLEY PLUMLY

**From the beginning,
about nothing
but the end.**

Got a tombstone hand,
a graveyard mind,
I'm just twenty-one
and don't mind dyin'.

THE IRONY IS, I DID. Mind. And while I no longer recall the moment with the kind of clarity certain to comport with contemporary standards of historical scholarship—the moment I was given the news I mean—I remember clearly enough what I felt, as I do, to a lesser extent, what I thought.

Keep in mind that death, the death of the young that is, was far commoner in those days than it is now. My sister had died in infancy, my blessed mother in her prime, and among people of my acquaintance, such was more the rule than otherways. Death—its constancy—was different then. Not only was it more daily, more ongoingly ubiquitous—I haven't the statistics to support the claim; you must only trust me—it was more personal. It was, that is, something with which all of us were intimately familiar, and so something we felt no need to be embarrassed by or shrink from, let alone gainsay. Not that it wasn't feared—there was fear aplenty—but it wasn't feared in the same way, the way it is today. Death had yet to be outlawed, to be stigmatized, to come attached with a taboo, to be declared bad form, as if it were the fault of the person doing the dying. It was, then, still considered a part of life. A perfectly natural part.

That said, I wanted no part of it, not at the time. Not because it was so alien—as I say, it wasn't alien at all; every sentence begs its proper period—but because I had other plans, and dying, much less dying young, decidedly was not among them. So that what I felt in the moment, the very moment my uncle, dear man, broke the news, was mainly disbelief. Disbelief and, curiously enough, wonder. (The anger and anguish, as the despair, would follow later.) Wonder, that is, at how vulnerable I suddenly felt. And how powerless. It was the powerlessness that threw me, rocked me even, and the sense that now, I must do everything possible to render myself less so.

Which, in the end, was why I consented to go West. I wasn't hunting a cure—I knew consumption precluded that; self-delusion, more's the pity, never was among my many failings—I was searching a way to feel less mortal. And so—more irony still, for how feel less mortal, without feeling less human?

Of course, I didn't reckon any of that at the time. All I knew was that I had been dealt this . . . joker, a card that ought rightly have been discarded from the deck, one not meant to be part of the game, and that I was saddled with the necessity of playing it, come what may and all the same. Whether at last I succeeded in doing so is not for me to say. The point is, literally overnight I had been presented with a wager that I knew I could not win, but which required that I make it, and do so sans delay.

Which was the other thing, for suddenly I was on the clock. Suddenly I had no time to waste. Suddenly everything was more precious, momentous, imminent, more . . . everything. More here and more now, as more finite and final. *We pass this way but once.* Well, indeed we do, and it is in the choices we make along the way, however bleak or desperate, that the soul of the matter lies.

There is no one more self-obsessed than a dying man, 'less it be a poet, and when the poet is the one who is dying—then even death itself, that vulture, must be given pause. And it is in that pause, while death, however briefly, hovers in advance of its descent, that one is afforded the opportunity to gain the upper hand. So it was that when I boarded that train, it was precisely that hand I was determined to track.

A needle in a hayrick, perhaps, but I had no doubt that once I found it—and I vowed to myself that I would—I might with the dexterity of a surgeon, this act of prestidigitation—thread the mortal iris of its eye. For this much (the only practicable wisdom my father ever gave me) I knew: even vultures have their day. When a poem is ripe, only then will it fall. And in the meantime? Keep from drowning. Stay afloat. Swim. Uphill. Under water. In the dark. But swim, stroke/by breathless/stroke.

—Doc Holliday

After inhalation of droplet nuclei a tubercule bacillus set-
tles in an alveolus and infection occurs with alveolar
capillary dilation and endothelial cell swelling. Alveolitis
results with replication of tubercule bacilli and influx of
polymorphonuclear leukocytes which disseminate through
the lymph system to the circulatory system, leading most
typically to caesation—the conversion of necrotic tissue to a
cheese-like material. The caseum may localize, undergo fi-
brosis or excavate to and form cavities, the walls of which
are studded with multiplying tubercule bacilli. If so, in-
fected debris may spread throughout the lungs by the tra-
cheobronchial tree.

—PROFESSIONAL GUIDE TO DISEASES

The Thief of Life.
The Evil Predator.
The Obscene Mystery.
The Mortal Affront.
The Germ of Death.
The Lethal Pest.
The Fell Destroyer.
The Galloping Scourge.
The Great White Plague.

By any other name, consumption (or cachexia)—originally ph-
thisis, from the Greek *phthiein*, "to waste away"; later scrofula, or
struma, the King's Evil—is a pulmonary (lung) disease, the origin
of which recently has been attributed to the Middle East where
some 8,000 years ago, it is thought to have occurred in cattle.

At present, its morbidity rate remains alarmingly high; once
contracted, consumption almost always is fatal. (Statistics indicate
that presently it is the leading cause of death in the United States,
accounting for approximately one out of every five fatalities.)

However, recent advances in our understanding of the etiology and morphology of the disease have enabled us to diagnose its presence in its more embryonic, incipient stages and to recommend a course of treatment which may allay its progress and prolong life, often significantly.

The Oxford English Dictionary dates "consumption" to 1398, with references to "bloodethynning" and "wastying." Over time, it has been suggested that everything from humors to vapors, ferments, agues, biles, spleens, cholers, colics, galls, biliousnesses, rheumatisms, jaundices, gouts, grippes, croups, pleurisies, purulencies, malaises and miasmas, but most especially melancholy, were among its causes. Today, we strongly suspect a hereditary link, a familial predisposition that in conjunction with such "irritations" as an unfavorable climate (cold/hot, damp, humid, rainy, windy), a sedentary mode of life, excessive alcohol intake, an immoderate and heavily spiced diet, smoking, defective ventilation, deficiency of light and depressing emotions, may trigger the onset of the disease.

Those diagnosed as consumptive are now regularly, if not yet routinely, advised by their physicians to undertake a variety of measures which an ongoing body of anecdotal evidence strongly suggests can and often does retard and arrest if not entirely eliminate the symptoms of the illness. Such measures include:

1) moving to a mild, dry, sunny and salubrious climate (the mountains and deserts of the American Southwest—Colorado, New Mexico, Arizona, Texas and southern California—are considered most beneficial); at the very least, moving from an urban environment to a more rural one;

2) participating in a daily regimen of gentle outdoor exercise (long walks, hiking, horseback riding, picnicking, hunting, etc.), augmented by self-monitored periods of rest;

3) increasing the amount of time spent out of doors, including, as it may prove practicable, sleeping "under the stars" or in tents;

4) adhering to a mild, bland, moderate diet (including avoidance of salt, sugar and seasonings, and strict abstention from ardent spirits and alcoholic beverages) heavy with milk, raw eggs and cream;

5) refraining from smoking, chewing or snuffing tobacco products;

6) "staying busy," i.e. deliberately engaging in activity designed to divert the mind from dwelling inordinately upon or becoming overly preoccupied with the disease.

Physicians currently describe the pathology of consumption according to the chronology of its symptomatology:

1) throat irritation; dry, persistent, hacking, harassing cough; chest and shoulder pains; slightly accelerated pulse; febricula; fatigue; difficulty breathing during and after exertion; increased appetite absent weight gain;

2) deeper, more moist and protracted "barking" cough, often coming in fits coupled with "hollow rattle" in the chest; expectoration of sputa progressing gradually from thin, white phlegm to thick, opaque green mucus streaked with yellow pus; intermittent "hectic" fevers spiking twice daily; algor; noticeably accelerated pulse as high as 120/minute; ruddied complexion—"pink flush" to "red tint," alternating with periods of pronounced "ghostly" or "spectral" pall; throat ulcers; habitual hoarseness; generalized body pain severe enough to interrupt and inhibit, if not prohibit, regular sleep; difficulty breathing, especially at night; depressed appetite and ac-

companying weight loss; mood swings ranging from febrile energy gushes and surges of exhilaration, giddiness and euphoria to prolonged periods of languor, lassitude and listlessness; (in some cases) exacerbated sexual desire;

3) general emaciation and rachitism—"shrunken" chest, "spindled" limbs, "sunken" cheeks, "hollow," brightly glowing eyes; chronic rattle in the lungs; constant, corrosive deep coughing (known colloquially as the "graveyard" or "sepulchral" cough); bloody sputa progressing in quantity from a teaspoon to cupfuls; "deathbreath"; generalized and ongoing deep joint pain; racing and weakened pulse; inflammatory fever; excessive sweating; difficulty swallowing; loss of appetite; bouts of debilitating lethargy and enervation; colic pain; diarrhea becoming more chronic and severe; oedematous legs; strangulated breathing; deliriums; hemorrhaging from nose and mouth.

There persists, despite the best efforts of the medical community to debunk same, a significant and growing body of mythology associated with this disease, doubtless owing to the imprecise and still indeterminate nature of its etiology. This is unfortunate, as it not only adversely stigmatizes the sufferers but negatively impacts the thinking and behavior of those who may have occasion to have commerce with them.

In this regard, the first and most critical point to be made is that there exists as yet no scientifically conclusive evidence that consumption is contagious or communicable. Unlike such diseases as leprosy, anthrax and gonorrhea, the genesis of which more recently have been proven to originate with a microscopic bacillus, consumption possesses no such etiology. One cannot, as far as we know, become "infected" with consumption through contact with consumptives. It remains a disease of the individual, not of the community. It contains no epidemiological component. It is not a "pestilence," nor is it possessed of the potential—as, for example, are cholera and smallpox—for rampant outbreak.

Moreover, the condition is itself neither expressive of nor a reflection upon the moral character of those who are its victims. The misconception, still all too prevalent, that the illness somehow "taints" its sufferers, on the one hand, or "ennobles" or "etherealizes" them, on the other, is purely fiction. Consumption is a physiological fact, not a philosophical concept. There is nothing inherently moral or immoral about being stricken with a life-threatening disease, just as there is nothing "aestheticizing" about living with its consequences.

Neither is there the least basis in scientific fact for the misbelief that the condition most often occurs in those who are "temperamentally" disposed to it. Consumption is a democratic killer. It does not target those who are "oversensitive" or "highstrung" or "refined" or "ardent" or "love-starved" or "delicate" or "emotionally vulnerable," or, indeed, those who, having been "born weak," are deficient in vitality, virility or somehow excessively morbid and not quite "lifeloving" enough to cope with the vulgar vagaries and rough-and-tumble vicissitudes of the real world. Consumption may render a weak man weaker and a sad man sadder still, but the joyful, robust and brutish are no more immune to its ravages than are the melancholy, the asthenic or the tenderhearted. There are, obviously, consumptives—that is, individual victims of consumption—but to assert the existence of consumptive tendencies or a consumptive character, is utter nonsense, however much those who suffer may suffer their symptoms in common.

Finally, as the disease is specifically one of the body and not of the mind, soul or spirit, it cannot be cured by thinking, feeling, praying or willing it away. There is no "inner logic" to consumption, save as all such pathologies chronologically run their course. Consumption is consumption and consumption alone. It is not, as it still too often is erroneously maintained, the manifest expression of some ongoing interior drama—an emotional wound, repressed longing, misspent vitality, excess passion, destructive energy, mental dislocation. Consumption, in other words, is not a metaphorical code the meanings of which are to be deciphered, but a somatic condition, a diathetic disease the symptoms of which are to be treated. And whose cause and cure in time—and that time is increasingly nigh—we shall positively determine beyond all scientific speculation.

(THE PRINCIPLES AND PRACTICE OF MEDICINE, 1880)

I should like to die of consumption, because the ladies would all say, "Look at that poor Byron, how interesting he looks in dying."

—LORD BYRON

From: phlegm to mucus
mucus to sputum
sputum to pus
pus to blood
blood to the must of a lifetime.

'Tis the Captain of Death
—JOHN BUNYAN, *Pilgrim's Progress*

"I'm actually afraid of his lungs."

—OLIVER GOLDSMITH, *She Stoops to Conquer*

It is the dread disease which refines death . . . in which the struggle between soul and body is so gradual, quiet and solemn, and the result so sure, that day by day and grain by grain, the mortal part wastes and withers away, so that the spirit grows light and sanguine with its lightening load . . . [and] in which life and death are so strangely blended, that death takes the glow and hue of life, and life the gaunt and grisly form of death.

—CHARLES DICKENS, *Nicholas Nickleby*

Death and disease are often beautiful,
Like . . . the hectic glow of consumption.
—HENRY DAVID THOREAU

We are the wounded soldiery of mankind . . . [our] world
is a disenchanted place.

—ROBERT LOUIS STEVENSON

The Southwest is a land that has brought healing to the
hearts of many. Invalids don't come here to die, they
come to live, and they get what they came for. There is
something in the air that makes the blood to run red, the
heart to beat high, the eyes to look upward and the lungs
to swell large, clean through with the strength of their
clarity.

—FRANCIS X. AUBRY, frontiersman and fur trader, from his
journals, published in the Daily Missouri Republican
circa 1847

Men come here not to buy land but to buy lungs. Why
not? The air here beats any fattening compound on the
market. Were all the consumptives to leave these parts,
the entire area would become once again what it was but
a few short years ago—a depopulated blank spot in the
desert fit for nothing but savages and scorpions.

—LAS VEGAS Gazette, 1879

My lungs is broke,
I've lost all spunk,
I'm plumb stove in,
I'm ganted out—
the way I breathe
'll be the death of me
yet.

I know a man who went [West] to die but he made a fail-ure of it. He was a skeleton when he came and could barely stand. . . . Three months later . . . he was a skeleton no longer, but weighed part of a ton. . . . His disease was consumption. I confidently recommend his experience to other skeletons.

—MARK TWAIN, *Roughing It*

My head and lungs have come to an agreement without my knowledge. . . . I'm mentally ill, the disease of the lungs is nothing but an overflowing of my mental disease.

—FRANZ KAFKA

Spitting up blood for
time to bleed, its
clock unwound, down
to human seed.

O Brothers of sad lives! they are so brief;
A few short years must bring us all relief:
Can we not bear these years of labouring breath?
—JAMES THOMSON, *The City of Dreadful Night*

It is the pining to die away. The desire must die away, then, the desire for the in and out, the up and down of erotic love, which is symbolized in breathing. And with the desire the lungs die away . . . the body dies away be-cause desire increases the illness, because the guilt of the ever-repeated symbolic dissipation of semen in the sputum is continually growing greater . . . because the It allows pulmonary disease to bring beauty to the eyes and cheek, alluring poisons!

—GEORG GRODDECK, *The Book of It*

cough up your T.B. don't be stingy
no trifle is too trifling not even a thrombus
—SAMUEL BECKETT

Poe and Thoreau, Shelley, Keats
R. L. Stevenson, Emily Brontë
Chopin, Chekhov
Lawrence and Kafka
Stephen Crane and Ernest Dowson
and
Leander H. McNelly

UNTIL 1882, WHEN the German bacteriologist Robert Koch for the first time microscopically observed the tubercule bacillus and described it as "beautifully blue," the color routinely associated with the disease had been white. Much as the bubonic plague some five centuries earlier had been tagged the Black Death, so consumption was known as the White Plague owing to the glowing, ghostly pallor with which it was said to imbue its victims.

Chaos, coma, a secret, silence, wish or thought unformed. What never was, is or is no more. Collapsing star, burnt out, bald. Ether, enamel, fridge, egg. Bone. Bedsheet. Nacre of needle's eye. Snow wrack, prayer, dawn's moon half fled, contrail, milkglass, panavision of the blind/and of the dead. White heart, says the poet, white dwarfs, winding sheet and linen. This paper. The porcelain space between   these   words.

Unspeakable. Anonym.

Or the whiteness of virtuous witchery; aerogram and smoke signal, their billows white as Warhol.

Death's shadow then, its syntax. Or Doc's: "I will say this much for dying, not only does it keep you on your toes, it is the single thing I have ever found, love included, that truly lasts. Outlives us all. Look around: the dead have got us outnumbered." Or this, to himself, on the occasion of his 30th birthday: "I think of Poe, *l'âme perdue*, so called, the wrecked and ruined soul. Some people are like that, just are, melancholy born, born . . . down, and so drag themselves through it as they inevitably must depart, disabled by fear, and alone. Perhaps they know something it would behoove the rest of us more candidly to consider. After all, are we really given this life that we might enjoy it? Or to savor its failure, and before we die, spit out what remains square in God's eye?

"Myself, I have no answers. My life was scripted in advance, as my grief is the weather I move through. Survival is hard, to endure one's survival unthinkable. I awake each day to the dying light of Armageddon.

"And to this credo: *let it come*. Let it, all of it, let what will come come tumbling down. Let the whole world avalanche across the face of my soul until it lies knuckled and white at my feet. *Après moi, le déluge!* Let the world die when I do, and then, all of you, adieu."

This is how he calibrates the hours now: in the loss of color and weight and sleep and sweat and the precise amount of expectoration in a day. And the ache embedded so deep in his lungs it is the gathered pain of all of life having hastened, narrowed there, to the cave of this small/white/place.

So is everyone influenced—

    the robust
    the weak
        all constitutions—

by the very fibre of the flesh
       &
    chalk of the bone

We are what we were made . . .

It is a sign of strength to be weak,
to know it,
        and

            OUT *with it*
          —AFTER MELVILLE

Men make use of their illnesses at least as much as they are made use of by them.

        —ALDOUS HUXLEY

He once was overheard: "To conceive of oneself as already dead affords one a certain carnivalesque license." He dreamed in tickertape and calliope colors, dreamed his own death so often, watched his funeral parade through his brain doublelooped at such length, it was like riding a carousel.

Remarked to any who might listen: "Who among us might be possessed of the grace to accept one's death as one's due?"

How lust after life when you are deprived of the language for its living? When its resonances fail to register? When its text is one of deletions, its score whole rests, each dawn the hour of mourning?

When one thing is wrong, how can anything be right? How get on with it, until you get over it? How accept that you've done anything, when there is one thing more to be done?

Its grace notes jarred off his back.

He carried the world within him, lesion on his lungs, bacilli boating each lake of his brain, and looking around, mused aloud through the laughter, "Apocalypse. Everywhere, Apocalypse."

One among the many tense moments to come: "Well, boys, what are you waiting on? Have at. Feel free. I have been dead so long I am not like to heed a few extra shots at it on behalf of the sorry likes of you. Every woman in giving birth gives life to death as well. The whiff of that involucre. I was a goner *in utero*. What you see here before you is but the part walked away wrecked from the womb."

"So what sort of fingerprints y'reckon the hands of time leave? Bloody, I'm betting."

It quickly became an exercise in extremism. And skill. Those two. To locate within himself the flipped coin that falls repeatedly on edge. Continuum of that brink. Its node of perfect balance. To discern the line at all times, take its measure, then cross it, cross back, recross it, each time a step further. To weather its altitude, control it, master the nausea while riding saddleless the haunch of its wind: typhoon, cyclone, prairie twister, gyre. Each breath a tonguelick, gust a lipstroke, each pant the one that might paint him pinto pony, rave him bareback to life at last. Fletched, feathered, arrowflown shamelessly from the dead. What he required of himself was the aim of the archer blind at birth.

There was his recollection of the future as his premonition of the past, and this stranger wedged at the angle of his brain, straddling its corpus callosum, spraddling the synaptic cleft, squatting mute and immutable in the rift of its Sylvian fissure. Troll.

And it waves wires, electric seaweed blue as tungsten, this anemone dance on the shore of its oceanless sun.

His brain a bulb
about to burst.

The plague full swift goes by;
I am sick, I must dye.

PART

Two

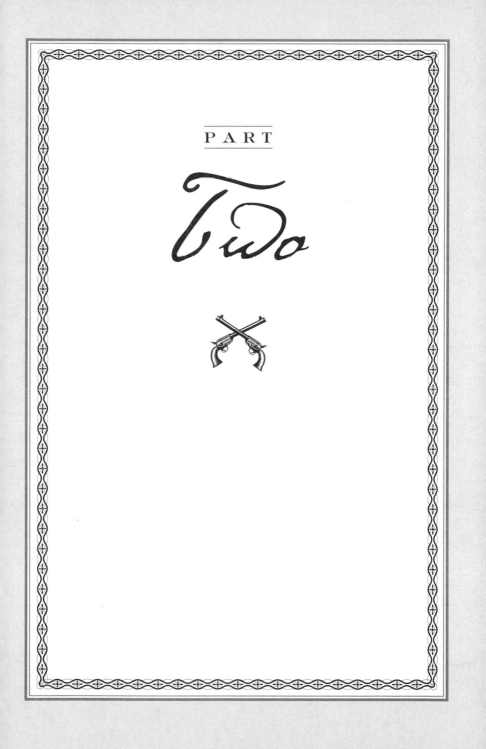

Everything is debriding itself to shape,
the drift of silence
through the debris of structure

He approached walls, floors and ceilings as an artist approaches a canvas, but at times his methodology shocked his clients. Once, deciding that he wanted a dismantled, piecemeal, among-the-ruins look, he built an ornately furnished, opulently finished dining room, then hired a wrecking crew to demolish it. The resulting eviscera, this impeccable shambles—from the dangling electrical cables and overhead trusses to diverticular glimpses of plumping pipes and crumpled ductwork, unpainted Sheetrock and exposed joists and lathings—what he called the art of *deshabille*—remained his favorite work. "Life goes on," he explained. "You go into the wreck of a place and you . . . experience. Get it?"

—FROM A NEWSPAPER OBITUARY: "SAM LOPATA,

RESTAURANT DESIGN GURU"

When I was a painter, my most successful paintings I left outside and let them get rained on. The ones that weren't so successful I just gave away, but my most successful ones rotted, returned to leaves and twigs. I'm just interested in decomposition.

—JIM DICKINSON, in a magazine interview

Devil may care and to hell with the hindmost, or so all the books say. What's truth yarned in books but wove fabrication?

He lived wholecloth the fabric of his own.

In facing our demons, as we all one day must, each of us sees different people as the devil, it matters little who. The devil is the devil and he's out there for us all, goading us to act as we will.

Pleased him to feel more alive to flirt with the Beast. Wanna give the finger to Lucifer? Gotta chase him down first.

Knowing
In his breast
The infinite and the gold
Of the endless frontier, the deathless West.
DELMORE SCHWARTZ

No one should brave the underworld alone.
—EDGAR ALLAN POE

SO HE WENT out there, cut adrift, endangered species, indebted to no one as he was pledged to nothing, his future furtively mortgaged on nought but borrowed time; this life, on loan, and each day numbered, if those but few, and those few fewer still. But of course the West had no vernacular for him, no parlance or nomenclature. He was an incongruity. Fatherless, unsired, unprecedented, he squared with no rubric or taxonomy, no phyla, no codex or established criterion. It never had seen such silks. And so could only wonder: whither thou-est, Doc, before you were born? And where'd you come by them duds, dude, default?

One day he was just there, the way a mist is there, the way a fust is, pale as parachute; each morning waking chewed up and chawed on, the sunslant blanched his lungs bleach blue.

Clean start, clean slates, starched shirts, second chance and fresh beginnings. What was it called? Tabula rasa? Yeah, that was the West, no presuppositions about where a person had been before, who or what he had been, may have done or dodged. You made that up in the making, riffed and improvised, summoned it in licks as you strode, as you found you had cause of it. Fashioned of your life a form of jazz: the Man with No Name, and from Nowhere. And, too, a Man Apart.

Such was the peculiar grace of the place, to take in those outcast, welcome the orphan, embrace the exile, suffer the pariah or pilgrim: defrocked priest, lapsed madonna, nameless anonymity, leper or fugitive lunger. That was its ethos and euretics: leave it be, leave it lie, leave it alone, leave the hell off. Portfolio, pedigree, provenance; lineage, credential, curriculum vitae; such documentation would not stand you a beer. And it suited him, to leave his own remote, as it would, in time, to avail himself of its license.

The deference paid self-invention here, reinvention, the berth granted self-imitation—why, you could live self-estranged, make of that your banner, exist *à rebours*, repose your faith in futility or a propulsive and positive chaos, and no one cared a damn. It happened all the time: life could be cheap, truth a matter of self-interest, justice swift and arbitrary, beauty but caprice, but so long as his lungs held out and he did not first take a bullet in the neck he might live high and dry. Aspire to the lift of a form of half-lit, lighter air.

But that was later. At the outset it was the same as being churned by a dust devil. He couldn't see five minutes in front of him. None of it made the kind of sense he might make sense of, frame, put a context to. It was like sailing a rudderless ship on dry land through wracks of sandblow—all of it, strange topography, moonscape, arid and alien. No vector or locus, pilot or polestar, moss, north wind, weather, horizon or season, no contour or traction at all. And the sky so undifferentiated, so white, it was like disappearing down a volume of emptiness or beneath a parchment of waterless lake. Nothing to compass a course by or map towards some sense of a center, but everything bereft of relief. The texture of the moment—sound, scent, color, the taste in your mouth, that feeling of waking up over and over in a strange bed in a strange place and not knowing all day day after day where you are or how you got that way.

Save that it sure wasn't Georgia. (Or anywhere else in the bedashed, deflowered South. So contented himself, night after night, with putting the Past and Its plans in their place—far, and further away; demonized the lies of his childhood; chose not to sentimentalize "home.") This outland so foreign to him that he felt absurd in it, apart from it, stripped of history and profile, station or audience. Just this lonely passing through, anonymous cloud in search of its sky, enough definition to fill in the corners, bevel the edges, gray the margins around the patternless, procedureless white. His discovery of a new reality: how much wider the world keeps getting when you're in it on your own.

Still, he was free now, if as morbidly alone. In a room. Any room. No matter. Along abouts. So, nothing better to do, he decided to be . . . new. Why not? To begin again, start over, the same as unnumbered numbers before him, trade himself in, exchange one Self for Another, easy as strapping on a gunbelt. To conjure one up, God knows how, out of thin air perhaps, a summoning, as from the misbegotten blue. Every thought this whisper to forget himself, replace the rest with what remained, to believe something, anything else, moment to moment, to somehow . . . sustain.

And so as his skin was too thin he must shed it; he'd cobble a life together somehow, out of leather and bark perhaps, sutures of nerve, scuts of blood, dredge so deeply the lost image of himself that his shadow might wrest free of its shade.

One night . . .

One night as night was hardhurrying towards morning, this pistachio light over the Planter's Hotel in Fort Griffin off the Brazos a block east of where he then was dealing faro at John Shannsey's Cattle Exchange Saloon, he played solitaire and nine times running ran the deck through besting his own record by one, then as if in self-congratulation made complex, encrypted love to three women, indulging the peculiar delights relinquished of each, all the painted perfumed idiosyncrasies, deviance and deviation, the small surrenders, large capitulations, the wet fires he aroused.

Throughout his life his lovemaking—which, believing that one owed it to oneself and one's partner to aspire to some art in the act, is precisely what it was—would remain irregular, the prolonged periods of abstention punctuated by appetitious bouts and binges that knew neither decorum nor decency. He devoured a woman differently from the way that he consumed a bottle—joylessly, doggedly, without flag or compunction; each instance of congress, this session.

As a lover he was passionate yet particular, unguarded if self-regarding, imagined himself imaginative, was ridiculously reliable, immodest to a fault. He considered his vulnerability a virtue, knew how to be playful, considerate, selfless, appreciative. If he could not claim originality, well, who could? Innovation tickled him all the same. He could take or be giving, ravish, play rough or not. He encountered women who found him unendurable. He was too uncommon, too able to indulge and bestow, too rich, perhaps, an extravagance, or one too unconstrained.

Even so, it gladdened him to cater and oblige. He would accommodate anything, wished to do anything, transgress or risk all, all of which two people could conceive and were anatomically capable; become acrobat, aerialist, oralist, gymnosophist, ecdysiast as well. He was possessed of the suppleness of mind to encompass it, for he lusted with his soul, this sodomy of each of the senses. At such moments he shone as do some women. He never would reveal what he owed women, save to other women, to Kate, for it was glidepaths and orbits, constellations, mapless worlds replete.

No plainsman, frontiersman, no so-called prince of the prairie, he eschewed buckskins, chaps, chivarras, chinks and dungarees, sombreros, coonskin caps and 10-gallon hats, bib shirts, yoke-backed ulsters and shearling coats. He didn't wear spurs, know how to twirl a rope, throw a lariat, drive a herd or punch a cow, how to live off the land or plow it for pay, scout a trail, bust a bronc, foal a mare, track a fox or skin one, sink a well, raise a barn, mend a wagon or tie off a fence. He knew neither how to wrangle nor ramrod, could not bring himself to ranch, and thought rustling the last refuge of roughnecks.

Weather bored him wishful, landscape scarcely less so; his heart was not buoyed by all he beheld, wildlife and scenery, the vast vistas and so forth. He felt no stir of kinship, no communion with flora or fauna or fieldfare. "A man could go blind with the desolation," was much his opinion. Wide skies unnerved him, all that high-toppled cloud. Snowbrowed mountain, desert, high chaparral, llano, range, purple sage at purple sunset depressed him. Terrain so open and raw, so all of itself alone made him feel swallowed up, gulped down and small, like "an immensity of nothing." He didn't sense God in the grandeur or delight in what nature had wrought. Didn't even cotton to rainbows, really, find them phenomenal or occasion for pause. "Gaudy," he'd remark, "gaucherie. The worst of the worst of God's stunts." Well, he was no man's buckaroo.

The object, it seemed to him, was to travel through it un-weathered, sojourn over it, preferably by train or stage, to abide it untrammeled, where not completely untouched, not live in it, get to know it, study its ways or wear them like skins. (He owned a horse, once, briefly, but never bothered to give it a name, content to lease them from livery stables or breed ranchers whenever he found himself saddled with the need.) At a loss to locate north with both hands of a compass, he preferred to haunt pike roads, a habitué of hotel rooms, denizen of saloons and drugcribs, dance-halls and bawdy houses.

He was discovering the culture; he knew it needed knowing.

He carried a faro kit satcheled inside his saddlebags along-side his armamentarium of costly Chevalier dental instruments, several maps, a mirror, an assortment of abalone and alabaster handcombs, gold, silver and ivory collar studs, an array of colorful string ties and satin cravats, an allotment of silk pocket kerchiefs bearing an acanthus motif in each of the primary *and* secondary colors (if none in black or white), two bars of unscented tallow soap, a pair of sterling matchsafes, several uncracked decks of Hart's Squared Linen Eagle Nonpareil Pharo Cards, and his shaving gear, including a Sheffield straight razor, with which he latterly had thought to shear several shavings from his ubiquitous shadow. One of those men who wear their profession, their obses-sions upon their person, within an arm's length, always at the ready, in reach at a moment's requirement, balanced on their hip, in a holster, say, or up a furtive sleeve, cocked inside their coat, shoved deep down in a pocket, derringer, near at mortal hand, *this very instant.*

One of those men who understand how in terror we lean in the direction that is most unlike us, clutched and cringing, clung to our tackle, our truck and our trim, our trade, no torture larger than living, running past our own character, into pain.

Upon dissolving their partnership, declaiming it his intention to abandon Dallas for "longitudes west" (this in the spring of '74), his erstwhile partner, Dr. John Seegar, bequeathed to his safekeeping—"with abiding affection," as he inscribed its frontispiece—a well-thumbed if hard-to-find volume from his private collection for which Doc on occasion had voiced a positive admiration. Entitled *The Anatomies of the True Physician and Counterfeit Mountebank (or The Tooth's Footache)*, the slimmish, lavishly illustrated book contained in particular one passage that, because it tickled him so, Doc—once having committed it to memory—would as the dynamic of the moment determined take to reciting with no little fanfare, the relief afforded by such theater being in his estimation preferable to that bred of such lower hilarity as knuckledusters, daggers or derringers. His regard for the word was boundless; he dreamed in *mots*, wordclots, he dreamed clogged with the syntax of litanies.

Rabble and quacksalvers of base wit abject perverse and sordidous scumme refuse and runagate cut-throats and graverobbers slowbellied monks Simoniacal and perjurious shavelings busy St. John-lack-Latins thrasonical and unlettered chemists shifting and outcast petitfoggers lightheaded and trivial druggers and apothecaries sunshunning nightbirds and cornercreepers dull-pated and base mechanics ribald resurrectionists stageplayers jugglers sub-conjurers astrologers ganymedes pedlar prittleprattling barbers filthy graziers curious bathkeepers common shifters and cogging cavaliers bragging and lazy clowns one-eyed and lame nursekeepers toothless and tattling sweeps impudent chattering charmen scape-Tyburns dog lechers counterfeit mountebanks and riffraff lewd and antic zanies factotums Merry Andrews and artful dodgers quick-witted and unscrupulous wachums who make the stars vouch for their virtue foretellers of starcrossed futures amassers of worthless fortunes glib purveyors of fake nostrums and remedies imposters pretenders frauds shams artificers hoodwinks hokums humbugs hoodoos hooligans hucksters ballyhoos bunkums connivers flimflammers charlatans chicancers grifters boondogglers hornswogglers swindlers scoundrels scalawags skullduggers cutpurses and low artists of high scam ruse con and dupe and those practised of brass brazen brash effronteries silly routs touts tumblers and hoopvaulters vain and boastful tricksters and harlequins dishonest blunderers and crooked and deceitful buffoons hamfingered bunglers journeymen jesters knavish jack-a-napes jimmyjammers jape-and-jibesters bloodletters cupdrawers bonesetters corncutters peruke-and-periwig makers cutlers occulists cunning physicks and all suchlike baggage who comprise *the professed sanctionless dental claque* and unto whose hands no wise man dare commend himself . . .

Embarking, then, upon his career as a "Transient," an "Itinerant Empiric" as they advertised themselves at the time, a "Floater" or "Portable," a "Pocket" (as he preferred), much less one compelled to canvas for clientele upon a rude frontier deprived of right technology, he was flirting with farce, as he was skirting the prospect of penury.

In a city, a skilled dentist could bank on netting more than $2,000 a year, tax-free; an enviably handsome living. In a wide-open cowtown where a cowhand typically made $30 a month, who knew? Certainly not enough to do aught but scrape by. Folks in general were not apt to place much stock in toothsmiths, reckoning them deliberate purveyors of pain where not downright crackpots and quacks. And while the latter as a class was one that in its credulity the West was wont to regard overfondly, the dental profession, as a profession, was roundly reviled. Certainly he had heard the description often enough: "a disagreeable taskmaker of unpleasant operations upon a recalcitrant and skeptical patient."

And small wonder, for while he toted with him such tools of the trade as he was able—forceps, pelicans, speculums, elevators, excavators, screws, keys, cannulas, trephines, gum lancets, scrapers, scalers, gravers, punches, pincers, raspers, chisels and files— his access to the latest in foot-pedal treadle-and-pulley-driven drills (an apparatus decidedly too cumbersome to practicably pick up and cart) much less to one of the newfangled electrics that the S. S. White Dental Manufacturing Company latterly had begun advertising in its catalog, was nonexistent. (He prided himself on remaining marginally abreast of such innovations, maintaining his subscription to the Southern Dental Association magazine, *Swish & Spit.*) Instead, he was obliged to make do as he might with the old jeweler's bow drill, an implement as backward in its application as it was problematic in results.

What was worse—and it was, inestimably worse—he hadn't recourse to the proper anesthetics. Not ether, chloroform, nitrous oxide or cocaine. Nothing, in fact, save such liquor as lay at hand. (Opium might be had, chiefly in the Chinatowns, but was prohibitively dear, and in light of De Quincey's account of the manner in which his own addiction had been prompted by "rheumatic toothache"—*Opium Eater* had been mandatory reading back in school—he refused to use it, dismissing its employment as "contraindicated and unethical.")

At last, despite the lot he knew about caries and pericementitis, pyorrhea and Riggs' disease, gingivitis, pulpitis, abscess and impaction, gumboil and ranula, tartar, plaque, and the manifold evils of bruxism—mainly, by and large, for the most part, generally speaking, as a rule of workaday routine—he just went ahead and YANKED them.

HAVING FLED THE Flat at Fort Griffin, Tex., "in a singular hurry," he came to alight for the summer in Dodge City, Kan., where he stood the price of an ad in the local rag (the D.C. Times), rented a room (No. 24) at Deacon Cox's Dodge House to double as a parlor/office, and began, however halfheartedly, receiving patients.

So, Mister Clamm—it is Clamm, is it not?

Yes sir, that it is. Zack. Zack Clamm.

Well then, Zack—may I call you Zack? You don't mind my calling you Zack, do you?

No sir. Fire away. Zack it is. Zack's jim-dandy. But say, how 'bout yerself then?

What's that?

Yerself. The moniker. Whaddya go by? How're y'called?

Why, Doc, Sir, I most generally am called Doc. Christian name's John Henry, though since careering West I have sought as I might to get shed of that particular past. Still, you know what they say: however much we may believe ourselves well rid of it, the past I mean, it is far from done with us—and I have no trouble believing it. Before I came out here, Mister Clamm, came West I mean, I never spared a passing thought for names. I had been given one, always—or so it seemed to me—had had one, was glad enough to go by the one I had been given, and whether it particularly suited me, I could not in all candor have said. A stray sequence of sounds in the mind, a few elementary movements of the lips and the tongue, some tracks on a page sutured there like a semaphore of serialized scars, serifs or bone chips strewn like a stampede of dice, nothing but a spoor of pronunciation comprising the phonetical map of its sum. That's roughly what I took a name for, Mister Clamm—a designation of simple identity. But then, as I say, that was before I debouched West, and once I had, what began to dawn on me was that what a name really is, is a repository of meaning. Just that. Singular meaning and metaphor. All the stuff that gets stuffed inside of its syllables like diacritical apples up the craw of a hog. The crap, Sir, closely crammed in the crapper, the enporcelained shit jammed to its bowl. Reputation, yes. Persona. Image and icon. The rest. All the associational refuse accrued unto it as if by some magnetic, effluvial pull. And so I began to ask myself, as well I might, how it was that such a thing could have happened. This unbidden appropriation of my name. The very one I had so naively assumed was no one's but my own, alone. How, that is, the cognomen Doc, when paired with its counterpart, Holliday, had become but a chamber pot for the stale of others, their projectivist scumber and subliminal stool. Because frankly, Mister Clamm, frankly I was beginning to feel reduced to nothing but a dump or a landfill, a waste site for toxic debris, a scow, Sir, for the scat of the ongoing past as it had come to yesterlimn the leavings of some barnacled yore. I trust, Mister Clamm, that I do not lard it on overthick, but what I wish for you to understand is that no name is exempt from the tricks that memory plays, or the burlesque it can make of one's life. What's in a name? Why, sooner ask what's in a septic tank, a slit trench, a cesspool or latrine. It's what's disposed of, what deposited, what reposes in the hollow of its hold, the manure of such meaning as history—or fiction—has succeeded in squeezing down time's passage like excreta through a bowel, until it obtrudes from the pore and dilated portal, that perforation in posterity's hole. And when one is dead or long departed, become but a memory—or a mem-

71

ory of a memory's myth, scarce a gesture of masquerade—what's in a name is all the flotsam others choose to fill it with. Before it is forgotten, or indurates to fossil, or some remnant of ossified dung. Doc, Mister Clamm, you may feel free to call me Doc, for now that *is* my name, and I bear it as best I am able, like a vast and inevitable fatigue.

Yeah, well, uh, pleased to make your acquaintance there, Doc.

So then, Mister Clamm, down to business, shall we? What seems to be the nature of the complaint?

Got me an ache. Bad ache. Like to be all of a misery. Back here, up top, down under one of my teeth.

Yes, Sir?

And whilst I rather be scalped than sit for a dentist, it's got here lately so I jus' can't stand it no more. Nights 'specially. Like it's, I dunno, jus' jumps is what. Pounces like. Pain of it. Shoots so's my head comes a-jacking off the pillow fixin' to fly clean off my neck. Haven't got more'n a wink all week. Thought to have a pass at it myself, knock it loose with a rock or hammer or whatnot, pry it up with a pliers, maybe cut it out with a scolpers, but a friend of mine seen your ad in the paper:

FIRST CLASS
PROFESSIONAL DENTISTRY
IN ALL ITS BRANCHES
Teeth filled or extracted
without pain or peril
J. H. HOLLIDAY hereby respectfully offers his services
to the good citizens of Dodge City and surrounding country
Ladies and Gentlemen are invited to call as convenient
Charges moderate and warranteed
Where satisfaction is not given money will be refunded

And, anyways, as this friend of mine give you such high marks, I thought, what the hell, might as well give her a shot, so . . .

So here you are.

Yeah. S'pose so. Here I am. And at your mercy.

Indeed my mercy. But not to worry, Mister Clamm, not to worry. We—the profession, I mean—have evolved no scant distance from the days of dosing and purging, blistering and blood-leeching, cautery, scarification and hot knives. We no longer avail ourselves of the Plumbeum Odontagogon Extractor, or, as Fauchard was wont to prescribe, recommend gargling with the early morning urine of young boys. We know that caries is not caused by scurvy, humors or worms, and it has been some time since we ceased treating abscesses with arsenic and enemas, or, you shall be cheered to hear, filling cavities with molten lead. We have evolved, Sir, beyond the Improved Magneto Electrolux Machine, Pratt's Battery, the Oxydonor, the Radiolux, Dr. Scott's Toothbrush, Greenough's Antiscorbutic Tincture, Burchell's Anodyne Necklace, the Violet Ray Machine and Baunscheidt's Lebenswecker. But here, first things first. Take a slug. Help yourself. That's it. And another. Laudanum and rye whiskey. Torture on the lungs, taffy for the brain. Healthy pull now. Bottoms up. There, that'll do. Now, you take a seat, get all comfy, head on the bolster, open wide, keep still as the grave, and you'll be out of here in no time, back on the street no worse for the wear, my professional guarantee. By the by, if I might be so bold, your friend, the one who put in the kind word for me, might I inquire after the gent's good name?

Reckon so. Why the hell not? Masterson. Bat Masterson.

Ah yes, but of course, the notorious smiling man and noble sheriff of our fair Ford County—Mister Billy Barclay himself.

Why? You know him?

Know him? You might say, after a fashion, though it would

perhaps be more accurate to observe that he knows me, or that he knows Wyatt, who in turn we know mutually.

Wyatt? You mean Wyatt Earp?

I do mean. The one and the only.

Why, that longfaced, rainyday bastard not two days ago knocked me for a loop right out front of this here same building. Coldcocked me with his damn gunbarrel. Laid me out flat in the gutter is what. Not the first time neither. Though don't it beat all, missed my tooth and cracked my skull.

Ah yes, quite so. I can feel the lump, just here. Reared quite an egg. Buffaloed you, did he? Can't say I'm surprised. He does have a peculiar positive knack that way. I trust he had fair reason.

Well, I was heeled, see? Didn't know it was agin the law 'round here. Once I come to, cost me a sawbuck to the magistrate.

But didn't you see the signs? They're posted all about, big as billboards.

Saw 'em, jus' didn't think to pay 'em no heed. Lots of towns got pissant rules like that and don't think to enforce 'em regular. Plus which, while I ain't normally the contrary sort, this god-howlin' tooth had me feeling heeldug and cranky and wired for a row. Still, if I'd've knowed it was Earp's law hereabouts, I'd've parked my piece straight off. In my experience, don't pay to tangle with no Earp. Cross one, you've crossed 'em all, and being they're so many, damn brood like a tribe, they got you outnumbered on the snide. That, and the way they keep on a-comin'.

Indeed, Sir, that they do, they do indeed, as they seldom back down. A word of counsel? So long as there are Earps in this world—and from the look of things that could be a good long while yet—might I suggest that the most sagacious policy is to remain, as you may intuit it in the moment, upon their sunny side—sunny, that is, as they may abide. Think of it as a matter of self-preservation. It always has worked for me. There now, that should do her. Your number 12. First bicuspid on the left side. Dead black at the nerve. I trust that it wasn't all too much of an ordeal for you.

But I didn't feel a thing. Not a twinge. Don't that beat all, though. How'd you do it, Doc?

Trick of the trade, Sir, trick of the trade. But here, another swig, swish and spit, you can use the spittoon, just there.

So what's the damages, Doc?

Let us subtract insult from injury, shall we, Mister Clamm? Call it even. Consider it equitable compensation for Wyatt's precipitous public humiliation of your thoroughly fictional, if legendarily pint-sized person. All I ask in recompense is that when history comes a-calling, as it surely someday must, that you do all in your power—your infinite power as a fully realized figment of the fictive imagination, that is—to set the documentable record straight. Tell them, Mister Clamm, as they may be disposed to listen, that though Doc Holliday was dying and drunk and preferred to exercise his prerogative to gamble his life away—when not engaged in the occasional sportive gunplay—that insofar as his chosen profession was concerned, he caused far less pain than he allayed. Here then. Your molar, Sir. Go ahead, take it. I believe it was Cervantes who once remarked that every tooth in a man's head is more valuable than a diamond, though might I suggest that in your case likewise the yanked tooth in your hand. As you will note, I have, improbable as it may seem, tooled and filled with goldfoil—my COA as it were—the pro forma trademark inscription into the surface of its enamel: *J.H.H. 6/9/78.* I admonish you to hold on to it, Zack, as a memento, a fetish or trophy, a piece of corroborating evidence so to say. Any man will eventually find himself down on his luck, and then, who knows, you may discover that such an artifact is like to fetch a fair penny at your corner pawnshop. The West cannot sustain forever, Sir, indeed might I suggest that we are living out the last of its myth as we speak. And once it is over and done, once it has played out its string, once they call cut and print, then mark my words, what once was flesh and blood and bone, and, yes, dead tooth as well, must only be worth its weight in gold. In the meantime, do yourself the favor of looking after your teeth. No need, as Pliny the Elder once prescribed, to eat a mouse twice a month, but you might want to look into green corn. Toughens the enamel as it sharpens the edges. Just the thing for biting the hand that feeds you. Believe me, I know whereof I speak. Leaving them laughing is fine, but it is bleeding and battered and shot up clean through that makes the more lingering impression.

Thanks, Doc. You're a right fair hand at the teeth business. See you around, then.

Not likely, Zack, allowing as I am on my way to hell, and you to God's Own Author knows where. The two of us may know the distinction matters less than our respective critics may condescend to concede, but as you have your own fish to fictionally fry, so have I my own in fact to fritter. I wish you Godspeed, Zack Clamm. Godspeed and narrative-life everlasting. I wish you, Sir, you and your creator, the immortality of poems.

The Cautious Gunslinger
of impeccable personal smoothness
and slender leather-encased hands
folded casually
to make his knock.
He would show you his map.

—EDWARD DORN

FOR 15 YEARS around the West, Doc was a knockabout drifter—
"the Man with Soles of Wind," as Kate called him—bannerless,
unbounden, bereft, selved singly to the hood of his own hook,
homeless as a poker chip, displaced in his person as he was dis-
possessed in his soul. And the drifting seemed to suit him; he
juned more terrain than a cartographer.

> Dallas, Tex.
>
> Denison, Tex.
>
> Denver, Col.
>
> Cheyenne, Wyo.
>
> Deadwood, S.D.
>
> Breckenridge, Tex.
>
> Fort Griffin, Tex.
>
> Dodge City, Kan.
>
> Las Vegas, N.M.
>
> Prescott, Ariz.
>
> Tombstone, Ariz.
>
> Pueblo, N.M.
>
> Gunnison, Col.
>
> Leadville, Col.
>
> El Paso, Tex.
>
> Glenwood Springs, Col.

"He changed zip codes with the weather," is the way one lat-
terday old-timer put it. "He blew with the breeze. But then, being
slatsided as a wand, racky as a reed and more delicate than most
women, s'pose he didn't much see the point in trying to stand his
ground."

There was extant in those days a recognized "gambler's circuit," and Doc typically could be found ponying its carousel through one town or another, inside one hotel-dancehall-saloon or another, at one table or another, day or night along its trail. Even on those uncommon occasions when he had no cause to dodge the law, he seldom overstayed a welcome. What Doc clearly had a knack for was making a killing, pocketing his winnings, pulling up stakes, packing up his scruples and moving on; catch you later, catch as catch can.

Once he left Georgia—and when he left, he left for good; he never, not once, returned to visit family or friends—there exists no evidence, scrap nor shred, that it ever crossed his mind to "put down roots, feather my nest, and lay in the larder."

"A booking target is harder to hit," was all he ever offered by way of explanation. "A shark, so it is said, sleeps upon the swim, and the moment it ceases such ceaseless motion, in that moment, so may you lay odds, it likewise has purchased the oyster farm. Hang your hat, unpack your ruck, pull up a chair, put up your feet, sink your claim, stay put too long in one place and the next you know, death's up and got the bulge on you froze dead in its sights, set to take your life for its trump. 'Tis true I am no nester. I always have been a slicker hand at leaving than at roosting. For this I offer no apology. Death is not a human condition, not lived day by day. Living life is hard enough, living death scarce to be borne. Mortality will unmoor any man.

"You'd feel much the same if you'd spent your whole life getting worse."

It wasn't wanderlust. No horizon called him, no greener pasture beckoned, he had no hankering to giddip-and-be-gone or itch to git-himself-yonder, make far-apart tracks for the high-and-uncut, hightail it, light out for the territory or skedaddle to parts unknown; he wasn't one to blaze new trails or gypsy fresh frontier, and the only elbow room he required was enough to belly unmolested to the bar. Unsettled perhaps, restless no question, a wayfarer, yes, but not wayward, no gadabout, shiftless derelict, vagrant saddle tramp, maundering bandit, scuppering vagabond. He knew where he was headed at all times, his sense of true north was as impeccable as his attire, and the compass of his thought, even when most besotted, he generaled with the witting clinicism of tumblers in a lock. As with many professional gamblers, his mind was a map, its geography clean as mathematics, Bedouin to its desert, and he was no less attuned to the subterra of its subtlest detail than that demanded by the dentistry that was his trade by formal training. It was as if he believed that to move, any move at all, was to act. That movement was possessed of a purpose, and in its migration, meaning. This art of passing through.

At last nothing could have been simpler: in his mind there always was another place, if seldom one more welcome, to get to. He had a footloose, itinerant, nightprowler's nature, and as he couldn't be troubled to believe in the past or what it might portend, he felt free to walk away from wherever he might be at any given moment as if it had never existed. He was, as he always was, on his way to someplace else. And if where he was headed was bound for nowhere fast, still, he was ill-disposed to be waylaid or otherways detained. He had a hunch he fobbed off as a theory: even Nowhere has a name.

And so there, wherever there might prove to be, he meant to go, lest time arrive there in advance and blast to flinders such future as might have him. He was, you see, doing his utmost to remain out front, a step to the fore, to outrun the waning of his days and the shadow that dogged them so like landscape. One of those men who never believed in death up ahead, *but eternally behind: in any moment that stops and thinks.*

DOC'S CIRCUIT

The Alhambra
The St. Charles
Bogel's
Johnnie Thompson's Varieties & Bella Union
(Dallas)

The Beehive
John Shannsey's Cattle Exchange Saloon
Wilson & Matthews'
Charley Mayer's
Bower's
Jones & Rush's Busy Bee
(Fort Griffin)

The Theatre Comique
The Little Casino
The Arcade
The Argyle
The Turf Exchange
Murphy's Exchange
The Mint
Cricket Hall
Patrick O'Connell's Missouri House
The Oyster Ocean
The Palace Variety Theatre & Gambling Parlours

The Metropolitan
The Denver House
Chase's
Chucovich's
(Denver)

The Gem Variety
Nuttall & Mann's No. 10
The Little Mint
(Deadwood)

The Bella Union Variety Theatre
Greer's Gold Room
The Shingle & Locke
(Cheyenne)

The Dodge House
Ben Springer's Lady Gay Saloon & Comique Theatre
The Long Branch
The Lone Star
The Billiard (later the Saratoga)
The Junction
The Oasis
The Alamo
The Green Front
The Main Street
Pierce & Thayer's Gold Rooms
(Dodge City)

Close & Patterson's
(Las Vegas)

Cobweb Hall
The Palace
Sazarac's
(Prescott)

The Gold Coin
(Globe)

The Legal Tender
The Fashion
Congress Hall
(Tucson)

The Crystal Palace
The Oriental
The Occidental
The Arcade
The Alhambra
The Capitol
Campbell & Hatch's
(Tombstone)

Tom Kemp's Comique & Variety Theatre
(Pueblo)

The Little Casino
The Little Globe
Cy Allen's Monarch
Hyman's
John G. Morgan's Board of Trade
The Texas House
The Casino Gambling Hall
The Church Casino
Phil Golding's
Pap Wyman's
Carbonate Concert Hall
St. Anne's Rest
Coleman's
Louie Mitchell's
Cole & Alexander's
(Leadville)

Taylor & Look's Gem
The Coliseum Variety Theatre & Gambling Saloon
(El Paso)

———◆———

See where you are,
look around.
This is what it is like.
—PAUL BOWLES

So watch out
and be there.
—STEPHANE MALLARMÉ

The quality of living, however fast or fully, a mainly missing life.

(How far West can any man wander? How far is ever far enough? What sundown too near? For any man? This man? This forsaken, solitary, particular, this sunstricken westering man?)

ALTHOUGH I ASSISTED him substantially on several occasions, I did not do so because we got on or because I admired him any too much, but on account of Wyatt, who perennially did. Personally, I found him hotheaded, impestuous, quarrelsome and reckless, his temper disputatious at all times, well-nigh ungovernable when drunk, which save when asleep was most always. He was selfish to the point of perversity, with the disposition of a dog that's been kicked twice too often, selfish and self-obsessed, and if there were those who considered him heroically so, which appears now the going rumor, I was content to count myself last among them. The strange part was, even at his worst—which commenced upon his waking—he more often was in the right than the wrong.

Doc wasn't everyone's cup of chamomile, that's a fact, but then men like him, so desolate and fleery, so all of themselves and nothing else, men so bent on going their own way, doing what they damn well please, fuck-all, men such as that seldom are. Outside the Earps he hadn't a real friend anywhere in the West. He was as petulant and hectic a pariah as I have ever known, and as desperate a one in a tight place as the worst of the worst of the breed. All in all, he bore close watching, the way you would a polecat; wherever he was at any named moment, that's the one place in the world you did not want to be, because if he wasn't real safe to know, he was a positive danger to have dealings with. Put a tolerable crimp in your plans for the evening, Doc would, like that.

No, far as I was concerned, Doc Holliday didn't have but a single redeeming quality—he'd soon be dead. If not nearly soon enough. Sounds mean, and I mean it to. Yesterday would have been eons late to suit me.

I say he was desperate, as so surely he was, desperate each day to cheat death, and yet to tag him a true desperado, one of those whose trade runs to mayhem and felony, would be to hem the facts to the hawings of fiction. He had his occasional run-ins, but it wasn't breaking the law that he cared about, it was breaking the bank, going for broke, beating the odds, it was prying the all from the nothing. We all of us gambled, it was in our blood, but Doc was a gambler, the table was his domain, and if he wasn't its sovereign, he came as close to it as any I ever assayed; when he wasn't playing it was as if he was lost, lost as a dog who's lost his last bone. The rest of us played for money, or laughs, or because we couldn't stop. Doc played to be perfect. It was just that simple. He believed in the chance of perfection, and more, in the perfection of chance. Could have been he was after something personal, an ascension maybe, private transit, his ticket stamped somewhere in the cards. Maybe what he was betting on was a moment of transport, that sacred investiture, the grace of a deliverance.

Only asked him about it the once. "Just trying to get it right, Billy," which is what he always called me. "Just trying to get right what's sure to go wrong in the end anyway." Which was pretty much the way Doc thought—that all was pure hazard, or craps.

What he really was was a hopeless romantic. Hat brim to boot heel. Not one of those shaggydog saps or dreamy-eyed dopes— because he was all of most anything but—but a romantic at the end of his rope, one who had literally exhausted all hope, and he romanticized that hopelessness until it had blossomed backwards into a full-bore despair. Had every right to do so, but too often it left him a liability in any particular situation, made him mood-swung and willful and too gladdish to be mean. Darkness and isolation, that's what he took solace in. And chaos. He was cussed and contrawise and we all knew he was cursed (as he knew that we knew); trouble followed him about like a bird dog.

Fallen. Reckon that's the best I can say in his favor. Like he'd known a height the rest of us couldn't have scaled in our dreams.

(He'd have said pratfallen, save it was no laughing matter, none atall.) But he'd been up there, had a taste, breathed it in, and there were times I might have envied him for it had he not been so hellbent on falling so much the further and taking the rest of us with him.

At best people put up with him, in part owing to his reputation as a killer, most of which was bunk, but mainly on account of his being a member of that frontier class which, though it seems queer to us now, at the time was so highly esteemed. Back then professional gamblers were a gilded species unto themselves, the lily-fingered fraternity as they were called, their chief characteristics being an absolute aversion to day labor, a smoothness of manner, an easiness of tongue, a quickness of wit and a penchant for fussy and finicky dress. In those days it was considered not only a legitimate business, but one that was honorable, even honored, a real profession, almost an elite or aristocracy, being on a par with medicine, and clearly outranking lawyering, dentistry, banking, undertaking or preaching the gospel. And at the top of the heap, the very highest caste, the real Brahmins and Mandarins, were the faro dealers, who if they were true aces, could fashion for themselves a right fine and steady living.

And the most famous faro dealer of all, the ne plus ultra of the type, was John Henry Holliday.

(WILLIAM BARCLAY BARTHOLOMEW "BAT" MASTERSON)

While still a child, he had been variously tutored in the intricacies of the folk games habitually played by the servants indentured to his family—Skinning, Up and Down the River, Put and Take, Get You One, others—each of which he had taken to with such ardor and aptitude that it had astonished even the most seasoned hands among those slaves (slaves making, in his estimation, much the most excellent servants).

"Genius comes guised in a gaggle of get-ups," he once remarked. "We all are granted our gifts and greenthumbs. Fate determined mine was for counting cards, ciphering the odds and wagering the bluff of my fellows. For better or worse, I recognized this from an early age."

There existed in the Deep South of his day a "roster of manhood," a litany of imperatives that constituted a code, this unspoken covenant with, as we might say now, a certain cultivated decadence, and one flouted its conventions only at unthinkable cost to one's soul. One drank, one rode, one wenched, one knew one's way around pistols and knives, and one gambled. And one was content to carry each to excess even as one prided oneself upon the capacity.

Liquor.

Horses.

Women.

Guns and daggers.

Cards and dice.

In no particular order.

It was once at school that he found himself at the latter roughly around the clock, and had he been less successful at the outset, had his classmates—not a few of them scions of a monied eastern seaboard set possessed of pockets deeper than he could have conceived—not been such willing marks, the way things fell later might have cut differently. But he won. Won just enough, just often enough, to delude himself that he had the knack, the touch, the gift, the juice, that talent, Old Mister X, its kismet, some magic, the Mojo, IT, whatever IT might be—shazaam, alakazaam, abracadabra, hocus-pocus—whatever he thought IT was. That is what he thought he had. Or IT, him. It was only later that he would come fully to apprehend that there is no IT, nor ever has been, for IT, decidedly, isn't. Or as it is, is never, not ever, enough.

In time he was to acquaint himself with every kind of gambler. The rabbits, softhands, jacklegs and hunchmakers who mistook it for child's play. The stiffs, shortstops, dilettantes and dabblers who were content to break even. The veterans who, having come to know better, wished to quit but could not. The hardrocks, mercenaries, cutthroats and swashbucklers who were out strictly for blood. The crazies who took less pleasure in winning than in the losses of others. The plungers, speculators, earthquakers and shortriders whose only play was the all-or-nothing gold dig. The grifters and gaffers, hustlers and nutmen to whom cheating was second nature. The sharps, mechanics and sure-thing riggers for whom the Swindle was high art. The chiselers, mopes, railbirds and lobs who frequented the fringes to prey on the unwitting. The weasels and stoats, welshers and fencetakers who were the worst of the lot. The coffeehousers whose best play was the gift of their gab. The students and calculators who thought it a science. The deans, professors and philosophers who had seen it all twice before. And the fanatics—the dreamers, schemers and true believers who had pledged themselves to a "system" at whose altar they worshipped firm in the conviction that it must shift the edge in their favor, break the bank, and secure them their fortune if only they could ride the lean times through at all cost before it cleaned them out bare to the bone.

"Common belief holds," he once wrote his cousin Mattie back in Georgia (this before, having taken the veil and the vows, she had become Sister Mary Melanie of the Order of the Sisters of Mercy), "that all it takes to make a successful gambler is the cunning to dope out the risk, the skill to sense the run of the game, the nerve to play the stakes to the showdown, and the judgment to quit the action in the black. That's not gambling, it's religion.

"No, what distinguishes the true professional from the rank amateur is the disposition and willingness to lose, lose big, lose everything, then lose again, hold fast, refuse to rattle and keep playing. To *work*. The sport who is the artisan, and for whom gambling is a craft, always will find a way, riches or ruin, to sustain his resource, to grind out the play.

"Each time I take to the table I repeat to myself the same four words: nothing left to lose, nothing left to lose, nothing left to lose that you've not lost long ago. And believed it, to the seat of my soul.

" 'Tis not the eternal hope of winning that draws me to the cards, but my abiding faith in the game. Not the promise of the payoff, but the action of the play. The action is its own reward. I simply desire to keep my hand in, to be a player. The play is score enough.

"It is said that a winner knows when to quit, when to hold 'em and when to fold 'em, but a professional hasn't the luxury of the license. He can never quit because for him it is less a matter of earning a living than of inhabiting a way of life, it is the same as breathing, the rhythm gathered of the moment. The money comes and it goes, the game remains. The money is no more than the medium, a means, an instrument and a tool. High stakes add a dash of spice to any wager, but in the end, money is but the language used to express the syntax of the game. As long as one has enough of it to keep from going belly-up, it is of scant consequence. Every true professional knows this, just as every true professional seldom speaks of it.

"As to Lady Luck, she is the old siren's song, a temptress and a tease. Dame Fortune is a whore. She will catch your eye with the flash of a thigh, lick come-hithers in your ear, finger your prick, then string you along on a wing and a prayer before leaving you flat busted and broke. I have heard it said that luck breaks even. Perhaps, over time, the course of one's life. But in the moment? No, the only luck I have ever believed in is bad luck.

"Chance respects no man's history. Nothing is certain owing to what has come before. Each throw of the dice, each spin of the wheel, each flip of the coin, each turn of the cards is unto itself virgin, the immaculate moment of singular possibility. Chance, in all things, is chaste.

"One player may well loathe another, but the cards themselves are no more friend than foe. Deaf, dumb, mute, blind, bereft of heart and soul, they simply do not care. Win, lose, draw, your life is a matter of complete indifference to them. Lest it be going at it with pistols, when a game is played straight up and on the square, I can think of no activity, sex aside, that can make one feel so alive. Or healed.

"Look here, Mel, it's just a job, and it's not Sweet Lorraine. It's what one does for a living, it's work, the work of a lifetime, perhaps, but not Primrose Lane. And if at times I feel for it a certain passion, a measure of compulsion, still, it is seldom a pleasure. It's turning a buck, sweat of the brow, bucking the tiger, it's on with the show. Singers sing, gamblers gamble. It's what they do, what they must do or suffer their souls' undoing. This, from the Heretical Gospel of Thomas: *If you do not bring forth that which is within you, that which is within you will destroy you.* The aura of the gambler is a flame, and unless it is given leave to vent itself at the tables, it must only fuel itself elsewhere, and then leaping, roaring, and much to the injury of all.

"I fancy I am much as the poet, the one who spends all day

every day writing poems, and when his wife asks him of an evening to compose a little verse on her behalf, says, 'Go to hell.' That's the way I feel about gambling. It's my business, I take it seriously, and while it can be gratifying in the moment or profitable over time, it never, ever, is fun."

———•••———

AT ONE TIME or another he flirted with most of them: pedro, pooloo, paddle wheel, wheel of fortune, birdcage, brag, blackjack, backgammon, banco, keno, casino, canute, Kansas Lottery, equality, roulette, monte, Spanish Monte, lansquenet, rouge-et-noir, all-fours, crown-and-anchor, rondo, red dog, fan-tan, tarantula, Diana, seven-and-a-half, seven-up, over-and-under, hi-lo, hazard, hieronymus, highball, horsehead, old sledge, el sapo, Van John, Van Tuama, vingt-et-un, chuck-farthing, chuck-a-luck, chusa, craps, dice. But it was poker, stud poker, that he was pledged to, as it was faro, the so-called prestige game, that he worked. And why not? It was not unheard of, after all, for a high-end faro dealer to make as much as $1,000 a month, minus the "rake" percentage kicked back to the house and the payout to his "staff" (or where hired on as the house steady, a flat $25 per six-hour shift).

Faro, while not overly complex, is far from an uncomplicated game, and if it was the most popular form of gambling in the saloons and sawdust joints of the time, that was only because it was reputed to be the one run most on the square while offering its participants—called punts or producers—the best odds at winning, odds broadly advertised as even (though the house in fact enjoyed a slight statistical edge—some 3%, more at times, as on the last turn, when it rose another 14).

A hybrid game incorporating elements of baccarat, roulette and blackjack, faro required both a "staff"—a banker/dealer or "mechanic" possessed of a sufficient grubstake (customarily 10,000);

a casekeeper or "hearse-rider"; and a cheatspotter or "lookout"; plus a "rig"—an oilcloth, greenfelt or flatboard layout or "spread" painted with the 13 cards of any suit (typically spades, though the suit was irrelevant); a rosewood-and-boxwood, abacus-like device called a "case," the doughnut-holed, rod-strung, ivory discs of which tracked the cards that had been played during a deal (an activity called "riding the hearse"); a spring-loaded, side-slotted, open-topped mahogany "banker's box" or "card shoe" holding a 52-card deck; and the chips: the 25-cent white, $1 blue, $10 red and $50 or $100 yellow, the latter employed only in no-limit, North Star games.

Play began once the punts had placed their bets on the board either "straight up"—playing a single card to win, "coppering"—playing a single card to lose, or "coppering the heel"—playing a combination to win and/or lose at the same time. (Such combinations were six in number: the king/queen/jack—the "big figure"; the ace/deuce/three—the "little figure"; the six/seven/eight—the "pot"; the king/queen/ace/deuce—the "grand square"; the jack/three/four/ten—the "jack square"; and the nine/eight/six/five—the "nine square.")

Once the bets were down, the dealer discarded the top card of the deck—the "soda"—and drew the next two cards—a "turn"—face up from the slot in the shoe. The first card of the turn was a loser, the bank raking in all wagers laid upon that denomination from the layout. The second card was a winner, the bank paying one-for-one on the wagers made by the punts on that denomination. If the turn produced a "split"—two cards of the same denomination—the bank took half of the wagers made on that denomination. If it resulted in a "wash"—two denominations on which no wagers had been laid—the punts could stand pat or redeploy their wagers before the next turn.

After 24 turns, three cards remained in the shoe—a loser, a

winner and the bottom card or "hock." In a special bet called the "cat hop," the punts could wager on the order in which these cards would turn up, the bank paying winners two-to-one.

<hr/>

IN 1882 THE *Police Gazette* published *Faro Exposed, or The Gambler and His Prey.* Believing it his duty as a professional, Doc took it upon himself to read: "All regular faro players are reduced to poverty, while dealers and bankers who do not play against the game amass large fortunes. Almost every player has some peculiar system which he strives to believe will beat the bank and which does sometimes realize his hopes. In the end, all systems fail."

In the end, all systems fail.

"I thought it a helluva fine epitaph," he would remark later, "and so thought to mention it to Kate, who readily concurred."

But apparently nothing came of it. The original inscription on his headstone, the one still to be found there, in Glenwood Springs, Col., 6,000 feet up in the Old Linwood Frontiersmen's Cemetery patrolled Cerberus-like by the twin, one-eyed golden retrievers, Cody and Kayla, reads now, word for word, exactly as it did then: "He died, in bed."

bucking the tiger: 1. playing the odds at faro; the professional frontier gambler carried his faro outfit in a mahogany box upon which was painted the likeness of a Royal Bengal tiger; tigers also were pictured on the aces of his cards, his chips and his oilcloth spread; as a form of advertisement, saloons that featured the game typically displayed a tiger marquee over their front doors or in their windows (Dick Clark's Alhambra in Tombstone kept an actual tiger, stuffed, on a shelf above its backbar, and the Arcade in Denver boasted a skylight inlaid with a tiger beveled of stained glass); the game thus became colloquially known as *the tiger*

There is no more honest game than that among those who know best how to cheat, for then the distrust is universal and equitable in its distribution. Not that they must be by regular practice cheaters themselves, but that they know how to call one out, how to detect the funny stuff.

Professionals dare not swindle other professionals, it is too risky a business. Everyone knows the same feints and ploys, dupes and ruses, decoys and misdirects, the same gambits, pretexts, stratagems, sleights and trickwork, knows what everyone else knows, knows the moves, when they are apt to be made and how to spot them when they see them. It is mutual suspicion that keeps the square game square.

It is for this reason that I dislike playing with amateurs, particularly those who consider themselves something more. It is the very aspirations of such ilk that render them first careless, then desperate, finally unpredictable, and so, in consequence, most dangerous.

—DOC HOLLIDAY

The Mechanics Grip

Mitting

The Pickup Stack

The Riffle Stack

The Overhand Shuffle Stack

The False Shuffle

The Overhand Runoff

The Pull-through and Fast Cut

Shifting the Cut

The False Cut

The Cold Deck

The Second Deal

The Double Duke

The Peek

The Bottom Deal

The Palm

Trapping   Spotting   Holding-out

Cheating, as an art, is strictly for amateurs, small-timers or technicians, or those deprived of the wit and imagination to apprehend that miracles can happen, and those that do, do. There have, of course, always been those prepared to excuse—insofar as they may be executed with the requisite skill—the palm- and handwork: the false shuffles, locations, the crimps and cuts and doubledealing, while in the next breath scorning marked cards and stacked decks, the use of rings and mirrors and the employment of any manner of setup rig, holdout device or advantage tool, as distinctly beneath them. Such standard paraphernalia as the crooked sand-tell, coffeemill, end-squeeze and horsebox faro shoes, for instance.

For my part, I never have recognized the distinction. As most men do not play cards, but rather play *at* them, and as not one in 10,000 really knows or cares to know anything about what constitutes gaming in each of the interior chambers at its heart, why bother? At last, all

that is required to prevail against such opponents is a
steady hand, a keen eye and a modulated measure of
nerve. Faith in the chaos of the moment and the acumen
to aesthetically manage it, a mastery of chaos until one
has become much its connoisseur—you are possessed of
those, and there is no call to cheat. Ever.

—DOC HOLLIDAY

belly strippers/humps

bevels/bricks/cut edges/shapes

big touch

blank-out/bloomer

readers: blockout work/cutout work/daub work/edge work/light work/line work/outside work/peg work/sand work/scroll work/shade work/strong work/trim work

burn a card

busters/tops/T's/misspots

cackle the dice

case card

case the deck

check cop

chippy

cinch hand

clip

clocker

cold deck

copthrower

crimp/ear/wave

crossroader/basedealer/handmucker/holdout artist/second dealer

countersinks/flush spots

dispatchers

dogger

dragdown

drowned

dry

fairbank

false cut

fast count

firstflops/flat passers/loads/six ace flats

flat joint

flatty

free ride

freeze out

freeze-out prop

gaff

get behind

get out

go south

grind

hook up

hop/shift

inside work

iteming

jake

jinx/jonah

kick/poke

kicker

laydown

live card

locaters

lumber

Memphis dominos

Mexican standoff

Michigan bankroll

mitt

office

old bill

oneways

on the cuff

overlay

paints

perfects

phonies

prop bet

pull down

pull through

readyup

ring in

rock

rope

rough it up

rumble

running strong

sandbagging

screen out

shiner

shortcake

slamming

sleeper

slick ace cards

slough up

sorts

spit

spring

steer game

stripped deck

trap

trims

trips

vig wire

workdown

Trade jargon. This private vocabulary, secret text, the Braille inside which he breathed himself whole again whole again whole again, arcane and immaculate, healed.

HOLLIDAY ON POKER: THE 21 RULES
(gathered here for the first time, anywhere)

1. Play and play often. It is the one sure way of sharpening your skills.

2. Five Card Stud—one down, four up—is the cleanest, the clearest, and the only true game. It requires more instinct, more judgment, and more raw nerve than any other form. The rest is for amateurs and with extreme prejudice to be scrupulously avoided.

3. Don't get in over your head. Long experience beats raw skill nine times out of ten. Tinhorns and old hands don't mix.

4. Know the rules of the game, the rules of the house, the rules of the table and the etiquette governing all three. As there are no codified rules in poker, to do otherwise is to beg embarrassment and humiliation, if not to be fourflushed and fleeced.

5. Always sit with your back to the wall.

6. Trust no one. Suspect everything. Betray nothing.

7. Believe in the superiority of your hand, not the inferiority of your opponents'. Don't try to beat your fellow players, let them try to beat you. Assign to them neither too much nor too little skill. Study them. Assess their style of play. Appraise their technique and its idiosyncrasies. Calibrate their strengths and weaknesses. Take account of their tells and tics, habits and mannerisms. Read their eyes. Hear their thoughts. Play the man, not the hand.

7a. Keep your opponents entirely in the dark about every aspect of yourself. Aim for inscrutability at all times. Play possum.

8. Know all the angles beforehand. Cover all the bases. Recognize the odds and play them, but don't become their hostage, or you will soon become their stooge. What is probable is just that. With a 52-card deck, nothing wild, the number of all possible hands in a game of Stud is 2,598,960. There are no sure things.

The smart play is always the smart play, but it is not always the right play. There is more to winning than mathematics.

9. Treat every hand anew. Sometimes everything loses, other times nothing at all wins. Forget what has come before.

9a. Avoid going on tilt. Resist the urge to recoup, pull even, make up lost ground, or you will wind up chasing rainbow pots, throwing good money after bad.

10. Concentrate. Focus. Pay attention. Every card received, every bet made, every gesture in every detail has in the moment a critical meaning that it is your task to rightly decipher. Never miss a trick.

10a. Read and memorize each card and its relationship to every other—your own and your opponents'—and how it affects the odds.

11. If you are the player holding the best cards at the beginning of a hand, you are the player most likely to hold the best cards at the end of that hand—but only if you play to maintain your edge by improving upon it at each opportunity.

12. Better to fold too early than too late. If you have nothing, get out, then stay out, all night long if need be. Where you have something, the moment you detect that your opponents have more, drop out. But avoid playing so tight that you find yourself seeking any excuse to do so. Winning can be a matter of timing as much as talent, catching the right cards in the right order at the right moment. Learn to cultivate patience while avoiding timidity. You don't have to be the best to beat the best, but you can never be the best unless you develop the stamina and discipline to wait, to outlast, to pursue and persist, to strive to the last limit of your ability in the face of every adversity. Defeat in the moment means nothing, not if you get what you want in the end.

13. The more players at the table, the higher the hand required to win.

14. Be wary of bluffing, and of being bluffed:

   never bluff a player on a streak, winner or loser

   limit your bluff to the fewest players possible—one, no more than two, and always on the end

   bluff the man, not the hand, the man whom you have determined is most bluffable

   never bluff an amateur; he almost always will call

   never bluff on nothing

   never fail at a bluff with the same players more than twice a night

   never show your hand after a successful bluff

15. Always bet a winning hand to the hilt (the less you bet, the more you lose when you win), and every other for precisely what it is worth, no more and no less. But do not be overly eager. Press the action, but pace yourself, or you will knock your own kilt even as you chase off the big money.

15a. Be assertive, alert and aware, but never aggressive. Adventuresomeness does not pay in the long run.

15b. Determine what the moment calls for as the circumstances may require, then raise accordingly: small hoist, big boost, high kick, or upon the infrequent occasion, the go-for-broke boot.

16. Draw fully upon both your experience and your skill. Bring to bear all that you have learned and all that you have honed. Rely upon all that has gotten you this far, but do not ignore the wisdom arisen of your gut in the moment. Heed your intuition and sixth sense. Playing an educated guess is different than betting a blind hunch. At the right moment, cheek and daring are commendable. Recklessness and abandon never are. All may be hazard, but only a fool throws caution to the wind.

17. Never play a system, it makes you predictable. Vary your play, improvise, but in a premeditated way. Be deliberately pro-

vocative, but remember—purely random play guarantees purely random pay.

18. Don't think of it as money, think of it as what it is—chips, stacks of colored chips. There are those who hold that poker is purely a proposition of money management, that the cards are but tools for manipulating money, and they are right, to a point. It is a money game, but money is a way of keeping score, nothing more. The game is played, a score is kept, but it is in the playing, not the keeping, that the heart of the matter lies. Players preoccupied with the score are certain to score badly in the end. Attend assiduously to the action of the play and the score will look after itself. Money possesses no value whatsoever save as it may back a hand, and those who covet it for its own sake cannot help but concern themselves less with playing well than with playing not to lose. Disposed to assume the worst in every situation, they will pull in their horns, screw the pooch and freeze themselves out, play so timidly, "tight-weak" and close to the vest, that the big pots must regularly elude them. Never forget, if money was meant to be held, it would come with handles.

19. Never look for the big score going in. Be content to grind. Winning medium most of the time pays better than winning big and losing big some of the time.

19a. Never go in looking to win more often than is reasonable. No one wins all of the time, not the best player in the world. Lower your expectations. The object is not to win always, or even at all cost, but to win consistently, consistently enough to keep playing in a way that consistently pays, pays enough to keep playing consistently. The best professionals can make a decent living, but no player who got rich ever got that way by gambling all his winnings, and the quickest way to land in financial difficulty is to believe otherwise. Sometimes it is better to husband what you have than to squander what you do not.

19b: If you play enough, accept that from time to time you are going to go bust, because from time to time, everyone, even the best of the best, does. Every professional eventually is faced with having to hardnose the highway.

19c. *In order to win, you must be prepared to lose sometime— and leave one or two cards showing.*

20. Play to win, or don't bother. Check friendship at the door. A "friendly" game is a misnomer. If what you are looking for is recreation or entertainment, there is the theater. If what you want is camaraderie, there is the bar. If it is companionship you seek, there are any number of likely whores.

21. Played properly, poker is hard work, but it is not life. In many ways it mirrors life, certainly it is a part of life, and for the professional it may be a way of life, but it is not life, all of life, itself. And to permit the game to hijack one's life to the extent that one is willing to sacrifice one's own upon the point, that is the ultimate fool's game.

When you know about the secrets, that's when they're most beautiful.

Supreme self-command, overriding impassivity and a guarded and vigilant detachment—these, so far as we may reckon them, are Holliday's cardinal qualities as a gambler. And where he is otherwise swift with his violence, it is rather the result of policy than of passion.

Good-humored and unflappable, the coolness of his cunning is matched only by the steadiness of his nerve. He is as ready with his pistols—which he never fails to wear prominently advertised (whether as fair warning or bald taunt, we dare not say)—as he is with his gold-plated toothpick. Yet he is reluctant to use them save as he may be obliged in self-defense, and then he would kill a man as quickly and mercilessly as he would brush a fly from his immaculate silks.

He accustoms himself to do without sleep despite the prodigious amounts of whiskey he consumes, and if necessary, for all the damage done his mutilated health, is content to go for several days and nights without a wink of rest.

He deals his game, be it faro or poker, with perfect sangfroid, no less when he is suffering his heaviest losses, and whether at or away from the tables is studiously neat in his habits, with but the subtlest inclination to foppishness.

At last we might observe that if by truest nature he is more wag than scoundrel, he nevertheless is one unlikely to shy from backing the bark of his wit with the bite of blade or bullet. Nothing could be plainer than that he is no man to be crossed, cursed, met lightly or trifled with. Not a word of guff. No. He is wont to abide not a single one.

(MARSHAL DAN TROOP, *PEN PORTRAITS OF PROFESSIONAL GAMBLERS*)

There was a trick with a knife he was learning to do.
Tried it that first time on Charley Rich in Deadwood.
Then on Budd Ryan up to Denver. Warn't 'til Ed Bailey,
though, that he finally got it to come right. Just so. Way it
pleased him.

I believe he wished to refine the rhythms of his
knifeplay the way a vintner vets his wines.

—KATE ELDER

HIS FIRST DOCUMENTED kill was of the wildly popular Fort
Griffin sport and bravo Ed Bailey during a hand of draw poker
between faro sessions inside Harelip John "Shanny" Shannsey's
Beehive on the corner of Griffin and Fourth. As in: Within the
Hive/we are alive/good whiskey makes us funny/Tie your horse/
come on inside/taste the flavor of our honey.

Fort Griffin, a buffalo town—200,000 hides traded each
month—was known (to those in the know) as Old Sodom;
Shannsey was a bearishly bluff, singularly unsuccessful ex-
prizefighter (heavyweight division) and later mayor of Yuma, Arizona; and this was shortly after Doc had met Wyatt for the first
time when the latter had stopped by the Hive while out goose-
chasing the bounty on the homicidal killer Bad Arkansas (pronounced are-CAN-zass) Dave Rudabaugh, soon to become a
crony and prominent associate of Billy the Kid's.

He had warned him twice to "quit monkeying the deadwood,
Ed, and play poker"; to "kindly keep your greasy paws off the dis-
cards, Sir"; and so the third time, as accorded with the gambler's
unwritten prerogative, had raked in the pot without saying a word
or showing his hand (he had been set to fill an inside straight),
upon which Bailey blustered his objection, choosing to skin back.

The taper of Doc's unlimbered knife eased now impromptu
through abdominal wall invaginating Ed's belly, eeling unleashed

up young Ed's gizzard, nicking Ed's rib, then through range of muscle, skewering tissue, pigsticking organ, out the gorge of Ed's vena cava, presenting no more resistance than uprooting a radish. And Bailey now clutching his brisket like picking at lint, then to hold his insides in, outflow of entrail, exo-offal, inchpin/out, the gasp of air its puncture *whooooosh* collapse loud as whaleblow, the fall of his face as a settling of shadow, the bruise that it leaves when it lands, jaws ground to grimace, the cup of his mouth brimming blood past its rims down chinfront shirtfront sausaging through, lacing off fingers pissing himself downleg pitching sidelong onto his back thrashing smeared slippery asquirm in the slurry of himself, the slush—*O my God O my God O my God*—words choked out through chew of red sewage kicking agony everywhere eyes going eyes gone spooled back in their skullsockets the world uncorked akilter whitening to wax on his blood pillow.

Bailey had left a shot of whiskey untouched upon the table and now Doc tossed it back, lifting the empty glass headhigh as he remarked offhandedly, "Well, huzzahs, young Ed. Welcome to the archive. Welcome to history. Welcome to the wonderful world of Holliday."

Cold. Cold as pigiron.

Arrested and confined to the Planter's Hotel would have lynched him sure but for Kate who set diversionary fires then bailed him out at gunpoint the pair bedding down overnight flat as flukes in the rushes and reeds by the Brazos the sky a star-cape wrapped 'round a rhumb of raw moon.

Whether fit or ill, flush or gone soak, hotter than kilnbrick or colder than chrome, each time he sat to play, cased out his place at a table, ensconced himself there so much like statuary, he sought his opponents' blood. He wished badly to bloody them, as he presumed no less in kind, with this distinction: that he was a surgeon, not a butcher, he was a calligrapher—he preferred the stylus to the cleaver. "You can shear a sheep countless times," he liked to say, "but you can only skin him once."

There is card sense, but there is common sense as well, there is horse sense, business sense, and the successful rounder appreciates the balance to be sustained between the two. To endeavor to gore one's opponents hand after hand not only is an open invitation to be gored in turn; it places one at risk by exposing one's grosser weaknesses, draws undue attention to the flaws in one's game, and in the end turns potential gain to certain loss by spooking off the prey.

If it is one's ambition to craft a career over time, one cannot afford the flair of too much flamboyance, and so his style was to nick—slit, lance, slash—to incise subtly, a guerrilla of lancets and razors. It was blood all the same. He bled them so routinely they scarcely noticed. He was just that good.

Thus does one keep the quarry alive, with sutures and thread, string the losers along, accumulate capital steadily, without fanfare, over time. In the profession it is called grinding. He ground.

His image—fastidiously cultivated and as impeccably maintained—was calculated deliberately to mislead: the deep Georgia drawl, the attire (the brocaded weskit, pewter-gray cutaway tailcoat, diamond lapel stickpin, gold-plated toothpick, jewel-crowned cane, the silk cravats and kerchiefs), the mordant, darkly cynical humor and exaggerated manners, the pair of nickel-plated, ivory-handled Colts holstered showily in their seesaw up-and-down shoulder harness (typically a self-cocking bird's-beak-gripped .38 called by its manufacturer the "Lightning," and a double-action .41, its cousin the "Thunderer"), even the conspicuous displays of heavy drinking and racking fits of coughing—all of it was a form of disinformation. Procrypsis. He projected an impression that ran counter to his methodology, the bulldoggedness of his play.

Thus as he intended was he routinely misapprehended, under- or overestimated, either of which might cut to his advantage. Those who thought him a swashbuckler played him too tight, those who dismissed him for a lunger and sot, too loose. He was all focused control, fine motor, cool balance, monotonality of purpose, all fixity and fastness, and it made him singly dangerous; he played cards like a sniper.

People, if one knew enough to read them aright, were, he believed, utterly predictable. Each bore their spoor—it was all over them like signature—and the vast lot made of it a gift, served themselves up, open as orchids. People were all self-disclosure. Even those who endeavored to remain circumspect incriminated themselves in the gesture; Braille to the blind.

He could discern the intentions of most of them by their physical presence alone, or such tempers of mind as distinguished them. Among the sane, human behavior may fluctuate, but it always is finite. Human nature may be erratic, even oscillate wildly, but only within discrete limits. It was, as he knew, simply a matter of watching and listening, of properly interpreting affect and posture, metering attitude and inflection, modulating carriage and comportment, calibrating disposition and disportment, of extrapolating the precise measure of a man from the mode of his manner. He used to say, not as a brag, that he could "peg" most people—"three in four"—inside a minute and a half; he was more often correct than otherwise. (But then, as he sometimes thought, what man had ever been more of a mannerist than he? There were times, indeed, when he conceived of himself as but a vessel of pure affect.) What governed him in this was sixth sense; he sensed the bathymetrics of a man—that inscape—in the gauge of his surface. It wasn't mind reading, but something akin, that heightened sensitivity, the hidden receptivity of an open channel. He was possessed of an affinity for the language of signs. This gift of sensorship.

"I play the player, the person, the human being, I play the character and behavior, the foibles first, only then the cards."

It was in the face mainly, sometimes the mouth, but always, always the eyes. It was not uncommon to encounter individuals who might with some diligence harness or tailor the pitch and cadence of their voice, the cast of their brow (upon the rare occasion he had run across those with stock repertoires, a rehearsed wardrobe of deadpan demeanors and miens; it was comical), the mannerisms and pantomimes of their body, but few were those who could keep their thoughts and feelings from lighting in their eyes like chandeliers.

The cards were different. Any hand, no matter how foolproof, could con you, mislead, have you on, send you up, spoof and sabotage, subvert and undermine, run you off cliffs and up blind alleys, into dead ends and detours, around hairpin curves, jump up and bite you when you least expected it. Statistical probabilities, the law of averages, knowing the odds, working the percentages, algebra and calculus, tabulation and deduction, ratio and ratiocination—you could know the math of it better than the features of your own face, but the numbers could be manipulated only up to a point, and that point was constantly shifting. The lines of command and control required the acumen of an aerialist, that they be played like a kite, or a fisherman's fly; each of the subtle corrections, these maneuvers in mid-flight.

Because at last there was something else, something . . . other, another element, the unaccountable, the rogue X embedded in the cards like sex: the possibility of perfection. This flesh of miracle. That was the allure, the seduction before which the true gambler was powerless in a way that his nongambling counterpart was not, nor ever would comprehend. The redemption to be squired in the moment, or the next, or the next, all of it on the line, riding upon the next turn of that next, right card: water to wine, gold spun from straw, fire arisen of ash.

There is, here, a measure of madness, madness and obsession that never can be fully appreciated by those who do not inherently share the predisposition. The impulse in part is childish, and one must be partly a child to succumb to it, and yet to succeed one must be the shrewder still, for the fall of the cards too often is a matter of caprice; nothing, no matter how far-fetched, might safely be discounted.

Each card, as he considered it, was a perfect neutral, the way a musical note is, taking on heft and hue only in relation to the notes contiguous to it, cognate and congruent to the morphology of its moment, those played before and after, each as possible, plausible, as fitting as the next, but all of them somehow inevitable. For there was to be reckoned—not a logic, exactly, but a coincidence of design—what he called "the architecture and commerce of the hand." There is, perhaps, a music hidden inside chaos, and its chords keyed through his mind with each turn of the cards like the mapping of an unwritten poem; he could, like that, convert theorem to verse.

There, in his mind, he drew a line, fluid as spine—this, the locus through his loom—and in the face of every parry and counter, strove never to stray too far from it. It was the grain of his style, and those he played against seldom could detect the fluency and flex of its warp; he played behind a meridian of cords. Which is why it worked as well as it did. Having none or next to none themselves—no *estilo*, as he was fond of saying, no style—as they watched him hour after hour brack up ravels of blood, the while pouring yards of whiskey down his throat, they assumed he had no discipline. In fact it was just as everything was crumbling around him, the moment of dissolution, the losses mounting mounting mounting become insurmountable, it was then that he slipped from his pocket his abiding sense of the serendipity of the moment, its noumena, that place in which every chance is certainty and every whimsy rote, his faith in *what is right in what is accidental*, and hewed to it.

And so he had no system, but a style he did, a credo and aesthetic, and it made to him the kind of metaphysical sense he found himself at a loss to explain easily to others. Fenced within its horizons—the borders of a table—circumscribed by that boundary, he sensed things he sensed nowhere else, where thought was second nature, and second nature skill. To become, in a sense, chemical, concentrate, but always to meld with the flow and the rhythm: shuffle, cut, deal, bet, check, raise, call, the forces at play like a diagram on the air above the table, this rapport with the repartee of cards, what cardplayers call one's kilt. Deep in his element, charged as ion, half knowing every move beforehand, all the conceivable plays at each point arrayed along the way, yet fully prepared for the inconceivable. That zipper of lightning.

It was what combat must be like, he thought (not wishing for a moment to phenomenalize, much less aestheticize it), the instant of reckoning engendering a sort of terrible ease, a more real, better, more natural way of being. Then he could begin to breathe again, as if his life depended upon its every draught, as indeed it did. He noticed that he did not cough as much when he was playing, though at times he found himself doing so for effect, like punctuation, to pace himself with its commas, phrase himself to the tempo of the game; around the cards, cough became a form of song.

At last it was a matter of the millions of possible hands coupled with the odds of their occurring at any named moment that
over time had imprinted themselves upon his brain like insignia,
this stencil through the blood, and, in turn, his casting the iron of
his character upon their spontaneous arrangement around a table
to his best advantage. To achieve this edge he found it necessary
to establish what he called "a lock on things." To play not only his
own hand, but his opponents' as well, even their down cards,
pocket cards, hole cards, especially their hole cards, the ones that
could be almost anything, but that always were the one thing only.
He must know without knowing—and know first, before anyone
else—both what lay facedown in what order upon a table, and
what lay buried, left over, in what order unplayed inside a deck.
Of course, he could not know with absolute certainty, not without
resorting to swindle, but he could know better than his fellows,
and when he knew better, that is when he won.

And sometimes—not often, really, but sometimes he had the
sensation of watching himself, being outside himself, of entering a
zone from which he could look back or down, his brain performing a thousand small surgeries, scalpel to their thoughts, laying
them open like rupture, yet with the exactness of cutting gems.

He could take the whole room in at once then, everything that
was happening, would happen, must happen, anticipate every
move so precisely that he could manipulate play like puppetry.
Sometimes he even could see the specific composition of hands.
Not intuit or discern or envision them, but actually *see* each card
in every hand around the table, reach simon-pure through the
moment and read them like alphabet, clear as graphs. Then he
need not worry the outcome or study the competition because it
was inevitable—he could not lose.

Like an addict, he lived for such moments, the convergence of
their alchemy, that narcotic of skill and wit and style, savvy,

shrewdness, guile, the craft in the absence of control, base alloy hammered to gold, and as it arose—as too often it did—the orderly management of the occasional violence. He knew what lay on the other side of risk, the gain that transcended the game, and it was a high he aimed to ride until it had bucked him off, and meanwhile, its hazard for all it was worth. Because the rest was just walking around, laying track, slinging hash. The rest was just breathing in pain.

And every time he pushed away from a table, every time he announced his intention to call it a night, cash in his chips, turn in, give it a rest, every time he signaled a halt and stopped play, he felt to himself like a stranger. And he felt, once again, like a lie.

He was by temperament and habit a nocturnal creature, and it was not unusual for him to gamble fueled by liquor and the occasional cheroot until dawn, four, five, even six nights a week. But there was a price to be paid: all those noon hours when he awoke to the squalor inside his skull, his every draught dewed, this wallow of residue like a resin that manifested itself in the certain feeling that his brain was about to

s

h

a

t

t

e

r

From:

saloon to tavern
taproom to dramshop
groggery to alehouse
bistro to honkytonk
barrelhouse to watering hole
doggery to publick house
ginmill to rumjoint
roadhouse to

the way to the last whiskey bar—

> *he staggered, superbly balanced*
> *drinking himself over borders*
> *dazed with loss of altitude*
> *down anonymous drifts, dunes*
> *across transparent skies*
> *flaring like a star*
> *into obscurity*

Won't say I liked him. Fact is, found him right disagreeable. Still, drunk or sober, he was the most surefooted human being I ever knew. Radiated aplomb like an atmosphere.

(JOHN P. CLUM, EDITOR, TOMBSTONE EPITAPH)

It is said that whiskey has pushed more money across the table to sober players than all the stupidity and bad luck in the world, and many's the time I've seen right proof of it. But it didn't hold with Doc. More he drank, seemed like, more he won. Never saw the like. He was the most ambidext, nimble-witted drunk I ever knew, and raw quicksilver upon the draw. I witnessed a magician once unfold birds from a bandanna. That was Doc. Pure facility, right and left alike, these acts of sorcery.

His hands contained miracles.

(NED BUNTLINE, PULP WRITER)

Seen him fish barehanded once, no hook or pole, weir or net, jus' ketch 'em up in his hands, pluck 'em, you know, minnows, pinch 'em up by the tail's what he done, tailfins, 'tween his thumb and forefinger. Did this same trick, over and over, musta been a dozen times running, and never, not once, missed. Blind drunk the whole time.

(FLINT McCULLOUGH, TRAIL SCOUT)

Why don't you stop, Doc? I asked him once. Why don't you just stop with the drink? Make the next one your last. It's beneath you. Anyone can be a drunk. Oh, to the contrary, Sir, was much the nature of his reply. Anyone can be a teetotaler. It takes a certain genius to be a sot. Indeed it takes the utmost discipline. Discipline and endurance. It takes stamina. And the proper pacing. The so-called virtues of sobriety are much overrated. Why, a man could go mad and never know it.

(JACE PEARSON, TEXAS RANGER)

Nights was he hit the whiskey so hard you'da sworn he bruised the bottle. He was prodigal, Doc was, like he reckoned the one way he could last was by persevering, preserving himself, staying pickled, by embalming himself alive.

(JOHN YUMA, EX-REBEL)

Look at him, will you? He came West, and one way or another, he's been killing himself ever since.

(WILLIAM W. OLDS, JUSTICE OF THE PEACE,
LEADVILLE, "CLOUD CITY," COL.)

And you drink this alcohol that burns like your spirit
Your spirit you drink down like spirits

—APOLLINAIRE

Forty Rod

Tanglefoot

Two Blend

Nitro   Pyro   Metho   Diablo   Tabasco

Swockeye

Cheapjack   Potato Jack

Knockback

Anklegrab

Black-n-jackle

Mouthwash   Brainwash   Bellywash   Throatwash
Tonsilwash

Sourmash   Tatermash

Gulch Cider

Barleycorn

Sneaky Pete   Stagger Lee   Buster Brown   Navajo Joe
John Hall

Brown Tea

Cornlikker

Floorlicker

Lickspittle

Prairie Stew   Swamp Root   Thistle Dew   Range Swill

Hog's Breath   Sheep Dip   Tiger Spit   Bull Piss   Painter
Piss   Gnat's Pee   Frog Pizzle   Snake Milk   Mare's Milk
Bug Juice   Skunk Juice   Jig Juice   Joy Juice   Juniper
Juice   Spider Juice   Eel Juice

Horsekick   Goathair

Thunder Cat   Mad Dog   White Mule   Scorpion's Bible

Woodgrain

Rearback

Pocket Splash

Gut Oil   Neck Oil   Lamp Oil   Tongue Oil

Apache Tears

Eye Mud   Red Eye   Tongue Knot   Headmelt
Bloodclout   Rotgut   Nose Paint

Nip-n-tuck

Nockum Stiff

Didn't Ought

Roockus Juice

Whiskerburn

Cap'n Hooch

90 Proof

Kerosene

Candle Sweat

Pistol Whip

Git-along

Shag Ass

Angel Teat

Hide-yer-hat

Flingdangle   Fuzzdrizzle   Slumguillon

Julep Water

Widowmaker   Mother's Ruin

Who-shot-John

Taos Lightning   Old Touse

Aftershave

Fogcutter   Dustcutter

Coffin Varnish

None of which he would have anything to do with. Taking his
liquor as seriously as a poet his prosody, he would sooner have
been spotted drinking sarsaparilla and rainwater than having
strayed from the topshelf. He was partial to Joe Gideon or Jim
Beam, less so to Clark's and Anderson's, would settle as compelled for the Old Overholt, Hermitage, McBryan or Monogram
brands, or where he could find it, it being a mite hightoned for the
kinds of places he was accustomed to frequenting, absinthe.

Believing it made all the difference to the grain of one's
drunk.

--------•-•-•-•--------

Why drink so, two days running?
two months, o' seasons, years, two decades running?
I answer (smiles) my question on the cuff:
Man, I been thirsty.

—JOHN BERRYMAN

I make no apology for indulging as I do. 'Tis no secret that to
the bottle I am as a fly flown to flypaper. What of it? It comes as
naturally to me as does mother's milk to a baby. That it may in
certain quarters be construed for a form of vice detracts not a whit
from the truth—that as with most vices worth the bother, there is
a gentleman's art to the practice, an orthodox aesthetic, a decorum and etiquette, that protocol by which I always have striven to

abide: namely, that the drunker one may become, so much the more sober ought one endeavor to behave. That is, so much the neater.

I am no mere lush, whatever the consensus to the contrary, for I drink only to the point and with purpose, as a sacrament, for the self-possession it affords. Those who have not the vocation never can understand this, nor would I presume to persuade them otherways. It is true all the same: drink enough, often enough, drink past the point of mere drunkenness, the slurs and the staggers, visions and shakes, and eventually one ascends to that holy place, the plateau of perfect equipoise, the moment of alcoholic eptitude and control that permits one to remember that which, when sober, one labors so conscientiously to forget.

I drink for the focus, because it helps me concentrate, to think properly, not to forget or wash away the sorrows. You fight through it, fight through the fogs, and eventually you emerge out the other side at an acuity of cold perception, a lucidity like diamond, its core of clarity enameled as a lake. The whiskey, you see, is the way back to the beauty in myself, bleak as it may be, and insofar as it may require my passage across the river Styx, so be it. That is one toll I never have been reluctant to pay. No, the only time I have a drinking problem is when I can't get enough to drink.

Let others consider me a drunkard as they will; such presumption more often has cut to my benefit than otherways. Men always will underestimate a sot, assume they can abuse him to their advantage, have their way with what they construe for the beleaguerment of his impairment, the nullity of his reasoning or dullity of reflex. And certainly there have been those luckless few who, sensing in me their huckleberry, have dared seek to do just that. That it behooved me on such occasions to dispose of their poor souls is only regrettable. I might have preferred that they learn how it is that true gentlemen conduct themselves while in their cups in some other, less drastic manner, but more's the pity, 'twas not in the cards—not, at least, for them.

For a place so enamored of its drink, the West is singularly sloppy with those possessed of no right aptitude for its right handling. It remains, alas, a land of scant couth, coarse and common and low, a land, at last, of low-down, loutish, copper-common drunks. In the meanwhile, as there be nothing in this world so detestable in my eyes as the sight of an empty bottle—lest it be an underfilled glass—I intend henceforth to preside over my own dissolution and disintegrate as it may please me, if always with such discrimination and discretion as my debauchery may deliberately allow.

Both as comfortably numb, as elegantly wasted.

Cheers.

Lonely
lonely eyes
    mouth
    lips
    face
lonely, lonely love
        days and nights
this lonesome
lonely
life
   of a dead-end
       loveless
         place

YOU COULD—SO ran the rumor in those days—delve, D

                                                    E

                                                    L

                                                    V

                                                    E   your

nails into the bill of your skull, hook the horn of both hands down
through flesh into bone among breath, dredge beneath scalp, fix flo-
rets of barbed wire dug to your forehead and *tug*, peeling, peeling,
peeling, peeeeeeeel off the scrim of dermis, that skinmask, exposing
what lies subepithelial, down to the subepithelial truth, extract the true
face, true nature of the true face drug up, up and up, up to the surface
like moon, moon beneath moon inside moon mucked from seaplain
and never dive deep enough to unmask the moon of its beauty.

Who are we? Am I? Who do I think I am?

My image its identity? Identity, image?

Wherefrom our notion of indelible self, where does that lie?
What, perhaps, inhabit?

Heart soul brain genitals? Face? Foremost the face, prow of
beauty, the first foot put forward's the front of the face a drape of
flesh some features afloat in its folds.

Think of another any other dead or alive, what do you think
of, what do you picture?

Look in a mirror what do you see?

Comb your hair apply your makeup posture primp prink
preen for the camera, marshal yourself to meet the day upon what
does the eye alight? This human salute to the world.

If one could divest it elide it erase it, rake it flat, iron it level,
efface its features, make it pancake discus platter easel, tile slate el-
lipsis, if one could rub out the clockwork on the face of time what
would anyone ever have been?

The face of beauty boils with blood, so *–it is the face which
must be taken off the forward-pointing of it, history.*

J. H. "Doc" Holliday,
Dallas, 1874
Buffalo Bill Historical Center,
Cody, Wyo.
Vincent Mercaldo Collection

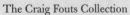

The Jeff Morey Collection, from the
original in *Human Life Magazine*, 1907

The Craig Fouts Collection

EVERY SO OFTEN, still, these rumors of image: a rummage sale in Atlanta, a housecleaning in Valdosta, a bank vault in Las Vegas, an attic trunk or cellar deskdrawer in Dallas or Denver or Dodge. It seems to be the face we still want. 150 years later. To excavate more face, as if the truth were a form of portraiture, as if identity were image, as if face had a value, value enough that we might take him at it, at last.

Naturally they never pan out. It always is someone else, somebody's uncle or brother or father or cousin or—who knows, except not him. Never him.

His life was a blur. Where not that blur's shadow. Where not that shadow's negative. That was the plan. To live it that way. Why expect more, then, as if the past, his past, has nothing better to do than slow down long enough for us to catch up to it, catch up to, exhume and frame it.

And so, as of this writing, the three compiled here remain the only "western" photographs of him known positively to have survived. The rest, and over time the rest have been legion—as they doubtless will continue to be—are either forgeries, fakes or counterfeits, having by the accredited experts, one by one, each and all, been inauthenticated.

The first, top center: commonly called "The Cavalier," taken in Dallas, summer of '74, when he was 23. Name of the studio, unknown, though according to the fashion of the times the image retouched or "enhanced" to make his thinning, naturally ash-blond hair appear both darker and thicker. Though Wyatt thought him "remarkably handsome," and Kate "the handsomest man I ever seen," the West was not long to lay eyes upon anything approximating the picture of dashing good health here.

The second, lower left: taken six years later, in Prescott, Ariz., where he then was rooming with Acting Territorial Governor

John Gosper. Prescott was the territorial capital, Virgil Earp was its town constable, and the faro table at Cobweb Hall on Whiskey Row was one Doc was partial to. Had Kate left a memoir, she would have written of his having around this time "gone on such a remarkable jag of good fortune that afterward we celebrated. Much champagne. Hatsful of licorice and chocolates. Bought me several unmentionables, himself a new suit. Set to D. F. Mitchell's for his portrait." It was 1880. He was 29 years old—and looks 40.

The last, lower right: taken in Tombstone, early 1882, at Kate's behest. Studio, that of C. S. Fly. As in:

Fly's Photogs and Shooting Gallery
24-hour processing, M-F
Daguerreotypes, Cyanotypes & Ambrotypes
Stereographs & Cartes de Visite
Black-and-white prints
Tintypes free with every order of 12 or more
Transfer your likeness to glass or silver plate
For a trifling expense you can favor your loved ones
with a memento mori they can keep long after
you have gone to your reward

Just looks sick. And old. Old as water. Five years later the well had run dry.

⸻

THOMAS CARLYLE ONCE remarked that he typically found "a portrait superior in real instruction to half-a-dozen biographies." Perhaps. And yet how much of any photograph might be said to constitute its fabrication? Are any of the three faces here true? To themselves? To the photos that contain them? They may each, to an extent, after a fashion, be his, but is even one an authentic or accurately rendered reflection of the literal appearance of its image? *Vultus est index animi*? Really? Or might they be mistaken? If every posing for a portrait is but a playing at being portrayed, might they be masks instead? Masks conceived for the choreographed click of their moment? Is it so inconceivable? Might Nietzsche be right? That "every profound spirit needs a mask"?

How can any photograph be sufficiently trusted absent a surer knowledge of the circumstances of its taking? Where the X-ray that scans the soul? Does any photo really deepen our appreciation of its subject, or rather bring us face to face with our feelings of ambivalence towards it? Perhaps we only see in these photographs what we wish to see. Perhaps knowing all that we know about the person in them—or all that we do not—we cannot help bringing that knowledge or its absence to them, superimposing it upon them in ways that remain to us unclear. Might it be, could it, that there is no photograph that exists unencumbered by a past that pours over it like pigments? What, finally, is being replicated here?

A picture is worth a thousand words? Fine. Here they are, these three. Here are some photographs of him. Can we elucidate, deconstruct, adduce, so much as describe what we see? Of course, to a degree.

Now, what on earth do they mean?

You fetch out an old snapshot, dust it off, square it away, put it to the light, put clothes on its ghost, recall each furrow of its features in the flesh, you can even frame it, but you still have to live on for the future.

Every photo is fractionally a phantom. This tissue bred of poisons. The tripod, blackbulbed box, the powderpan, abeam. The cyclops chamber there. Its empty eye mawed back at him, its monocle his lair.

Photography—or "drawing shadows upon stone" as it figuratively was described in its infancy—always is in some sense (the way it interrupts life, interrupts and holds it, holds it back, suspends it, freezes and frames it, stays time's hand, if only for a moment, the moment of visual eavesdropping) about death. By means of chemical torture, sifts mineral designs from the salts of the dead, as if the dead were not dead at all, but up and dancing a dirge to the beat of the shake of their bones. Engraves, that is, the stone with shadow.

Similarly, so in some sense (the way in which it defies death, outlasts it, prolongs life, preserves it, even when the life it is preserving is that of the dead, the active dead, in their inactivity) is every photograph about life.

And so these photographs in their stillness *do* speak to us, but what they speak of is little besides their own silence: I was here, but now I am gone. I am elsewhere now. I have left the frame. You cannot speak to me. You cannot touch or taste or smell me. You cannot hear me cough myself to death. You cannot cure me; too late, your vaccine. Because I have dissolved. Eroded to wave. Reverted to vapor. My exhaustion has evanesced to exhaust. Save this. What I chose to leave behind—my face, its form, these features. That which you see here, this, just this, alone. All that it is and the everything it is not. This I left, and this you can have, this and no more, these three. These all, that are nothing.

Every photograph is a picture of that which has since died or passed on or decomposed and disappeared, or which inevitably shall. The replete absence which has in every perishable and permanent aspect of itself been unrecognizably altered, forever.

And so these are the end, the only photographs, the photos of the last face, his face. The film has run out. There are no more exposures. Everything has faded. Everything dimmed to the perfect anonymous   white.

Everyone knows by now that photographs lie: rayograms,

superimpositions, solarization, bleaching, burning, blurring, airbrushing, morphing, photoshopping, multiple shadows, photomontage, double exposures; everyone knows by now that seeing is disbelieving and that all reality is virtual. But what if everyone is wrong? What if it is the lies that count? What if it is the lies that count most of all? What if Wilde was right? What if "a mask tells more than a face"?

See Doc, then. See him. Face the facts, each facet. Face the facets of the facts of his face. Here: see Doc die.

Now, get the picture?

he was a handsome man
    and what i want to know is
how do you like your blueeyed boy
Mister Death
        —ee cummings

PART

Three

There are several dubious assumptions about the early West. One is that . . . it was rough, ready, unkempt and ribald about anything not as unkempt as itself, whereas in fact there was never a time or place where gentility . . . was more respected.

Not if it was the real thing.

—WALLACE STEGNER

The ladies all thrilled
twittered
applauded then trilled, O
the Doctor's a dream
his tool's a ream
and I open up wide
where he drills me

Now Kate, Kate just wanted him free. Freed. To be free. Feel frantic or flattered, indulge wholesale his cravings, curry his appetites, hover or float as he would, drift or parade, turn on a dime, shift sands at will, sail off edges of altitude or plumb latitudes of depth along with him. To be whomsoever he might choose in the moment, do with her whatsoever might outlandishly please him. In her he realized unbidden a great gift—the peculiar grace of his fashion.

Kate was sunlight. Luteous lux and lumens. Like fucking sunlight. Her heat was as a fever brushed across her body with a wand. And that body had come through wars, hard buffets, the roughshod wear of the West, but oh, how she wore that weather well. Wore it like a lacquer. All the golden grace notes, bones of music in each movement. Lord! The moments of hallelujah, volts of velvet, each jolt a *shout!* These hosannas high through the hinge of her hips.

Her presence, leavening his anarchy.

———◦—◦◦—◦———

THEY MET BY chance, Kate come up on him back of the Hotel Dakota reckoning him one more stray new in town just blown in thinking him yet one more fallen-down drunk . . .

this stark lone stranger, sheer as mirage, scarce a needle of vapor, bereft on his back, corpse-flat and hatless, crisp-pressed suit, fresh-blocked black Stetson on the ground beside him, and his arms rigid as axles, as axes upthrust in alleluia to the air, coolly unloading the contents of both six-guns a single shot at a time (left after right, .41 then .38) with the precision of unraveling a nerve, emptying the brace of their bullets, hurling blunt wire at the sky to wound it (so he said later), rout it, irrigate, perforate its bull's-eye, make it bleed noonlight, vomit red scream out its shatterproof jaw, any damn thing to stop the grate of its glaring, unsight the sun, enucleate the shell of its glower, unyolk the yellow, blast the sun blind, and what the hell she'd seen things before seen her share seen plenty but what the Sam Hill was this here some anonymous drifter shooting the eyes outta the sun as if they was skeet or clay pigeon, silver coin, tin can, lit wick of wax candle propped on a fencepost she could not have said on a dare and having pumped dry both chambers (each round to its orbit) through blue smoke coughed himself upright, bracked up char and red ash, dusted himself off, spat a chest's worth of sand, wiped the blood from his lips with the back of his hand, then bent down to hook up his hat and palmbrush the chalk from its brim glancing her way wading over spilling his smile like seed all around cool as mint, as mineral, a forward fresh kid cocksure as a coxswain bowing at the waist gracing her with an angle of arm (its offer or menace) and a pair of smart words—"Shall we"—the arm she hooped into right off not knowing why not . . . quite, saying nothing, quiet, quietened, but in his hotel room later, postcoital and consummated, twice-spent and fleshdrunk, oiled clean through slick as spitshine sweat runneling in rills sharing the bottle in bed turned to her remarking each word a wing finning delirious through rye, "Sure, I know it seems a queer thing, but try to understand: there are times when I no longer can abide the strain, each corona a camera paving through cornea, its crescent like a crust as it crests, the claw of those cleats," this blow of blue flame blundered obliquely from the barrel of both lungs

   . . . that being the only time he would foot payment for her favors which proved at once so unprecedented they immediately became regularly attached.

   For once having had the best—and knowing it in the having—once having transgressed, obliterated thresholds to arrive at the rim of imagination, how abide for so much as a moment anything less?

Coitus with Kate was clover-sweet,
unhurried, redolent, wet
with heat, and
salacious as all hell;
peach-sweet the penetralia of
the severally penetrated
Kate.

(Still, had he known then that their fortunes were in the future bounden to become so inextricably bound . . . up, it is doubtful he would have pursued with such purposeful élan what his passion impelled him to; he would not, for all his failings, like to have inflicted his life upon another for whom he felt capable of caring even that deeply. But she was Kate—the promise of something from which there was no escape. The first dream he once had dreamed, without knowing it.)

The first time she went south on me
ledged to a bed in Deadwood
legs overboard, thighs
                che V roned
and she in genuflection thirsting
slow into the spread of their saddle
her mouth sheathing, throat
a sleeve
       sleeving to the arm of its host
whoa, I said, say
what?
her face sliiiiiide trombone, its
bell an orchid O'd
open, path to its polestar (cynOsure)
gliding me glis
           s   o
           s   d
         s   n
        s a
        s
as a march over maps: portolano
                mappamondo
                words like meals in the mouth
(en)compassing   whole   longitudes

the quiver of her face, the
globe of its four directions
taking the arrow of me in, hefting it
ahoy hats on (being both more clothed than not)
bracketing her head with my hands
entangling the reins of her hair like

raising a tent so high
                    oops
her hat spills off
hooprolls the rug and
I am smitten
harpooned
left behind in her, white
as the swallow of a whale

Most of what we was called don't bear proper repeating, but some, them few what does, included the following:

soiled doves

calico queens

shed birds

sportin' hens

brothel bunnies

Cyprian Sisters in Sin

demi-mondaines

nymphes du pavé

errant charmers

fallen angels

upstairs gals

painted nightcats

frail enticers

alas/alack lasses

ladies of the half-world

scarlet fleshpots

brides of the multitude

women of spotted and easy virtue

damsels with distressed and wayward pasts

We didn't take it personal. Come with the job. Strictly business. Market economy. Capital exchange. Customer and commodity. Patron and purveyor. Client and vendor. Men had the want and the wherewith, women the wares and the inventory. We hawked such product as we made a profit off peddling—on which, 'less you count sheep or other livestock, we had most of a monopoly—they ponied up for such as what pleased them. Warn't no high finance to it; model of simple commerce. Worked, too, being we was such a limited but renewable resource, slim but choice pickin's so to say, and they such avid, indiscriminate pickers.

So there it was. A lot of men—almost all of 'em, 'cept them that was married, and most of them too—had a lot fewer women. But then that was the point—we was there to be had, and we was, over and over, about as often as they come down with the itch, which judging by the rate of consumption must have been always, or whenever they was feeling flush, if mostly for the price of a poke. Backhumpin' work, not that I'm complainin'. Least I never got carved on.

And then there was Doc Holliday and Beak Nose Kate El-der—though why Beak Nose, I never could reckon, cuz it warn't, to comment—and together they scrapped all the rules. Cuz Kate was a whore (and less than a whore, which is what we called a whore who so clearly relished being one), and Doc was a gentle-man (of a beset and beleaguered sort), and though neither would consent to marry the other, still they chose to pair up in a fashion that give the impression they had, and had might as well for all the carrying on they done as a couple. Didn't make a whole lotta sense—a whore who enjoyed being a whore too much to give up her whoring, giving it away free to a gentleman who was too much the gentleman to pimp her in the meanwhile, warn't real shy about showing her the knout of his hand (where not the snout of his boot) and who on top of the rest was like to drop dead as dice on the spot.

In some ways it was kinda cute, if mysterious, but mainly it was real sad, and even pathetic, where not flat-out perverse, and what it come to in the end was what it always comes to—a fester-ing want of the right self-esteem. (Author's Note: In Doc's case, his mother's early doting, combined with the parlousness of his condition, had saddled him with a permanent sense of delicacy, a hyperesthesia he strove as he ever failed to conquer. And Kate, however headstrong and independent, knew that she was what she was, and what she was was a whore, and little more.) I like to

147

have lost my appetite whenever I seen 'em together. Cuddlesome as they could be, and they could, often past the point of propriety, too often they was just a war waiting to happen.

Rumor had it, after the Ed Bailey business down to Old Sodom, Kate saved Doc's hide by torching half the town to spring him from the hoosegow, though Kate give out later as how she'd hitched up with him some before that, in Deadwood, winter after Wild Bill'd got hisself burnt. Way she told it, they'd wound up in the crib, made a nightlong of it—though a lunger Kate said he was a laster—and next day Doc netted up on a streak that rolled him well on into spring. After that she said he told her she was the best luck he'd ever been around and wouldn't she consider stringing along with him henceforth onto glory or straight to hell whichever come first. Which words sound awful . . . cooked, 'cept that comin' from Doc, they sound exactly like the truth. Either way, they was hooked into each other on account of something, and whatever it was was keen enough to make 'em as much a team as any couple can be who never took the vows and content to go their own way as the wind might chance to blow.

Kate told me once she'd gone and married Doc in secret, back in Carolina or Georgia somewheres, but I didn't credit a word of it. Could be from time to time, when things was sailing along sweetcakes and sass, she might've thought of herself that way, but that neither one was the marrying sort, the nose on your face is less plain. 'Sides, I never heard Doc call her his missus, and if Doc had had a wife, a real one and proper, you can wager the farm and family to boot he would've called her that much, at least.

Way I reckoned, they liked it that way, absence making the heart grow the fonder and all, liked the space and distance, the lifting of those limits, that missing one another, loved the other more for all the farewells and separations, as, too, the heat in them rekindlings, the relighting of them fires when they flared. The yearning charm of trysts. They was precarious, that's what they was, as unstable and rabid a couple as any you might hanker to see.

Truth is, I was kinda sweet on him myself—nor the only one—and so quick to take heed of such. Cuz Doc Holliday had manners, more manners than any of that trash he palled around with, those Earps I mean. Traffic enough in the contrary, lot who wouldn't know a your-leave from a let's-go, or worse, the pretenders who do, and the real thing's as easy to spot as red on a fox. A sot, yes, sad to say, that he was, no question, but even then, drunk as Bacchus, he had manners, he had breeding, and . . . cultivation, and when it warn't seeping from his pores with the fever, he moved around inside it like an aura. To this day, and with all my soul, I believe he was without a vulgar bone in his body. Certainly he had no tolerance for it, that sort of vulgarity, in others. Doc was just a cut above, that's all. Don't hear much about it anymore, ain't much call, but what he had full spate was what they used to call gallantry. He was gallant, Doc was, a by-God, free-fallin' gallant.

Which is why his commerce with Kate Elder rankled so, cuz even amongst us hens, she was the one got cold-eyed and clucked at. See, there was certain ways, call 'em wiles, certain tricks to the trade that most of us—hell, well-nigh all of us—just would not have truck with nor stand for, some for the sake of common decency, sure, but most on account of common cleanliness. The West warn't never no untrammeled haven of high health and sanitariness, that's a fact, but while it may have been rude and plumb wild for its whores, most was a lot tamer in the sack than you might like to think—'cept Kate, who not only warn't shamed by it, but seemed mortally to hunger for it, dared even to brag on it, like it was some brand of art form or feat. None of us was what you'd've been real comfortable calling Christian exactly, but Kate wanted for the fear of God hisself, if less for a dose of the staph.

I been with enough rough trade in my day to know there's no tellin' jus' where their lusts may lead 'em—swill this, spread that, take it this way, that and up the other yonder—but it was hard to feature how a man like Doc could've been brought so low he'd have gone at it from each of the angles that might've kept a quim like Kate Elder quietened in her contentment. On the other hand, he was dyin'. Could be he just hankered to sample all the sweets, every whichaway, before he up and did.

All the same, he sure smelled good. We all knew Doc was for the worms—warn't much for keeping the news to hisself—so you mighta thought he'd stank of it: whiff of old gone-to-rot, macerate, old ghostmeat on the hoof, but he didn't. Tell you what he did though. Smelled like sage. Yup. And didn't use no scent. Sagebrush and spicegum and cactus flower full fan in its bloom. Ain't that the wonder, though?

He smelled like fresh-cut daisies.

(A DODGE CITY WHORE)

Only man I ever known to sparkle. Sparkled more'n most women, and without but half the try. Up from down out of hisself, up from way inside. Put you in mind of snowlight, tinsel, spangles, sequins; French champagne; spun sugar and silverine flossing; this suite of glycerine stars. Resolved, as ever, to emit no light before his time.

(DODGE CITY WHORE #2)

There's all manner of tale—idle broadside, unfounded presumption, baseless surmise, swirling rumor, salacious hearsay, base innuendo, groundless accusation, malicious gossip, unascertainable slander, whispered calumny, an actual news brief or two—that he whaled on me something awful.

Did solemnly consider it, time to time.

Tree ain't a table and considered ain't done to. Not saying we didn't have our scuffles and scrapes, go-tos and dustups. Sure, we had our rows. Any couple will as every couple does. But Doc ever laid a glove on me I'd've laid him out sidewise and he knowed it. He was the weakest man, musclewise, I ever known. And each day getting weaker.

And this was a knowledge we shared. Still, however much it may have made for some extreme occasions, I would not have mixed in a partnership with a woman that was not full of sparks, nor one that was not in its several ways wanton. At last, each admired what soared strongest in the other while abiding that which did not, and though that sometimes made for fractiousness, we were mainly up to it. The dander enlivened things in ways we both required. That said, I must contest that we were other than an uncomplicated pair. Turbulent, yes, tempestuous, perhaps, tumultuous and always torrid, but—permit me to put it this way: if we were short on tact, we were long on scruple. If only in our fashion. Strikes me, the art of living boils down to that one thing—juggling morals and passion. On occasion, we all of us drop the ball.

See, I known Doc had other women, same as I did other men, time to time. Warn't neither of us pure as no driven snow. (I was once, but oh, how I'd duned up and drifted.) He was naturally a fatal attraction to females. Any fool could see it, way they hussied up to him, vamped, way they sidled over—flirty, flouncy, flaunty, flitty, fluttery way they get when they're hot-buttered up on a man. Why wouldn't they? Doc warn't no tomcat nor skirtchaser, not like some, out to run up the score fuck-all, but he did so dearly love a woman, all women, even the old ones, even the plug-ugly ones. Just loved being around 'em, sound of and shape of and smell. Loved the whole *idea* of 'em, whole ideal. Doc had his own way, and in them days in those parts warn't the sort you saw much of. Kind to bow, kiss your hand, offer up an arm, kind to lay his cape kindly at your feet. Doc could be real chivalrous when the mood come over him.

Wasn't a mood, but a manner. The *code* of it. That so long as she was with me when she was with me, so long as she purposely chose to be, that is all I asked, and the most I dared require. When she was not, when she was elsewhere, what she did, who she did it with, I did not know nor care to know. I considered it none of my affair. I am not by temperament a jealous man—envy in such matters is unpardonable—and as we were loyal to one another it was largely as neither demanded, carnally speaking, fidelity of the other. That others may have found it queer, I can readily feature, but the arrangement suited us, I might presume to comment, in roughly equal measure.

We was tied without the knot, is what it was. Soulmates I heard some call it, so that's what we was then, soulmates. That skin hunger, the lust a-loose through the blood like a bat. See, Doc had certain proclivities—inclinations, appetites, what have you—and they was widely frowned on, then as now, so the wonder was the way they matched up tongue to groove with my own.

Luck of the draw I reckon, luck for us both. We felt kinda sorry for everyone else in that regard, having what we had and the rest of the world famished. Sure, there was times we about drove one another crazy, but even then bedtimes was swell. "You and me, darlin," he'd say—I can hear him even now, clear as shields—"are we not some likely pair? I should say we are unrivaled through all of time. Why, dear Kate, we are a pair of royal aces." And we was. It was like he said, what we had, it made flamingos fly.

In my experience, Kate was a lover like no other. I had never really known what was possible, and in discovering what was, she reminded me of what it felt like to feel good again, to know something of lushness and extravagance, the rapture of that open-assed bliss, and for that I thanked her, as often enough I cursed her for having fired and kept stoking in me the need. We were leagues beyond ardent. We were fervent. What we shared, I'd call it combustion, and any burning I may have suffered on account, well, so it goes when a man is drawn mothed to the flame.

Doc was so thin-skinned, he bruised so easy—too easy, bruised more'n most women—you coulda ripped him up like that you had half a mind. His heart I mean. And that heart was mainly a fine one. Not that he didn't behave badly. He was—what's that word? mecurial? mercurial?—and then he could be mean, nasty as a scorpion. Had a real knack for it, as who should know better'n me. And naturally, should it come to it, he always was primed to skin back. As it so often did, come to it. Because he was all but a magnet for all manner of woe. Never known a man to invite being picked on so. Made him quick to offer insult, take offense, quicker still to pounce, keen to go straight for the throat. Still, he didn't dote on brutality, and believe you me, I've seen the doters, and the distinction is everything. No, a decent sort, that was Doc, decent enough. Had to be around him some to appreciate it, see him daily in situations, circumstances, from different angles, had to be there with him in the moment, but anyone he let close could've told you that when he done wrong it was only out of grief or on account of the drink or some slight he would not suffer or score that owed settling. Or simple contrariness, spite or malice, which don't count, or ought not.

Permit me to suggest that with respect to any wrongdoing, I more often was the abused than the abuser. I seem to recall a time in Tombstone—what it was we had fracased about I could not say; Wyatt, probably; in those days we fracased about Wyatt rather a lot—but being roistered by the row, she blew off directly and proceeded with some enthusiasm to drink herself so frolicsome, she roostered on 'til dawn stole the wings off her rudder. Thus did my enemies, seeking their advantage—that fuck Behan in particular, though I later was informed Johnny Ringo as well—crowd her into signing an affidavit swearing to my having confided my complicity in the two murders connected with the Benson Stage robbery. So I was arrested and tossed to the sharks. Spent an overnight in the jug. *Juzgado.* Hoosegowed. Old news. When she sobered up enough to get wind of the mayhem she had authored—told me later she felt just like the cat had kittened in her mouth—she was properly mortified, meekly enough recanted, I was released, she immediately asked my forgiveness, I immediately gave it, we put it behind us, never mentioned it again and moved on. Stand by a person, stick around long enough and eventually things are going to happen that neither one could conceivably have intended. The disappointments, deceits and deceptions, duplicities, dissimulations and dissembling, such bruits and betrayals are inevitable, but if you want to be with someone enough, if you find that you must be, then that is what you do, you forgive them and move on. You weather all the forgivenesses, suffer their wear, relinquish all faith in redeeming the past, but the bond—bloodied, bruised, bent, a bit bowed—remains sound, and sounder still for the scarring.

We were together—what?—10 years, and you got the gall to go and mention that one time? Not fair, Doc, and not sporting. So you name me another. Go on. Name me one other time, a single one, that I ever went against you.

I mention it, dear Kate, only as being illustrative of my abiding magnanimity. And because, while I forgave you the entire incident long ago, the memory of it lingers. Lingers and looms. I might have been hung.

Might ain't was, and rue your damn memory all the same. That was the problem right from the set-to, you remembered too damn much. It was never your heart, Doc, but your mind. Never seen the like. Mind like a cesspond, sewer and slum, mind like an unwardened prison block. Each thought, every one, all of 'em tow, live-fire fobbed from a tinderbox. It's them what done the violence, presumed the worst, threw in their lot with the lost, felt condemned and abased, suckled on shame, held themselves in fast contempt, sop to self-ridicule, saint to self-blame. It's your mind thought love a menace, delight a spy, connection abominable, cursed the light, tilted at shadows, marched off to war, sought the succor of the solace to be had in a lonely and unmindful death. What you exacted of yourself in the moment, Doc, thought you thatched 'cross the top of the act like a pleat, that's what done it, about drove you plumb mad. Life's a slippery slope, and your mind was 20 miles of bad ski trail four hours after the sun's set and the last run gone sheet-sheer to glaze ice. There was just no way in creation you should have been allowed near it alone, and the fact made for all sorts of mischief in a time and place that bred mischief like heartache. My God, man! You *were* your own assailant, and of the assailing content to create some kind of tortured . . . art.

Perhaps. Perhaps to an extent I was. But then, I'd had a whole lifetime of practice. It was what I was good at. Became good at. What choice did I have? I could turn it all back on myself, or I could go in search of my daisy. I sure as hell couldn't pray it away, and I'd be damned if I'd play the part of Mister Pitiful the Poor Pitied. I was straddling the razor either way. Helluva thing for a man to feel cornered by his own life. Won't say I was born against my will, but I damn sure was living under protest.

So you want to talk daisy. Here then: you were dying, every day, and the way you managed its truth was to make of its fiction your friend, but don't pretend you were betokened to some deathwish. I know better, and most of what I know is how much of it's codswallop, all of it, codswallop and claver. Hellbent on meeting your match, sure, reckon you had your share of reckless moments, but whenever you come close to throwing in your hand, all you could think was all them others deserved to go first. You remember so damn much, you oughta remember this: "I do that, darlin', and the devil wins without having been called. Hell, live long enough and eventually your time comes around all on its own." Remember?

What I remember is the poet: *No hope could have no fear.*

Used to tell him, ain't no sin to be glad you're alive, Doc, ain't wrong to believe a life can be beautiful.

NOR IS IT, no sin atall, so long as you remember 'tis but a single step to terror. So long as you recall 'tis but the agony that lasts. So long as you remind yourself each sunrise that what you're living is but prologue to what's perforce your past. Truth is, I had no talent for it, no talent for living at all. Not that I couldn't appreciate it in others, see the right way of things, way they ought to have been, might have been, if only . . . But how get to it, when you know in the end that none of it—not love, beauty, truth or freedom, neither joy nor laughter nor scruple—that none of it matters a lick? The trouble with life is simple—it's so much itself, requires so much breathing to get through, or so much fight to avoid, that by the time you go to actually live it, there's not a scrap of it left to abide. There was never a moment—not one—when something did not seem to be missing, yet not a clue as to which or what-from. Always left me cold, I suppose. Couldn't seem to warm up to it. Or it to me.

And that ain't even the real tragedy, which was that when the consumption begun to take him down, when his life begun its slide from spectacle clean to trauma, that's when the shell he'd spent his lifetime a-hewing, the one he wore yoked to his back like an armor, that's when he found it was too late, that it'd hollowed out all on its own, like the fairies come along when no one was looking and hauled it off leaving but a husk in its place. See, I never known Doc when he warn't in a state of ailing, failing, feeling poorly, freefalling all the levels of his own sickness, sometimes more than others, but always someways sick, and not just his fleshly self, the one everyone seen and known about, but his whole self, the one hid back of his eyes, that deeper deep-set self, the deep-set self inside. He was delicate and dying, always dying, but I never known him to be ashamed of it. He may never have stopped thinking about it, bemoaning it, availing himself of the license he presumed it give him, but you had to hand it to him, if he couldn't be bothered to look on the bright side, he seldom backed down from making the black worst of a dark situation. Doc was not appalling, he never was, but he was scads beyond audacious.

Lest you forget, I was a gambler. I was gambling, that's all, gambling my all on the everything that is most merciful in death—the absence of any more violence. And why not, where it profits a man, why not believe in the wages of death?

Had a name for it, remember, Doc?

Hmmm. Not offhand. No, can't rightly say I do.

The Wire of Hopelessness, that's what he called it, and a man, he believed, could learn to walk it, all day, every day, day after day, without tumbling into the pit of despair. Forget the past, avoid the present, shun the future—it wasn't easy, but with right effort, the perfect balance could be struck, just so. A man could learn to stop holding on, let go, and just . . . float. Because that's what it took, letting go of the memories, the dreams, all of the stories and promises one has ever been told, the acts of love one's been shown, all the beliefs and wisdoms, each of the permanencies that create the lie that any of us once existed, or still do. And so just trust and go on trusting, trust to the futility of it all. And if to get there, if to realize that trust required God or money or gluttony or sex or booze or dope or madness or violence, then what matter, so long as a man had the integrity of imagination and clarity of character to wager everything on the edge to be gained in the moment. A man could spend his life burying himself alive and survive, live airless and empty, that's what Doc believed. And he proved it was true, for a while. Existence? Hell. Far as he was concerned, that was just a word for a way to use up your life.

Hah! So now you begin to see why Wyatt thought her such an inimical influence, as he used to put it. Would have had me throw her over, old Wyatt, "for your own good, Doc," so he said. "She'll be the death of you yet." As if she were some species of pit viper. He was wrong of course. When it came to dear Kate he seldom was anything other. Didn't understand her, couldn't trouble himself to try, and hadn't the imagination to envision the kind of man, the better man she helped make me. Wyatt wasn't right about every last thing, and the last thing he was right about was women, a shortcoming, I might add, in which he was scarce alone.

And you reckon you are, that it?

Not atall, not for a moment, just more right than Wyatt, who hadn't a clue. No, I was no different than any hundred men, with this exception: that I understood that for what men and women share, there are no blueprints, itineraries, no almanacs or manuals, neither chart nor graph nor diagram. That the jig of their relations, our relations, does not come blocked and choreographed, painted by number or annotated by orchestral score. What I knew that perhaps the next man did not, what I *accepted*, was that such matters cannot be metered like a boardlength or epoxyed like a tooth; that love, in short, is never long division. None of us know to what we ought attribute our arrival at one another, why we have arrived once we have arrived there, nor to what that arrival, in time, may of its own accord aspire. Sadie proved the woman for Wyatt, the one right and only one, and to his credit he was not too thick to recognize it, relish it, and do by it the proper thing. But he didn't know a thing about you, dear Kate, as he knew all the less about us. Not that it was incumbent upon him that he do so. It was, after all, none of his affair, and that he did know and mainly respected. That respect was the single thing I ever required of Wyatt Earp, and though it often pained him, because he was my friend, that respect he freely granted. He had to have done no less or we could not have remained cordial.

Better for you if he hadn't. Better for us both. I never met an Earp I'd've crossed a street to pee on if they'd've burst into flames, a miracle, by the way, I prayed might occur on many an unrainy day. I don't much cotton to sharing a man, 'specially with another man. Don't leave enough left over when the time comes to shoot the moon.

None of us get everything we want, so we take what we can get. I got you and felt more alive on that account than I had any right to feel, than I would ever have dared to feel. Besides, you were good for my game. Gave me something to play for. To spoil when I won, and when I lost, to listen. You don't hear me complaining.

And you don't hear me playing the fool. I know better than to believe you ever loved me right and proper. You never loved anyone that way, not a soul, 'cept maybe yourself, and more likely, not even that. Warn't in you was what I finally come to. Couldn't do it nohow. Too took with your own mortality, too much the reckoner of your woe, and too damn vain besides. A perpetual fascination to yourself, eh, Doc? Well, to love you gotta surrender, self-abandon, gotta let the best of it go, and you was never up to it, abandoning yourself, not all of yourself, not any part that mattered, mattered most, leastways not to me, or even, I reckon, yourself. Heard a phrase once—the ruthless need for autonomy—highfalutin, but there you go, that was you, hands off your heart every beat of the way. Moats, Doc, you lived behind mazes of moats so elaborate, there was no hope of ever breaching a one. Wonder's the way I was so willing, willing to suffer the famine, feast off the bones, willing to take such as I was able and put the rest away. Warn't everything, warn't much atall, but guess it was enough, enough to get by on, barely. Turned me scavenger, Doc, that's what you done, turned me vulture. Night after night, these buzzard dreams, gnawing on nothing but air. God forgive me, but that's what it was, so help me Jesus, it was like living with visions of carrion.

And what would you have had me do? What ought I have done? Done differently? If part of loving someone means honoring such freedom as they may require to enable them to love freely in return, how can such honor take seed lest one first suckle that freedom in oneself? And as in myself such a freedom'd been stillborn, what was I left to nurse but a corpse? The life and death of it's what flummoxed me, the desperation people feel, the *panic*, to render of their lives but a scrounging for affection, as if how well-loved one is, or how well one loves back, is the measure of one's worth, or might embroider one's death with its meaning. No, I knew what was required, as that I hadn't the right chips to play. I had misspent too much, squandered myself, exhausted each resource along the way. My soul, call it what you will, all that had gone insolvent, long before. I loved you the way that I loved you, that's all, the way that I could. What I loved was the way you made me feel—adored, every inch the Sun King. No, not even; more. I loved you because you would have me, me no more than a lunger. The avidity of your ardor, that was the miracle. And what you called me, "My wonder. My wonderboy. My ever-dying wonder." I may have sought grace with a gun in my hand, but oh Katie, you made me feel like a sultan. Cynical about all the wrong things, dear Kate, that was you from the start, save the one thing against which you found yourself helpless, the man you took into your heart.

Kate Elder knew what she was about, as she knew what she was not, and knew, too, that she did herself no dishonor in priding herself upon surrendering to her natural inclination to do her utmost to please and to pleasure a man, or indulging her appetite to bestow such tender parts of herself in the name of being thought the more indispensable. She knew, knew long before I told her—this most base as most human of truths—that if you want to be treated like a princess, please don't, dear love, love me like a king, but fuck me as it may please me, fuck me, oh Kate, like a whore. And being one from the outset, content to abide much the same.

So she soothed me less than she sated, so what? The sating was everything, and the everything it was was miracle. Paeans to true love come cheap as they are prolific, and chivalry blooms only in books. No, it is the virtues of lust, that vampire rapacity, the slash and the burn and scorched earth of it, that too often go politely unpoemed. Kate always knew where she stood with me—prostrate, facedown on her knees.

Upon this, thank God, we both in philosophy and practice agreed: strip away his costumes and crepe, and man is scarce more than a beast. Between the sheets we are as wolves in high rut, and the only truly romantic moments to be savored in this world are those that arrive in crest after crest of the most coilsprung and soaring carnality, shanks asplay, thighs agape, cunt akimbo, slicker than a skyful of starglide.

No man wishes to be understood too completely, especially by a woman, especially by a woman like Kate, and from the first, as the both of us knew, she could read me like a rune. No matter. She was never less than my abiding darlin', and though the trail was sometimes bumpy, strewed with sage or gone to seed, we rode it through, hearts hitched high in the saddle, straight on to trail's end.

So if, as Baudelaire has said, love is but the desire to prostitute oneself, Kate loved me well enough and dearly, but then she understood what we both understood—may have understood it best: copulation, coitus, coition, congress, this carnal form of innermost knowing   more   what matters   most.

Poor Doc, he warn't what most folks would have called a good man, warn't much interested in giving himself the chance, but he was a gent, he was a gentleman, and if he wanted for the contentment and calm that the storm in his head strafed to tatters, still, more than most knew or wished to believe, when he felt safe, when the nightmares let him be, when he give himself permission to be held tight, hugged, rocked off to sleep, he was a gentle soul too.

Mainly though—you'll pardon the parachronism—he was just the bluesiest song you ever did hear an old troubadour sing: *A thousand wounds, a thousand wounds, and each one bleeding lyrics.*

Never forget it, what he told me once: "Loss of belief cleanses the mind, loss of faith the spirit." Well, his life may have been little more than a slog, lament by long lamentation, but at least it was that, at least it was something, at least it warn't some burlesque or self-parody, proverb or parable, piece of dime novel drivel or conceit of a celluloid lie.

And here's what you did not know: had a birthmark, shape of Australia, this target smack in the midst of his back, and a soft spot where it sunk in like, that place on a baby's head, that fontanelle, right there on the left side of his chest. And sometimes, here lately, I caress it in my sleep.

Lying here where
a moment ago her
loins so loudly loitered
lovesounds
littering the sheets, liquid
across yet one more hotel room bed
downtrail
the way her lyrics
linger
stun the night to
cinder
as he cools the heels
of his songless heart

Let me introduce ya to somethin' new (I told him)
cuz the way ya seem to like it
that's the way I like it too:
pore and pure portal, aperture, cleft,
orifice, ostiole, vomica, vent,
socket or seam, geode or druse, notchlet or nocking, rosette and
    fuseau,
moist joint,
slit crease,
concavity's sleeve,
the long loaf of you lumber eased
timber! up my muscle of mouth

                        (this knowing instinctive,
                        the way each of us arrives as we will
                        at the entrance that beckons:
                        backgate
                        oubliette
                        hatchway
                        trapdoor
                        cellar window
                        flue—
                        or down this chute of open skylight
                        burnt black before we hit the ground
                        sprinting
                        furled in flame)

please!   don't!   stop!
shatter me, RUIN
me,
my mongrel brain tripping backwards
bent bare over barrier reef

into bedroom choreography
this rumpus of coral sheets,
now plumbing my monocled O,
now plunging the sphinx of its sphere,
and as the stars collapse to   stardust
and the body breaks to   bread
feel that?
ab
intra
anum
as water when it travels or
starlight when it leaps,
the planets when they scatter
your seed when it escapes

watching his shadow stem
across the wall at his back
this rev of piston, ancient as
a bloodstar or
a thorn torn free of its rose

Being a Georgian well-bred he
always had been susceptible to
orphaned women of
independent means and
dubious virtue
fled West
down the Mississippi from
Iowa
fluent in Hungarian and
steeped in the wiles of surgeons

the way they fist
stilled hearts to life
again

apparent from the moment they tangled

born Mary Katherine Harony (or Haroney), 11/7/50, eldest of seven children of Dr. Micheal Harony and his second wife, Katharina Baldizar (or Boldizar) devout Catholics from the Pest section of Budapest, Hungary

family immigrates to the U.S., arriving in Davenport, Ia., 11/63

two years later, both parents since deceased, resides briefly in nearby Scott County with half sister Emelia, 23, and her husband, Gustava Susemihl

1866, stows away on a steamboat southbound down the Mississippi, debarking at St. Louis

as Kate Fisher bears a son to Silas Melvin, an 18-year-old attendant at the St. Louis County Insane Asylum; when the baby dies in infancy, abandons Melvin to become a "working girl" at Joseph Henry's Theatre Comique at the corner of Biddle and 5th

1874, works as Kate Elder in Wichita, Kan., first at a "sporting house" run by Sallie and Bessie Earp, then at Tom Sherman's Dancehall

probably while wintering in Deadwood, Dakota Territory, 1876-7, meets John Henry "Doc" Holliday, a consumptive, Ivy League-educated dentist, professional faro dealer and alcoholic saloon gambler, accompanying him that summer to Ft. Griffin, Tex.

————

AFTER BOTH OF her parents perished in a boating mishap, hauled down every crucifix, painted saint and plaster madonna in the house, bundled them in a duffel, then heaved the lot into the Mississippi, sparing only that which she wore on a gold chain about her neck. This I later lost in a game in Dodge, which, considering, did not seem overmuch to concern her.

Her brother Alexander, though a year younger, is permitted to take the boat onto the river while she is made to row in circles tethered to a tree on shore. Naturally she grows up to be an expert swimmer, one attracted to riptides and undertows who seldom misses an opportunity to bathe naked in stream, lake or river, or jackknife from escarpments and cliffsides. No surprise, then, that she bore her own rivers within her, the way she coursed, secret and wild, the subaqueous cross of her current.

Remembering the ocean crossing as a kid: "I warn't scared, not for a second. Didn't feel to sea. Just kept wanting to jump on overboard and go swim with those dolphins."

One night, half drunk, confides she left Iowa after having had "a bellyful" of her half brother-in-law. The deadness in her voice and eyes, their opacity, those shark eyes, I had seen that once before, in the Kid, as I was to see it once again, in John Ringo. Just never on a woman.

Melvin took her on the job with him once, the bughouse in St. Louis. There was this nigra there, patient himself, cut hair, shaved the others, never spoke, but walked around touching things, tapping them with his fingers, way you'd drum a table. Finally he waltzes up to her emboldened as you please and starts in on her face. Eyes, nose, lips, chin, tapping and flicking, drumming faster and faster; maniac. "Like he was playing a trumpet. Making silent music. That's what it felt like. Like he was playing the cornet of my face. Funny, I plumb forgot about it 'til now."

She'd swim the Colorado in the dead of winter, but having once had a bad experience, refused to ice-skate on a dare. It was winter, but warm. For winter. And if the ice was weak on the river, her ankles were weaker still. So when she fell, then fell straight through, her ankles came tumbling after. "I sank like a sack of washers. A bag of BBs. I sank like a box of ballbearings. A crate of slugs. And then my lungs began to fill with water, so I thought sure I was a goner. Felt my heart engorge, and then explode. So that's how I almost drowned. Every year some kid did, and that year it nearly was me." But they hauled her out, laid her on the ice, someone tucked a blanket about her, and a muffler, and they rubbed at her hands as if to strike sparks. She had visions of viscera being sucked in ventilated scraps out her lungs. "And later I caught a catarrh that nigh finished off what the river'd just only begun." Told her I knew exactly what that felt like—every day.

That first winter in Deadwood: "Never did know what love was before, and now I got a case of looks-like-far-too-late."

Apparently it was the European fashion of her mother—plus which most of those cowboys were not overly particular about the trimmings—but I told her, "If you intend for us to team up, then you must kindly shave your arms and legs and such, for I cannot abide a woman of hirsute parts." My quim? she asked. "No," I said, "not there, for I am much partial to a full bush. But should the blade distress you, I would be pleased to do the honors myself," an offer she saw fit to decline. When next we made love, her skin was smooth as seal.

She knew her way around the terrain of a man the way most do their own kitchens. "Good at what I'm good at is all," she explained. "Once I come West I faced my choices—dressmaker, laundress, seamstress, milliner, servant gal, waitress, schoolmarm, nursemaid, midwife. Couldn't feature a one. Reckoned if I was going to whore, why not be the best piece money could buy." Which she was, knowing every trick in the book, and all the ones outside.

She typically wore a pessary until one of her many abortions so ruined her womb parts, it all but rendered her barren. She bore her childlessness as well as any woman could, like a badge. And later, same as a banner.

A moment's comical indiscretion: "It's true I like showing off my butt, if only to give my face a rest."

The way she slept, shining, her flesh lit up from beneath, bright, brightening, lined on the inside with suns. I loved sleeping beside her, that boulevard of skin, bone hammocked to bone, globed ivoried to the hive of her. She shed years in her dreams. Breathing her in, tasting the humidities, her smell on me lush as burst peaches. Sometimes, being mindful not to wake her, I toyed with her hair, coasting my fingers through its cape, curled a tress to my tongue, buried my face up under its tentflap nuzzling the notch of her neck. Endless as an orchard.

She smelled of civet. We all have our private scents; that was hers. Read once where it comes from the glands of a cat's ass. Figures.

I'll confess I wasn't always up to her. "C'mon, Southern Boy," she'd say. "Don't just sit there a-whistlin' Dixie. Serve it up, hand it over, gimme some, gimme a taste of that ol' Southern hospitality. Make me see stars and bars." She knew the grammar of sex as if she had invented it, each tense and preposition, pronoun and predicate—invented it expressly to inhabit it.

Skin Poetry: in the right mood, on a good day, hit the right spots, just the right way, she could cum that way. Nape of the neck to the base of the butt, round and around, performing slow orbits, tracing the terrace of her back like a cartographer maps, or a palmist palmreads palms. Hours at a time: line, shape, speed and pressure, motion and depth, fingers and nails, knuck of 10 knuckles, pad of two thumbs, heels of palm, lips and tip of tongue, teeth, nose, soles of feet, their heels and, as often, toes. Touch, caress, palp and plane, scratch and press, strum, hum, blow, sigh, knead and nibble, forage some, or graze. In and out of hollers, along cleft and crease, rift and seam, wedging (or wending), through crevice, crack, crook, crevasse, node upon nick to her crotch; ranging ridges—rack of a shoulder, dowel of a rib, ring of waist, down slopes, 'tween folds and spreads, o'er rolls and rises, curves and bends, fussing with her freckles, arc of scar, lapping moons, mouthing mounds of flesh like figs. Just meandering, precinct and parish, shire and ward, each lobe and bulge and tuck, flank and shank, haunch, paunch, pavilion, porch, vestibule, suite, hill and glen, each dell and every dale. Burrowing her bottomland, its bracts and bunds, its berm, ramp of rump, or riding high a jut of hip, lingering there, stalled upon a loin of lower thigh. Sometimes I'd use my prick for a probe, or in place of a feather or fruit. A column of down boa-ed her spine, whose cobbles were as knuckled as knobs, and she bore a birthmark, as did

I, tucked up under a wing of scapula that resembled one of the lesser continents, though which one, I never could decide. She was where I retreated, routed, where I went to surrender, to be gathered in and up and unto, refueled and refreshed, refortified, to be ramified and released. We were mad as kings for one another, lunatic, each for our high throne of flesh.

Pillow talk: "Wanna make love again? Now, right here—come."

"What? No. Wait. All right. But without touching, OK? This time without touching. Let's fuck each other holy with our eyes."

Told me she kept hold of a meat cleaver to fend off forwardsome men, nor have I a reason to disbelieve it. But I never saw her brandish it, not once, nor spoke with a soul who had.

This much later: "Appears it's not ours to grow old together, but I'd give both arms to walk you hand-in-hand on past the sunset. And all for the adventure."

A particularly bad attack after a long night out, my mouth and lips, my chin bloody, and as I go to wipe them, she staying my hand, shaking her head—"Here, let me"—kissing me flush, full on the lips, parting them with her tongue, her tongue everywhere, minnow, salamander sliding past teeth over roof of mouth rooting down throat like sucking poison from wounds swallowing red salts carrying the taste of it diseased and fluid planted to another, deeper place.

Never saw her shampoo, ever. Hair just seemed to rinse clean by itself. That miracle, resplendent, self-cleansing hair. The way it smelled of root beer in the morning. And later, bourbon and *jit*.

Over-heard to the mirror: "If that's what it takes, that's what it's come to, I don't want to tempt you to be true. I'd rather you just . . . fake it."

I did not, as did she, subscribe to the totemic favor said to emanate of amulets and talismans, but once, one of the few times we were to go out riding together, her horse had stumbled almost throwing her before pulling up lame, having thrown a shoe. So that later, back in town, I thought to have the smithy fashion from its iron a miniature in kind of its U before stringing it like a locket to a silver chain; this lucky charm. But she consistently refused to wear it, complaining of its weight, until I grew so irked at her ingratitude, she was obliged to quiet me by disclosing the truth. "Last thing I need is Holliday luck slung like a noose 'round my neck. You understand, doncha, Doc? No woman likes to be yoked." Still she kept it, appreciative of the gesture, and much later, as accorded with the wishes enumerated in her will, was buried with it. Not hanging at her breast, but clutched—this fist of misfortune—cradled in the clasp of her hand.

For a while she was having the same dream, weeks running. Up on the same white horse, but painted black. Bareback, stark naked through the streets, people thronging parade-like, their eyes into her like hooks, and suddenly this crack of thunder, the one, and then it's raining—flowers, gumdrops, whirligigs, scented candles, colored balloons, tin whistles, showering silver dollars like the sky's a piñata and folks scrambling to the loot, and she just keeps on riding down the street. Godiva. Rides out of town, not a backward glance until the applause, applause like songs, songs her daddy used to sing her back in Hungary. So whirls around and waves herself awake, unwoven—same place, same moment, never fails, every time.

My consort, perhaps; *never* my concubine.

DOC AND BILLY
A True Story

The Kid's mother had died of consumption when he was 14 or 15, so I reckon we shared that, the always ache of it, and it's the ache that doubtless queers my estimation, but notwithstanding that I knew he had all manner of blood on them, it may have been his hands that won me over. (Plus, too, we both were Micks, Irish from the North, the Kid's true name being McCarty. Henry McCarty.)

You noticed them right off, because though small and flawless as a girl's, they were so infernally alive, lethally alive, more alive than any of the rest of him, as if they were fed by an extra heart, some heart of their own, sleepless, supple, never at rest, weaving arabesques, in their ease and dexterity seeming almost to glow, expressive in the moment of the boy as a whole, a form of language to themselves, alone. And the fingers, oh my, just beautiful, ten of the whitest I ever had seen, smooth and white as rime, as ermine, and he henned them like a new mother her get. His saddlebags were stocked with creams and lotions, lanolins, mysterious ointments and unguents (mysterious, at least, to me), oils and come-by Native potions with which he salved them several times a day. I had known only women to do that before. Wrists too. This ritual.

The main thing about him, the one true thing, was his senses, for it was at once apparent that they were of such a highsome quality—shaved raw, carved keen, polished to a positive pitch—that they occupied some higher register or range; like the blind, he could glean things with them in advance of others. It made him too sensitive, tactile, tensile, it made him too extreme. He said his skin itched all over all the time, that insect noise jammed his head and the respiration of others, every fluxion and frequency, that to think through it was dizzying. He didn't sleep, he told me, just reposed with his lids half closed. And how the motion of his blood as it traveled his veins and the drift and sway of the scents on the air, the musks and mosses and musts, sachets and pomades, was so thick at times, so . . . plush, it got so he could hardly breathe. Everything was too clear, flavorful, pungent, too loud or too soft, hot or cold, overprecise, so magnified and concentrated, so wholly exposed, that to think through it confused him.

He was all nervepoint.

So he had stopped, he said, just stopped that kind of thinking. "Ain't but clutter nohow." Thought, mind, calculation, in the Kid such as that had been muted and forestalled until what was clarity in most people had become in him a raw and elemental alert. Everything about him embodied wariness, his brain repeatedly breaking up, yet reconciled to a dissonance that crowded out meaning in favor of instinct and intuition, reflex and reaction. Sixth sense. Yet one he had managed to harness that he might direct it as the moment required, in an eyeblink, moving inside the disorder of its discipline, unplotted, plotless, yet hewn to the living shape of each detail. I had heard the phrase once before: "an organism of inexorable purpose." That was the Kid all right, pure raptor. There was no abstraction in him.

It was while in Dodge, this some after I'd rescued Wyatt's backside, that my lungs took to kicking up again—there is, believe me, no dust on God's earth so devilish as that arisen of Dodge City's peculiar squalor—and having wangled the invitation out of my old acquaintance John Chisum, I thought it the better part of prudence to repair to his spread upon the Pecos to rest up some, recover, take the hot springs near the new Las Vegas, explore the notion of opening my own saloon thereabouts—Dodge was all played out for me by that time—and avail myself of the latest in those remedies advertised, as Chisum had himself put me onto them, by the West's very first "Lunger's Club." (Chisum was the first of the cattle barons, so called, biggest and wealthiest in the West; paid 100 cowboys to run 100,000 head on a ranch stretching 150 miles along the South Spring where he lived to himself, save for his daughter, Sallie.)

This may have been the Christmas of '78, '79, don't believe '80, somewhere along in there, a time when the Kid and John still were cordial, Chisum having been an ally of the Kid's former boss, a Brit named Tunstall, before Tunstall was stomped by Chisum's rival, Murphy. So Chisum took him in, but the murder of John Tunstall had by then led to what was called the Lincoln County War, one of those numberless, interminable range feuds that flared from time to time, and the details of which are best forgotten save to mention that the Kid directly succeeded in getting himself mixed up in them to the extent that he took to roaming at will about the neighborhood raising mayhem in the company of a band of roughnecks and hellraisers that went by the name Regulaters. By the time I met him he was a much-wanted man, one with a mounting reputation as a rakehell desperado, though the Mexicans, the señoritas in particular, worshipped him for something like a god. El Che. El Chivato. That's what they called him—the Guy, the Kid. Well, he did speak a surprisingly elegant Español.

You had to ride out to the Chisum place, there being no convenient coaches or trains, it was in the middle of no damn where, hard flat land, bench-flat, like steppe or savannah, you could see the house clear 40 miles off, so I hired a horse in Vegas and rode out there, being in no singular hurry, a saunter, a Saturday, sometime after breakfast.

The Kid was nowhere in evidence when I arrived—not that I noted the absence, being ignorant of his connection to the place—and John was himself briefly away on some business, or so I was informed by Sallie, who before I had so much as dismounted strode out across the front porch all salutation. Wind-tanned and tall, long and oblong, big-boned and clad always in white—as I was directly to learn, if never the reason—Sallie Chisum was tons more than mere confection. Her hair was some shade of bran and she wore it looped at the neck so it fetched against the field of her gown, swagging across the fan of her shoulders in a way that played up the twayblade she'd fixed at its crown. (Where she came by orchids way out there, Lord knows.) She was not by any calculation my notion of comely, but she was possessed of devastating manners, and once we had exchanged pleased-to-meet-yous she inquired if I had eaten—the Chisums were famous for the larders they laid on for their guests (Sallie authored a green chili stew ardent enough to melt candles)—and whether I wouldn't appreciate a tall one to cut the trail dust. Someone had tutored her well.

Sallie was partial to varmints and critters, had a genuine weakness for mavericks and strays, and at John's behest she collected them like coins, birds in particular, mainly of a species no one had heard of. Over the next several days I would be shown toucans and cockatoos, quetzals and macaws, hornbills and shoebills, marabous and rocs, gadwalls and wagtails, peacocks and lyrebirds, a stork, two herons (rex), something called a jacana, another named an ibis, a golden condor from California, as well as an ostrich, a pair of pihis and a one-eyed old Tengmalon's owl. Oh, and an albatross she'd cognomened Lucky. (I should not have been startled had she kept pterodactyls.) These, in all their convolvulus chirm, she kept penned around back where the help had carpentered an avenue of coops and keeps, a sort of homemade aviary, her offer to take me on a tour of which it pleased me to decline—the ride in had about fetched the fine points right off my fettle—content to amuse myself instead with the parrot, a dockwinged Green Amazon perched on a pedestal-stand in the dining room. Damnedest thing, she remarked goodnaturedly, won't talk 'til nightfall, then won't shut up 'til dawn.

Butlering me to my room up the broad-curving stair where with my acquiescence she poured me a hot bath, she suggested I "take a liedown," offering to wake me when her father arrived, some few hours still, or so she rough-reckoned. As a rule I am contrarily disposed to naps, but I must have dozed off; when the rap came at the door it was nigh onto sundown. Father's just come in, she said, if yer agreeable, come on down as it suits you. No rush. She turned to go, then wheeled back round all of a motion. Oh, and he's brought someone with him. He's a character too.

I was about to ask who when that "too" sank in and distracted me. A character too. So I was a character then. Well, by Sallie Chisum's lights, reckon I was. Stole myself a smile on that one and decided right then to like her immensely, even found myself wondering about her life, all alone in that big house, miles from anywhere, solitary desert flower, and about all those birds, though I knew she was not the sort bound to appreciate it, being thought after so. That gal may not have been some Helen of Troy of the West, starved to near perfection, orange sherbet to the eye or a ravishment beyond the telling, but there was something plainly beautiful about her. A beauty in her being. Sallie Chisum was and always would be scads more than just the head on any man's beer.

I found the three of them downstairs deployed around the block-long dining-room table—John, near 60 then, marshaling its head, Sallie midpoint down one side, and at its south end, leaning back full-stretch in his chair so it teetered on its hindlegs, his ankles X'd and propped by a single boot heel on the table's edge, a boyish-looking, long-haired fellow with bucked, grossly maloccluded teeth that were none any too white. Could be that was the feature lent the crookedness to his mouth, or may be what caused it, but it ramped at a promiscuous pitch that once you got accustomed to it—and allowed for a pair of lips so thin and thinly drawn they appeared all but impoverished—was less overtly cruel than frankly unattractive.

Trigged out Paladin-like, an investment in black—bib shirt, neckerchief, felt vest, silver concho belt, gunrig (the border of his holster was emblazoned with blued metal grommets and carbonized studs), pants, silver-toed, fancy-tooled Mexican boots—he was engrossed at knifepoint policing his fingernails. But what I noticed first, noticed before all that, was how rumpled he looked, even for that time and place, extraordinarily rumpled. Like a tramp, way it struck me, a rattletrap tramp; like he'd spent the past three nights running sleeping it off in a Goodwill bin, or the historical equivalent thereof.

When I entered the room—I was watching him without lending the impression, for he was facing front-on—he did not glance up, or shift, or tilt his posture but an nth of a inch, even as John launched from his chair and, hand out, strode bluffly over welcoming me hail-and-well-met to his home. Doc, he said, ushering me over, I want you to meet a friend of the house, Mr. William H. Bonney. Billy, this right here is the fella I was telling you about. This here is Doc Holliday.

Now, it has been my consistent experience that in real life so-called legendary encounters almost always are a letdown, and this one about fit the bill in each detail. There was no trouble, not even a detectable sort of testiness. I wouldn't call it an exchange of animosities by any means. We both knew that if we were not meeting a friend for life, neither were we confronting a foe, and so felt no need to one up or engage in an inkling of rivalry. There was no challenge in it, no affront, no dare or sizing up of the other. We weren't about to match wits, vocabularies, reading lists, c.v.'s, to compare nether parts or joust like the champions of yore. I'd say it was a mutual regarding to which we were about equally indifferent.

Billy holstered his knife, wiped a hand—right hand I seem to recall—on his shirtfront, lazed to his feet—the way he slouched at it, like some damn humpback, made him appear even shorter than he already was, the Kid in no way troubling 5′5″ stood on tiptoe; Wee William, Pee-wee Willic, Half-pint Will, Sawed-off Billy, Runty Bill, Itty-bit, Inkspot, Knee-high, Bean sprout, Cow chip, Peanut, Pissant, Pipsqueak, Popgun, Small fry, Shortcake, Squirt, I did not call him any of those things though I confess to being in the moment sorely tempted—and raising his hand like a pledge and squinting up south of his brow with eyes that beckoned you to wade through the ore-blue of them into black water, said simply, How-do. Or, as he was wont to pronounce it in a voice indeterminate and gleeless as glass, at least so it sounded to me, How-duh.

I was to learn later that he never shook hands. Ever. Something about not trusting to another man's grip, how the gesture made him nervous, his policy being to keep his hands to himself at all times, keep them freed up and "on the prowl." I told him I could nearly see his point, but how it left him wide open to misinterpretation, to which he shrugged and remarked, Well sure, happens, fuck-all.

The Kid had his ways, and while they were largely inscrutable, they likewise were distinctly his own, and if each one made him more what he was and that much less like everyone else, still, that didn't make him what I since have heard bandied about—some kind of stub-peckered chucklehead.

We retired to the porch after a while, each encumbered with a café con leche and trying our damnedest not to slosh, the porch being the one John'd recently had built out there 'cross the breadth of the roof, narrow stair leading up to a railed-off catwalk or crow's nest, Captain's perch, what back East they call a widow's walk, and John clambered into his rocker where he set to dragging on his pipe like a calumet, head half hid for the smoke flange, furling out the sweet fragrance all burleys and peats, while Sallie proposed to keep to the steps below content to dig at the ears of her hound, the basset Augustus, Augustus or Woodrow, I forget which.

Billy meanwhile, having once unburdened himself of his bandoliers and gunbelts, plunked himself down tailorwise up top, where he bent hove to his labor, fishing from his ruck all manner of truck—handtools, rulers and levels, brushes and whisks, steelwools and sandpapers, ragcloths, lidded canisters and container tins, cork-topped glass phials filled with candy-colored liquids, baglets of rosin and chalkdust, he even—God's truth—hauled out a jeweler's loupe and calipers, the lot of which he proceeded to align in some arcane order that he alone was privy to. This child at play with his toys. It was a routine, Sallie told me later, a kind of ceremony she had seen him perform on numerous occasions in the past.

I had heard tell that Wild Bill was about as fanatical with respect to the minutiae of his rig as a man could be, but in my own experience there never was a soul paid closer heed to each immaculate detail of his hardware than that disheveled 18-year-old. Hours he was at it (slackjawed the while; owing to a misknit nose the Kid was a ferocious mouthbreather), a marvel of fine motor skill and manual dexterity, this closework of the true artisan— bluing the barrels, filing the hammers, shaving the sights, hairing the triggers, removing the guards and safety catches, adjusting the grips, oiling his leathers, the lot—until, as I studied him, I swear I was saddled with a nosebleed that rendered it politic I pardon myself and stagger on down to bed.

Now, anyone who knows me—nor need the knowing be

overtly familiar—knows I've a weakness for custom-tooled gunnery, and any man who permits rust to rigor his ironware is a slaggard and sloth who deserves what in time he has coming, but everything the Kid was about in his single-minded compulsion boiled down to one thing only: speed. To be the one to skin back, throw down and pop off *first*. Fast, faster, fastest. And he was. Fast. Jackrabbit fast. He was, I daresay, electric. That boy was faster than the gunhand of God. I am myself no slouch in the velocity department, but sweet Jesus, Billy the Kid was a blur. More's the pity, then, that none of it mattered for snot.

Because he was reckless, pure firebrand, and monumentally indiscreet with his talents while possessed of the religious belief that he could never be had, inevitably a fatal combination. I will not say he was a fool—he was, after all, a mere juvie—but he was by every standard that matters headed headlong in the direction.

Truth is, fast is no vice in itself. Better too fast, after all, than not fast enough. But fast is no more than fast finally does, and fast alone is but half of it. Fast but dead-calm, cocksure and cool, that's the whole package. Wyatt called it best: taking your time in a hurry. Collection and composure, deliberation and method, calculation and odds, all in a wristflick. Oh, the Kid had nerve, five minutes alone in his company and you knew he had that—guileless, unprepossessing, deferential, diffident, the Kid was none of those—but that nerve was too sheer by half, and to his everlasting detriment it was of a sort that I quickly surmised he had neither the horse sense nor temperament to curb. At last, the speed that was his gift was likewise his curse, and for me it made him a figure stained clear-through in crimson, as one fingered long past by death's host.

I was right of course. When I heard later that Garrett had got him, much as I regretted that a boy like that—one capable of inspiring during his brief go-round such a lode of timeless and terrible myth—had gone and got himself capped, still it made to me perfect sense. I knew Pat Garrett some, enough to know that he was that rarest of exotic birds, an academic killer, a sane, if you prefer, assassin, every stitch the equal of Tom Horn, and that Billy, by comparison, was an amateur. A ruthless amateur, no arguing, but an amateur all the same. The Kid may have done for the 21 they say he did, or he may have done 21 more, but as Paddy Garrett was a man, and the Kid was, well, a kid, the outcome was the result of a mismatch, and of that mismatch foregone.

Later, there would be those pleased to suggest that what had perished with him that day was a form of precocious sagacity. Perhaps. Dead at 21. Shot violently, brutally dead. Assassinated in the night. Bleeding out 'neath the wane of midnight's moonlight. Myself? I'm slow to grasp the wisdom there. Suffice to say he was no daisy. No, Sir, your precious Billy the Kid? That poor boy was no daisy atall.

In any case, such was the first night. There were others, for I lingered most of a week, languishing in the hospitality—first water all the way—the quality of that air as the absence of activity doing my lungs a world of favor. The Kid was coming and going the whole time, stealing in and out, he seemed to have free run of the place, disappearing only to materialize unannounced at the most irregular hours. I had heard it remarked that he rode like a centaur, as if riding was an extension of the body as much as an exercise of the mind, but you couldn't have proved it by me. I never once saw him astride. He had the habits of a yegg.

I recall one night in particular, he drifts in more hopped up than usual itching to play cards, and though it already was too late, way past one in the morning, what the hell. So John rustles up a deck and some chips, has Sallie fetch a bottle and some glasses, and we hunker to the dining-room table, everyone—save

Sallie and the damn parrot, who is squawking up a blue streak—drinking too much, way too much, too all-at-once too purposefully, especially Billy, who as a rule was not much of a drinker and so hadn't the seasoning to stomach it.

Now, the Kid fancied himself a player, which he decidedly was not, but that night he's winning in spite of himself, pot after pot, I cannot catch a card to save my scalp, John's faring no lick better, and the Kid is on the rush of his life, just scorching, hellbent on a streak the likes of which I have seldom seen and sometimes so it goes and no prevailing. But he behaves as if he is accustomed to it, manifests no particular emotion, does not crack so much as a grin, his eyes are narrowed to the sort of slits you use to sight down the barrel of a Winchester or lock a world of confusion in your crosshairs, save that as the night wears itself out he is getting drunk and drunker and beginning without knowing it to show it.

At one point he heaves himself out of his chair nigh capsizing for the trouble and goes to swerving across the room down the length of the table hanging onto its edge like a ship's rail before drawing his gun and waggling it at the parrot, the parrot that's perched there narrating the night, challenging the parrot to its face that if it doesn't shut the fuck up, well, he's sure he's got a recipe for parrot stew right here someplace. Which might have been comical if he hadn't sounded so much like he really meant it, then haired back the hammer sliding the barrel through its beak into its mouth down its throat pinning back the black of its tongue and actually pulled the trigger, once, to no effect—empty chamber—which is when John motions Sallie sidelong to fetch the bird off to the kitchen make it fast and close the door.

Finally about four, John, who by then is pretty loaded himself, suggests bed—Sallie had turned in hours before—and Billy slurs Aw right and the three of us get up and head off, but then I see Billy stumble and nearly go down only to right himself on the swivel and make a wrong turn coming out of it so that he bangs off the wall making a terrific THUD! before caroming ten feet on the oblique winding up slewed completely around in advance of disappearing veering *backasswards* through the front door out onto the lower portico forfeit to the night.

Which, right there, was the last time I ever saw Billy the Kid. Alive or otherwise. And John saying, Oh leave him be the gilas won't get him, and me, later, lying in bed upstairs through my open window hearing the sound of vomiting, someone heaving himself up over and over, barfing his young, mythopoeic fool head off—the true Eventual Kid, as I heard someone once call him—which was the last sound I ever heard Billy the Kid make, as I say, alive or otherwise.

And get up and go grope to the window, can't see a damn thing, no moon, asking Billy *¿Quién es? Quién es?* Who is it? Who is it? Kid? That you? Anything I can do? And getting no response, not even more chundering, close the window against the wind that's spanking now so steady I hear the sand like seed, raw rice, like birdshot, the desert like spit teeth at the glass.

So there's a tale for ya, and hope it fanned yer fancy.

You make the air dark
with the beauty of your speed,
Gunslinger, the air
separates and reunites as if lightning
had cut past
leaving behind a simple experience

. . .

the result of such ferocity, a stutter
of some deep somatic conflict, this owner
was ill-advised to use a gun at all
and least of all to let it speak for him

—EDWARD DORN

. . . and who knows, Gunslinger, who daresay how long, on the higher frequencies, may your story be sung, your tale be told—this one, that, some other (for all arc one, as *of* one)—or once more suffer their sounding.

Drawn to the much-touted benefits of its 22 hot springs, Kate and Doc found themselves in the summer of 1879 in "New Town," East Las Vegas, New Mexico Territory, on the Santa Fe Trail, where, having recently closed his dental office on Bridge Street, Doc opened the Holliday Saloon and Gambling Concession, "a legitimate experiment," as he wrote his cousin Mattie, "in on-the-square capitalism." A failed experiment, as it proved. Toothless Montana Mike Gordon was no Billy the Kid, he could not have blacked the Kid's boots, buckled his belt or so much as bundled his bandoliers, but he spelled trouble all the same.

———

Why certainly I remember old Mike. Classic case of queered timing, poor soul. I had been in a mood all day, don't rightly recall the reason why, and here comes Old Gordo as he so despised being called, like some damn cartoon out of a dime novel, and it was more than I could stomach. Mike always had been bad medicine. Word on the street was, he'd disposed of his share of innocents, few of them face-on, though according to Kate his real genius lay in the rate at which it pleased him to deposit among the local whoredom his singularly purulent brand of crotch rot. The Scourge of Vegas, that's what the hens called him. Montana Mike Gordon was a living pestilence, a walking plague, and I have no regrets whatsoever about the affair. A man who cannot be bothered to keep his disease to himself is one who begs inoculating, and I was happy to serve for his vaccine. But as you are asking, I will confess—no, it was far from my finest hour.

—DOC HOLLIDAY

It had become his custom commencing on opening night to station himself straddled to a stool at the far end of the bar, this fixture clad grimly in gray, content to keep his own counsel, and so respectfully granted, as he from the outset insisted, undisturbed berth to drink and smoke and play solitaire as it might suit him, the while surveying in portentous silence both his staff of recently hired working girls and the clientele they served.

He worked them hard, these young women, but paid them tolerably well, extending them a courtesy and deference to which they were unaccustomed and upon which they might often be overheard to comment amongst themselves. So far as they were concerned, he was as a boss "a square-shooter and a gentleman"; he had yet to lose a single girl. Indeed, save for the occasional easily quelled rowdy, the enterprise was going more smoothly than he could have anticipated. More lucratively too; in the past month, owing largely to the late arrival of the Santa Fe Railroad, the place had proven a motherlode.

But that week had been a rough one—he had failed despite Kate's nagging to manage a single session at the hot springs north of town—and that Tuesday night in particular his lungs were at him like currycombs. As he routinely did when they assailed him, he resorted with increasing frequency to the bottle. He knew the rye solved nothing, but damn if it didn't soothe him in the moment, bullnose the edges a bit, and that was solution enough.

He was pouring himself another—number five or, no, six— when the pair of shots sprayed through the front window skittering spiles of glass across the floor in sufficient quantity to encourage staff and patron alike to scramble for quick cover. Errant bullets were one thing, flying glass quite another; no one wished to catch a spelk in the neck.

Apparently unperturbed, he continued pouring, hoisting the glass to his lips while keeping an eye fixed upon the front door;

partook of a prolonged sip. Which is when, as if on cue, Montana Mike Gordon, not a tooth in his head, barged through, gun drawn and still smoking. He was, predictably, quite obviously liquored up. Predictably, because he was Mike Gordon. Obviously, because just as he swayed where he stood, so did he slur when he spoke. Also this: his eyes, rashed red as radishes with rheum, swam in their sockets like slugs. And he was drooling, from mouth and nose alike. In addition, he smelled of freshly let piss and miscellaneous, still ripe evacuation. The sight and smell, while repellent, was one that had become around town so commonplace of late that it had inspired a name, "the East Vegas Look," and everyone acknowledged that Mike Gordon was its Brummel. The unhappy consensus? Toothless Montana Mike was unrivaled.

Toothless and unrivaled then, drooling and pissing himself—Lord alone knows what else—Mike Gordon, formerly of Montana, stood there swaying rebarbatively in place.

"Why, Mike Gordon, what seems to be the matter?"

Mike Gordon appeared to register . . . something. A voice perhaps. Down thataway. At the end of the bar. He turned his head in the direction of the voice, blinked once slowly, then again more slowly still. Once more he appeared to register . . . something. An image perhaps. Down that same way. A figure of gray. A blur at the end of the bar. A man perhaps. A gray man perched on a stool, more still than a shrub. For the first time, Montana Mike Gordon spoke up.

"Huh?"

Then he fell quiet, blinked again and, wobbling like a gyroscope, essayed a single, unsteady step forward. His gun, in the meantime, had ceased its smoking.

"I said, what seems to be the trouble, Sir? Is there anything I can do for you? A drink perhaps. How about it, Mike? Put up the iron and we'll have us a drink. The good stuff. Topshelf. Stiff one. On me."

"Ain thirssy."

"Ah, I see."

"Ain thirssy and would'n drink with no lunga iffn I was."

"I do see. On the other hand, no, I do not. What do you want then?"

"Prish. Wan my Prish."

"Pardon? You want your what?"

"Prish, goddammit! Rye now! Come to gimme my girl."

"Ah, Priscilla, you've come for Priscilla, then, have you?"

"Rye. Mean to have her too." He paused. "Mean to have her goo."

"But you cannot, Mike. You cannot have Priscilla, good or otherwise. She presently is working, you see." He fobbed the watch from a vest pocket and thumbed open its face. "Let's see now, shall we? At present it is nearly midnight. She gets off in another, what, four hours. Four hours, Mike, four hours from this very moment and she will be yours and all yours. I am certain that in four hours she will be glad to accompany you anywhere, anywhere you might choose to name or wish to go."

"Now! Wan her now! Wan her quits and come along!"

"Hmmm. Here, I know. I'll cut you for her. How's that? Low card wins. You catch it, she goes with you. I catch it, she finishes her shift. Fair enough?"

"No cars."

"Lots, then. We'll draw lots. Or draughts. If you prefer, we'll throw draughts. Bar dice, darts, caroms, you name it."

"Fuck all that! I ain skeered a you, Holliday. You don skeer me. You don skeer shit."

"But, Mike, you misapprehend me. It is, I can assure you, the furthest thing from my intention to *skeer* you, as you put it, to skeer you or your shit. It is my intention, rather, to ask you to holster that smoke wagon, turn right around, all the way now, and leave by the same door that you a moment ago entered, just there."

"Ain goin. Ain goin nowheres. Not 'til I gimme my Prish."

"We have been over this ground previously, but in the event that I left the least detail unenumerated the first time, I shall try again—you cannot have Priscilla, she is working, you can come back for her when she has finished working, you can have a drink, you can play cards, you can stand there reeking of yourself and dripping from every aperture and pore until hell freezes over in each of its manifold corners and cubbies, or—and this I wish to make clear is much my personal recommendation—you may do all of us a favor, yourself most of all, and just"—he waved at him as one might bye-bye to an infant—"leave."

"Nope."

"Nope? The best you can do is nope? Well, then . . . *GORDO*, you leave me no choice. After all, it matters little to me to which god you pray. As it matters so much the less which card you may play. You can look all day long for the name of your muse. At the end of the night, it's still just a ruse.

"Come along, then, hop to, Gordo, follow me. Let's see if we can't reckon us a way to stow your problem in some moonless place where the sun don't shine and what's brown turns green in the shade."

Doc slid from the barstool and strode straight past the befuddled Mike Gordon favoring him with nothing so much as a let's-go-bub before disappearing directly through the swinging front doors. Upon which the next voice to be raised—in light of the sequence of events the place had frozen itself into a paralytic hush—was once again Doc's: "I haven't got all night . . . *GORDO*."

Mike Gordon blinked and looked around. The gray figure at

the end of the bar was no longer there, and now his voice seemed to be coming from somewhere outside, out in the street behind him, and the voice was calling him Gordo, a name he detested, and the tone of its overenunciated two-syllable delivery somehow made it worse. A taunt.

It was then, just as he had begun to swing in the direction of the voice, that he saw her. She was crouched beneath a table near the middle of the room, and the sight of her made him blink.

"Prish," he said, softly.

"I'm waiting," said the voice in the street, not softly at all.

She forced a smile, shrugged, nodded her head towards the door. "Go on," she said. "Go ahead. Go on out there now, Mike. When you're done, maybe then you can come on back. Right now you gotta go. Finish what you started." She brushed the heel of a hand at her eyes.

"Finsh," said Mike Gordon, who never could quite bring himself to say no to his girl, especially when she switched on the tears. "OK. Be rye back." And turned, and walked, and zagged towards the door, zigging each step of the way.

He made it through, through the door; he did not make the street.

There was the report of a gun, just the one, the brief discharge of its echo, and then Mike Gordon was back, back inside the saloon, standing there, staring hard, saying nothing, trying to see—who, or what, or where—to piece it together, hold it in place, inhabit a focus, a moment of grace, to make something out, miles off, but the something was too gray, and too fast, and too fleeting.

The gun had gone limp in his hand, and its barrel dangled obliquely, oddly angled to the floor, and still it was not smoking. Like a fog, the floor was afloat, slowly flooding up to meet him, softly rushing now, rising, he could hear it deep inside his eyes, and he blinked, and his mouth began to move in silent chews, and when the blood appeared, it was in a mangle, and in the instant before he dropped, sprigs of reddened spew.

And then Doc was there, striding past the lifeless clump that appeared so much smaller if no less objectionable in death, side-stepping the puddle of blood as it pooled and spread, and though he looked no paler or more ashen than usual, yet he appeared somehow disappointed, chopfallen, aggrieved; indeed he appeared betrayed. This brinksman: yet one more void dispensed with, one more abyss faced down. And as he returned to his place at the bar, he lifted the glass to his lips. But before polishing off what remained, he glanced her way and said, "Priscilla, you would do by me a most singular honor should you consent to take the rest of the night off. With pay. I regret that I killed your Mike, but your Mike was no daisy. No, ma'am. I fear that your Mike was no daisy atall."

<hr>

LESS THAN THREE months later, the Holliday Saloon and Gambling Concession had closed its doors, victim of its competitors' success at blacking both the name of the establishment itself and that of its notorious proprietor. Holliday's Sanguinary Abattoir & Ossuary, that's what the town took to calling it, a stroke of counteradvertising genius that, though it had cost him the easy money, even Doc could appreciate.

And when he rode out of town, he did so with a chuckle on his face.

THE LETTER ARRIVED while they were in Prescott, Ariz.—would have been the late summer of 1880 by then—working the tables at the Cobweb on Whiskey Row. Apparently Wyatt was thriving, down in Tombstone with his brothers, making a killing off the silver mines, and he encouraged Doc to come down there, as "there are no dentists here and I believe you could do right well."

———◦•◦•◦———

SAID KATE: WELL then, you aim to hobble yerself to them Earps, hie off, go to it, git on down to Tombstone, Doc, sounds just the place to suit your style all the same. But I shall not. I am going on to Globe, for I have it in mind to open a boardinghouse there.

Well, said Doc, for the present I think I shall go down there. Something about the name appeals to my better nature, though I do not expect much to like it, nor intend to stay. You will see me in Globe, likely sooner than later.

Their last night in Prescott was a raucous and ruinous one. They were to part early in the morning and the strain of the separation, as it invariably did, wore upon him horribly. Kate was to describe it later as "one of the worst bouts he'd had 'til then. I was awake 'til dawn tending him, his fever a-ragin' the while. I swear it was like he was sweating out every resentment he'd ever had, every grudge he'd ever nursed, every erosion and hatred all at once. His dreams was at him like beaks. Times like that, and I'd seen 'em plenty, I known there was nothin' for it but the poetry, that only the poems could soothe him, but when I went to fetch 'em, ones we'd toted with us'd got lost or somehows stashed aways, God knows. That was the time, think it was, I tried the music, way I known his mama had, singing to him best I could remember those words."

It ain't natural for you to cry in the midnight,
It ain't natural for you to cry, way in the midnight too,
Into the wee, small hours, long before the break of dawn, O Lord.

"And he was raving, out of his head, railing at the sun, the way it come breaking through the glass in the window hooking at his eyes, impaling each thought, way it set 'em ablaze, pleading with me to 'kick out the pane, kick out the pane,' and let him breathe; just let him—breathe."

> *The cool room, Lord, is a fool's room,*
> *The cool room, Lord, is a fool's room,*
> *And I can almost smell your T.B. sheets,*
> *And I can almost smell your T.B. sheets,*
> *On your sickbed.*

"He asked for a drink then. He was crying, coughing—he was deep in the blood fits, those red throes—and he said he wanted whiskey, that he needed the rye. I went and fetched him a glass of water, and when I went to give it to him, he knocked it outta my hand, screamed it was piss, it was poison, and why was I trying to kill him, called me a manqueller and a moerdrice and said he didn't need no help, he could see to doing himself in all on his own. And then the fits was on him agin, and he kinda keeled back and bunched, curled up in a ball, and coughed himself bloody to sleep."

> *You'll be all right too—uh-huh, yeah,*
> *I know it ain't funny, it ain't funny atall, baby,*
> *To live in a cool room, man,*
> *To be laying in a cool room,*
> *a cool room,*
> *cool room.*

IN THE MORNING they boarded the Kearns and Griffith Stage, Kate traveling to Globe and Doc on down to Tombstone where he immediately took a room at Fly's Lodginghouse, landed a job dealing faro at Dick Clark's Alhambra and, looking more like death than ever—if feeling much the same—her words a harmonica burred blue through his brain, he entered history as shucked of documentation as the best cobs their corn.

Walking away from it all—the blight of his past, his scaffold of pain—rale and rhonchus, so cool.

PART

Four

We began with myths and later included actual events.

—MICHAEL ONDAATJE

He set out to master the fine art of draw-and-shoot as cold-bloodedly as he did everything else. He practiced with his Colts for hours at time, even at night, for he wished, so he told me, "to gain a feel for how to shoot straight in the dark," and indeed it got so that he could close both eyes and hit his target above half the time—no mean feat. He was hands down the fastest, deadliest man with a gun I have ever seen, the Kid included, a true gun-sharp and pistoleer, and because he was haunted by the knowledge that he was dying, indeed that he could die at any time, the most utterly fearless.

—WYATT EARP

It was a peculiar thing about the Doctor. Although he was a gentleman-through, a finely skilled dentist and overall a friendly soul, yet outside of us Earps it seemed he hadn't a friend anywhere in the world, though he had enemies enough to suit any ten fellows. Tales were told far and wide that he had murdered men in different parts of the country, that he had committed all manner of vicious crime, and yet when asked how they knew it, not one could point to more than hearsay. Nothing of the kind ever could be traced up to Doc's account, and in all the years I knew him, not once could it be proven that he had broken either tittle or jot of the law.

—VIRGIL EARP

I have over the course of my life had more killings laid at my feet than I could have dreamed, or would ever have wished. But if you will trouble yourself to fairly examine the facts, you will find that whenever I was charged with murder, I was always a long way off, never near at hand. Odd, isn't it? And why? Because I never murdered anyone. Ever. Not a soul. Any killing I ever did—and I did far less of it than I might have had I chosen to avail myself of every just opportunity—was well inside the right line of the law. I never once shot a man dead 'less there was no way around it. Not that I was averse to the gunplay. There were moments of virtuosity, flashes of a silver brilliance for which even I could not account. But my reputation far outstripped the facts. For a while I found this amusing, and after a while I did not. It was like walking around inside a suit of stone—in the main, kept the bugs off, but there was absolutely nowhere to run.

—DOC HOLLIDAY

The killed attributed to him (by journalists, biographers, historians, conventional wisdom, popular legend, etc.) numbers, roughly, 30:

while still a teenager, three Negro boys, with a shotgun, at a whites-only swimming hole on the Withlacoochee River in Georgia; two men, one the former City Marshal, over a "row" at cards, with pistols, in Dallas; with a knife, Budd Ryan in Denver; an unnamed cavalry soldier from Ft. Richardson, Jacksboro, Tex., circumstances unknown; Ed Bailey, with a knife, over a hand of poker in Ft. Griffin, Tex.; the Cowboy who drew down on Wyatt's back in a Dodge City saloon, often identified as Tobe Driskill, a single pistol shot through the heart; Kid Colton, shot down over a hand of poker in Trinidad, Col.; two unnamed Mexican highwaymen along the Santa Fe Trail while traveling to Las Vegas in the company of Kate Elder, method unspecified; Mike Gordon, with a pistol in Las Vegas, and his Mexican cohort when he sought retribution the following day; Jim Crane, "Old Man" Newman Haynes Clanton, Dixie Lee Dick Gray, Bud Snow and Billy Lang, as part of a deputized posse during a firefight near the Mexican border; three men in Tombstone, one named Conley, method unspecified; the McLaury brothers, Tom and Frank, in the Tombstone fight, the former with a shotgun blast to the ribs, the latter of a heartshot; Frank Stilwell, Morgan Earp's bushwhacker, in the Southern Pacific railroad yard in Tucson, with pistols; Florentino "Indian Charlie" Cruz, Stilwell's crony, south of Tombstone near the South Pass in the Dragoon Mountains during the Vendetta Ride, with pistols; John Peters Ringo, the Cowboy Hamlet, a few miles outside of Tombstone in West Turkey Creek Canyon, a single pistol shot fired upward at the right temple exiting through the top of the skull; Johnny Tyler, with Wyatt's assistance, along the Colorado River outside Glenwood Springs, Col., following Tyler's attempted bushwhacking of him in Leadville, Col., and his companion Perry Mallan, a self-styled bounty hunter who formerly had arrested him in Denver, in '82, method unspecified; Constable A. J. Kelly of Leadville, method unspecified.

The killcount in fact comprises . . . two, two positively confirmed—Mike Gordon and Tom McLaury, another two—Ed Bailey and Frank McLaury, some probable fraction thereof. (Bailey, whom he knifed in Ft. Griffin, never was verified as officially deceased; Frank McLaury, shot by him in the heart during the Tombstone fight, more likely was killed by Morgan Earp's near-concomitant headshot.)

As for Henry Kahn, Budd Ryan, Kid McCoy (alias Kid Colton), Charley White, Milt Joyce, Bill Parker and Billy Allen, each of whom he at one time or another either pistol-whipped, knifed, or shot, they all are known positively to have survived such insult to their person as he may have offered.

his rapsheet
this cicatrix,
its every charge a weal,
inside each wayward word

another notch of the noose to his neck

the dark brand on him,
bloodtext,
tabloid down the spine of his life

the transmogrifying power of fiction?
aw—
what delusory newsworthless shite

thinking of
Doc

Doc
shoots
to kill,

But unlike the Kid, to
the seat
of his
soul

Doc
's
shot

torn so fast
it sounds
silence:

steams

hissssssssss-
zing, a
shuss

as if
to heat the sky
thermal

(bring the sky's
blood to its boil)

that becomes—shhhhh
ush

listen now

silence—

called also—

a kill.

WYATT BERRY STAPP EARP: clansman, clan head, Lancelot of the brood. (1) James, (2) Virgil, (3) Wyatt, (4) Morgan, (5) Warren. The Five Brothers. Yet it was always Wyatt, Wyatt alone. Why? Why was that? His, the piston of narrative drive.

> *Wyatt Earp was the meanest ill-begot bastard I ever known, and I known my share. Ask around, ain't just me allows such. Didn't call him the Fighting Pimp for nothing. Had such a born-tactless knack for making enemies, times was it seemed the whole West was crawling with nothing but them out to take him down. Never kilt more'n handful hisself, but buffaloed 'em by the hundreds, cold-cocked 'em by the score—clobbered, clouted, clocked, cauliflowered 'em upside the head with the barrel of that long gun of his. Heard him 'til it got like a mantra: "Well, boys, think I'll grab the old iron and go crack me some skull; need the exercise." He was all blackjacks and brass knucks, that one. King of the drygulchers.*

> —WM. MUNNY

Mind of a Fundamentalist. All scruple, sinew, summary judgment. Muscular, cold, clear, clean, literal as new rain. Unmolested by too much imagination. Content to kill to justify his unnuanced faith in himself. In pursuit of what he considered right anything was permissible. Self-doubt, pangs of conscience, such did not occur to him. No arrival at him save through that lens. His private morals.

Not volatile. Had a temper, but seldom betrayed it. Cool, even, steady-as-she-goes. Not brilliant, but steeped in common sense and an overriding instinct for self-preservation. Prided himself on his mental clarity, mental sobriety. (Preferred the inside of a saloon to that of a church, but rarely drank past a certain point,

seldom heavily.) Less that he valued the ordinary than that he favored order to disorder, imposing his will upon it. Less that he
liked things in their proper place than that he enjoyed putting
them there, heavy hand be damned.

Believed reason was useful only as it presupposed the threat
of force, but favored bluff to intimidation, intimidation to brutality, brutality to killing, yet never backed away from meting it out.
Undaunted by desperate men. Would not hesitate to face them
down, manhandle them eye to eye, yet supremely disinterested in
showing them up. No bully or chest-thumper, but damned if he'd
permit the other fellow to gain the upper hand. Enjoyed the role
of professional enforcer. Liked the power. The wielding of it
settled the part of him that required settling. Where the law was
practical, admired and upheld it. Where (in his judgment) it
proved an impediment, glad to bend it to breaking to make it
work more efficiently.

*As a lawman he warn't incorruptible, warn't no Bill
Tilghman, being too raw in his ambitions and limited in
his talents. May have been his worst characteristic, way his
private aspirations was forever outstripping his natural
abilities. Overreached too damn much. Still, he was better
than mediocre, more fair than middlin', better than most,
doubtless on account of his innate understanding of the
criminal mind, his own according with much the same
conniving self-interest. Image that got mythed up around
him later was of the hard-driving, straightshooting moralist, one who known right from wrong in the churn of his
gut and never failed to cleave to the former. Whole nation's
heard it, all childhood long:* **brave, courageous and bold.**
*Well, that was a song, a theme song at that; facts match up
with the lyrics 'bout as well as most folks' marriages.*

*Which was, he was a harebrained, starry-eyed, backalley
schemer and smalltime hustler forever on the make. Wyatt
Earp was all pipedreams, few of them pleasant.*

—ETHAN EDWARDS

Had a keen and persistent mercenary streak. Few interests besides monied and commercial (and, in consequence, political)
ones. Prone to playing the inside angle before the odds. Not
averse to a hustle or con, but wasn't a swindler or fraud. If Doc
was self-involved, he was self-interested, self-promoting and tribal
to a fault. Where his family was concerned, not to be trifled with.
Then he took everything personally. Take him or leave him, he refused to change for anyone. Inflexible about most things. Im-
placable, relentless, unremitting, redoutable. A man's man. There
are such men; he was one. Two-fisted. Stoical. Resolute. Stern
stuff. Less physically imposing than strong, sturdy, well-built;
solid as good furniture. Blond and blue-eyed and, at six feet, tall-
ish for his times. Demanded deference—perhaps because he believed the worst of people until they had proven him wrong—and
got along well with those who displayed it, if only to his satisfaction. Happy to extend the fair shake as he alone defined fairness.
No man is an island, but toss in the brothers, and he about flirted
with it.

*For all his repeated failures to make the killing he felt
himself entitled to, he never stopped walking around as if
to lord it over the rest of the world that he was Earp and
they was not. Had a right exalted opinion of hisself, like
his own weren't the only one mattered a damn, but the only
one could ever be right. Ought come as no surprise, then,
that he weren't atall popular with people. Not that he
didn't have his cronies—man like him breeds cronies—but*

says all you need that while he always was chasing after one office or another, he never got hisself elected dogcatcher. Polarizing, that was Earp, being the sort to demand worship, and if he didn't get it, that toadying, glad to let you know he thought you unfit to lick his chamberpot.

—PIKE BISHOP

All business. Never laughed, seldom smiled. Seemed to have little or no sense of humor (though he had a peculiar weakness for any kind of ice cream, pistachio especially, and spumoni). Always wore black, undertaker black. Used profanity regularly, "son of a bitch" liberally, but did not overabuse it as he was not witty or original in its expression. Not much of a talker. Content to leave the jawing to others. Had an abiding mistrust of words; they spelled trouble. Longest speech he ever made was in court, under duress, after the Tombstone fight, then only because his life depended on it.

People talk about how much they disliked Doc Holliday, but the way they disliked Doc was the way you dislike a rabid dog or cornered rat—you never knowed when he was going to blow, lash out, strike back, or just what might set him off. Way they didn't like Earp was on account of his being such a long-running drink of water. Guess he was like a lot of bores. Finding hisself endlessly fascinating, he felt he was doing you a favor by gracing your life with his presence. Doc made people nervous, Earp made 'em roll their eyes. Or yawn. Because the man was a glump. Pure glunch. Oh, you could get him to smile, some, a little, maybe, once a coon's age, but I only ever heard him laugh once, at something Doc said, he alone being able to tickle it out of him. He was probably the single most literal-

minded person I ever knowed, and as incapable of appreci-
ating a moment's irony as Doc was the opposite. "It is not
that Wyatt lacks the capacity for amusement," Doc once
told me, "any more than I want for fellow-feeling, but that
he is possessed in abundance of an unnatural aversion to
its display. That others may find this an irritant, I can
well understand. But I do not, not atall. I rather think it,
well, endearing." Typical Doc. To find something affecting
everyone else thought irksome as hell. No, a hard case, that
was Wyatt Earp all over, or where a notch or two softer,
still all of a son of a bitch.

—KATE ELDER

A schemer at heart, eye fixed fast upon the Main Chance, committed to dodging pillar to post after every rainbow he had ever seen or heard rumored, indefatigably on the make, yet he spent most of his life being a farmer, teamster, stagecoach driver, shotgun guard, buffalo hunter, lumber hauler, saloonkeeper, procurer, pimp, gambler, faro dealer, prospector, detective, bounty hunter, bodyguard, Wells Fargo agent and horsebreeder. And, for a number of years, a peace officer. An officer of the law.

At 19 a toe-to-toe with his father culminated in his leaving home and eventually marrying Urilla Sutherland, who died in childbirth nine months later. He promptly went out and stole two horses from William Keys. (He consistently had queered luck with women. He would drive his second wife first to drugs, then to suicide, bicker incessantly with his third. Where they did not exist for his pleasure alone he seemed to presume they had been placed on earth for him to cuff around as a form of recreation, a rug in search of its beating, where not a mattress to peremptorily stuff. He neither understood nor, save carnally of course, appreciated them, and considered the effort a supreme waste of time. Women, much as he might seek their companionship—and such seeking was nearly as constant as it was mindless—did not make him happy.)

The horse-stealing episode was in Missouri. Lamar. He was 23. Arrested, he made and skipped bail. And then for a number of years little was heard of Wyatt Earp. He had fled somewhere in the Indian Territory, the so-called Nations. What happened out there no one knows. No one saw or heard from him. But there were rumors. He had disappeared (some said) down a bottle. Let his mind swill there, stewed, stayed drunk for two years, supporting himself as a hide hunter slaughtering, skinning and butchering buff. It was said (by others) that he lived for a time with the savages, marrying several of their women and siring a brood of breeds, learning to eat dog and decipher his dreams, becoming infected with the pox, a venereal disease. None of this can be verified.

At the end of two years he took stock of who he was, of what he had become, and was appalled. He was sick of eating dog and being told it was a delicacy; it no longer agreed with him. Insofar as he could manage it, he willed himself to stop dreaming. He had badly abused each of his wives and now they left him, taking the children with them. He became a pariah, an outcast, anathema among the tribes. But he felt he had settled a few things, inoculated himself against certain dimensions of himself, dredged their backwaters and altered the currents of their course. He had answered for himself questions he formerly had not known existed. And when his mind was substantially back in his body and he had regained enough of his wits, he returned to "civilization," took the mercury cure—bismuth and arsenic, actually—and became a lawman.

For seven years he was a Deputy Marshal in Kansas, in the

cowtowns of Ellsworth and Wichita and Dodge. He killed a 23-year-old cowboy named George Hoy in the line of duty, treed Ben Thompson and Clay Allison, failed to run to ground Bad Arkansas Dave Rudabaugh, became friendly with Bat Masterson, Bill Tilghman and Luke Short. And with Doc Holliday, who saved his life. He married by common consent Celia Ann Mattie Blaylock, who in time became addicted to opium and, after he left her for Josephine Sarah "Sadie" Marcus, a teenage Jewish stage actress in Tombstone, killed herself.

He came to Tombstone, then, in the full flower of himself, knowing exactly who he was and who he was not, and, too, who he wished to be. All he was capable of, all he aspired to, all he was about to become, prepared to the last to pay off on every debt, to cash in on every promise he had ever made himself. He was 32 years old and it was high time he aimed to make his killing.

Killing.

It's a matter of going to pieces
without losing track of the parts;
how else go about pulling yourself together again?

—DOC HOLLIDAY

If, briefly, he was Wyatt's best friend, he was never his soul-
mate, sidekick, ramrod or whip, smoking gun or extra hand. He
was not his alter ego. Nor was he, ever, his silent and faithful companion. They were not, to be clear, the Two Musketeers.

They were not in one another's lives five years, and during
that stretch their days as a definable pair, as pals or pards, were
markedly circumscribed. From time to time their paths crossed:
Ft. Griffin, Dodge, Vegas, Prescott, finally, inevitably (as it seems
to us now), Tombstone. Their paths crossed, that's all.

They frequented similar circles and circuits, shared some associates, interests, appreciated aspects of the other that were perhaps less apparent to the rest of the world, and then each went his
way. Neither managed, controlled, "threw in with," "ran herd on,"
deferred to or exerted some invisible hold upon the other. If there
was fraternity, as there was fidelity, then of fealty there was none.

Bat Masterson once observed: "Damon did no more for
Pythias than Holliday did for Wyatt Earp. His whole heart and
soul was wrapped up in the man." Masterson was wrong. Doc
might risk his life for a friend, but his heart and soul were
"wrapped up" in no man, save perhaps himself.

Doc once lent Wyatt a hand when the latter found himself in a
tight spot, one of the few times Wyatt found himself at a disadvan-
tage, outnumbered while out lawing. Doc took it upon himself to
cover his back, the back which in that instance Wyatt had left so
inexplicably exposed. It happened . . . *likethat*. Doc was fast, far
faster than Wyatt—Wyatt himself often enough attested to the
fact—and it was a moment's reflex, that flick of pure reaction. Wy-

att lent his own assistance to Doc by dint of the infrangible fact of his friendship and the loyalty it inspired in turn. For a while it was almost enough to live on, not moment to moment perhaps, but day to day; for a while it provided a connection, a hitching post, something to hang his hat on, something more decent to tether to.

In time they would come to owe much to one another, and a fact people too often overlook, they genuinely liked each other. Doc could make Wyatt laugh, no minor matter; Wyatt let Doc know he thought him staunch enough to be mortally relied upon. Others found it odd, considered them cut from contrary cloth; they never did.

DOC: We stood by one another, no conditions, qualms, questions, equivocation, we stood up for one another as the occasion required. Sometimes when you save a man's life you get to feeling kind of responsible for it afterward, not the man himself, but the life, protective of it, the piece you had a hand in saving, the piece you consider your own. It can get . . . personal. Possibly I felt some of that towards Wyatt, a certain interest in my investment, though I never knew a man who stood for less nursemaiding than Wyatt Earp.

Funny thing was, what sealed our friendship was but a trifle from my angle, and anything but from his own. I had made his acquaintance once before, down to Old Sodom. He was passing through on the trail of Bad Arkansas Dave [Rudabaugh], not that he made much of an impression on me at the time save that he was a bounty hunter, a breed I had—and have—scant use for.

But I found myself in Dodge that spring, where in the meantime he had taken a Deputy Marshal's job, and come that August or September a pair of Texas herders come rolling into town that Wyatt had locked horns with once before, back in Wichita. Tobe Driskill the one, Ed Morrison the other. So naturally the two proceed to drink themselves sidewise, a cowboy characteristic—this was inside either the Comique on the South Side or the Long Branch on Front Street, I no longer recall which—and go to jamboreeing the bar. Which is when Wyatt strolls in and, as was and remains his specialty, goes to head-dusting Morrison, at which Driskill skins back and I—sitting there the whole time playing poker with Cockeyed Frank Loving—beat his play, shouting to Wyatt, "Watch it!" and shoot the pistol from Driskill's hand, shoot him in the hand actually, in and through it, which he likely would have missed anyway being so rozzled. And that's it. The whole story. Like I said, not much, except to Wyatt. Being Wyatt.

Discounting Wyatt, Doc didn't have friends, not a one. Not that he wasn't friendly enough. He could be cordial when it suited him, was always courtly, prided himself on being civil (no more so than in the most uncivil of circumstances), could even affect a certain jocundity as the moment might strike him, but he wasn't congenial, affable, wasn't amicable, couldn't bespur himself to be commodious or accommodating, and he was far from warm. He was too wary, for one thing, too aloof, not unapproachable exactly, but too disaffected, and too centered in himself, too enfolded there, too alcoved at the expense of everything, and everyone, else. This sanctity of one.

Certainly he felt no itch to be part of something more, something . . . other, to affiliate with a flag or banner, party or denomination, to cultivate a circle of friends or fraternity of colleagues, to identify with a community, or even a family, to attach himself to an idea larger than himself. He didn't believe in causes, lost, righteous or otherwise, rather was possessed of a keen aversion to them, and while he might take exception, as the mood struck him, to certain forms of indecorous and loutish behavior, felt himself incapable of what others presumed to call moral indignation or outrage. If on occasion he felt himself compelled to intervene on behalf of such women, children and other defenseless critters whose abuse had been drawn to his attention or suffering he had chanced to observe, well, he admired fairplay almost as much as he despised bullies and boors.

Still, whether it be slaughtering the buff or plundering the mountains, fencing the prairies or massacring the last Apache extant, the fact was, he could not be troubled to bestir himself. Such matters piqued his complacency; he hadn't the conscience to encompass them. (About himself he once remarked that he was possessed of "a passive sense of justice, a quiet moral center the language of which bespeaks the eloquence of a careworn and abstemious silence." Whatever he may have meant by such a statement, it was clear: he routinely exhibited the ethical instincts of an occultist.) It was less that he lacked for conscience than that he did not wish to care. To *belong*. Because caring left one vulnerable, and to belong inevitably meant to suffer the loss of belonging, and he had suffered too much loss already. He could not bear it. He could not bear to lose more.

At last there was only this: that he was willing to lay down his life for a friend if he believed the gesture would be returned in kind, as he believed it of Wyatt Earp—and of no one else.

He spent most of his life in saloons in the company of lesser men from whom he deliberately withheld those parts of himself most worth sharing, lived sealed off from those around him, unallied and unaligned, detached, distanced, undisclosed, inside himself, to himself, voyeur of his own experience, an experience he found too farcical for earnest comment. It required a strong stomach, stomaching himself, and he had over time contrived the wherewithal. Certainly he had been at it long enough. "Ever get lonely, Doc?" a reporter once had had the brass to ask him. "Nah," he replied evenly. "Not to comment. Only around people." Thus did he sharpen the blade of his wit and burnish the bark of his irony, employing both in the service of a personal code of behavior that placed a premium upon antique words like honor and valor and gallantry, and the refusal to flee from the specter of his own demons. The West is rife with ghosts, but Doc's phantoms belonged to himself alone.

And so Wyatt's friendship was to him a miracle, a gift he had neither solicited nor sought, but that lasted and sustained, and in which he might abide. He wondered at it, the grace of it, but mainly he honored it, curried it constant and steadfast and close. Still, even as he invested in it, he refused to need it, would not permit himself the luxury. However sad or regrettable, the truth was, he could walk away from anyone, as he had so long ago walked away from his own family, from his dreams and from his future, and he could do so without compunction. If it was, as he knew, scarce a virtue, it was nevertheless an expression of a certain sort of mettle, and one for which he had perfected the capacity. All his life people would comment upon the inclemency of his coldness. That was the source of it, and its severity. The resource to live with the breakage, without himself breaking. To live . . . bent, devastated and dauntless, every day upon day of his life.

And yet . . .

It has been suggested that gentility, like hemophilia, is bequeathed to the son through the mother, and that, like hemophilia, once inherited it is a quality so invested in the blood as to be immune to cure. He was genteel. The way some people are phlegmatic, or bluntspoken, or garrulous, he was genteel. And it was only after being a while in the West, that most roughneck and ungenteel of places, that he understood that what he aspired to was a life as precisely lacking in moral breadth as it was steeped in genteel manner, in urbanity and insouciance, bonhomie and savoir faire. And so he was acutely conscious of manners and of manner, of the art of self-collection, composure and composition, the several ways one may choose to present one's face to the world, and how much of any self may constitute its fabrication. He lived less like every day might be his last than as if he wished to clear his life of its contents, drain it as dry as his lungs, the better to breathe life into that which might remain, the isolate o as dead as the whole that holes through the vacuous O; the X that prefixes exist. That was the mask, and what lay behind it was less the tissue of contradiction than a quality of chiaroscuro.

At its best his life was an exercise in the manufacture of a self-conscious style—in his case the poise of aplomb—and either you appreciated the weave and weft of its form or judged it harshly for its absence of heft. Not that it mattered to him. He understood too well each of the wormholes in his character, and content to let its fabric . . . fray.

So he sidestepped the regular company of others, seldom observed their rites and routines, their rituals, commemorations, ceremonies, celebrations and sacraments; *would* not join in. Refused to be any man's tag-along or fifth wheel, never rode with an outfit, kept a crew or captained a gang, allowed himself to be bossed or aspired to the bossing of others, never hitched his star to another man's wagon or attached himself to his coattails. Nor did he, ever, bask in another man's aura, possessing of that an excess of his own. The incidentals, niceties, the lubricities by which others were buoyed along the way on the round of their days were lost on him. The so-called small moments, the consolation of that communion served only to embarrass him. He scorned the mundane, deplored the prosaic, the day in all its dailiness, considered common sense too common to merit uncommon comment. Well, better murder than monotony. His fellow man, this humiliation.

A thinking man horrified by his thoughts, albeit one sane as stone, he was insanely intolerant of unkemptness and muss, could not abide three-day-old stubble, dirty fingernails or those hung or ingrown, flappy shirttails, slackly knotted ties, unbuttoned weskits, baggy knees, public expectoration, body odor, halitosis, head lice, scuffed or unpolished footwear, hats worn uncocked, crisscross, cowlicky or whichaway hair, dandruff and/or scurf, snoring or the chewing of tobacco in his presence. A man who neglected to floss, he believed, was one who might be relied upon to display a slovenliness of character and dereliction of self-regard that must in time prove disastrous. If he was a lion for the sort of hygiene that verges upon ablutomania, perhaps it was owing to his professional training, or because those around him so uniformly were not.

He could not bear being touched in a casual or overfamiliar manner, much less without advance notice or permission; a decidedly prickly, peculiarly modest, almost abashed man, and one whose internal stirrings were scarce of a practical nature, for he took to his bed at odd hours, slept past noon, could only sleep in TOTAL darkness and so seldom slept soundly, though he religiously eschewed naps and in consequence often found himself adrift in the doldrums, which, considering the alternative, he welcomed.

He whistled little-known melodies in the dark, Celtic airs many of them—"Raglan Road," "One Irish Rover"—in moments of despair read French poetry in the original French—Baudelaire, the soon-to-be-published Rimbaud (though whether he was aware of the description of that adolescent *voyant* as "the Billy the Kid of Literature" is highly doubtful), a little Mallarmé, or recited Poe by heart. Was partial to capes and canes. Polished his teeth with millet after meals. Did as he damn well pleased.

He went unmarried and unbetrothed. Childless. Froze out his family relation. Never had a home or place of his own, shop, business, office. Never held a day job or served his country. Did not attend church, or vote. Finally he identified with nothing, nothing around him, nothing that he might name, and so left the impression of being disinterested in life, too disinterested even to be bored by it. At last, the universe could not locate itself in him, for he was become pure vacuum; there was no air there. Well, he knew existence was a riddle and was content to leave it at that, fearing that were he to arrive at its answer, he would find it too banal by half.

What choice, then, but to live his life at arm's length from itself, to hold the hostility of it, the horror of himself at bay; a man who kept his distance yet who missed very little. However absurdly, he considered this self-estrangement—and the self-exclusion it fostered—the source of whatever marrow of character he might possess. It was, at last, less a retreat than a secession, no amnesty, armistice, moratorium, no quarter asked for or given.

He didn't care about any of it, didn't give a damn, and so sought no man's solace, solicitude, confraternity, fellowship, ever. When he sat to a table, bellied to a bar, walked a darkened street, waltzed through a door, death waltzed with him; this genteel killer.

It was one helluva way to live, but it was his way. He didn't know whether it was a particularly good way, and no question could have seemed to him more pointless. It doubtless was not a good way. How could it be? It was bound to come to a bad and abominable end and to that he was passionately indifferent. The world, to the extent that it concerned him, could go to hell; he was dying—no contrition, no remorse—still dying, and without a solitary notion of how properly to go about it. Obsessed with his own mortality, dogged by an absence of purpose, what else was left him, but—content in his discontent—to vacantly abide? "I can't go on. I go on," a wise man once wrote. Though he had every conceivable reason not to, Doc *went on*; he chose to buck his tiger.

Wyatt, better than anyone else perhaps, was capable of appreciating this, though why that should have been, he never really knew, as he knew he did not need to know, but simply to embrace it. The martyrdom of self-crucifixion was the furthest thing from his style—not for him, the Way of the Cross—but until Wyatt came along, it was Doc's worst enemy that was his only friend.

thirty miles north from Old Mexico
'cross Goose Flats Mesa
San Pedro Valley
scorpions, rattlers, Gila monsters
turkey buzzards, tarantulas, horny toads
chuckwallas, whiptails, jack-a-rabbits
coyotes and lobos
ovenbaked earth, air/aft as off a forge
hardscrabble scabland
alkali caliche
furnacebox of borax, borderland of bone
skilletscape: scrub, rock sage, mesquite, cacti, piñon tree
the seldseen horizoned Apache
blues misting off those mountains: Whetstone, Dragoon,
*   Pedregosa, Mule*
sierra *and* desierto, *wind-mown* despoblado
a place more fit for reptiles,
reptiles and red savages
than humankind

he took to it straight off

pop. 6,000 (est.)
375 businesses (63 saloons: mescal, tequila, pulque, habañero)
tennis courts
bowling alleys
skating rinks
ice cream parlors
raw oyster bars too
and theater: the Rolling Pinafore on Wheels

silver mines by the score: Lucky Cuss, Tough Nut, Hard Sell, Flat
  Bust
3,000 claims dragging up
$500,000 each month—estas planchas de plata

come up on it over-ridge to a rimrise
fer outskirt of town
hand visored, salute
to the insult of the sun:
"Seems they got the name right,
all right"

wild red with
all this wonder
drudgery of
quotidian slaughter

their highnoon wrought
of midnight's wreaking
having placed his soul
in soak

BY THE TIME Doc come to Tombstone he was insignificant and pitiable-looking, what with that chalky face, always a kerchief to his mouth, coughing that way he had, all bloody and brokedown, like a rail engine going up a grade. Couldn't believe a little fella like that could make such godawful noises.

One thing, cardsharpers knew better'n try anything with him, diddle him or whatnot, any fancy stuff, 'cause he would not have it. Would *not*. He weren't no dabbler nor dilettante, but all pro, and he could shoot, shoot like no man I ever seen. Shoot the buttons off'n your fly if he had to, and he did, have to, knew he had to be right able in that regard being he could not have whipped a 14-year-old girl in a go-to, go-as-you-please, bareknuckle fistfight. Practiced all the time, right and left alike, offhand, what they call that there ambidext, so's he didn't favor the one for t'other. In the mornings he'd sit up there at his hotel window and shoot things. Shot from stagecoaches when traveling: jackrabbits, prairie dogs, lizards on rocks, spikes off a cactus, horns off antelopes, what-haveyou. Pooch anything that moved or stood still. Anyone tried to stop him, they was told they was welcome to go to hell as he'd be happy to help 'em along with the headstart, don't mention it, no trouble, his pleasure.

If you happened to be standing beside him at a bar and saw into his eyes, it was like looking close at a new corpse. Give you the holy bejabbers. Gooseflesh. Them horripilations. Say this for him, made no secret of how to him people was just dirt. All people. Just dung. Got to admire a man who'll do that, not keep the feeling to himself, go along to get along, put on the airs, pretend he cares when he don't, fuck-all.

When he come to live with us on Fremont, with Mother and me, he rented out a spare storeroom, but we seldom seen him much. His custom was to get up real late and take a long time dressing. Arrangement was he should have a pot of coffee, black, black and strong, and a single slice of toast, rye, no butter, burnt a certain brown, and this Mother would put down for him outside his door to take in when no one was looking. I think he must have been shy. That's what Mother thought.

About two in the afternoon he'd come out into the light of day, looking hurt, wounded some, broke-like, racked and aching, yet half singing to himself. And always the same lyric—*Blue as a bottle-nosed dolphin/black as a methane-lit night*—and then he never failed to salute politely if he met up with one of us, tip of the hat, flip of the cane, wink sometimes, but never said a thing, not a word. He'd walk across the street to the Occidental, it having the smartest dining room in those days, and he'd take lunch, soups and stews mainly, crackerbreads, fruits and cheeses, he liked that Black Diamond brand, then sip at a snifter of their driest sherry. Read a paper, smoke a cheroot, then settle into a corner to play patience or solitaire or do card tricks for himself before going over to the Crystal Palace or the Alhambra or wherever he was dealing or decided he wanted to play that evening.

He'd come home sometime during the night, afore sunup mainly—lived all upside down that way—if anything more quiet than when he'd left that afternoon. Because we never heard him. Not once. All those months he lived there, we never once heard him come in at night. Nor cough, which was queer, on account of coughing's 'bout all he did otherways.

He was about the quietest boarder we ever took in, quietest and most well-mannered. Least 'til Beak Nose Kate come over from Globe, and then it got so we had to ask 'em to leave, which is when he went down and got himself a room at Fly's.

Always felt bad about that. Up 'til then, 'til Kate, weren't more trouble than a shadow, and after, more'n a hatful of rattlers.

(HASSYAMPER, TO THE SWEDE JAN OLOF OLSSON, AFTER HIS MEMOIR, *WELKOMMEN TO TOMBSTONE*, TRANSLATED FROM THE SCANDINAVIAN, 1956)

Despite being built as close to the bone as a man can be and not fall apart for want of the flesh to cobble it to its frame, he never appeared in public looking anything less than just showered, shaved and fresh-shucked to the nines. He was dapper, Doc was, natty, snazzy, a walking wardrobe, like it was with him a first principle. Might say he was conservative that way. That phrase, "keeping up appearances," that was him, mindful of his rig and his raiments, the old first impression, until he'd kept at it so long, he'd plumb exhausted each one. These appearances like suits.

Did keep a certain distance, though. Held himself off-from. Not higher, but over to the side like. What's that word? Aloof. Like all the world was a stranger to him, like he warn't to home in it no damn ways. Couldn't get comfortable, find the right fit, like it wouldn't let him breathe, which I reckon it wouldn't.

But it made him an exile kind, orphan, a fact he made clear without no need to say, cuz he was *not* one for being got at or gone up to. Wouldn't stand for it any more'n a puff adder. Come too close, shoot you a look—Jeeeee-zuz!—shoot you a look give off he was the meanest man in six states with a straight razor. Which he was, or so they said.

I thought him a cactus sort of person, breccia-like and broody—burred as the shag off some bark, of flint/made fire, that gunfire all through his breath—broody so you'da thought he'd have hacked off enough hard cases along the way to be laid to sod long since. Well, he was dying, a fact it stood everyone well to keep in mind, especially in his vicinity. Course, all of us are doing it, dying, all the time, just ain't doing it in the same way, day by day, hour by hour, breath by next battling suck of breath. Must've been a self-dwarfish, downfallen, longish sort of death, and going through it couldn't have helped but fray him raw. Might say his mortality was more a misery to him than the rest of us, like he was the walking-around embodiment of his own 24-hour-a-day eternal loss of future.

Might.

On the other hand, what was so damn queer, leave him alone, left to hisself, he'd have liked to charm you out of your boots and braces both. Had a way of seeing humor where there warn't none, not a chuckle, then making you see it too, same way, and content to use it like a shiv. Still, put a gun in his hand, and he was as comical as anthrax, capable of just about anything. A more consistently desperate man I have never brushed up against, for he always was overreacting, like*that*—in an eyebat, a fingersnap—to every fancied threat that happened past his vision. Understandable, maybe, when you consider how much of a physical weakling he was, and when going around unheeled, how piteously defenseless, but cold consolation to those who wound up blistered on account.

What I remember, cuz it struck me so odd, is he had a particular stick up it for cats. Got his dander up. Strangest thing. Seen him at it over and over—blowing 'em up, shooting 'em down, hanging 'em by the neck, setting 'em afire, drowning 'em down wells and creeks, flinging 'em off rooftops, running 'em over with wagons and horses, laying down poison for 'em, anything he could think of. Save to eat 'em. That he would not do.

Told me once how he hankered to impale one sometime, one or more, on a picket or pike. Or a prong. A pumpiron bolt. Spiked post. On an antler or horn. How he itched to skewer one sidewise through the neck right where it cuffs to the throat, on a tusk or a meathook, an axle, a bicycle spoke. Told me he'd take a rat or a bat to a cat anytime.

But why, Doc? I asked him. Why hate a cat?

But I object, Sir, he answered. I with vigor object to the word hate. Whilst 'tis true I mean them only ill, and worse than ill, I would no more squander such depth of noble feeling upon so grotesque and hateful a beast than I would shed a tear over the death of a high-stanking yalluh savage. 'Tis not hate, but envy. I envy them their temerity. The each of their profligate nine lives. My God, can you fathom the arrogant greed of it? Nine! 'Tis wholly unnatural. These eight lives too many. Why, for a cat, I'd say none's roughly plenty. So call it my way of evening the score, of righting the ship, of restoring to nature a kind of creaturely, cat-less balance.

Oh, and they give me the fucking hives.

It could not have been easy, being Doc. Beak Nose Kate told me once that the only time he ever was truly at peace, only gladness he ever knew was when they were hard at it in bed, and while she was right fond of his ways on that score, she was not too taken with herself to confess how she wished with all her heart that he'd done everyone a favor, himself most of all, and never come so God-dang far west.

Come down to the last of it, the one thing you need to be understanding about Doc Holliday ain't all that complicated. Only that there was his self over here, and here was his life over there, and that the one did not much cotton to the other. Save to spit in its eye. That there was what the Doctor done best, spitting back at himself. Spitting back with all the spit a mortal soul could muster.

(INTERVIEW WITH JOSH RANDALL, AUTHOR OF
MEMORIES OF 50 YEARS SPENT STRAPPED TO A MARE'S LEG)

Sometime after 3 a.m.

Fly's Lodginghouse.

Fremont Street between Third and Fourth.

Room #7.

Kate, recently arrived from Globe, awakens in the half-dark, and reaching over to turn up the lantern, turns to wake Doc in turn. Ordinarily, he is a light sleeper.

"Doc, wake up. Wake up, Doc. Hear that?"

"What? What, darlin'? Hear what?"

"That noise. Hear it? Some sound, second ago, like outta yer dream sounded like. I dunno, sounded like a bomb went off. Inside yer dream. Firecracker maybe. Shellburst. TNT. Sounded like some damn explosion."

"Mines, must be. Out to the mines, dynamiting."

"Nah, closer, close-by. Right here inside. Shook the walls, Doc. Look here. Over there too. See it? Cracked the plaster. Good Lord, buckled the damn floor. Look here, the bed's all busted. You musta heard it, Doc. I know you was dreaming, but you hadda hear it."

"But, sweet Kate, Sugar, I wasn't dreaming. I wasn't even sleeping. I was just lying here. Staring straight up at the ceiling. Breathing."

Make the fiction fallow
harrow it with ash
trump the truth
take the trick
play the facts for clowns

    'cause

where time is up for grabs
no longer up to snuff
where time's become a jester
it wants to ham it up

    so

we tell ourselves its stories
recalibrate the clock
embroider them with meaning
tick tock   tick tock   tick tock

THE ONLY ORDER IS
THAT WHICH WE
IN OUR HUBRIS
ELECT TO CONFER

    and

continuity unravels
amidst the chaos
unveiled
behind a single   vehement   gesture
our imagination—smoking!   in ruins

plant a rumor
weed a myth
water a legend
watch History flower

The most famous gunfight in American history.
Yet how map out its meaning? Account for
Doc's part in it? Negotiate this traffic of fact?
The way it comes at you—in snarls.

———

THE EARPS—JAMES, Virgil and Wyatt—arrive in Tombstone, December 1879. James opens his own saloon, Virgil works as U.S. Deputy Marshal, Wyatt rides shotgun for Wells Fargo until July, when he is named Pima County Deputy Sheriff. Morgan arrives and takes Wyatt's job with Wells Fargo. The Earps file mine claims, buy land, acquire water rights, purchase property, construct homes in town. They maintain a high profile and make no secret of their Republican political alliances and ambitions.

That July, Virgil, Wyatt and Morgan recover stolen U.S. Army mules from the ranch of Frank and Tom McLaury, brothers who operate as "fences" for a loosely knit cartel of 100 to 200 rustlers, horse thieves, highwaymen and stagecoach robbers known locally as the Cowboys. Based in Galeyville, 75 miles northeast, members of the claque often patronize Tombstone, getting drunk, raising hell, wreaking havoc, terrorizing its citizens, but they also spend freely in its saloons, dancehalls, gambling dens, brothels, hotels, theaters and retail establishments. Prominent among the leaderless combine are Curly Bill Brocius, John Peters Ringo, "Old Man" Newman Clanton, his sons Ike and Billy, and Frank Stilwell. No arrests are made in the recovery of the stolen federal property from the McLaurys, but heated words are exchanged.

———

In late September—Virgil having been appointed Tombstone Assistant City Marshal in the meanwhile—Doc arrives from Prescott, rents a room at Fly's Lodginghouse on Fremont Street and takes a job dealing faro at Dick Clark's Alhambra Saloon on Allen. A few days later, John Behan, a former Democratic territorial legislator, arrives with his live-in inamorata, "Belle of the Honkytonks," 18-year-old stage actress Josephine Sarah Marcus.

After Virgil's boss, Tombstone City Marshal Fred White, is fatally shot by Curly Bill in late October, Wyatt buffaloes and arrests him, ushering him to Tucson ahead of a lynch mob. On the strength of Wyatt's testimony, the shooting is ruled an accident and Brocius is acquitted of murder and released.

When Wyatt resigns as Deputy Sheriff, Behan replaces him. A week later, having been soundly beaten in the November election, Virgil resigns his position as Assistant City Marshal.

That December, during a particularly ugly standoff, Wyatt recovers his stolen horse from Ike Clanton's younger brother Billy.

In January (1881), Wyatt purchases a one-quarter interest in the Oriental Saloon, where he deals faro and serves as "bouncer."

When a new county, Cochise, is annexed from south Pima, Tombstone is named its county seat, and John Behan—having previously promised Wyatt the County Undersheriff's position in exchange for his commitment not to filibuster for the top job—is named its first sheriff. Reneging, Behan instead appoints a known Earp antagonist, newspaper editor Harry Woods, and names Cowboy Frank Stilwell one of his deputies.

On the night of March 15, during a holdup of the Tombstone/Benson stage, the driver and one of his passengers are murdered by Cowboys Jim Crane, Harry Head, Luther King and Billy Leonard, the latter a known acquaintance of Doc's. Captured by a posse that includes Behan, Wyatt and Bat Masterson, King confesses, is remanded into the custody of Undersheriff Woods and promptly escapes.

Throughout the spring and summer, Behan, Woods and the Clantons, exploiting Wood's editorship of the Tombstone *Nugget*, orchestrate a smear campaign that fingers Doc as the mastermind behind the stage holdup and murders. When Kate arrives from Globe, she and Doc quarrel. After plying her with liquor, Behan induces her to sign an affidavit implicating Doc in the holdup, a murder warrant is sworn out, Behan arrests Doc, Kate sobers up, recants, and Doc is freed after spending the night in jail.

When Tombstone City Marshal Ben Sippy skips town to escape creditors, Virgil Earp is appointed his replacement and names Morgan his deputy.

With the November election for Cochise County Sheriff four months off, Wyatt, angling to bolster his chances, secretly approaches Ike Clanton and Frank McLaury with a proposition to which they reluctantly agree: in exchange for the $6,000 in reward money, they will disclose to him the whereabouts of their fugitive friends Crane, Head and Leonard so that Wyatt might take credit for their apprehension. Before the arrangement can proceed, all three turn up dead, Crane in a border shootout with

Mexican soldiers during which Newman Clanton also is killed. Doc taunts Ike, insisting that it was he who killed his father.

Josephine Marcus leaves the philandering John Behan, taking her own rooms in town.

That September the Tombstone/Bisbee stage is held up for over $3,000 by four masked robbers, two of whom are positively identified as Frank Stilwell, Behan's deputy, and Cowboy Pete Spencer. Apprehended by a posse that includes Wyatt and Morgan, the pair are placed in Virgil's custody in Tombstone, but judges there and in Tucson refuse to indict or jail them.

Frank McLaury, in the company of John Ringo, Ike and Billy Clanton and his brother Tom, threatens Morgan Earp on Allen Street: "If you ever lay hands on a McLaury, I'll kill you." Tom McLaury makes a similar comment to Virgil.

Wyatt begins seeing Josephine Marcus.

Around midnight on October 25, Ike Clanton—fearing that Wyatt has confided the details of their abortive collusion to Doc, whom he fears will in turn make them public, thus exposing him and the McLaurys to the retribution of Brocius, Ringo, et al.— finds himself in a verbal exchange with Doc inside the Alhambra. Doc berates Ike as "a son of a bitch of a Cowboy," "a goddamned lying varlet" and "a thieving, whoreson knave of a high-stanking, caponized sow cunt." Ike threatens to take Doc "on sight and man for man the next time I see you." After Doc retires to Fly's, Ike continues to play poker through the night with John Behan, drinking profligately. When the game breaks up around 7 a.m., Ike retrieves his rifle and revolver from a nearby hotel and, braving that day's increasingly frigid winds, spends several inebriated hours, until well after noon—and in flagrant disregard of the town's anti-carrying ordinance—first staggering from saloon to saloon on Allen Street loudly threatening to kill Doc, then camping unsuccessfully in wait for him outside Fly's. Virgil and Morgan eventually track Ike to an alley on Fourth between Fremont and Allen where the former buffaloes and disarms him before dragging him to court where he is fined $25 and his weapons confiscated. Wyatt, having joined his brothers in the courtroom, accuses Ike of "so threatening our lives that I think I would be justified in shooting you down anyplace I should meet you." Upon leaving, Wyatt encounters Tom McLaury in the street, they exchange words, Wyatt slaps him across the face with his left hand, buffaloes him to the ground with his right and walks on.

A block away on Allen Street, an oblivious Frank McLaury and Billy Clanton, just arrived in town and on their way to the Grand Hotel for a drink, are accosted by a recently awakened, cane-twirling, cape-clad Doc, who before entering the Alhambra across the street to open his faro game, pauses long enough to bluffly shake each of their hands: "So how are you gentlemen? Some weather, is it not? Cuts cold as blunt spurs. Of course"— addressing 19-year-old Billy Clanton—"should the brother of this young buck have his way, I suspect it may warm up considerable." Sighs, shakes his head, pretends to ignore the pair of openly bewildered looks. "Seems old Ike is back on the warpath again. My, but his story does get old. Like he was raised on sour milk, poor soul. All piss without the vinegar. Wine not worth its press. But here, don't let me keep you sports from oiling up your bellies. Perhaps as you are feeling the itch you might care to stop by later and have a go at bucking the tiger. You know my game. Sky's the limit. Roof gets in the way, blow her off. Couldn't say just why, but I have that certain feeling, like today's your lucky day." Smiles, lightly touches the crown of his cane to the brim of his hat and, lilting, walks away.

Backup a sec; retrace a step—

Inside Room #7 of Camillus S. Fly's Lodginghouse on Fremont Street, it is dark and chill and climbing quickly towards noon. Naked beneath featherbeds, Doc is slightly asleep, Kate beside him, brown bottles on the floor, one tipped upon its side, sprawled there as if irate at finding itself so empty, the other left standing if staggered, still half filled with rye.

The gunrig is at his head, an arm's length off, a mere lunge away, both holsters occupied, slung like a stuffed bird by its leather wing upon the bedpost; this rig to its rack, rubbed slick with civet.

A scythe, decor, adorns one wall.

When the knock comes, Doc scarcely stirs, but Kate, naked, slips out from under, slinking into the folds of her robe, holding it shut with crossed arms as she slippers to the door. Asks who.

"Mary. It's Mary, Miss. Mary. Fly." The landlady.

"Yes?" Through the door. "What then, Mary? What is it?"

Doc murmurs, curmurrs, susurrates, rustles some, this sound softer than jostling. No, however, stertor.

"I think you oughta know."

Prepared to be exasperated, Kate opens up and steps into the hall swinging the door softly shut behind her. Cold as a meatlocker; when she speaks, the words knuckle out, white fists upon the air. "Know what? What is it, Mary?"

"That Clanton fella, that Ike? That was Ike Clanton we noticed. Around back by the photo gallery. Yup. Sure was. Ike Clanton, out back around there."

"Wait. Ike Clanton was here?"

"Outside. Like he was waiting. Waiting on something. Someone. Waited a good long while too. Uh-huh. Ike. Ike Clanton."

Pauses. "Mr. Fly thought, well, thought maybe Mr. Holliday, I thought maybe you should know."

Inside, a cough. Just the one.

Kate whispers, edgy. "But he's left, then? Ike? Ike's gone off? Where'd he go? Know where he went to, Mary? Mary, it's important. Where's Ike now?"

"Went away. Minute or two. Went off down Fremont, looked like. Up towards Fourth. Didn't appear none too steady 'bout it neither. Appeared 'bout ready to go callus up his elbows. Ike, he ain't here no more."

"Thanks then, Mary. Doc'll appreciate it, your thinking to warn him. Thanks, Mary." Turns, grasps the doorknob.

"Oh, and Miss?"

Still ahold, turns back around.

"He had himself a rifle with him. Ike did."

A beat of silence, a second, and then: "He was heeled?" No whisper now, but the alarm through her voice high and taut as a wire. "Ike Clanton was heeled?"

"And a pistol, Miss. From what me and Cam could make of it. Had a rifle and a six-shooter both. One of each, that we seen."

Stares a moment, Kate does, eyes aglaze and narrowing, a single long blink, nods her head in thanks, presses a hand to Mary's, complice, steps back inside.

"Doc! Goddammit, Doc, wake up! Wake up and get dressed right now! Ike Clanton's been here, Doc. Been looking for you, Ike has. Flys say he was prowling around out back, skulking around drunk and heeled to the hubs. Say he had a Winchester with him, Doc. Ike's out there, he's out there somewheres, and he's a-hunting you."

Hauls himself up, this anchor, weighing. Sits backpropped by pillows. Coughs. Coughs again. Again and again. The blood comes in thistles. Sprockets his chest. Yellow. Brown. Red. Colors of debris.

"He is, is he, the strabismic son of a bitch. Well then, dear Kate, if God will let me live long enough to don my adornments"—the words clear a path around the coughing—"he shall shortly see me.

"But first, here"—pats, pets the bed beside him with the palm of a hand—"care to do the honors? Kate, darlin', after all, would you mind? Let us to it. First rites, first."

It was 2 p.m. when Virgil ducked into the Wells Fargo office on Allen Street, three doors down from where Doc was dealing faro at the Alhambra, to unlock and retrieve from its rack within the stow the company's standard-issue Richards's 10-gauge, *single* shortbarrel shotgun—a sawed-down affair, sawed or sawn off—loading it right there with a single shell containing 12 buckshot. He dropped another shell, maybe two, no more than three, into his coat pocket.

It was 2 p.m. Roughly.

Emerging from the office, he walked five doors further on to Hafford's Saloon on the corner of Allen and Fourth where he joined Wyatt and Morgan who were standing outside on the sideway, their hands to their hats against the whipsaw of the winds; that corner was known to be peculiarly at the mercy of their crossbuck.

So that what you had here, congregated upon the spot, was a pride of Earps—prideful, primed, armed to the eyes and feeling perilously provoked.

Over the next half hour, a procession of civilians—H. F. Sills, a visitor just in from Vegas; Ruben F. Coleman, a silver miner; William Murray, a stockbroker; finally John L. Fonck, an ex-L.A.

police captain—this parade of bystanders would in no agreed-upon order approach Virgil with what amounted to the same piece of news: as Sills put it, "There are four or five men wearing guns in plain sight in front of the O.K. Corral and they are threatening by name to kill you and your brothers on sight—'the whole damned party,' in their words—should they meet you. They seem to mean trouble, and I thought it best that I raise the alarm."

Conferring with his brothers, Virgil spotted John Behan emerging from Barron's Barbershop across the street and called him over, inviting him inside Hafford's, where he alerted him to what he termed "the unfolding scenario," as in "We got us an unfolding scenario here, Sheriff, and it is my intention, as accords with the city ordinance, to take their arms off and arrest them." He then requested Behan's assistance in doing so. It was now 2:15 p.m. Roughly. And by the minute growing colder.

"Are you mad, Marshal?" Behan replied. "Those men will never give up their arms to you, and should you attempt it, should you dare go down there, blood will flow through these streets on this day. And that blood, Marshal, that blood will be on your hands and no other. On yours, Marshal, on yours and on each of your brothers'."

"So," said Virgil matter-of-factly, "I take it you're of scant mind to pitch in."

"Being of *sound* mind," replied Behan, "you are to take it that I am of no mind atall. What I *shall* do is go down there right now and disarm them myself as they may require it, or persuade them to leave town as they may be disposed to do so."

At 2:30 p.m. exactly, Doc, having closed down his faro game, left the Alhambra and, noticing the Earps huddled on the corner, strolled over, cane in gloved hand, nonchalantly irrigating his teeth with a gold-plated toothpick.

"Gentlemen?" He tugged in salutation at the brim of his hat.

"Well well, so what have we here? A gathering of the clan, I see. But why the long faces? Don't tell me, there has been no death in the family, I trust."

"No deaths, Doc," replied Wyatt. "Not yet anyway."

"Then what, Sir? Why all so interminably drear?"

"It's them damn Cowboys, Doc," said Morgan, earnest as always. "Clantons and McLaurys. They're at it again, all morning long, insults and threats, talking trash, on the streets going heeled."

"Ah, the Clantons, you say. Why yes, I did hear something of the sort." He coughed, using the back of his hand for a bulwark. "Apparently old Ike was caught lurking about Fly's this very morning. Sporting a Winchester, so they say. Spooked Kate no end. Had it in mind to *bushwhack* me, I suppose, is that not the word? So, anyway, I decided I had best keep to my bed, receive a brief spot of head, until he got bored and went away. Which, being Ike, he in due time duly did. The man has, I must say, the attention span of a flea, a pest, permit me to add, that as a personality he all too perfectly personifies. So then, what do we propose?"

"Appears they're all gathered down to the O.K. Corral even now," said Virgil. "Armed and aching for it."

"Well then, we must only oblige them, would you not agree? Call their bluff, open the ball and bring the game to a close. Afford them the opportunity to play their hand, should they be so bold, or what is more likely"—he looked from brother to brother and back again—"fold."

Virgil squinted hard at Doc, chest-up and chuffy, then shook his head, grudged a smile and outlimbered his left arm. "I'll take the shillelagh, Doc." He offered for the cane. "Here." Holding the shotgun on the vertical, he passed it over. "You man the street Gatling. Hold down the flank."

"Dammit, Virgil, I know buckshot means burying, but I do despise these scatterguns. The kick of these greeners is too mean and too mighty, and I am not, as you doubtless have failed to notice, a well man."

"Oh," said Virgil, wry, "I've a hunch you'll bear up just aces. Might consider keeping it hid 'neath your cloaks, though, just for the trip yonder. No need to be rankling the town more'n it's riled already. 'Sides, by now, could be Behan's . . ."

"Fuck Behan!" spat Wyatt. "You know damn well Johnny Behan couldn't disarm his own grandmother. Hell, the man couldn't locate his own arse with both hands."

"Why, Wyatt, do I detect a stab at humor?" Doc's grin collapsed, then convulsed to giggles. "And at a moment of such high gravitas! I must say that I am stunned, Sir. Why, Morg"—mock-fanning himself with a hand—"prepare to catch me as I swoon."

"All right, Doc, all right." Virgil was all sand. "If we're going, then we're going. Now."

"But of course, Sir. Fair enough. I seem to have recovered quite nicely in any event. So then, lead on, Marshal."

And so, a slight bow at the waist, a light cluck of the heels, a swoop of the open arm upon the flourish. The effortless execution, if you can believe it, of a single, perfect, entrechat. And as they shoved off: "After you."

Action is not life,
but a way of wasting
a kind of strength
                    —RIMBAUD

There were the four of them abreast, three Earps, one Holliday. This is how I recall it, even now, way it remains, such remnants as do, always have, way the reel gets drug up, feeds its frames, them daily rushes in my mind, as I say: three Earps, one Holliday.

Virgil, carrying a cane, then Wyatt and Morgan, a fencerow of black, black topcoats, cravats, black flat-top hats, pants. Anthracite black. Shoulder to shoulder, so you couldn't rightly tell 'em apart. And to the outside, outermost, separate a ways, Doc in gray shoulder-capes, windruffed and billowing, divulging the scattergun.

At the time it was midafternoon, 2:15, 2:30, 2:40 maybe, four days before All Hallows' Eve, three or four days before. Five maybe. Either way, it was unseasonably cold that day. Snow parched the ground in patches.

Up Fourth Street, 300 feet, give or take, had to be Fourth, moving in unison, raven. Like a wing. Then as they turned left— think that's west, yeah, should be—onto Fremont, the south sideway there, past the post office, halving into pairs, tandem, Virgil and Wyatt first, Morgan and Doc in arrears.

It was a painting. Not at the time of course. But thinking back. It was a painting, this mural, tableau vivant, a moving picture. Why, it was a damn diorama. Wished then, like I wish now, that I'd've had my camera with me. You should only have been there: pure Broadway.

The Earps, each one walking cool and deliberate as you please, all business, no bluster, brisk pace, square gait, whisking you might say, almost a march, no moseying here, forging you might say, or imagine striding on stilts, determined-like, grim as gravestones. Their faces clenched and set-jawed. This very flint of history. Like I say, thinking back.

And then there was Holliday, One Holliday commonly called Doc, and though it sounds mad, twice mad to beat the damn band, the man was strolling. Don't know what else you'd call it. Strutting maybe? Cockwalking? Cakewalking? Like he was on his way to a quadrille or something. Like he was on sashay.

I was close, close enough to see and hear—I'd clambered up onto one of those low roofs there, might have been the Capitol, could have been, may have been the Capitol, the saloon at the corner, made myself a one-man grandstand—and when he passed by, not only was he strutting, I swear, he was smiling too. Not broad like a grin, but tight, slight, half, telltale-like. What I'd call wistful. Wishful. One or the other. But not so's to share it, that was the thing. More to show just enough to keep it to himself.

He looked like his mind was onto other things, is what it was, if you can believe it, a time like that. Not bored exactly, not bored stiff, but off somewheres else. Spooled out beyond itself like none of it, this, the moment, what he was about, what he was doing *now*, like none of it mattered shucks. It was like most of him weren't really there at all, looked to me, but out ahead, onto some different future.

And there was a sparkle in his eye I caught the glint off right away, both eyes maybe, and that's when I remember thinking, "like mica," and his face filming sweat in flows, pilling like a sweater, and then, I swear, right there for a moment on the air opposite, etched clear as mirage in relief against the facade of the buildings, not his shadow, but its projection, its reflection, this refraction prismed and alight—his anthelion, or parhelion, it didn't last long enough for me to catch which—and then it winked out and he commenced—more madness—he started in . . . *whistling.*

I know, I know. But like I said, I was hardby enough to hear, and though it was a chore to pick out or pull a tune from, no mistake, he was whistling. To himself, but still, clear enough, and then fife clear. I could not reckon then and I cannot reckon to this day how a man in his boots could have managed it, the breath or spit, cheek or gall, but beat all if he wasn't whistling.

Now once I caught onto it, I knew right off that that there was a melody I knew better than I know Auld Lang Syne, Rock of Ages, Jimmy Crack Corn, Yankee Doodle, the Battle Hymn of the Republic, Old Dan Tucker and the Star-Spangled Banner all together. Some folks said later they heard it too and thought Garry Owen. But it weren't, not atall. I know Garry Owen, and I'm telling you now, Garry Owen's one thing it weren't. Not a riff. Not even close.

It was what it was, and what it was—and why not?—was ol' Dixie. Definitely, Dixie. Dixie definitively. Its notes outspun, fluting ahead of him like bugles, their bells like beaks, curved birds above his head, vining there, unfurling like flags on the air carved into its bark, this lumber of his own nonchalance. Boy howdy, that strut of rebel song, damn skippy those Stars and Bars, by *God* it was his banner.

And then of course here comes Johnny Behan angling up. Met 'em right up under the old striped awning of Bauer's, the Union Meat Market there, and when he tried to wave the four of 'em off, why, the four of 'em just brushed right past, crewed on by without breaking stride nor missing a beat of the dance.

And then I lost all sight of 'em.

(CAMILLUS S. FLY, PHOTOGRAPHER)

THE COWBOYS

And you glimpse it on the horizon
something dark winging your way,
and you tell yourself it's coming
getting closer by the day,
and you tell yourself be careful
use prudence
take precautions
to play it at least reasonably safe,
you tell yourself to cover your back
watch your step
endeavor to save some face,
and as you fail to raise your arms to prevent what's come from
    coming down
you know that what you've feared is here
bang!
you're dead
and not a sound

So as the hammer falls
that is where death waits
in the middle of the day
in the middle of the street
this low thing
                ruthless
                      and cool

Thus do the barracuda school
sheeped to their shoals,
their gaping
ignorant as theological truth

What will history reveal? Little, count upon it, save through violent means: you must smash it to have it . . . we have no other choice; we must go back to the beginning; it must all be done over, everything that is must be destroyed.
—WILLIAM CARLOS WILLIAMS

Archaeology, of necessity, involves violence—the uncovering of past lives . . . seeking the grammar of the fragments.
—ROBERT KROETSCH

Genuine understanding occurs only after taking things apart, breaking things down before puzzling them together again. The dismantling of the constituent elements. As the cogs of an engine or mechanisms of a clock, chronology of a crime or dimensions of a life. But the seams remain. The rifts. These individual breakages like gills. The vents where meaning breathes.

Iconography, unlike celebrity,
is conferred on the stellar few and
does not accrue until
after the stardust has settled, each
clue been weeded   through,
residue
weighed
each wayward rumor
received its due

so that

the events and those who preceded them
survive un-nicked by time
having dodged posterity's bullet
the way a star embalms the light
in an autonomous desert town
one drab   indifferent   anonymous
                                                                        autumn
                                                                        afternoon

and we, stunned dumb,
beguiled by the sight:
the showdown of their shadows
and of those shadows'
flight

It was all over before it began, ancient history in a moment, and yet quite endless. Beyond the individual rosettes, a career of blood. The way it went on and on, meaningless as sky.

—DOC HOLLIDAY

The gunfight was a spiritual exercise.

—WILLIAM BURROUGHS

TOWARDS JUST WHAT holy extremities, the poets have asked, does an experience unlike any other, be it public or private, imagined or real, numinous or profane, towards what consecrated ground is the profound strangeness of such an occasion apt to shoulder us? When one bestrides the realm where that rough god goes riding—and ragged muse presumes—towards what is one finally propelled but its threshold, that outermost edge, the inevitable margin of violent uncertainty

he was thinking, Doc was (or something uncannily akin), when of a sudden he was fetched up short by the scruff of his reverie—so much so that he ceased his whistling in mid-warble—by some, some, some anonymity—nameless, faceless, featureless, futureless—some de-archived, undocumented someone hollering, "Here they come!"

And so they do. 2x2. Closed rank and trig. This folded wing dead-on down the jackpine plank sidewalk, clobber of boot heel knocketing hollow, occasional tug of a hat brim against the windshear breathing steamfields like winded horses willowing white the air about their heads. Until once past Fly's they indent on the catenary curve towards the vacant lot adjacent just beyond and west of it, strait or salient, this narrow, cramped quarter no more than 15 feet across, mere isthmus of alley, bare dirt mews formed by W. A. Harwood's clabord house to its rear.

Save Doc, who wings open, finning right towards Fremont, deploying as previously appointed to warden the flank, to prowl and patrol it, parry any gesture towards dodge-out. This, while the Brothers Earp *barge*, quickening their stride curvilinear in concert—Virgil headmost, vanguard, at 38 the eldest, the City Marshal, the LAW, prowing the fore shadowed by Wyatt then Morgan—pivoting left off the sidewalk dumping directly into the lot whose occupants clear off abruptly backpedaling, eyes widening, jittering front, back, sidewise in disarray and alarm, their incredulity klaxon, rattled as ricochet as the three approach, square around, post up, face off not seven feet from them blackly clad and bristling. Firing squad.

Smells highly of horse in here. Ripe. Rank. Their stale and their stool.

Across, over there, hemmed in, the few feet of killing field, men stand like straw targets, cardboard cutouts, props off a backlot. Configured left to Earp right: Billy Clanton, all of 19; his brother Ike, 34; Frank McLaury, 33, to the front of his horse; and brother Tom, 28, adjacent the sidewalk and so nearest the street, semi-obscured behind the shield of his own mount.

Deeper inside the lot, apposite the rear landing between Fly's and the photo gallery in back of it, Behan and Arizona Billy the Kid Claiborne loiter, apart.

This is the chessboard as play begins, though the unfortunate few who are, so to say, non-Earps, are in the fresco of their moment, the space of this frieze, mere sub-sketch. They are cameos, ciphers, stickfigures, mannequin, virtually indistinguishable one from the other. They are interchangeable, about to become more than the less they might otherwise have remained—if not for this day—but still, ultimately, disposable; bit players, walk-ons, extras, scarce footnote—entries in an annal, tallies on a toteboard, notches on the grip of a gun.

And it is for that very reason that one might wish inside their heads, to sample the text of their thought, sense the texture of its flesh, its rondure and stratigraphy at the moment pre-fireflaught, if for no reason other than to ascribe to them, to accord what, after all, is only their due. To turn up the light on the lamp of their feelings and behold the human outflow of heart.

Cowboy heart.

Impossible, of course, unthinkable, and so, say, instead, that between them such thought as may abide is reduced to instinct, reflex and reaction, their will to survive the moment, this moment as it connects to the next, to weather the approach of what appears the weather ahead—Earp weather—ominous, at best.

"Boys," barks Virgil, "throw up your hands. I have come to disarm you. I want and will have your guns."

Well, now wait. Perhaps not quite   so   fast.

The gunhands of Billy Clanton and Frank McLaury have all along been fidgeting, fiddling with and fingering the handles of their six-shooters. Now Tom McLaury's insinuates furtively (insofar as he can stage and manage it) for the Winchester, the stock of which is jutting up big as all Montana just . . . there, from the scabbard slung from his horse's saddle. Which is when the sound, a sound unmistakable in its carry and so familiar to each of these men—as it likewise is kerosene-clear in its meaning— intromits; the *snik snik* of single-action pistols being thumbed back by their hammers, full cock.

Ike Clanton sleds a hand inside his shirtfront.

Wyatt jacks his gun from concealment, the trove of his coat pocket.

In the street, Doc swings the shotgun out from under his capeflaps, braces and levels it.

Billy Clanton draws his gun in ape of Wyatt.

And now the world is narrowing, whittled to zoomshot, vectored through the collapsing funnel of a telescope—convergent, magnified, graticule: seven feet of dust-addled alleyway, two dun-colored horses, eight men and their hardware, and the immediacy of Mexican standoff. This theater of war, pre-abattoir.

No telling what one may encounter on one's way to the Apocalypse at the arse-end of the raggedy-ass earth.

"Hold!" roars Virgil, raising Doc's walking stick shoulder-high and dexterways with his right hand, his shooting hand, hanging it out there stiff on the horizontal outthrust before him, this gesture of a drum major. "Hold on, that's not what I mean. I don't want that."

But it is getting awfully late. The tripwire has been tripped. The domino has tipped. The degree of shift imperceptible, yet too swift, its pitch spun irreversibly earthward. The physics of fate awaits the one faulty move of the improvised gesture that will deface the long face of time.

O—

something is about to fall like rain,

and odds are, increasingly—

it won't be

flowers.

And then he winked. *Winked*. Doc did. Warp-eyed, nice touch, and they descended each into their story, all of it going d

o

w

n

around them

•─•••─•

ONCE UPON A time.

In the West.

Old West.

Wild West.

Wild & Woolly West.

Before one had to queue up, shell out, fork over, pay admission; before Remington and Wister, Broncho Billy Anderson; before Ford, Hawks, Leone and Peckinpah; before replica and simulacrum—once upon *that* time, two shots, as is classically said, rang out.

There were two gunshots, a co-authored pair (though that was not at once so apparent), the reports registering so percus-

259

sively compressed, consonant and piggybacked, so proximate each inside the other that they passed to all who heard them—soundwave-to-ossicle—for one.

But one, Billy Clanton's, sprayed wide, fluming hot and windily between Wyatt and Morgan, knotholing with a distinct *chud* the wall of Fly's Lodginghouse at their backs, while the other, Wyatt's, mowed subcutaneously through, gouging some before embedding itself roughshod among the interior cores and tissues, fibers and fabrics, fascias and visceras, the shims and lathings of the human brisket.

And so Frank McLaury, himself a crackshot, yaws yawn-jawed and goggle-eyed, blood a paint smear, spatter, then a billow darkly wet, this seepage out the sewer of his shirt where Wyatt's bullet has naveled him an inch right of the omphalos. The agonal moment, black as orgasm.

For some reason, or perhaps none atall, it is during this sequence, somewhere along about . . . *here*, that Frank's hat jolts off, the wind tossing it like leaf lettuce. Tumbleweed. This concretion of throwaway detail.

Virgil transfers Doc's cane to his left hand and unsatchels his gun with his right as Morgan draws his own.

The two horses bluster, dodgy and spooked—the noise and smoke—start badly, nicker and rear, preventing Tom McLaury from retrieving his Winchester. Its stock is suddenly goose oil, axle grease; he cannot orchestrate a grip.

All this elapses, so to say, in less time than it takes to read about it: 10 seconds. Roughly.

Then, save fluster of horseblow and hoofstamp, nothing: —————————————————————————————

Flatline. Asystole.

Nada, nil, null, nought, negato, néant, non. Nolition.

Lull.

A suture of silence. This arrest between beats. Its surcease and caesura. The quietus of oblivion. A world unhinging, arrived at the last act of its axis in advance of Ike abruptly lurching forward, hands skied, brow florid, shrieking maroonly, "But I ain't heeled!" Pouncing on Wyatt's gunarm, grappling, Wyatt's pistol inadvertently firing into the ground at their feet before he can right it, get shed of him, shrug him off long enough to growl, "The fight's commenced. Go to fighting or get away."

And so the 20 seconds that remain begin their plunge into chaos. The commoving of their choreography. All of it but red cloud spooled from its reel—the foment, torsion, turbination too, everything about to succumb to the aesthetics of vesania.

Tom McLaury, nearest the sidewalk, is trying to calm the buck and wrench of his horse enough to beguile it for a bulkhead or breastwork; out in the street Doc's eyes track, inspect and inventory, hawking him. (The way history, it is said, stalks before it strikes.)

Ike's maneuver, while momentarily screening Wyatt enough to block a follow-up shot by Billy Clanton, likewise clears an avenue of fire for Morgan, who, availing, plunks Billy in the chest perforating lung and hurling him like sacked laundry backwards against the Harwood house. Pneumatically rasping, Billy is cashiered a second time by Morgan above the right wrist; the shot compels him to transfer his gun to his off hand.

Blood blurting, Billy's torso falls mute.

Ike, as scrambled in thought as he is panicked in spirit, abandons his baby brother, sprinting across and out of the lot down the sidewalk, retreating first through Fly's front, then out its backdoor, shagging across a vacant backyard through Kellogg's Saloon and onto Toughnut Street, two blocks distant. This scurry of a roach.

When a stray bullet shreds onlooker Billy Claiborne's uncuffed trouser leg, John Behan yanks him towards Fly's open backdoor and shovels him inside, diving in on his heels.

Frank McLaury chamfers Virgil's right calf, upending him— he goes down like stepping into the path of a cowcatcher—then clews up the reins of his horse, tugging it snorting from the lot, across the sidewalk and into the street.

When Morgan wheels to follow, Tom McLaury from behind and over the cantle of his saddle unleashes a single bullet that plows beneath Morgan's scapula, clipping a vertebra—the eighth thoracic—before punching out his right shoulder. The shot scuttles him. Sprawled on the sidewalk he hollers, "I am hit!"

As Wyatt slews towards Morgan, edging into the street, he yells at him to "hug ground," then laces Tom McLaury's horse in the withers, coercing both its bolt onto the sidewalk and subsequent lunge for Fremont.

Managing a knee, Virgil further distresses Billy Clanton with a shot that smacks meatily into his gizzard, gorging it. Billy crumples, flumping buttfirst to the ground where muddled and dazed he lazily braces his gun on a kneecap and, fugued, persists in blankly firing while calling his brother's name, the word that 18 years before had been his very first.

The lot is fogged, churned with smoke, the air is cogged flinty with metal. The horse smell has been burnt off, displaced by bouquet of gunpowder, human feces and urine. Bullets whing by, whizz, whumpet and zing. This singe of velocity. Sear of ballistics. Shellcasings clitter like cleats.

Tom McLaury, refusing to turn loose its reins, is dragged by his horse sidewise into the street obliquely exposing him to Doc, who opportunistically dredges the opening with buckshot pumping an even dozen into the pocket of Tom's right armpit obliterating the triceps and torquing him, pirouette, around.

Zigzagging mortally downstreet west towards Third, Tom

festoons blood in his wake; a trail of red bees. Crashing blindly into a telegraph pole, he slumps against it, downslides and dies. It is but a matter of seconds before he is hived by hundreds of black flies, feasting.

Observing Tom's flight and thinking he has missed, Doc mutters an obscenity—"Cocksucker!"—flings the shotgun to the ground in apparent chagrin and on the crossdraw pulls his pistols, raiments of nickel and ivory.

Beyond Doc's back, further out in the street, Frank McLaury fumbles the reins as his horse skitters, balks, breaks, then gallops east down Fremont. Wyatt levels, aims, fires at Frank, misses. Frank's reply riddles Wyatt's coat-tails. Frank shoots at Morgan and misses, low. Then, overcome with languor and enfeebled by blood loss, he reels drunkenly to the ground, clumping there flodged and faint.

Doc turns and commences his stroll, arms outspread. Cruciform.

As he approaches, Frank, his breathing impossibly labored, musters such part of himself as in the moment persists and fetches leadenly to his feet. Weaves some. Then, as if raising a barbell mired hilt-deep in muck, hoists his gun: "I've got you now, you assfucking pimp."

Doc tsks his tongue, rueful. "Such vulgarity, Sir." Then grins good-naturedly. "So, please, proceed. At your leisure. Blaze away. You're a daisy if you do."

Using his left arm as a buttress to steady his right, Frank fires pointblank. The bullet glances off Doc's leathers creasing his right hip. Doc, staggered, sags, appears about to buckle, knows at once that he is bleeding, suspects badly, but resists going down.

"Oh my," exclaims Doc, mocking, "the burn. I believe I can only be shot right through. How very game of you, Sir, how . . . intrepid. Bully for you then. A-plus for effort. But now, poor soul, why, it can only spell your doom. Let's see, just how sordid shall we play it?'"

Frank, tumbling backwards, is about to achieve the sidewalk on the opposite side of the street when two gunshots—a co-authored pair (though that is not at once so apparent)—concomitantly jar his body, effectively combing out every thought he has ever had or will have, clean as sand scoured from its shell. One, Doc's, peels open his chest. The other, Morgan's, murries his head, mulls it, splatting just beneath the right ear.

The air slurries with slush, snaggles with propulsions of glair.

Frank, befallen, shudders, spasms, gasps. There follows his risus and calcitration, anoxia and cyanosis; he blues.

Doc stands over him, gnaws at a thumb, punts at his ribs with a boot toe as if they are made of stone, this stump, as if blood had breath.

"So die," he says indifferently. "Go on then. Every rat to the trip of its self-triggered trap. Die, Cowboy, die. Down the greased chute. And stew in the cesspits of hell."

And so he does. Frank does. He dies. Nor so much as rattles as he does so. Just dies and decides to stay dead.

The business is over. 30 seconds, 31 shots, each bullet bright in its bluing; 30 seconds, not even. A brevity. An eternity. An enormity and farce. For that was the fiction, the calumny and lie— that it meant something, any of it, added up to jacksquat, that it changed anything, led to a sort of wisdom, or altered the course of one's life. Or that in the doing, it made one feel doubly alive.

He'd felt like shit. He felt like shit still. He'd felt like shit yesterday, he'd feel like shit tomorrow. And the next day. Where he felt anything at all. Men were dead. He'd killed them. And he? Well, apparently he wasn't. Yet. So it went, so it goes. And so what. Why was he standing here? His hip burned like hell. His lungs were on fire. His balls were blue-numb with the cold.

Holstering his pistols he felt for the wound, found it—mere graze—winced, stared at the blood on his hand

blood on his hand

blood on his hand

blinked once in disbelief, once more in recognition, yet again with the first stirring of the relief that he sensed must prefigure regret, appalled.

He knew: the magnitude of any triumph can be calculated only after accounting for the formidability of one's opposition, as that there is no escaping any provisional or contrawise account of something that has happened once it has sunk its fangs so deeply into the 12-point type of black print bound into 1st editions as to become perdurable.

So, fuck this. It, all of it, felt so vomitously familiar. "Fuck me." Fuck it all. Sidewise.

Triumphant? Hardly. He needed a drink.

So let it end; in the street, somewhere else, the mask falls.

He never second-thought his having backed the Earps in the business, suffered no knot of remorse or knurl of regret later, no . . . pang. He had made his play: all in. In that he strode content, it had been his place.

"This is none of your affair, Doc," Wyatt had told him on the corner outside Hafford's earlier that day. "It's our fight, not yours. There's no call for you to mix in any of this."

Already it seemed weeks ago that having been alerted to Ike's homicidal blustering, he and Kate had made love. She had finished him off like draining a neck of champagne, he had bathed and shaved, brushed and polished his teeth, gargled with anise and branch, emeried his nails, enjoyed a leisurely brunch, played a few hands of solitaire and checked in at the Alhambra feeling fresh as May flowers.

But now, well, he couldn't believe what he was hearing. What did Wyatt mean, not his fight? If it wasn't his, then whose was it? They aimed to kill him, didn't they? They wanted him silenced, his tongue and guns besides. Wyatt! No, it was his fight all right. Just because he refused to pin on some cheap patch of tin . . .

"That's a helluva thing for you to say to me," he had shot back. "If you are going down there, then I am with you. I would not miss out on such sport for the world. Besides, I've nothing more pressing at the moment. I could do with a spot of diversion."

"Could get nasty, Doc," Virgil had remarked. "They may resist."

"But I am only counting on it, Virg, that's just my game."

Well, it had proven a mite more than that, and afterwards it was only Kate, Kate alone who could console him. Returning to his room at Fly's, he had perched on the bed white as she had ever seen him, the trauma, its tremors all through him; sleet.

"My God, darlin'," he had whispered, "it was awful, just awful."

There was neither shame in his voice nor chagrin. He still was reeling, feeling shelled. "I hated it, Sugar, hated what I was doing, half loved the very thing I was hating.

"But why? Why should that be? Why, Kate? Why do I always want . . ."

"What, Doc? Tell. What is it?"

He seemed at a loss, in need, perhaps, of a name. A naming. "Don't know." His chin lolled some. "What can't be reconciled, I suppose, what won't comport. Conflict, maybe. Chance. Its music. Hazard of that edge. The wonder of its gray.

"Can't seem to trust it somehow, that sort of clarity. The black of it and white, the shelter of those categories. Feel like, I don't know, like I'm missing something, what won't add up, come trig, come plumb, square away, life outside the frame, what refuses to be corralled that way. What won't be parsed, or tamed.

"Didn't you ever want to saddle-up a tiger and just ride? Ride it hard? Ride it so hard that . . ." He let the image trail, wrung clean and reduced, drowsy in each of his bones; he was sapped, suddenly 100 years old. Then, in scarce a whisper, added, "I know I'm babbling, but goddammit, Katie, a man should be able to read himself right without words."

"Men do," she said softly. "Most men. Reckon yer like them? Any of 'em? No, you been flirtin' with the silence yer whole life, tryin' to bluff it one way or t'other. Silence, that's the real tiger. Today you was called, that's all. Forced to show yer stripes.

"Yer alive, Doc. Resent it all you want. You survived. Rest of it's just talk.

"Law'll come for you now, you know that. Ain't the first time, 'spect it won't be the last. Reckon you'll rig a right way to play the hand yer holding."

And as only she knew what to do, now that's just what she did. In silence they shared most of a bottle while she fetched him a hot bath, undressed him gingerly being mindful of his wound, gunrig and all, this hardware that was so much a part of him she thought of it as grown onto his frame, then helped him slip into the fur-glove of its heat while his body, embraced, opened as slowly as something long-froze, the cold sweat, white dust, the freshly let blood lifting off, skating away, skimming apart in a film across the water's skin as the nerveshock, hipthrob, bruised bone, the wound to the muscle cinched up and slackened. Thawed. The site already was darkening towards plumbago, this lick of dusk. A tongue of curfew.

He let himself be taken in, slide down, his back hard against the hard back of the tub until his head was completely under water eyes closed against the soap sting, unthinking, thoughtless, thinking hard on nothing, arrived at bottom, beneath it, vacuum, resurfacing like a resurrection draping his arms over the metal sides not moving, just letting the water shift, sift, then still against the rack of nakedness until he had achieved that state of perfect skinmelt and he alit from the water, drydapper, stepping out, the bent rail of his body gant and sluicing, puddling the floor like windows while she wrapped him inside fresh towels. Bunting.

She crooned him to the bed, laid him down, arched over him letting her hair fall across his legs while her mouth, lips, tongue became active, stalking the root of what was forming in him, what was gathering, stealing onto the bed beside him still clothed, the travel and graze of her fabric across him like gauze, silk mesh, like bandages, the open O of her face lowering, taking the still-damp, the damp fit of him, in.

He closed his eyes and let her. The forgetting. Way back. Previous. It seemed years now. Ages. Bygone. Miles off. Another country. Marrowing. Abob. Inside. All of it undreamed. Letting it, the it of him, just, come.

THROUGH THE SALOON's front doors, night of the next day. Kate, draped, arms yoked to his neck, lightly snoring in his ear. Shifts her now, dozing in his lap, head deadfall on his shoulder.

"Look," whispers Doc to the convoked as they belly-up near, "what happened yesterday? The way it played out? It couldn't fit in a book. Words could neither capture nor convey it, covers contain it. Permit me to tell you about Frank McLaury, the unvesseled light leaving his eyes, the blood his nostrils and mouth, the bone glaring up from the skullbase, up through the cranial floor—none of it annoyed me more than a gnat does a walrus. What did, what genuinely rankled my rhubarb, was the way he just lay there, prostrate and inert, letting it happen. What curdled my cream was how easy he made it, as if to say, 'Why fight it any longer? Why resist?' As if his soul had no will of its own. His death was an insult, an insult and a gyp. I felt/I had been/gypped.

"All the same, I will confess, it was much the most marvelous sight in the world. Him, just lying there, cut to pieces, laid low. Oh, it was a charred occasion, make no mistake, a moment of pure evil, and had he been elsewhere, that evil would have found him, even so. For as mankind courts disaster, and no man more than he, when I gazed down upon his person, I did so indifferently.

"I could tell you that I will never forget the feeling, that I will carry it with me always, stigmata, a scar down the rest of my days. But that would be a lie. In fact, you may believe—let's see, ah yes—I have forgotten it already.

"And yet, yesterday you say, it happened only yesterday. Why, it already seems less than a dream. Tom irreduced to fillet you say, and Frank but an idiot's grin? His head tossed to salad you say, reticular, rhizomed, well-rucked? Ruckus of occiput? Ruction of dura mater? His rame rutted and striate, retted and scutched, his life come to scuttle, all scotched? Why, yes, I do seem to recall some such, something of the sort, though I thought, well, I was certain it was something I had read once. In a book. Or remembered. In a fuck."

Hefts Kate from his lap, stands her up, buckles an arm about her waist and, chuckling and shaking his head, drifts out, disappearing in advance of their catcalls and razoos through the swinging doors with a go-to-hell wave. For once having put them down, put them down like ponies, he was, with them, quite done. He never spared a thought, was bedeviled by no nightmare, never looked back. Not once.

Thirty seconds of no-account street brawl, half a minute of bloodbath, and for all the fuss and fulmination you might have considered we had won the war, invented the wheel, and discovered a cure-all for cancer. Strange how it played out, caught fire and spread, acquired a life of its own. Don't ask me, I have no answers. Even now, all these years later, I find it nought but a snarl of perplexity.

Maybe that's the way it is with legends: in the making they don't seem like much, nothing stellar or superlative atall, could be they even seem flat ridiculous, a few laughs over a glass of topshelf rye and once around the dancefloor before a fast fondle and farewell. Because when a thing is being lived, it just feels like life, nothing special, little of this, little of that, some good, some not, but you don't take the time to give it a second thought. It is only once it is over—or in that moment when you know it is all about to end—that you are wont to enlarge the picture, enhance the focus, add some scope, tweak the perspective, look back, reconsider, weigh the balance, impute a context, impose an order, fashion a shape, attribute motive and meaning, assign causation and draw crafted conclusions—account for the unaccountable, insist upon communicating the incommunicable, and so, in turn, turn it into something else, something it never was at the time, or was never intended to be, but that now, like alchemy, it has come to so inevitably seem. Or that you need it to seem. Something larger, something deeper, something more, or more obscene.

How wrest a meaning from a moment's mindless gore?

Wes Hardin, who ought know better than most, having done his fair share of the same, once wrote that it is almost as bad to kill as to be killed. He was right. No man who's half a person and lays claim to an ounce of soul—or a fig of fellow-feeling—no man feels good about gunning down another, no matter who he is or how it happens, no matter how just the reason or how many times he may have gunned one down before, because each time it happens something goes out of you, gets stripped away, frays off, flays, something more goes forfeit, one more piece of who you are, or hoped you'd still become. And you know that even while you're at it, it's something you're never going to recoup, because all you're getting in return is the absence, more and more absence, compounded sums of nothing, the recombinant zero, cubed. Until finally there is nothing left *but* the absence, and you're living on borrowed time, a lesser man than you ever could have conceived. (And the piece that persists? Bone-dry.)

Despite what some may say, and others have boldly written, do not believe it, or fall for the lure of that line. There is no romance in killing, no aesthetics, no gesture of the exotic, much less of poeticized bliss. Violence diminishes life, that's all, or where it may surrender up its knowledge, is never worth standing the price.

I wonder: how know anything about something save not only that you were there at the time—witness or actor, onlooker or participant—but that that which you witnessed and/or participated in was not blurred or colored or tainted or even—why not?—entirely mistaken? That what you experienced—or fancy you experienced—corresponds in each detail to what everyone or anyone else experienced? That you did not blink and miss something, your mind for an instant fog over and you fail to take but a fraction of the whole of something in, or indeed conjure—God knows why—what was never there at all? That you did not unwittingly impute to the circumstance of the occasion, in the moment, as it was happening—or it happening to you—some unconscious slant of interpretation? That first your eyes, then your mind, finally your memory did not play each in their turn some antic yet undetectable trick?

I *was* there that day, indeed, I was, and yet . . . mustn't what anyone, any ONE sees and experiences, necessarily be circumscribed? Truncated by one's own—point of view, perspective, perception—defined by one's own, alone? How dispute this? That no one experiences every/thing, all/at once, on every/level, from every/angle, ever. And if they did, or dared to claim, then how trust what they experienced for the truth—universal, actual, absolute, the whole and nothing but? And if the truth is not whole, whole and wholly true, then how can it be trusted? If the truth, in any sense, on any level, from any angle, is incomplete or adulterated, then is it not something less—or, at best, something other—than the truth? And if it is—less or other—then what in God's name is it? No, just as seeing one thing clearly means seeing everything else less so, so remembering anything at all means having first to forget the rest.

Such concerns are not original with myself, and insofar as most people live their lives without once participating in a so-called historical moment (whatever *that* may mean), they might easily be dismissed. But here: it is of just such "historical" moments that History is composed, and it is that History, the one hinged to its capital H, that is the communal one, the preserved, polished, publicly anointed one, the sanitized, edited, official one, the version revised and narrated by the winners, and so the one with which all of us are obliged to contend.

Which, perhaps, merits trying to get It right.

Or make true.

The truth? Men died that day, the way that they died was awful and bloody, and I had a red hand in their dying. Beyond that, so much depends. And what it depends upon in particular is a distinction that can seldom be so easily sorted.

Look here: a tree may be a tree, or what most of us have agreed to call a tree, despite the handful who may argue that it really is a giraffe, just as fire may be said to be hot notwithstanding those who claim to eat it or walk across it or leap through it or juggle it for a fee—but only *to a degree,* because everyone's experience of a particular tree, or of a positive instance of fire, differs.

To what degree then becomes the question, differs to what degree. Is it the commonality and consensus of collective experience that finally determines what is true, or is it rather the contradictions and inconsistencies, all the unaccountable irrationalities, blunders, ravings, raptures, visions, miracles, the deliriums and transports, contraventions, irresemblances and idiosyncrasies?

I would hazard I have been asked by no fewer than one thousand persons to describe what transpired that day, and the only frank and honest answer is that the facts must remain forever in dispute, a dispute that no amount of time might resolve or lay to rest, for in time, time passes, and as it does, as the future draws nigh, what once was fact—or fiction, and always *always* both—fades like a page of purged text, or a palimpsest, in a book. Becomes, that is, History, this . . . narrative. Though it doubtless is more useful to rightly call it Mystery. And what is a mystery, after all, but a contradiction that because it cannot be reconciled, is one we cannot bear to face, and so, being only human, prefer to mask.

Well, I am tired of masks, as I am bored by the facts, if bored further still by the numberless masks of fact, and what I am bored with the more so is the imagination that professes to order and arrange them as if life were little beyond the composition of its own story—lyrical, luminous, execrable! I am dying, you see, and haven't the time to squander.

Seeing is not the same as believing, nor is hindsight 20/20, and the truth where simple is seldom half so clear. I was there, I was there that day, I saw what happened with my own eyes as surely as I killed those who, afforded the opportunity, would have killed me first and shed no tear in remorse. But while I may recall or contrive the most concretely casual details of what in fact occurred, reconstruct or reconjure the experience with documentary scrupulousness, however persuasive the precision of my imagery, what guarantee of its truth? Indeed, far from becoming clearer, the more complete and keenly drawn my images, the more they seem to me inauthentic, artificial, the less faithful to the very past that inspired them.

And here is why: because most of it was absurd, or where not, equally perverse, for beyond farce, it was worse. It was mockery. As that, in turn, atrocity. The past may lodge inside the present as its countless versions invest but a solitary moment, but that is precisely the problem—how reach inside the amber without altering what its retrieval requires? Truth in the eye of the beholder? That only it were so. No, truth is cougar—slippery, elusive, evanescent, seldom to be had where a man might so easily glimpse it. Anything untrue, after all, speaks for itself, as the facts, more's the pity, never do.

Save this. That it *was* a horror, that it was, and whether you are inclined to credit this version, or that, or some other, as "factually correct," or "historically accurate," or "existentially authentic," or "true to the reality of the experience," or "verisimilar in its veracity," still, even now, I do not believe a single word of them.

Gunfighter Nation? The Way of the Gun? The Sacralization of Violence? No, there are no lessons here. Save one: that once there were such men.

In the end, one works as one might with the available light. One can do no more. Save to be mindful not to construe its illumination for enlightenment.

So come then
all ye fed on lies,

of dim imagination
as if facts   like God
were possessed of eyes . . .

On All Hallows' Eve, a few days after the fight (from which both Virgil and Morgan had been quick to recover), Doc and Kate visited Hoptown, the Chinese Quarter across Third Street. Opium was readily to be had there, was pandemically used by certain subpockets of the population and bore neither legal sanction nor social stigma.

In those days neither had yet suffered the misfortune of having fallen much prey to the habit—as a rule they seldom trafficked in the pipe—although Kate did on occasion use laudanum recreationally, while Doc (as we have seen) was partial to other passions, those poisons more congruent to his style. But there are a thousand ways to murder desire (as there are to fornicate with fear), and so on the heels of the shootout, having been arrested but out on bail, it was he who suggested they "indulge a bowl of the cockatrice."

"I could use the clouding," he explained. "I need a lift. A spot of relief. Just to float for a while, flat on my knees."

At Li-Tzu's, last of the true lotus-eating Celestials, he of the braided queue, blackened lips and blacker teeth, they were deferentially ushered to their stall—the *fumerie* so called—where they were served, though Doc demurred, a generous selection of herbal teas and candied and caramelized fruits. Redolent of a palanquin or howdah, swagged and canopied in opulently colored tapestry silks (depicting what Kate recognized at once as some of the more convoluted Maithuna positions), the intimacy of the space contained a pair of chaise-like pallets affixed with horsehide headbolsters called *chumton* or "dragon pillows," which proved negligibly softer than saddles.

Everything at Li's smelled lavishly waxed in resins and spices, phosphors and saps, the least stupid smell in the world. Thuribles suffused the booth in pitchily scented smoke. Terraced banks of joss sticks and paraffin candles burned vaguely inside colored jars, altar at their feet. Their flames, lantern-low and fitful, plied intricate shadows across the ceiling. Soft chimes, muffled gongs, finger cymbals, lap harps, stavetaps on water drums, the delicacy of panpipes sounded steadily at long remove, walls away. Calamist. They stretched out seeking the comfort of their bones, shrugging them soft in their sockets to shape a snug fit.

The "kit" was ushered in, its salver arrayed with the spirit lamp, needle, paste tin, scraper, sponge, shears and scale—and the *yen tshung*, the two-foot-long, sweetened bamboo pipe, its *dow* or bowl having been previously looped, rolled and packed with the pungent *chandu*, a choice blend of *fook yen* and *li yuen* that with the lamp was kindled for them by their "chef," Li's son; he had been designated by his father to "keep the pill cooking and pipes coming," and now he handed it to Kate like an oboe.

They inhaled, Kate followed by Doc, a succession of sharp, abbreviated drags, and as the world atomized to silver wet and glitter the moment billowed open like an eye, past the glaze, beyond the gloss, vision gone to gimbal and ratchet, evacuating the mind of its contents. Doc stepped through bottom to find himself alone, left wholesale for Lotusland, those psychotropics, slogging an estuary through which dream, time, space and sleep all coursed as distinctly as mirrors, a pouring of miniature mirrors that faceted and reflected upon themselves conversing in musical stanzas. Mirrors like amoeba trebled in trills, coloratura at his feet. He listened, and what he heard . . . glistened, the sound that glister makes.

He waded through mists of mercury into the language of water drawing comfort from the discourse chroming at his feet, chatting silver up his ankles, words like bangles, like barnacles clung to his soles. His toes entangled the seaweed of sentences, the drifts and dunes of their syntax. He was barefoot and dressed in white serapes and a yellow sombrero whose fit felt oddly familiar, and so alien did the familiarity feel that now he removed the headgear and sailed it, discus upon the waters.

The gesture disclosed a slot in the center of his calvarium about the size of a silver dollar, a third eye dark and deep as a chimney chute. An entrance.

Shrugging off the serapes he dove headfirst into the rift in his head and down the strand of its seam, surfing the warp of the wave there, imbricate wavebeams warm then cool, warm again, their several chromas those of gems or precious stones, this pathology of color: emerald green, sapphire blue, ruby red, topaz yellow, diamond white, obsidian black, and with these he merged and mingled buoyed along (as it seemed to him) upon a razor of wind ruffling several strata beneath his skin, bereft of direction or altitude, yet vibrant and vertiginously vivid through the shriven core of him until, arriving at the end of iridescence, he opened onto its absence colloidol and spat out, steeped in darkness, back once more beside the estuary, spangled in tinsels of incense.

He was like that for days, unable to move, not really wanting to, perfumed and tonically immobile. Vegetable. It felt like several days, though perhaps it was centuries more. How know for certain? The purity of form, clarity of meaning, intensity of thought, density of feeling, all of it was reduced to raw electricity, chemical impulse, blue aura of energy. To charged ion.

He felt (he felt) everything, pain and pleasure; heard everything, inside and out; saw everything, before and after; thought everything, all and each; knew everything, was everything, life and death and whatever was missing. He was linked to it all, its allness, its once was/still is/yet to be, connected to the everything he knew. For he had stumbled upon the secret wisdom that is the same for every man who willingly quests of it: that aside from physical suffering, there is nothing, nothing at all, that is real. And with this, as from it, the release of a new kind of oxygen. Nor a thing vatic or visionary, mystical or gnostic about it; just the raw wonder—he could breathe again.

It made no sense, of course. He could not reckon its meaning. There was only the purity of sensation and the certain awareness that here, in this lack of knowing, its lacunae, the erasure of all memory and reason, dwelt something like perfection; fraught through every tissue, an absence of vector, and of volition.

And lifting to the surface, lungs napalm once more, awoke beside his nodding Kate, her half-sleep, and burrowing his head to the hutch of her breast, bit his fist, the blood taste red against his weeping.

———◦•◦•◦———

THAT NIGHT IT was different, and the next, and when they made love now, or rather when he made love to her, it was absent his former lust and ardor. He was desperate, grateful, wished nothing but to please her. He had never been so selfless in his attentions, content to cater and oblige, willing to ingratiate, lavish, blandish, flatter, minister to her every whispered whim. Where he was excessive now it was out of consideration for the other.

Something had changed, an equilibrium been upended, its harmony unchorded, this unspoken understanding, the permission to empty the whole of themselves, immersed and unmindful one inside the other. No longer was there the mutual taking in the giving. That reciprocity. Its verticity. Only the empathy remained. And it was too much, too reasonable, and it was wrong. She was illicit, wished to be and was, and all he could muster now was empathy.

Neither had ever apologized for the avarice of their appetites, those extremes, the voracity, not once, there had been no need, nor a moment of embarrassment. She did not want a gentleman, a gentle man, not in her bed she didn't. And so it struck her as a betrayal, not only of their relationship, but of his nature, and it was that which she could not forgive. He had left her behind and outside of that which once they had so heedlessly shared. He had become thoughtful. But all she recognized, all she sensed, was timidity. His *mildness*.

Both of them felt it, possibly, and feeling it neither said a word, probably, for this is what it had come to at last. Laying his body down, yielding it up lovingly, knowing the mind must follow—it always had—the heart as well, his soul, and so it went, and so it goes, nor questioned, ever, why it was, or had come to be just so.

Their bail having been summarily revoked, Doc and Wyatt spent most of November in jail awaiting the outcome of a month-long judicial inquest into the shootout, and it was during this lull that Kate was visited twice in her room at Fly's by John Peters Ringo, the Cowboy Hamlet, "who after giving me $50," as she recalled later, "warned me back to Globe, confiding how should Doc win his release, Ike Clanton meant to murder him in his sleep."

<hr>

KATE: I found John Ringo to be a fine figure of a man any whichaway you trimmed him. Physically of course, on account of his being the proverbial tall, dark and handsome—he stood above six-three—but intellectually as well. I had known him for a rustler, heard talk of his being a murderer, had seen him raging drunk on more than one occasion, but his relations with me, as with all women, was never less than sober and considerate.

I believe he could only have been a gentleman born, for he had that way about him, not unlike Doc's, though wanting the wink or smile. Fact is, where Doc's eyes shone bright as nickel, even in the dark, John Ringo's lassoed the light so's to sponge it up, absorb it, just absorb and snuff it out. That was a mite unsettling, don't mind saying.

His reputation around town, among the hens, I mean, was of a prodigious nature, and I'll attest to that being not an inch shy of the truth. The Lord had formidably addressed him in the apparatus department, though for all the endowment of his credential, it was as much a source of aggravation to him as otherways.

May have been the drag of all that liquor—told me he'd been at it without much brake since a sprout—or may be had to do with the thoughts that seemed to aggrieve him on the inside, but he'd about lost most of the finish off his function. At last he proved one of my more spectacular failures, though he put out like he was appreciative all the same. Think what you will, with me John Ringo always behaved the gentleman.

You couldn't help but notice something about him, a longing-like, a morosity, like his thoughts was far off on something sad. He'd say, "Oh well," no reason, sigh at nothing particular, then shrug and smile sheepish-like and sorrowed. I been around enough sadness to know the real thing, and John Ringo's was the sort you call a brooding at the soul. Something was at him, gnawing, eating, something that had gone bad awry in his life, and him determined not to share it with a soul. Like Doc that way, though Doc the more content to sing it like a song.

Naturally I did not dare ask him about it, and it was only later I learnt just what it was—how as a boy he'd been there when his pa'd turned the shotgun on hisself, and how the family'd turned him out when he'd got towed under by the drink, and how his ma and sisters out in California wouldn't have but nought to do with him, damned and disowned him though he'd wrote a dozen times begging to come home.

In the end I thanked him about Ike Clanton, got word of it to Doc, then directly set out alone by buckboard back to Globe. May seem a mean thing now, bedding my lover's enemy, then leaving him in the lurch, his fate still hanging fire, but Doc agreed it was best that I should leave, and by then I'd had it up to here with Tombstone anyways. It was like Doc said, "Should I hang, I much prefer to do it alone, and should I not, matters must only go from bad to worse. It pains me to concur with a rotter like Dutch Ringo, but he's got the read on these winds right. Globe's the smart play."

'Course, I never did divulge to Doc the details of just how I come by my information about Ike, pumped, so to say, that piece of news off his foe, but I heard tell how once I'd gone, and after he and Wyatt'd got free of jail when the judge ruled them killings what he called "justifiable homicides," he somehow got wind of the nature of the tactics I'd employed. And that when he did, there was hell's toll to pay.

John Ringo I never did see again. Hell, I seen Doc only just once more, though by then he'd not only forgive me, he'd plumb forgot what it was he was supposed to have forgave. Being so otherways occupied. Dying.

DOC: Mister John Peters Ringo was that dark and curious exception that proves the worst in every rule, and while I did not know him intimately, you may believe that I understood him all too well. As Wyatt never did. Ringo was one of the few men I ever knew to nettle him because he could not rely upon his unerring judgment to predict what he might do.

Now Dutch was hardly dumb, but crewing with those Cowboys—a lot I might describe as so much scum, riffraff and rough trade, dullards and dolts, drumbles and drones, dotards dumber than dandruff, bullies and thugs, slackers and stiffs, lamewits and lunkheads and louts, hardback boils on the butt of creation, comedones the bunch, just the ilk I never could abide, but which it pleased me on occasion ignominiously to debride—well, he was sadly slumming. His right, of course. Still, he ought have known better, as in truth he clearly did. Pity of it was, he no longer cared a damn. Precisely why I understood him more than I might have preferred to pretend.

When I heard later that he had cashed himself in ahead of schedule, I cannot say I was startled. The fact of his own existence rankled Johnny Ringo more than any human being I have ever known. There were times when even I could not stomach it, and my stomach can stomach most anything, if my lungs abide the less. Still, I might wager that he's happier now, six feet under, happier than had he kept walking the world no more to himself than a curse.

I have heard it remarked—though it is as likely a thought of my own—that suicide is the culminating act of the born narcissist, and surely this is so. Poor Johnny was the only man I ever met saddled with a worse case of self-love than myself. Love may seem a peculiar word to pin to a man who hated himself so, yet what is the passion for hating oneself if not self-love turned square on its head? No, even in death, if not death most of all, there is the compulsion to vanity.

Poor Johnny Ringo, it was with him as it was with young Billy, that he should prove no daisy. No daisy, poor Dutch, none atall.

THAT JANUARY. ANOTHER high noon in Tombstone. Ringo, whiskeyed up as usual, comes carousing across Allen Street. Breasting up nigh, fetches from his coat pocket a kerchief, making a show of flapping it like a fish in Doc's face.

DOC: Why, John Peters, another round of lurching theatrics, is it? So what's gone and got our feathers ruffled this time? Feeling a tad under the weather? Under the gun? Under old Curly Bill's thumb? Feeling a bit sorry for ourselves again? Or is it just that time of the month?

RINGO: I have had my fill of you, lunger, and that is all a man can stand. Right here, Doc, right now, you and me, man to man. All I want of you is three paces out in the street. You know the game. Take hold a tug with your teeth, toe the mark and say the last of your prayers. I am the one to kick your damned lungs out once and for all.

DOC: My my. Such a pleasant thought. My damned lungs, you say. Why, dear Johnny, I do fairly tingle at the prospect.

Though you will pardon my observing that your act grows stale. Increasingly wearisome, Johnny. One note.

RINGO: None of your damned jaw. No more palaver. I aim to have a piece of you way one or the other. Again and for the last time, reach back.

DOC: I'm your huckleberry. That's just my game. But why the rush, Sir, when I have yet to determine how I am to oblige you? How about it, Dutch, where would you like it? I invite you to name the spot. Through the heart? The heart might do quite nicely. Or the neck. How about the neck, Dutch? The way you did Hancock up to Safford. What do you say? Bleed out fast that way. Then again, there is always the temple. Hmmm, yes, something about the temple rather appeals to me. Less mess. I'd paunch you, Dutch, shoot you in the kitchen, open up your sewer and let you shit yourself to death, but you know how it goes with the bellyshots, all the ruckus—or as your sort might prefer, *rookus*. Plug a man in the gut and he's like to howl stuckhog 'til all the cows come home. No matter, I defer to you the choice. Left temple, or right?

RINGO: Go ahead, lunger, gravel yourself to hell. You've been a swift rattle in my balls from day one and I only want your blood, same as I had your woman. Your hash is settled either way. Look at you, you're all but stiff where you stand. I'll be doing you a favor.

DOC: Oh, that you will indeed, if you can but make fair the boast. And yet you cannot, can you? No, never have I been more certain of a thing in my life. Why, I can see it just there, in your eyes. The failure. The foredoom. Lord, son, but you are a dismal soul. Too bad. I had such high hopes. Dared to think, entertain the belief, that perhaps you were my daisy.

RINGO: Goddammit to hell, Holliday, that's just what I mean. You and your goddamn daisy talk. Go to work, Doc. Throw down or I swear I'll blow your lamp out. I don't care. I don't give a shit. Fuck-all, I don't care about any of it.

DOC: Don't care? About any of it? Pardon my growing more antic, but whatever can you mean? Sounds like nirvana to me. So how do you do it, Dutch? No, don't tell me, let me guess. You feel the whole world was created deliberately to drown you in the rising tide of its shit. Am I close? Well, you may be right, but what of it? Your problem, Sir, if I may be so bold, is that you lack all sense of right proportion. You overvalue yourself, Johnny. The sun will rise tomorrow whether you are here to see it or have slipped under in the meanwhile. Might I offer a word of advice? You need to learn to let go, lighten up, just . . . float. Enjoy the ride, the drift of the dive, like me. Which is why you envy me so, you envy me the gift of my grace—your own being for nothing but spite. Well, if a man is to envy another, then grace is just the thing. Still, because you envy, you hate, and your hate I cannot abide. You leave me no choice but to pluck your flower for you. *Vaya con, mi maricón,* and give Señor Death my regards.

At this moment, the moment of truth (as the books like to say), nothing happened, for before either could make his play, partisans from both camps intervened, stepped providentially between the pair and, enjoining each by his arms, hustled the adversaries off in opposing directions amidst a flurry of shouted oath, derogation, epithet and execration, so blue the anathemas, not a word is recountable here.

Remember this: the past draws blood

—JIM CARROLL

Virgil Earp they gunned down in the middle of Fifth Street outside the Oriental Saloon. It was shortly before midnight three days after Christmas and the pair of double-barrel shotguns discharged over a distance of 60 feet blew apart his left arm, reducing 5½ inches of humerus bone to slart between the shoulder and elbow. Against the advice of doctors he kept the arm and survived, crippled for life.

Within days, U.S. Marshal Crawley Dake had wired Wyatt from Phoenix appointing him a Deputy U.S. Marshal authorized to "enlist as many deputies as you deem necessary to restore order." Three months later (Wyatt for once having failed to do so), they backshot Morgan Earp while he played pool in Campbell & Hatch's Saloon on Allen Street. It was 10:50 of a Saturday evening, Morg had just returned from a W. H. Lingard Theatre Company performance of *Stolen Kisses*, at Schieffelen Hall, and the single .45 caliber bullet dredged his lower back making sherd of his spinal cord, then shoveled through his left kidney tearing out his loin before lodging in the left thigh of George A. B. Berry, a railbird. It took Morgan Earp 50 minutes to bleed out in his brother's arms.

The next day, coincidentally his 34th birthday, Wyatt Earp rounded up Doc, youngest brother Warren, Sherman McMasters, Texas Jack Vermillion and John Blount, alias Turkey Creek Jack Johnson, and they began executing those whom they considered merited it.

On Sunday, the Vendetta Posse, as it was immediately labeled by the newspapers, executed Cowboy Frank Stilwell in the Tucson trainyard. On Wednesday, the Vendetta Posse executed

Florentino "Indian Charlie" Cruz, a Cowboy crony, in the Dragoon Mountains north of Tombstone. On Friday, the Vendetta Posse, after being ambushed by a contingent of eight Cowboys, shot and killed, among others, Curly Bill Brocius, at the Iron Springs watering hole in the Whetstone Mountains. (No one save Wyatt ever took credit for a single one of these killings.) On Monday, the Vendetta Posse holed up for two weeks at Henry Clay Hooker's Sierra Bonita Ranch, where Billy the Kid once had worked punching cows, and where, as Doc feigned horror, Wyatt Earp took his first drink of hard liquor in three years.

Ike Clanton and John Ringo still were at large, but for the moment, it was enough.

OLD NEWS

They are a roving band of dark repute—no-account banditti, highwaymen, blackguards, malcontents, cutthroats, ruffians and red-handed assassins, and their path is strewn with blood. Wherever they halt, common decency is ignored and human life ceases to be sacred. And at their disreputable heart rides the most disreputable of the lot, one Holliday, known far and wide as Doc.

(ARIZONA *DAILY STAR*, 3/21/82)

There is a prospect of a bad time and there are about three men who deserve to get it in the back of the neck. Terrible thing this Vendetta business, but the sooner it is all over with, the better.

(GEORGE PARSON'S DIARY)

The Earp Vendetta booms; and when the Cowboys and the Earps meet, it can only be hoped that the slaughter on both sides will leave but a few survivors, thereby lifting a great weight from the minds of all.

(SAN FRANCISCO WEEKLY EXCHANGE, 3/23/82)

I am heartily glad at the bloodshed and hope the killing is not stopped. Things seem to be coming to a head at last. Then let them come. The time is ripe and rotten ripe for change.

(GEORGE PARSON'S DIARY)

That a band of so-called officials with a high hand rove the country murdering human beings out of a spirit of revenge, this red-handed assassination will not do. It is an assault on every citizen in the country. If Holliday and the others can kill one citizen in violation and defiance of the law, they can do so with every citizen.

(ARIZONA DAILY STAR, 3/30/82)

One of the reasons the Earps found themselves in court after the O.K. Corral [was that] the law took different forms, and sometimes it had wars of its own.

—DAVID THOMSON

Revenge was necessary in the absence of justice.

—WILLIAM GASS

> *I find no hint throughout the Universe*
> *Of good or ill, of blessing or of curse;*
> *I find alone Necessity supreme*

—JAMES THOMSON

Despite his affinity for orthodoxy, or perhaps positively on account of it, Wyatt believed that there were times—owing to the corruption of the police and/or dereliction of the courts—when a crime could be considered not only conscionable but a moral necessity. Naturally he would not have called it a crime, he would have called it an act of conscience; the point is, he reserved the right to allow for those moments when one is left no recourse but to appeal to the church of one's own rectitude as the altar of last resort. Whether he was correct to do so, I would not care to say. Being a Southerner, I recall much the same argument being made in behalf of the nigra-lover John Brown, and as a Southerner, I always have shrunk from it. Still, I knew Wyatt, and knowing what I knew, knew that what he itched for beyond mere revenge or retaliation, retribution or reprisal, or even simple justice, was to put things square. He wished for redress, requital, what others have called a reckoning, and yes, a vindication, and to accomplish it, the recompense foaled of that accounting, he would do whatever was required, up to and including breaking the letter of the law.

In those days, in those parts, the resolve, as the restraint, could arise only from within the individual, and in this instance, Wyatt alone was the individual suited to the calling. Much was made at the time of what the papers took to denouncing as our Vendetta. It didn't amount to deadwood. A handful of Badmen who richly deserved what they received got their just desserts, yet people dared to complain then, as a good many complain still, about the ethical niceties and damned us for vigilantes.

Well, we were far from choirboys, the business we were about was scarce child's play, but where the law is bought and paid for by the murderers and assassins of one's own family, morality can get as murky as mull, rules of legality so bent that they break, and justice miscarry, gone forfeit to the fracture.

There was no law in Tombstone, none that a law-abiding citizen might recognize, and where there is no law, the best that one might hope is to preserve the peace and maintain some semblance of order though it require meeting fire with hellfire. How, after all, act above or outside the law when that law ceases to serve any but the interests of those who stand most to profit by its violation?

Ordinarily, issues of law and jurisprudence, as those of ethics and morality, interest me less than yesterday's rain, but I did have occasion some while later to touch upon the subject with Uncle Billy Tilghman, the only Western lawman I ever knew afflicted with a worse case of self-rightness than Wyatt himself. Deputy Sheriff, City Marshal, Deputy U.S. Marshal, Chief of Police, County Sheriff, Special Federal Detective, at one time or another Uncle Billy must have held every law post ever invented.

"You know, Doc," he told me, "Wyatt is a good man to work with, but a hard man to keep up with. He makes and enacts his own law and rule which beats all the written code we have or ever will have. Written law is made to accomplish a general purpose and in that regard generally suffices, but no lawman can follow the letter of the written law in every instance with efficiency or safety to himself. I have been in the harness all my life and I know. I know because I've tried.

"Wyatt is a man who can forget his badge, make his own law and rule, enforce them in fairness, and at the same time defend himself and his actions with the legal factions. I won't say he done wrong—I was not there and cannot talk to the way of things—but I know Wyatt, know his character, and on that alone, I'd be reluctant to condemn him.

"Still, I do count it distinctly a blessing that he thought better than to ask me to render my assistance in such a matter."

Whether our actions were laudable, I know they were honorable. Where the choice reduces itself to disposing with due process or rising to the defense of one's family and friends, well, that's not a hard choice atall, not for some of us. Most of us prefer to believe that we find certain acts morally repugnant because we are endowed by God, or nature, with the facility to distinguish right from wrong, this distinction we pretend to feel in our gut. Some call it the conscience, others the divine spark, others being attuned to one's own humanness, to our shared humanity. Well, I had been obliged to test that belief and found it spun of nothing more substantial than stardust.

Why did I do what I did? Join in the hunt to pick off those men? Better ask what ought have stopped me. A want of spine or resolve? The right opportunity? The long arm of the law? The conventions of conventional morality? Ought love? Religion? The fear of retribution, eternal perdition, the prospect of ensuing anarchy?

Tell you what I thought as I thought it: I'll take my shot and suffer the fall. Or not. Either way. What I will not do, what I cannot, is nothing at all.

This is the way that it was, and that way is always the same: you realize a thing is happening only after the thing is long done. No one knows what they are doing while they are doing it. Sometimes, in the moment, certain work begs its doing. You do it and nothing for it, or how face the future? One way or another, things get done anyway, if seldom the right things, in just the right order, in just the way you had intended. No matter. I still feel I did the world a favor. I know I did them one. Only the intellectually impoverished believe violence is the answer to nothing. On occasion it is the answer, the only answer, to some one thing. Trust me, we are all of us infinitely better off without them, as they are without themselves. It was a liberation, or so I chose to think of it. We were liberating them from their lives, as we were relieving them of their wretchedness.

Judge, jury, hangman. I know, I sound like God himself. But

not atall. Truth is, I had no especial feelings about those men. All equal, I would not have troubled myself for the waste of lead. But Wyatt did have feelings, each one bloodier than the next. His hurt was of the fraternal sort, and it lay so far beneath the belt of the heart that if it was ever to mend it required cautery, the anneal of hot lead. Once he had made the call, once it was settled in his own mind and the outcome set in motion, once the handwriting was writ upon the wall, my own actions were never at issue: to back the play of my friend. Because I had no other, no friend, not a one, and to the last of my natural talents—which in such sanguinary matters were not inconsiderable—I intended to ensure that the only one I did, survived.

I may not have been worth much to begin with, but I would not have been worth a pair of deuces, to myself or anyone else, had I played it another way. It was right, seemed right, felt right, to me, to stand alongside my friend. (Though I might have done without being deputized. Deputed, perhaps, a sort of freelance so to say, enlisted and attached, job to job, sub rosa, that I might have justified. But I was allergic to badges; they didn't wear well, and so content to leave the lawing to Wyatt. His was the company gun. I had no stomach for all the by-the-book bunk.)

A dirty business? Certainly. I was on to that going in. As dirty as I hope ever to do. But I did not feel dirtied in the doing of it. I did not feel anything at all, save relief, once it was over.

Any difficulty is seldom more than what one makes of it, no problem so steep it cannot be surmounted, so paralyzing that one cannot waltz—weeping, wailing, whistling, whatever—away. And this was the reality: someone had to do things, these particular things. I did not delight in their doing, drew no solace from doing them, nor did I then, as I do not now, endeavor to justify their having been done. But I will say this—it could have been worse, much worse, and perhaps I helped make it less worse.

Was I complicit? And what if I was? If I was complicit, then so, finally, were each of you. "In what blood shall I walk?" the boy-poet asks. Reckon we all of us contribute our tracks.

I did not think much on it then, I care to think less on it now. As a rule I find the past pointless, a perfectly pointless place. What's past is past, what done, done. What is this history anyway, but posterity's pest? No, I refuse to dwell upon it. If you speak, you die. Remain silent, the same. Why do I awake each morning? Why do you? Why? Why do any of us bother?

You will get no stories out of me. It pleases me to affirm nothing. Those men were found dead, and the tales of their deaths buried with them. Save this: that they were ridden down, and I was along for the riding.

— • ✦ • —

> *It's time to see the frontiers as they*
> *are, Fiction, but a fiction meaning*
> *blood*
>
> —JOHN BERRYMAN

That history has on occasion seen fit to extoll its knaves and exalt its killers is no concern of ours. We are a nation of laws, of laws and reason, not men. The past is replete with such devils and anarchists, not one of whom triumphed in the end. So it is with this Holliday business. An unfortunate interlude. A sordid distraction. The passing fancy of a fanciful press. The law shall prevail in this matter as the law has always prevailed. Our frontiers shall be tamed and brought to heel, and then he too shall pass, this Holliday person I mean, more forgotten than the most savage and godless Apache.

—CHESTER A. ARTHUR,
21ST PRESIDENT OF THE UNITED STATES

In the spring, Doc and Wyatt fled Arizona on horseback ahead of a posse that included the outriders John Behan, John Peters Ringo and Ike Clanton. Wanted for murder, the proverbial price on their heads, the pair crossed into New Mexico spending 10 days near Albuquerque at Frank McLane's place, a friend of Wyatt's from Dodge City days. McLane having loaned the pair $2,000, they hopped a train for Colorado debarking near Trinidad, where Bat Masterson was City Marshal. Eventually Wyatt went to ground across the Continental Divide, in Gunnison, while Doc insisted on going to Denver to gamble. There, while strolling the streets of a May evening, he was accosted at gunpoint by a bounty hunter, who, hoping to collect the $1,500 outstanding on his apprehension, delivered him to local authorities to await extradition back to Arizona. Alerted to Doc's plight, Wyatt contacted Masterson, prevailing upon him to intervene on Doc's behalf. Masterson in turn appealed to Colorado Governor Frederick Pitkin, who subsequently denied Arizona's request for extradition on the grounds that "should he be returned, he would be murdered by Cowboys before reaching Tucson."

<hr />

MID-JUNE FOUND WYATT still holed up outside Gunnison nearby the Chinery Ranch awaiting word of what he was certain must only be a matter of time: his pardon by Arizona authorities. For two weeks Doc was in and out of Wyatt's camp, down a draw, around a blind coulee, on-through an arroyo, over two buttes and a mesa, across a dry creekbed, a wash, a single gulch, a pair of deep gullies, the girth of a wide-waisted gorge, long way 'round a morro and moraine, the swerve of a swale, along a set of six switchbacks, through a rock-cut defile, a naked couloir, finally up a box canyon to the rimrock there—"Earp's Chicken Coop" as he took pointedly to calling it—spending most of his time in town dealing faro. But the action was slow, his winnings meager, he sorely missed Kate—it had been more than six months—and he sensed that Wyatt, while not outwardly reproving, had begun to suffer a subtle if definite unease in his presence, an unease never more unnuanced than on those occasions when he returned from town obviously liquored up, occasions which, he was not slow to own, latterly had become the more frequent.

Inevitably the night came. "I aim to go back, Doc."

It was late and they were outside, each spraddling a hogshead hunched to a mulish fire. Heaped too high with green wood, it refused to catch wholehog but just stoked along, smoking easy, half-baked and recalcitrant, a glowish orange. This bluish blow. Off west lightning spoked the sky with barbed wire, yet overhead stars shone like spurs. Stars, thought Doc, that this night were best left unspoken, as unspoken as God when he weeps.

"Once my lawyers draw up the petition, they'll get Pitkin to sign on up here, Bat too, then go on down to Tombstone, do the same with all the right people there. Everyone knows we were just doing what needed doing. We were doing our duty, and we did it, and it's done, long over, and the pardon'll come down in a few weeks, month at the most, and then I aim to go back, run for sheriff against Behan in the fall. He can't win, not now, not after what's happened on his watch. Besides, I've got too much property there to just up and leave it without a say." He fell silent, flung something dead he'd been fiddling with overhand into the fire. It scuffed up a flame, a scarving of spelds, flared out. "Pardon goes for you too, Doc."

"I do appreciate it, Sir, truly I do." He coughed awhile, not nearly sober enough to shoulder his end of such a conversation, if neither so drunk as the night before. Damned if he could remember turning in. He'd chewed it over all day. Couldn't half recall anything but rousing sometime in the night to make water. It wasn't like him to slip, make an extravaganza of himself, drink beyond his wits, if for no reason than that the quantity required to do so typically was so outlandish. Perhaps it was the mountains; a man slid down that slope slicker at these high elevations.

"I believe I have had as much of Arizona as my lungs can stand. Or should I rather say, Arizona has had a bellyful of me. Besides, I do frankly favor these mountains to those deserts. They say the altitude here does wonders. Who knows, perhaps it may be prevailed upon to work a miracle as well."

Wyatt grunted, hard to read, then frowned. "You feeling all right, Doc? Holding up?"

"Holding up and holding out, holding out and hanging on. I am not complaining, merely dying. One has nothing to do with the other. Despair, Sir, as you know, is the single thing of which I never have despaired." He paused, something left unsaid, still simmering. What was it that he had meant to say? Damn! His thoughts listed and capsized, bobbed like dockbuoys. Ah yes, of course, that was it. "And death, of course, which is no less than the ultimate mender."

Wyatt nodded, then fanned a slow hand down his face feathering the wings of his moustaches between bracket of thumb and forefinger in advance of whisking a backhand at the rashy bristle beneath the sill of his chin.

"You know, Wyatt, as much as I do not love what I have made of my life, I will confide to you a secret: I did so dearly relish each moment of its making. Or so I tell myself in those moments when I can recollect what the devil it was I thought I was trying with such ardor to make of it. The memories, Wyatt, for what they may be worth, we've made a few. Of a sort. But may be we should leave them be—for a while."

"Suit yourself then. Like I said, pardon still stands."

"If it comes."

"Oh, it'll come."

"And if it does not?"

"Then reckon I'll go on back anyway. Stand for trial. Tucson, not Tombstone. Face the music. Pay the piper. Governor's in my pocket, Fremont, Gosper too, Bob Paul, all the lawmen and court officers. As long as I get a fair show, fair shake, I'm not fretting."

"Even if it goes right, goes aces, Ringo's still out there, Wyatt. Ike too, Claiborne, few of the others. Not a fair card in the deck."

"Ach, Ike's all fuss and foam. With the McLaurys out of the way, Curly Bill too, Ike don't mean spit, and Billy the Kid the less."

"Dutch Ringo, Wyatt. He's spit. He's snake spit. Johnny's snake spit and venom."

Arc of lightning; its burrs, braiding. Encore of thunder rolling yonder; vowels growling up from a hungry belly. This hard gallop; sky hooves.

"I know what Ringo is, Doc, I've always known. Just never been able to reckon the why of it is all. Not that it matters. If it comes to it, I'll handle Ringo." A comma of pause. "One way or the other."

No, thought Doc, if it comes to it, no, you won't, not one way, not the other. Not you, Wyatt, you won't handle Johnny Ringo. A man like Ringo doesn't take handling. He takes being had. He takes being had and put out of the way.

Wyatt straightened up, spine curtain rod, then outstretched, knees clacking like cleats before stamping a boot to free up the fuzzum of a fast-asleep foot. "So, hear from Kate?"

"Not a word, Sir. I should imagine she still is in Globe. As you know, we did not part under the most auspicious of circumstances. We had done so before, of course, split up after our spats, more times than I care to recount, but this, this somehow was altogether different, different in a way I cannot quite explain, even to myself. For the moment"—a plaintive sigh—"it is perhaps best that we grant each other, Kate and I, the grace of our berth."

"Well, you know how I feel about it, Doc. Can't say I'm sorry. That woman . . ."

"All right then, Wyatt. Leave it be. I shan't have her spoken of ill, last of all by you." No irritation, rancor or reproach, rebuke, animus or enmity, no ire or wrath, bile, spleen, choler, gall, no vitriol, just—what?—this boding. "God knows what you think of her, as God only knows why, but that's where the knowing need keep. Do me the courtesy—do yourself the favor—best leave it lie."

Carry of a new breeze, its vespers. Fresh rain, turned earth, its elements, that mineral clean weeding through the peat. The approaching monsoon. "Weather's up," said Wyatt, fetching to his feet. "Reckon I'll turn in. Beat the rains. See you in the morning, Doc." It was a question, a querying.

"Not if I see you first. Night, Wyatt." He smiled. "Wet dreams."

Wyatt chuckled, shook his head, strode off through the dark repeating the brace of words to himself. Then, half swallowed on the wind, Doc heard it again, that most exotic of sounds: Wyatt Earp, laughing. It never failed, he could not help himself, he grinned.

And yet . . . no destiny now. That was the lesson here, the knowledge of this night. His only future lay in outlasting the past, and even as he vested no faith in his character, nor might vouch for his fate, still, he knew that he must try. He must, or face becoming a beast.

"So long, Wyatt," he said aloud, and lifting his face to the storm, sensed the skyfall, its plunge, the descent in wave after wave. He closed his eyes and took the brunt, full and hard on his lids. This weight of rain, cold as coins. He imagined each drop bore a bullet.

PART

Five

I know better than to claim any completeness
for my picture. I am a fragment
and this is a fragment.
The voyage of the best ship
is a zigzag
of a hundred tacks.

—RALPH WALDO EMERSON

The way any of us spackle a life,
composite its story of the cobbles

You've got a tiger; so unchain it
and then see what explanations they give

—JOHN ASHBERY

Doc was more famous in his day than any of 'em, save maybe Wild Bill hisself. (And Cody of course, 'cept he don't count, being a showman by vocation and calling.) The Kid was small potatoes by comparison, and there was them never heard word-one 'bout Wyatt Earp who you'd mention Doc Holliday—just the one word, "Doc"—they'd fall quiet as prayers. Won't say his name stood for something, but sure did *mean* something. Come as close to what you'd call a going legend as any man in the West, bar none.

Funny thing was, where both Bill and the Kid rode the myth of it for all they was worth, Doc couldn't be bothered. Resented the hell out of his reputation, like he found it an insult, 'specially after Tombstone. Publicity, celebrity, notoriety, *glamour*, the repute and reknown of it about drove him mad. Got my own hunch it's that what spelt the beginning of the end of him. He was so weak anyways, and obliged to shoulder the weight of that baggage, it about drug him under. Like he was drowning in his own notice.

He was the kind of man needed to be left alone, stand clear of folks, fend or fall on his own, fence off the space of his solitude. Kind who has to do and die in private. After the Corral fight, you had to think he would of sold off his soul just to be anonymous. I know the feeling. Price gets too high, like the rights to yerself got stole out from under and no way in creation to get 'em all back. Leaves you too available, too damn exposed, too much the occasion for trophying. That sort of attention? Believe you me, it can cost a man his life.

—J. W. JAMES

Now comes Doc Holliday, as quarrelsome a man as God ever allowed to live on earth. A Georgian well-bred and well-educated, he happened in Kansas some years ago saving Wyatt Earp's life in Dodge City and earning his gratitude, and notwithstanding his many bad breaks since, he has always found a friend in Wyatt. Doc Holliday is responsible for all the killings in connection with what is known as the Earp-Clanton Imbroglio in Arizona. He kicked up the fight, and Wyatt Earp and his brothers stood in with him on the score of gratitude. He produced a feud that has driven the Earps from Arizona and virtually made outlaws of them.

(SAN FRANCISCO *EXAMINER*, 5/11/82)

Holladay [*sic*] is a delicate, gentlemanly-looking man, slightly built and with prematurely gray hair. He wears a heavy, sandy moustache and seems at all times to have a nervous, frightened, catlike, extremely wary manner, as if convinced that some one, or some thing, were pursuing him.

(*ROCKY MOUNTAIN NEWS*, 5/17/82)

John H. Holliday, better known as "Doc," is known as a desperado and a hard man generally. Bat Masterson, who is generally known as "the man who smiles," and whose words are weighty in official circles, says Holliday is not so black as painted. In conversation here, Holliday said that he had never killed anyone except in protecting himself, and that all he asked was to be let alone, that his single purpose in being here is to remain at peace with everyone around him and that he hoped his enemies would allow him that privilege. Doc Holliday is a man of light weight, rather tall, straight as an arrow, smoothly shaven, and is always well dressed. Streaks of gray can be seen in his hair which grows from a head a phrenologist would delight in examining. His eyes are blue, large, sharp and piercing. He is well-educated and his conversation shows him to be a man of considerable culture. That he has killed a number of men in the southern territories, and that he is regarded as a dangerous man, there is no disputing. But his friends claim that extenuating circumstances existed in every case laid to his charge.

(PUEBLO DAILY CHIEFTAIN, 5/17/82)

Doc Holliday is one of the most noted desperadoes of the West. By comparison, Billy the Kid or any other of the many Western outlaws who have recently met their fate, fade into insignificance. For years he has roamed the West gaining his living by gambling, robbery and murder. In the Southwest, his name is a terror.

(DENVER REPUBLICAN, 5/17/82)

Holladay [*sic*] has a big reputation as a fighter, and has probably put more rustlers and cowboys under the sod than any one man in the West. More recently he has been the terror of the lawless element in Arizona. Holladay's [*sic*] appearance is surprising, as different from the generally conceived idea of a killer as could be. Dressed neatly in black with a colored linen shirt, he is a slender man, his face is thin and his hair sprinkled heavily with gray. His features are well-formed and there is nothing remarkable in them save in the eyes, where rests a well-defined desperation that an amateur could hardly mistake. His hands are small and soft as a woman's. The slender forefinger which has dealt the cards has dealt death to many with equal skill and quickness, and the slender wrist has proved its muscles of steel. But the first thing one notices about him is his soft voice, and the modesty of his manner.

(DENVER REPUBLICAN, 5/22/82)

Doc Holladay [*sic*] is a tall man who, coupled with a pleasing shape, a handsome face, and a sort of dashing, independent air, arouses in the mind of a beholder feelings of the deepest resentment. One cannot share his company without feeling he is enjoying the society of a human tiger. It is supposed he originally came from Georgia, though he refuses to speak of his childhood to anyone. Be this as it may, he turned up in the West some ten years ago with very strict ideas of honor, making himself known as a man who would stand no trifling and with whom contradiction meant gore every time. A man of daredevil courage, indomitable will and a roving disposition, his record of murders throws the deeds of Jesse James, Billy the Kid, or any other desperado, entirely in the shade.

(DENVER REPUBLICAN, 6/2/82)

Dressed in a dark, close-fitting suit of black, his hair was seen to be quite gray, his moustache sandy, his eyes a piercing, dark blue. His handshake upon reception was strong, free and friendly, and upon introduction he said, half-laughing, "I am not traveling about the country in search of notoriety, and I think you newspaper fellows have already long had a fair hack at me. It is my habit to avoid trouble. My father taught me when young to mind my own business and let others do the same. It pleases me to leave people alone, so long as they are disposed to return the favor."

(GUNNISON *DAILY NEWS-DEMOCRAT*, 6/18/82)

Bat Masterson is back in town preceding by 24 hours, so he says, a few other unpleasant gentlemen, one of whom is Wyatt Earp, the famous marshal, another of which is Rowdy Joe Lowe, and still another Shotgun Collins. But worst of all, worst by far, and enough to send a chill wind through every honest man's heart, is the famous killer Doc Holliday. Among all the desperate men of the West, he alone is looked upon with the respect born of awe.

(KANSAS CITY *JOURNAL*, 5/15/83)

"Doc" Holliday is a man who enjoys the reputation of being one of the most desperate and determined in the West. He has been the subject of more than one fancy writer of the day and his prowess is sustained by a long and bloody record. Weak, out of health, spirits and money, slowly dying of his lungs, he told this writer recently, tears of rage coming to his eyes, "There are people in town who desire to murder me for notoriety. They know I am helpless and spread the report I am a Badman to protect themselves when they do the work. I am afraid to defend myself and these cowards kick me because they know I am down. I haven't a cent, have few friends, and they will murder me yet before they are done. I am afraid to carry a gun for fear of being fined. I defy anyone to say they ever saw me conduct myself in any other way than as a gentleman should. But I think my life as good to me as theirs is to them and I know I would be as a child in their hands if they got hold of me. I weigh 122 pounds." It is due him to say that he has, while here, conducted himself very quietly.

(LEADVILLE DAILY DEMOCRAT, 8/20-26/84)

Few men have been better known to a certain class of sporting people. He represented a class of men who are fast disappearing in the New West. He had the reputation of a bunco-man, desperado and Badman generally, yet was very mild-mannered, genial and companionable. He has strong friends in some old-time detective officers and certain of the sporting element. He was a good-looking man and his coolness and courage, his affable ways and fund of interesting experiences won him many admirers. He was a strong friend, a determined foe and a man of quite strong character.

(DENVER REPUBLICAN, 11/10/87)

Known by his quiet and gentlemanly demeanor, the Doctor looked like a man well-advanced in years, for his hair was silver and his form emaciated and bent, and yet, he was only 36 years old.

(UTE CHIEF, 11/12/87)

The Doctor was as mild-mannered as Byron's Pirate and perhaps not such a Badman. Histories of him are very indefinite and highly unsatisfactory. The little that is known is suspicious. There are few facts that can be readily vouched for or reliably verified and even those are as scattered as sands to the desert. Of the several hundred sporting men who claimed to know him intimately, few knew much about his history, though virtually all had heard one story or another second or third hand. The Doctor was always a prudent man, though the homicidal tendency was always strong within him. He practised dentistry a little, but he also seems to have practised gambling. A quiet, modest man, his smile was child-like and bland and he was generally regarded as very inoffensive. He usually looked out to have the law on his side and only then blazed away. The truth seems to be that the Doctor seldom lost his coolness. He was not thwarted by a blind, yielding passion, but was slow and studied and consistently merciless. In later life, his health failing and skills eroded, his fate became that of the ordinary gambler and he did not always play in the best of luck.

(DENVER *REPUBLICAN*, 12/25/87)

And as for all those
who wish to return
to those thrilling days of yesteryear
please, feel free

but for myself?
I've had a bellyful
of heroes
whose feats are made of clay

and therefore
hereby
declare myself
henceforth and forever
withdrawn from historical commerce

become unicorn
monocerous: flagless semaphore
        fingerless Braille
        silent Morse
        airless smoke signal
        last rub of last erasure
less real
than the white of this
                anonymous   space

One day it dawned on him—
that gradually it was ending now
and that he was still out there
living it, dying
as he always had
on nerve alone
everything dark and whitening
the West having lost its last hand
its noose hitching the notch to his neck
and him mustering the sand
to craft the character of style
to continue to grind
as he always had
to wager
another card: just   this one   more
if only he could hang on
keep, hanging, on, hold, out
last long enough to summon the next fume of breath
down miles
off mountainsides
skimmed from cirrus sky
or lifted through altitudes
of thin   blue-white   wind
clear as ether
as anything   anywhere   ever was
save the arid/empty weather   of his lungs
BUT, O—
how events had aged him
35 years OLD
health a wreck
sick enough to be better off dead
as if overnight all the killing had caught up at once

the death and dying
dealing   defying
had by some osmosis diminished him
depleted and curbed
left to live, die dwindled and dazed with whatever was left/over
the interminable slippage
unceasing declension & ageless decline
its long, slowwwwwww slide
this sleigh to the foot of the slope
where it waited
to softly inhale him at last

He would be dealing or playing or having a drink or taking a stroll or eating a meal or practicing offhand—for he continued to practice as diligently as he ever had—and he would be recognized, accosted or pestered, not so much by regular folk as by those who considered they had some ax to grind or bone to pick or beef to make or angle to play or license to take and most often he found himself at the mercy less of some pretergressing, crapulous Cowboy than of those scabrously sober scriveners who refused to leave him be until he had given them more than a "not now" for an answer.

So you would get exchanges along the lines of this one with an unbylined reporter from the Boulder *Comedian*:

Don't your conscience ever bother you, Doc?

Uh, no, Sir, not atall. Coughed that up with my lungs long ago.

But all the men you've laid to ice.

Some few, 'tis true there have been some few, but had there been the same thrice over it would have been of scant account to me.

Then indeed you are a cold one, Doctor, cold as they all say.

Begging your pardon, but I have no use for what they may say or leave unsaid. Such dodgast comes cheaper than two-dollar whores. Nor does it alter, for an instant, the truth.

Which is?

Why, that each of us lives shadowed by terror, and that such terror is more real than love. It lives, it breathes, it walks the earth as brute and as monstrous as God. What choice, then, but to meet it upon its own terms wherever it may arise, to locate its lair and stealing inside, face it down with the best of oneself as one might. No, we are given but one choice in this world.

Which is?

Why, to determine precisely which sort of wreck we may wish to make of our lives. That is, with which tool we may choose to dig our own dungeon, our fate being our affliction, and our affliction the sum of our plight. It is not, after all, about being born into darkness and slouching towards the light. There is no darkness, as there is no light. It is about being born into nothing and slouching towards nowhere. Or not slouching at all. No movement, direction, no towardness. Just inertia. Stasis. Reposing in place. In situ. No truth, save entropy. Lapse, and lull.

Happy thought, that.

All the same 'tis true. 'Tis true and nothing for it.

But how live then, in the face of such a truth, beneath the weight of such a fear? Why not just end it, end it all right here?

And what, Sir, do you consider has been my angle these past 10 years? No, death at one's own hand resolves nothing. I learned this long ago. Better to give oneself the sporting chance to outlast the dastardly aims of one's foes. To die in increments, wager by call. The other way is too common, and unbecomes me. Besides, in my case, it would have been just so . . . redundant. Still, I shan't call it the craven's way out. Indeed, for a man of certain parts, one of valor and honor I mean, such a gesture is the last card that he might play, the solitary trump, the single way that he might best God himself at his own game.

GAMES INDEED. YOU have gambled professionally for the better part of your life, have you not? How much might you estimate, then, that you have won, won or lost, along the way?

But I could not begin to think. I paid scant attention to such matters at the time, and can conceive of no method of calculating it now. It has been said by some that I won more money than any sporting man in the West. Who knows? If so, then I lost more in like measure. The problem, you see, was always the same—that I loved the play for its own sake, much as the moralist does virtue for its. Quitting while I was ahead never occurred to me. I suppose by then it had all become as much a part of who I was as what I did. My career, so to say.

Ah yes, your career. Would it be fair to say that violence, violence and death, have shadowed it more than most? More, perhaps, than any man upon the frontier?

'Twas my sainted mother who favored me with the wisdom: Pass by. Pass by, John Henry, those whom you do not love. But then she never had been West. Live West but the once, and what one learns at the outset is that death trumps love, every time. In the end, it is death that takes all. You, no less than myself, are already has-beens, always have been, has-beens just waiting to happen. One way or another, life shows its hand—it is nought but a cold-blooded killer.

A hard path, then, the one you have chosen to follow.

No man who lives his life as it deserves to be lived, no man who truly does right by himself, is wont to escape its living unscathed. The world, Sir, is shit, as life, in sum, much the same.

How deny it? That there exists the world without, and another within, and each to the depletion of each, until what once was redoubled is undone and decoupled, left halved, and by wholes incomplete. What purpose in pretending otherwise? For myself, I choose to find it diverting, it amuses me, and insofar as others may choose to differ, that is none of my affair—save as it may merit my laughter. I leave it to others to leap, place their faith feet-first in the dance. A man in as delicate a condition as mine cannot afford to misspend the effort, bucking the reality, maintaining the facade, nursing the illusion along; he cannot suffer the strain of the pretense. In the end, that which is required to reconcile the fraud—the joy of this life, the wonder of just being alive, God in a grain of sand or the eye of a cod—so elaborate a hoax could take the breath away, and I haven't, you may rest assured, the spare breath to waste. No, better to celebrate, if celebrate one must, that it is all just a form of slow murder, to live life in such a manner that by the time one arrives at its end, one is not only willing but impatient to have it so. That way, when it comes, as it one day must come for us all, at least one can go out with a smile on one's face. For if one cannot see the humor in one's own death, then one has not lived any sort of life worth the long labor of its arrantly ridiculous living.

And after you pass, what then? How is it you'd like to be remembered, Doc? What would you have people say?

Say? Why, Sir, I should consider that they will say what they will, and as I shan't be there to hear it, not a word, what ought it matter to me? My legacy? The word itself posits my absence. 'Tis true I've ordered much of my life expressly to cheat Mister Death. But my legacy? Fame? Its barley-bree? (I heard someone call it that once: bree, broth, broo, the why in the rye of it, the halo on the head of the brew.) No, fame I consider a pest. The way it would have you inhabit your life, like an uninvited guest. That, or scatter your name like ashes on the winds of a pestilent past. 'Tis true the devil seldom pays court to those named John Doe or Plain Jane or Dumb Mary, still, all in all, here, take it, you can have immortality. Listen, as anything someone says about anyone while they are alive is largely a lie, I cannot conceive of the tangle of fiction that must get spun about them, the opprobrium and obloquy that must be heaped—much, I might observe, as manure is heaped—once they are otherwise. It would be plain discouraging, were it not meanwhile so meaningless. For if there is one thing I have learned in this life, it is that people do not change, ever. They do not evolve, improve or get better with age. At best they simply become more of the same, more of who they were in the first place. The rest, all of it, is nought but shit masquerading as syrup.

Then you mean to say, as I take it, that you are quite indifferent as to how history may pronounce its judgment upon you?

History! Sweet Christ! What use have I for history? Save to make it up as I go along. No, what I mean to say, Sir, is that while none of this may have been meant to happen—and certainly not in just the way that it has—what conceivable difference can that make now? The philosopher instructs us that as we may disapprove of our world, so ought we feel free to remake it to suit ourselves, and I have, I have availed myself of that freedom each day for the past 15 years, and so can affirm—such freedom as that?—'tis the same as being locked without parole in a cage. Do you know *The Epic of Gilgamesh*? "We must treasure the dream, whatever the terror, for the dream has shown that misery comes at last to the healthy man. The end of life is sorrow." Because life is impossible, you see. At its heart. Utterly inconceivable. And so one must only seek the shelter of its margins, dwell upon its periphery, that violet brink—and do more than just look down. But here, with your permission, Sir, I have . . . well, I would be curious as to your opinion as a man of letters. I call them my *membra disjecta*, scattered leavings you see, mere postils, really, these jottings that over the years I have troubled myself to *un*scatter, gather and order as I have found the time or been struck by the inclination, if not, to be sure, that I might claim for their quality aught but the rank amateur. Perhaps your readers might find them instructive. A moment ago you made mention of my legacy. I reckon I would not object too much were what follows to be considered in that light.

the path of death is always underfoot
—ROBERT LOWELL

He had heard tell of the Yampah Springs. Mineral baths. Underground salts. Steam and sulphur pots. Mountain spa, its marble-benched vapor caves south of the river there. World's largest hot springs pool, 615 by 75 feet, 2 percent dissolved sodas and sodiums, 120 degrees F., pumping out three million gallons a day, over a mile above sea level.

Someone had told him. Wyatt? Kate? Never mind. Someone. Yampah being a Ute Indian word meaning Big Medicine. Ever notice, he thought, how many Indian words mean that? Mean medicine, miracle, magic, mystical power, secret spirit, lucky charm, holy vision? How many words they had for wonder? That *duende*? Ever wonder, why wonder why?

Maybe it was worth a shot. To go to Glenwood. Glenwood Springs. Canyon of the Yampah. Where the Colorado and Roaring Fork conflute. Check into that tony hotel there, corner of 8th and Grand, one said to boast electric lights and hot and cold running water in each room. Take the vapors, breathe the healing, mend some. Look into the 22 saloons crammed into the square of its two-block downtown.

What could it hurt? Manufacture a little health. Why not? A little rehab and decumbiture. Regeneration. Remission. Ease of some convalescent lift. This lifetime's last roll of the dice. Last pass/at the last rampart.

Because here lately, his lungs, by pairs, were absolutely killing him.

Surely the dying must sense what a sham it all is, that nothing is really itself

—RILKE

Suffering brings out the showman in a person

—RICHARD POWERS

Earlier that morning he had taken stock of himself on the upright physician's scale that sentried the hotel's front entrance on the boardwalk outside. Fully clothed—boots, hat, pocket watch, hipflask (filled) and rig included—he had weighed exactly 113 pounds. Mere newel post. Hell, he had known shadows to weigh more at the height of high noon.

Now, retired to his room after a breakfast he had found himself too disinterested to make a dent in, the white-haired stick figure—sallow and sunken-cheeked, stoop-backed and slump-shouldered—sagged onto the foot end of the bed and grasped as might an invalid the knobs of his knees, steadying himself before reaching inside his coatflap to fish from its breast pocket a small, stub-handled handmirror. For several seconds he gazed wordlessly and at apparent depth into the image reflected there, then slowly harrowed a hand through his hair fingering the features of his face as if making their acquaintance for the first time. Terra incognita; he no longer bore a semblance of resemblance to himself.

Here of late it was becoming habit, ritual even, studying the remains, often for hours on end. Turning this way and that, scrutinizing each groove and hollow, bag and droop, sag and crease, pucker and pooch, squint-line and crow's-foot, every declension and declivity with a mortician's fastidiousness, or a forensic

325

pathologist's. And yet too confounded to opine whether that which he beheld was beautiful, or ugly, or simply nondescript. He no longer recognized the aesthetics of himself.

If only. If only there was a way to pry open the chrome, peel back the scrim of silver wide enough to permit what it contained to tumble onto the floor fractured at his feet where he might, with some considered reflection, undertake to piece himself together again. If only. Was there ever a pair of more pitiable, of more piteously profitless words?

The fit of hocking that in its fanfare consumed him did so as does water risen loudly to engulf a drowning man, the waves in their churn so violently convulsing his diminished, clench-eyed form that they threatened to spring each cuff free of its coupling. Ignoring as he might the racking, he groped limply for the flask at his hip, retrieved it with no little difficulty, fumbled hurriedly to unscrew its cap, and raised its mouth to his own pouring a drams-man's portion full upon the uptilt down the subfloor of his throat.

"Here's to you then," he said aloud, eyes fixed upon the mirror. "The final gallop."

Then . . . winked.

Having done, he did not smack his lips nor complain with an aaaaaah of the burn, but slowly opened like puncti each of his blood-razzled eyes; they swam in the sinks of their sockets as some yolks run red through their whites.

"Laudanum and rye whiskey," he said. "Torture on the lungs, taffy for the brain." A liability of the solitariness of his circum-stance; it scarce had escaped his notice that he had been doing more of it of late—talking to himself aloud.

The scrape and blow of his breathing, its anhelation no less labored than that of one who has just run a race, wheezed as the collapse of a bellows, yet he found the racket, the drone of it, oddly comforting, a reminder, however disquieting, that he still

was, if just barely, alive. It was sitting upright he was having difficulty managing.

Placing the mirror facedown on the bed beside him, he tapped
its surface twice lightly with a thumbpad, then capped and returned the flask to its hideout. "Roll of the dice," he muttered,
flopping back headfirst across the bed. He felt like a rag. He felt at
the wit's end of his wringing. "All of it, but a roll of the dice."

That the fix was in, had always been, that was old news. No, it
was who had put there, on whose say, and why, that was what he
never had been able to reckon. Not that it would have altered a
thing if he had. Time, after all, did not heal or mend, repair or put
right, but wounded—repeatedly, deliberately, deep and indelibly,
nor relented until the last blow proved mortal. Time was death's
jackal—he could smell the scat of its squat—and its day drew
nigh.

Locating the mirror with the flex of his fingers, he scissored it
towards him down the length of the bed raising it by its handle
before holding it at arm's length above his head; still he could not
make himself out, ascribe to what he ascertained there a name. So
strange, this stranger.

Was there, he wondered, such a thing as objective beauty? It
was not, to his knowledge, much-rumored, but could not what
appears ugly at first be but beauty masked by its moment? Perhaps beauty required time to reveal itself, invent itself, reinvent itself even. Time to emerge. Why not? Could not what appears
ugly today appear beautiful tomorrow? Or the next day? Or the
year after that? It might take centuries. Still, must beauty by definition be timeless? Was it so inconceivable that ugliness might be,
was merely . . . beauty, becoming? That flaw, this blemish, imper-
fection, mar, that pock or stain, mutilation, scar, could not beauty
lurk there as well, inside, underneath, in between?

"I believe that I shall agree with the poet," he said of a sudden. "Why, beauty is nought but the beginning of horror. And why? How so? HA! Because there is the look of too much blood beneath it." And in his head composed a poem.

> *And were your arm to wither and die*
> *what then? Would you shrink*
> *shy and ashamed*
> *from its shriveled stump being seen or*
> *shake it*
> *noisily*
> *like me*
> *for the whole world to see*
> *how it suffers*

He still was looking at the mirror when he disappeared. He disappeared into, up and inside of it. He did not quite know how he had come to repose, poured there, did not know why, did not want to know (not really), but as he looked down, he saw himself lying there, looking up, transfixed, rapt, yet still unable to recognize himself, or rather, recognizing what he saw there as unrecognizable, aware that were he to manage it, to fathom the unfathomable, it would only be to decrypt the reflection of the face he hated more than any other in the world.

Now he considered sticking his tongue out at it, almost did, stopped himself short. He was too afraid, afraid that in doing so he would burst into tears, begin to weep and never stop, that his tears would fall in flinders to the floor sharding there shattered in sherds—or splattered threefold in spales. Flakes of ice in a globe of glass. So then, what good is a mirror? he thought. What good is a mirror if it cannot be turned inside out? For how else keep what is caged there, captured?

And this was the way it was becoming: a face without features, body without definition, mind without ideas, self without opinions, voice without inflection, or an intelligible word to say. Or rather, all that, more, but none of it that he might decode. What was keeping him aloft now was purely a mystery. Unless it was the armature of his thought. Perhaps it was the architecture of his imagination that was keeping him propped upright. This ossature, each socket and spindle.

What must it be like to be possessed of an invisible self? He did not pose the question. Not quite. Not like that. Not yet. He still was applying himself, editing and so forth, coming to it, working towards it, circuit by compass by step. One does not embrace one's own disembodiment, after all, without the proper soul-sleuthing, or having lain with right rigor the groundwork. Still, what must it be like, to render oneself transparent? Comprise one's own vanishing act? Dissolved and deliquesced. Come to silica and silts, pollens and powders, the talcs that blanch white with the rains. What must that be like? To disappear before one's own incredulous eyes, pale as a wrist trailing alban through lolly, or a rose bleeding out at the vein? Reduced/at last/to divot. Become skywriting absent sky.

There is soon to be no more, he thought, no more at any moment of catching a glimpse of oneself—*grotesque!*—unfit to grace the mirror in this frame. For he was living solely off his body now, or his body off of him, the way a bird of prey—buteo, say, or bateleur—lives off the carcass of the land. Land, the eroding lay of it, that left little to be succored or profitably skimmed.

I must beware, be aware, take care the leap of faith that would fall repeatedly short of its mark. And yet where then might beauty reside, if not on the opposite side of this void? So run. Leap. Fly. But away from what? Or towards whom?

And had you been there to hear, you might have remembered his words: "Further," he said then. "I must run further. I must vault, yes, catapult, fling myself forward still-whole, out as ever-inward, I must plunge as I am able, after more."

———•◦•◦•———

He who has never felt, momentarily,
what madness is, has but a mouthful of brains
—MELVILLE

(Just this: being unable to control the *eddy* of one's imagination or key open the cuffs on one's passion.)

Upward
leaping,
ever upward through the loam,
to the blare of 100 blazing bugles
and one burnished blue
trombone

Come on in now, you last of the pains I will admit,
incurable, into my body's web . . .
You burn me, but I inside your burning burn

—RILKE

NO MORE FAIR days, damn few middlin' ones; the aubades have ceased; no respite, as no repose.

Each morning awakened now more weakened, diminished, deficit, and the sheets so clammed with sweat he is obliged to wade from his nightclothes as a swimmer through fetters of surf. The mountain clime, mineral baths, the alcohol and tincture of opium, none of it is working anymore.

He negotiates the days each moment fugued with fever. His eyes shine with it, burn, bore bright as open wounds. The pain he knows is seismic, diaphragm-deep, miraculously wrong, wondrously unwelcome, worlds beyond what anyone ought be required to endure, and yet the tangle of it—for he is stranded there no less hapless than a moth hobble-cobbed to its web, its verriculum of ambient punishment—scarce feels part of him. It is too other, unearthly, aerated, yet too infernally alive, so . . . present, so diabolically clear and uncontained in the blaze of its immediacy, so oceaned—or no, so skied—that it washes as in waves over ridges, drafting him up, up and up, dizzying the heights of him, each muscle of air this meal of pain. It bedazzles him, assails, spelds and humbles. He feels savaged by its splurge. Sea-ed inside its lymphs. His lungs are swallowing themselves at last. He breathes through batter, exhales exhaust, hemorrhages sprue, lung-thrushed. He is losing. It is in the cards. The final humiliation. Every gambler's instinct tells him so: the hand he holds ought have been folded, long ago.

He gives himself a matter of weeks. Bricked up. Bricked in. In hell. And yet, his mind/just/flying, athrum with anthems and encores, arias, with first rites and last acts, this denouement and finale. He must dredge as he delves it, describe the arc of the dive, shape words of the descent, quarry the clays of its gorge. While the wit yet remains, some few moments of pellucidity—this tremor of pen to epistle, where, in the accretion of words, then still more words, the dying souls of those departed sentences, every fiction refracts the truth, the truth mutes the lies of the legend, and such myth as persists aspires to its own reclamation.

9.3.87

Dearest Cousin
Martha Anne
Mattie
Mel
Sister Mary Melanie

I write you from my bed where more latterly I have been confined while death stalks me like a dowser. It would seem that my lungs, dear Cousin, have let me down at last, though perhaps caught up with me is more apt. The distinction hardly matters; each day I feel more the fossil.

Do you recall when I left home? (Home! Was it ever really that? I no more write the word than it conjures images of . . . nothing.) Can you remember then what I was told? Six months, they said, a year at most. Well, it has been some measure more than that, however mean and meager, and each thought now, the way they utter, "Dice Thrown!"

And still 'tis not enough. I reckon one always feels one's life cut shorter than is just, though how justice might be said to obtain in such matters, I would not dare suppose. (After all, where nothing sustains, everything obtains.) No, for 15 years I played with nothing but house money. How complain of it now?

I beseech you, Cousin, do not be distressed, but rather keep me close-by in your prayers. You know I am no right God-fearing man, nor ever aspired to be, but if I have not lived a saintly life—or even one much on the side of the angels—neither have I pursued one so tarred with sin as some would have it broadcast. I do not write you in Christ, then, late convert to the cross—my hypocrisy has its limits—but if you would deign to hear it at this distance, it would please me much should you consider the document before you a facsimile of that which those of your faith call, I believe, a confession. The Mind, it has been said, is the abiding hermit of its own purity, so here, as it may delight you, this pureness of expression.

But permit me, first, to remark how deeply I admire your recent renunciation of the world, and the beauty of the logic that can only have inspired the gesture—this way of getting right with the odds of the game by betting your all on His heaven. Oh, to aspire to such largeness of character myself, to be possessed of the breadth of imagination to believe that the angels will not welsh and that God must pay off in the end. Religion is a wager, is it not? A bet on the chance of the reward of true faith? A roll of the dice with one's soul? Where, dear Cousin, wherever did you find the nerve? I might gamble all day with the devil, but to call God's own bluff? No, I fear 'tis not for me, your church of cards, however much I might envy you the solace of having arrived at its shelter.

Cousin, notwithstanding such appearances as may redound to the contrary, believe me when I say, I never intended for my life to resonate, that it merit the attention of others, much less become the object of their curiosity. Fossil I may be, but to descend to the realm of artifact? No! May God forbid it!

I always have been a private person, more private than a

ghost, and now that I am to die—I suffer no discomfit in saying the word—I find that I am of all things most unthinkable, much the public personage! That my bones ought provide the occasion for their sacking, the remnants of my life be exhumed and paraded as a story for the idle amusement of strangers, its scraps scavenged and scrounged, sifted and scrumped for an order that might be marshaled iron and ink into type, such a prospect appalls almost as much as it galls me. To have it all reduced to peepshow, to extravaganza and spectacle, some huckster's idea of pastiche, to have it hyped and hustled and spun until I must myself but twirl in the grave—it sticks, dear Cousin, it sticks like a coign in the craw.

What can it mean, Mel, to recede into legend? To become but the mist of a myth? I cannot begin to imagine, though nothing good I'd wager. Perhaps it means to be reduced to one's meaning, a meaning that may or may not be true, but that can only be less than wholly human, as it must be wholly incomplete. There are those who would have us believe that as everything is possible, so nothing is certain, an admirable sentiment, surely, yet one that succeeds in getting it precisely backwards. No, most things are inconceivable, and those few that are not, inescapable, where not utterly beyond our control. Are you familiar with karma? Perhaps this is that, the way I am to pay off my debt, and go on forever paying:

it's not enough they take your life away with a gun
they have to take it away with their pens

It is said that in time it must become the object of this life less to die—any fool can do that, as in time every fool does—than to back out of it with the ease of a winner. And so I have a favor to beg of you: as the occasion is bound to arise once I am gone, remind them, would you, that I lived far more than their damnable fiction, that I was real, as fledged and fully flawed in flesh and blood, no more a piece of commerce than themselves. I am far from sanguine that you shall succeed in this, in righting the record—sooner, I fear, unweave a rainbow—but perhaps your voice as it may join with those of certain of my better associates shall be listened to in earnest by some discerning few.

That I invented some of it is regrettably true. An indiscretion of youth, nor a soul to blame but myself. Perhaps we all do it to an extent, fabricate ourselves, make it up upon the spot and as we go along. Certainly I had been given, or so I felt at the time, reason enough to do so. I found myself alone and dying, exiled to a strange and savage place, a place where it was one's reputation, however doctored, that helped one outlast the dawn. (I have read that what an exile really is, is someone who not only once lost a home—much as I long ago lost Georgia—but who cannot find another. The West was my playground, or my purgatory; what it never was, was my home. How make a home in such a place? Inconceivable!) And so, yes, I did, I manufactured my own, mindful of having trained my eye upon the clock, knowing full well that a man's reputation is seldom the man who inhabits it, any more than the cut of his cutaway frock.

Even so, I never did less than belong wholly to myself, relied upon no one, trusted solely to chance, sought no absolution, expiation, no remission of sin, atoned for nothing, counted upon less, save to live and die as I might choose, upon my own hook, alone and dragon, assailing the sun. Cousin, believe it, my regrets are few.

A thousand pardons should you find this letter so soon tiresome in its self-aggrandizing. All this brooding over one's place in posterity, the foofaraw of these last things, December's fanfaronade. I can conceive of nothing more wearying than to dwell upon penultimacy, save as it is the imminent state of one's own. I fear 'tis one of my most glaring weaknesses: left to my own devices, I lapse headlong into eschatology. Well, being dead, says the poet, is hard work, and I do not doubt it, though perhaps it is in the dying that the real killer lies.

You have, I shall presume, heard the talk. That once I was much the Bengal Tiger. It pains me ineffably to consider that you should think it so. I never was (though often enough I was hunted like one, chevvied pillar to post one end of the country to the other; it was a matter less of keeping one step ahead of their noose than two to the rear of their nostrums). No, if I mixed up in such as came along—and that I did my share of mixing I shan't gainsay, for I wished, 'tis true, to hasten my fate, not idly to outwit it—it was alone owing to it being the only way I ever found to forget myself. I grew to abhor the virtues of restraint, as I did that stillness that shimmers with silence. And so, not wishing to wait, I invited myself to the dance, however much it might prove but a dirge in the end. And for this I am condemned? Deviant, yes, from time to time. Decadent. Debauched, perhaps. On occasion even perverse. But depraved? No, that I never was.

I prefer that no man judge me. Indeed I have oft troubled myself to insist upon the prerogative. Dying will take care of itself, in the meanwhile it will turn any man dangerous, and I was dying every day. Suffering alters anyone, and the price of salvation is steep beyond counting when the cost of everything is all that one holds most dear. Still, I find it fascinating, the capacity the common run possesses for cherishing their killers while for the victims not a word in sympathy save in thanks for letting themselves be killed. But then, perhaps all men are killers of some sort. It is simply that a few have more assiduously perfected the art.

So my thanks in advance to no one. The world is not a school for the making of souls, but a crucible for their murder, and insofar as one pledges oneself willing to resort to the violent gesture, people sense this and prefer to keep their distance. How blame them? Most men, if killers, at heart are cowards too—their lives are ordered mainly by their fears, their flight from what they suppose may humiliate and beleaguer them—and their cowardice has largely suited me. But I am compelled to ask at last, is it my fault that people are so unimaginative that they find inconceivable the notion that one might make covenant with a positive carnage?

It is late, Cousin, and I ramble, but consider: life happens, however much we may object to its course, and then we may curse it for its happening to us without our consent, our permission or say-so, even, at times, without our really knowing it. It drags us along, or down, thrashing headlong and bewildered, brawling, bawling, braying at every furlong, or for the more fortunate few, basking upon their backs. We live not as we may, but as we must. What will be, will in time be undone. The best-laid plans, as the noblest of intentions, whiten to ash in our hands. Life is seldom sweet, or as it is, never near enough. None of us get the life we deserve, or as we do, live to regret it. Name me three things that are not unavailing, two that have ever prevailed.

I know, I sound harsh, harsher than I intend. And yet, is life in the living any less so? The world, Mel, is in error, as you well know, distorted darkly, knurled, warped as wayward wood, the griffin through its grain, its gargoyle in the burl.

So where the palliative, Mel? Tell me. Where the antidote? Dear God, Melanie, where the vaccine?

Once, as a youth, those days when we were both so young—do you remember them as clearly as do I, for in all candor, I remember them scarce atall—I had been possessed of the conceit that I might render of my life a minor masterpiece. Poetry, song, the savor of the fairer sex, such was my breeding as it was likewise the turn of my temperament. (As the poet says: I preferred flowers, and breathing.) I still can recall the promise I made myself: to think nothing but beautiful thoughts. I wished then for nothing but to live a courtly life and so dreamed of doing deeds of knightly valor, to garland myself in *glorie*. All I wanted, Mattie, all I ever wanted was to be the hero of my own life. More's the pity, then, that the hand I was dealt was littered so with jokers.

I was 22 when they bequeathed my life for the daisies. Well, I suspect it shan't be long before I keep my assignation with that particular species of flower.

Two subjects always have haunted me, though I never let on to a soul, not even to Kate, dear Kate, my Kate, especially not to Kate, who now is nowhere near. But you are, Mattie, you are near, you are here, I can feel it, you are here in this room, and so I will presume to make mention of them to you, a form of keepsake, for you, and you alone.

History, Mattie—hi story—that is the first. The idea of it, Mel, strikes me as utterly preposterous, where not the more pointless still. Pointless because by definition it is so delinquent, because it arrives at every party tardy, because it comes along too late to make a difference. History is unpunctual, it is surrogate, and each year it is increasingly scuffed. Time has trampled there; its footprints still run riot. No, history is slow, too slow to emerge, and when it finally hatches such overtrodden plots as it may please itself to orchestrate, they usually prove . . . nothing. Mystic Chords of Memory? Please! Spare me. The only history that ever mattered was that which went unrecorded, as my own—the poxed and pestilent truth of it—surely someday shall; this "Much Ado About Doc."

People can study the past until they are blue in the face and they still will make a muck of the present, squander their lives as if every hour were expendable and the future but a form of black farce. Time is not a salve, it resolves nothing; it is a solvent, it dissolves all. It does not dance, march, or so much as stately flow. It performs no steps, contains no design, manifests no direction at all. You will pardon the blasphemy, Cousin, but God is not a choreographer, and insofar as He may be said to have composed of the past a symphony, it contains but one sour note after another. No, what history does best is hide.

And so this caution: be wary, Mel, be wary of the ways of its telling, for at last, what is it but a form of weather? That which brooks no going back and cannot be replicated. That which once was what it was, and no longer is what it is, and with which one never can acquaint oneself sufficiently to so much as a single purposeful end. It is that which does what it pleases, imperfectly.

Filing system? Framing device? Staging area? Account book? No! History is time's dumping ground, that's all, the place where the lies lie heaped. History comes and it goes and cannot be possessed. It is time filling itself with behavior. It is time fulfilling itself in its own image. It is time over and gone and long past, never to come round again. Time bereft of its air, that is your precious history. DEAD time, then. As in: certainly I must die soon, and thenceforward my history—cut short, storyless, its silence nought but dischord—blacken like blood.

Oh my. Do I sound embittered? 'Tis not so, not atall. What I am, all I am, is tired. Merely tired. I am so deeply tired, dear Melanie.

And so we come, as come we must, to stories (for which, as I recall, you likewise share an aversion, save those to be found in your Scripture). After all, there are none—are there?—nor ever have been, not one, save those that we make up. And each of those too tidy to be trusted, where not too glib to be believed. Too wrought, overfraught, too clear and full of—what?—well, cunning I suppose, the cunning of coherence, portentous meaning, facile motive, or such morals as in their foxing make for drama, where not the pretext of suspense.

I wish to ask you a perfectly serious question: who needs a

story to mimic how make-believe characters feel or mime how they are purported to think? Who needs a story to . . . depict? I don't.

No, more stories—if stories there must be—ought strive for being, to just be, stand free, unto themselves, apart, *ex nihilo*, alone. Because a GOOD Story—one that's worth its storying in the first place—does not arrive plattered upon its silver, wrapped primly in a package, encased like kielbasa or a brat inside its sheath. No. Nor cherried with a bow. It does not come coiled neatly in a meat hive to resemble links along a wurst, or even soldier forward briskly in trim echelons like an army gone to war. A GOOD Story must be, well, it must be so much more.

Consider: anyone can tell a story all they want. Anyone can. Anyone can tell anything at all about anyone, tell a story one way, the same or some way. Can or could. As it's said they should. The old way, the way anyone could. So if you're going to tell one, why not tell another? Make its telling other? As other as it, itself, may suffer. Or why bother in the first place? We have spoken of the boy-poet before, have we not?: "Inspecting the invisible and listening to the unheard of is something other than reviving the spirit of dead things . . . Inventing the unknown calls for new forms."

The truth is, there is nothing to say, not a word, there is nothing worth saying about anything. So keep still, remain silent, act dumb, go mute. Say NO! (I often think that the gesture of purest aggression is that of simply withholding—affection, wisdom, grace.) At least that way I shan't become whatever the world wishes to make of me, what anyone might imagine everyone else wants to make of me, or insists that I must be—myth or fable, lore or legend, parable of the unpardonable past, yellowing now and shadowless, but a shade of my disinterred self. It was Mallarmé who said it best: Pursue black on white as one will, what else is putting down the quill, than the "rhythmical suspending of defeat."

If I were a story, one of those BAD ones I mean, I would go

out in a blaze of glory. I understand that. I understand that much at least. But no one does that anymore, if anyone ever did. Nowadays one just grows dim, dim as an old dime pitched down a well into darkness. (And as for the notion that stories can alter one's life—much less save one or transfigure the future—I have never heard such preposterous, pretentious, unregenerate rot in all my blackly born days. Stories are for suckers, suckers who prefer their suckling one finger raised to the wind, the other enamored of what lies north of their knees.)

And so I have only this instant decided: I shall come to death drowning, drowning in the dark. Why not? At least that way I shan't die inventing heartwrenching new tales or making up page-turning yarns. Imagine. The dampness in the loam there, where no man's lode lies coldly, where each man lies alone. Left/alone. At last. Tell me, is that not also a kind of victory?

Dear Mel, it is said that none of us may foreknow what is going to happen, or what time may hold in store, but perhaps we know more than we allow. That we shall not be treated kindly. That we shall buckle beneath a flurry of low blows. That we shall be left betrayed and sore abandoned to founder alone each in our way. That we will pray for direction and find none, for faith where none might be had. That we will shear our hair, rend our garments, slash at our breast with each loss and in the end, unredeemed, unreconciled, out of time and breath and mind, sip too deeply of the squandering of the best we might better have been.

North in time goes South. What once was sweet turns sour. Young to old, beauty to beast, truth to the falsehood of fiction. The condition of life is its loss, the condition of life is defeat, the condition of life is to grieve for its dying or destroy—ha! I had written it "de-story," so be it then, de-story those who would bring one to grief.

And so I ask you, dear Cousin, life being lived only at its
peril, might it not require as many miracles of faith to sustain it as
it does accidents of fate to expend?

Perhaps it *is* only an accident that I lived as long as I did, or
perhaps it is rather a miracle, though in the living it felt less like either one than a mindless exercise in marking off the illusion of
time. Or:

an indefinite reprieve from what was definitely coming

the way saddled me of waiting around while I ran out the
string

the plight to which I was sentenced, in my own way to waste

a futile stay of execution

a fiddling away of what I otherwise failed to fritter

a joke in poor taste turned back against its teller

a meaningless stretch of pointless incarceration

ongoing dysfunction

erratum ad infinitum

Golgotha, squared

a bungled experience in emergency management

an all too long visit without much to do

a spot of mindless diversion before events turned deadly
serious

a protracted period of ambuscade culminating in its own
holocaust

much ado about nothing very much

a temporary inconvenience

earthbound incapacity

the rub of the matter and rue

an inevitable passing through

the worricow borne through the blood

a whiling away beside the grave beneath the weight of a long
day's dying

a luxury the debt on which can never be paid

that which I arbitrarily was given that it might be deliberately taken away

nothing all so much to lose

an empty gesture in enduring what from the outset was obviously foredoomed

a determined casting about after serial disappointment

an as yet unwritten obituary

a death certificate awaiting its filing

that which filled itself with its hollowed self alone

a few moments when the soul kept the corpse ambulatory

being marooned on an eroding island not of one's own making

sowing the ground at one's feet better to receive one's imminent burial, piecemeal by piece

a mandatory period of pre-interment

being sick unto death of always feeling this way

squatting over a latrine rigged to blow, evacuating the decayed contents of one's soul—stir-about, gruel, black crawstone, cold stew

passing the same kidney stone night after night

an unpleasant interval between nothing and nothing

a harassment of self-conscious time

the wound that bleeds eternally backwards

contributing as one will in one's fashion to the farce of the ongoing fiasco

one long humiliation, beginning to humdrum end

And yet even so, though often enough I was accused of it, I never once wooed death, I never did, however much I may on occasion have contrived to endanger it some. (Though looking back, there was indeed the feeling that by dying one might at least escape the *longing for* death.) You are familiar, perhaps, with the

concept of necromimesis; it never was for me. And so—wha.
else?—now here it is befallen me, the last reproach for having had
the temerity, or cowardice, to dare live long enough to linger. Ah,
Cousin, what is man but the creature who knows that he must
die? I look in the mirror and the death's head grinning back at
me, though I no longer recognize it as that of the man I know
myself to be, can belong to no one other. Perhaps 'twas always
thus, the only gift I ever had—to ensure that in the end what is
bad turns out so much the worse.

And what an end, this one. Such a piddling period to place at
the end of such a tortured, unparseable sentence. This end to all
the outlasting. Or:

a break in the inaction

interim *ad nauseam* and middling *interruptus*

a permanent yawn

a lapse into timelessness

an unnatural hiatus from nothing

a cure-all for life and what ails it

longer-lingering mercy

a mildly interesting form of crisis intervention

a dousing of the flames on a fire long gone cold

unending intermission

a severing of the receipt of a garbled transmission

posthumous nonexistence

indifference in perpetuity

a certain minor difficulty in continuing to persist

a positive correction in life's ho-hum imbalance

a mortal error in divine judgment

replacing what was with who knows

a last moment of who cares before the next wave of nothing

the final affront of the ultimate defeat

a lowering of the curtain on a dark and empty stage

welcome, much longed-for relief

ongoing ennui

a senseless cessation of the senselessness preceding it

the fate of the fait accompli

inevitable predetermined indeterminacy

the closing performance of a play that never opened

the perpetual coercion of a little peace and quiet

lights out on what was badly lit from the first

the permanent vacating of a formerly occupied vacuum

the everlasting vanishing act

this, anthrax

travesty heaped upon farce

that which can never be known about which one did not know one knew until that instant, nothing.

Ah well, what *is* the noise that a shadow makes? A shadow, when it falls.

Here then, Mel, is what I mean to say: that while I would mightily prefer not to—I've grown rather used to existing by now, fallen into the habit so to say; after all, in the end, what else is there to do?—I am not afraid to die. I never have been, at least not so I can recall. And it is that single fact that ever made me, to the extent that it did, different. Not better, and perhaps even worse, but different. It was a difference that men in the main mainly sensed, and so content to keep their distance. Death, after all, was not *their* domain, they kept no covenant with its ablutions, were not familiar with the stink of its intimacy, the cold wind of its breath a blade to their necks. Or as they were, it rendered them uneasy, uneasy and fearful. Well, I never was uneasy. Nor am I fearful. 'Tis no boast when I say, it does not scare me.

There were any number of men along the way who mistook this for courage, and as it suited my purpose in the moment, I encouraged them in their error. But there is no point in pretending with you, Mel, not anymore. It never was bravery—that mysterious word—but that I had carried it around with me for so long, felt the germ of it growing inside me as I might imagine a woman must feel her own child in the womb, that I had come to think of it as part of me, part of who I was, and would always be.

I will not say that I succeeded in making it, the fear of it, my friend—though I tried, O God, how I tried—but that I enlisted it as an ally, honored it, endeavored to be worthy of it that I might face it each day with a measure of equanimity, some shred of dignity and low humor. I wished to come to it singing songs, you see, singing songs and saying poems. Well, it never was my friend, I know that now, but that I earned its respect, yes, that I believe I did do. In my fashion.

Surrender. Somehow I never could seem to bring myself to it with another human being, but I learned to do it with death—or its specter. It was the only way I could think to render it powerless.

I never was one to seek after all the answers, merely the few it pleased me to pursue, and those no further than so far. I never aspired to know everything about everything—a thing or two about a thing or two seemed more than enough to me. Why presume to what others would call wisdom when there is none, no canopy of explanation, wheel of truth, stair of accountability, well of being, no wisdom at all, save the one that so singly matters: *morior ergo sum.*

For 15 years I called death's bluff, and for 15 years I won. Fifteen years, Mel! For 15 years I was perfect. They couldn't touch me. Never made a dent, never caused a wrinkle, never gave me so much as a moment's sober pause. Aw, Mattie, they never laid a glove on me.

I may never have, despite the whispers to the contrary, been nvincible—none of us are—but perhaps I was something more. I was immaculate, and self-conceived. I have heard it remarked that the best revenge on death is to live long, live slowly and well, and if I have failed to exact my own with just the proper *pacing*, if I lived far too fast, and am dying much too young, and shan't be leaving behind such a comely-looking corpse, still, it was one helluva streak while it lasted, it was a streak for all the ages, and just because my last hand proved a loser

And here the letter endeth. Apparently it never was completed. Or as completed never posted. Or as posted never received. Or as received later lost. Or deliberately burned, "that the world might keep from knowing," as Sister Melanie later cryptically remarked when first the Gentlemen of the Press and later those of the Archive came a-calling, "a different man from the one who died forsaken and faithless, the figure of Western fame."

Sicker by the hour with the drama, the tremens of his trau
addresses his penknife adrift to the grain on the vertical sla
down the bedpost in his room having mustered enough of some
leftover passion to cleave it clean open through phloem into cam-
bium past xylem to the core of its duramen:

R

E

L

I

E

F

as if to whittle up some shelter
from the pith of the heartwood
in the blank eye of this whitening storm

the sunk untreasured chest
the hollow of its trove
where lungs churn breath to cream
its clabber centuries old
while all about it crumbles
hard as last hellos
the blighted bark
its silver moss
a man
unmanned to mold

Like a tiger whose leap has failed:
this is how I have often seen you . . .
a throw you made had failed. But
what of that, you dice-throwers! . . .
If great things you attempted have
turned out failures, does that mean
you yourselves are—failures?

—NIETZSCHE

And so, if only to reiterate: ***Un coup de dés jamais***
n'abolira le hasard.

I dream of the code of the West

—TED BERRIGAN

So far outside his own experience now, beyond the conceiving of any world he might invent, the laying on of metaphor, any healing word, so lost and unclaimed to himself that there simply was no avenue he might walk or way back of which he might avail himself that could help him traverse the terrain he still must travel.

He had come unhorsed. Unsaddled. His life had bucked him off.

Now he was dying, even in his dreams.

———·••·———

DEEPBENT ON ALL fours crawling a colonnade of trees hands ahead of knees down a gantlet of sky-vaulting trunks, their boles brightly emblazoned, giant crayons stood on end, Technicolor versicolorate colossi, this carnival stand of untoppled tall timber, balloon colors in a Crayola place, a rendering by Monet or Renoir—or, no, Matisse. And a wind rising wailing whirling, a wind swirling wild-high in a gunmetal sky banging about the boughs so he half expects to see sparks, tracers twirling, the shrapnel of rainbows, starstreamer rockets fly. And though the sound churns his thoughts to pinwheels, as to flags his finer feelings, on he creeps, head high and attentive, hunting for the source of the squealing. Sees them snagged in the upraised arms of the branches as if snatched clean out of the air, or lowered there as by nacelle emplaced like ornaments about a lair. Assumes at first they're shells, conch he thinks, or the eggs of dinosaur birds. Miniature planets, maybe, or a galaxy of albumen dwarf moons. So shinnies up a trunk to catch a closer look, only to find himself e to face with their unfleshed faces of bone, and each one his nd formless, his sun-whitened rame alone. And now the wind somehow inside his head, the sound of the sea in a shell, and each mask as it melts to his mien, each feature unfastened and falling, a wish down a bottomless well.

And then time's become taffy, Dalí's pocketwatch, adagio of anti-speed, oncoming walkers waltzing waist-deep in water, closer yet slower, closing but   slowwwwwing. *Peckinpah Indians!* Until stormed, swarmed, overmastered, overborne, eating the face from the earth. These swallows of loam, lungfuls of cloam, every bone in his body riprap, threshing each one in their sockets to scoria. So inhales bathybius, blinks back the malm, and . . .

watches

watches

watches them straddle his back like a workbench to lift the scalp like a lid from his head, his heart/beating/humus.

This sOUnd

of a hOle

being kERfed

in the tOp of his head

like a second mOUth

permanently a-yAAAAAAWn.

The rip of his rictus, shrieking.

And wakes up. Sprockets and pins, pivots and gears shifting inside his head—*clik/clik-clik/clik/clikit*—like tumblers scrolling a lock. And a shadow laid across his mind like a hand, the shade of a redhand enmeshed in its wheels and levers as if to halt the metronomic whirring of time.

Like depressing the brake on the stomach of a clock, a clock hourly rigged to implode.

Hauls himself up and dressed, shuttles lightheaded ·
telegraph office—barely shambling now, shuffling, bent and c
dering soon to be doubled over, each step another continent
wires Kate: *Darling. Please do. Come. Come now. Fly, Kate, fly.*
Fly like Mercury.

Man is a museum of diseases, a home of impurities;
he comes today and is gone tomorrow;
he begins as dirt
and departs as stench

—MARK TWAIN

By the time she got there, there wasn't much left: a skull with some face strung across it, this stranger's face now; a torch of hair whiter than the birch off some bark; a pair of eyes pinned to the floor of their sockets like suns; and at parade rest beneath the blankets a body so spindled in each of its extremities, it appeared—having breached its own breastwork—about to turn itself inside out sternum by stem. He looked, she thought to herself, just so damn . . . papery, like the wild'd gone spang out of his winds. He looked blasted. Mottled, cratered, abscessed and ulcerated, his torso was scaped, florid with fibroid and furuncle, chancre and carbuncle, bubo, botch, blain and gurry, papule and pustule, crepature, impostume, verruca and crewels. She dug weeping for the word, found it: lunate, lunoid, *lunar*.

What she had coveted above all and all along was little more than to get closer to him before it was too late. Which it was now, too late, for he was going under, slipping away, his mind fetched off to parts far-flung, its thoughts havocked to a faraway place— pillar, say, or post—and unless she was mistaken, they were unlikely to hitch their way home.

Instead, as he died—no timely thing, for his heart had a mind of its own; straitened as he was, he died much as he had lived, according to the lights of his leisure; it took months—she learned things it would better have pleased her not to. And if most of what she learned was the dross let of fever and hallucination, the gamboling of hobgoblins and ghosts, gremlins and ghouls, all the

imps and daemons that fin free when a man is fugued and p⌐
tomed with pain, well, that was of scant solace.

But he would not be silent.

And so sitting here, nurse, hovered beside him as he lay helpless and betrodden shaking himself loose inside this stupid
room—adjusting the bedsheets to suit him, plumping his pillows,
palping a procession of cold compresses to his forehead, shifting
his bones against the chafe and the bedsores—what he let slip
shocked her. Unnatural couplings with unavailable women, base
betrayals of unwitting men, expressions of a paternal hatred so
heartfelt it reduced her almost to weeping, ramblings in French
and Latin to which she could attribute little sense but that were
uttered with a ferocity so fervent she could reconcile not a one as
his own, scandalous secrets regarding the Tombstone days, indis-
cretions about Wyatt she resolved even then never to disclose
(nor ever did). The words spilled forth in flows.

And some of them were about her, those that had remained
abeyant behind dikes and levees, catchbasins and breakwaters,
dammed up, retained, held back all these years. And these were
not shocking at all, but surprisingly tender and affectionate, even
generous: the way she brushed her hair upon coming to bed exactly 99 times—67 with her left hand, 32 with her right; or how
she appeared in the morning light without her face on as she sat
before the mirror; or had fearlessly flirted behind his back with
some handsome bravo at the bar; or how a certain smile on a special occasion had seen him through 'til dawn; or the curve of the
lift of her bottom propped by the tilt of the height off her heels,
the unfairness of her body, the hundred times he would think so
each day.

It occurred to her that he was emptying himself of his past,
disposing piecemeal of those parcels he no longer could reconcile

had use for, lightening the load before it could crush him—images, moments, impulses, disconnected facets, figments leading nowhere but to their expurgation, as if a clarity or conformation might emerge from their divestiture that would enable him more surehandedly to face the labor at hand—the impossible necessity of keeping body and soul together a while longer.

Remnants, that's what remained now, vestige. She could see it plain enough: that this was the contest at hand, that it was more dire than murder, the contest of his lifetime, and that increasingly lost, he was losing it.

Doggerel and royal flushes and star-talk, brands of rye and gunnery, cat murder and long afternoons of fellatio, lingering grudges couched in the incommunicable rhythms of duels material and figurative. She felt she was being granted entré to an un-lighted sideshow fractured internally at oblique angles to itself, conducted on an unbearably intimate tour of a refracted nether region that left her almost as appalled as it did aggrieved, for it was too parlous, too private, finally too freakish, and could only end wretchedly. And about that she could do nothing, as it must avail himself much the same, because all that was little but life, just life, and this was death, his death, something momentous and vast, and so vastly more immense.

He had become half ghost, and that half dazed in daylight; a bereft self, or one so thinly drawn and insensible upon its bed of pain that it amounted to much the same thing. Reduced to his own self-canceled ticket, he was on a ride to nowhere, save precisely where he found himself—here, now, living the first act of his past.

She could not do for him any more, *could* not. She could do the little she could. She could sit here. She could sit and watch and listen and wait, wonder and worry and pray. She could take his pulse and count the hours and tally the number of breaths he took in the vilesome space of a day. She could hold his hand, whisper endearments and settle his nightmares when they sought to assail him. She could talk to him with her tears and stroke him with her tongue and take his words for what they were, a language of smoke, of shadow and secret, ribs of thought no meatier than the broast of brain from which they issued. She could buck up, not cry, and be brave.

But mainly this, this most of all, she could wait.

———•—•—•———

> When I wake
> I am breathing out of all proportion to myself.
> My whole body is a lung; I am floating
> —STANLEY PLUMLY

as flesh made whitened wind
come stillborn up for air
my soul in transmigration
yet no arrival there

ιere so Rocky-high
re alone than on an atoll
ights became as strappado to bastinado,
something to egg the mind surreally towards its final wrest,
a diminution not (wholly) dissimilar to those febrile occasions
when with a pulmonary flair
foaled of some pneumatic dare
he would (with brio) abate his breath
then plunge through pleura right and left
and pluck them out and
muck them up,
wrenched up and out like reeking weeds
on-reeled through ribs
their rot at root
both blasted as infested fruit, then
fling the fungal, air-lorn pair:

>   bronchus, bronchiole, alveolus,
>   lobule, milium, surfactant

come clean unhasped
piecemeal by emplundered piece—

>   airborne, disjasked, anonymous

unlunged
at last

Lathered awake in the dark he hears screams. But no, are none, save those that entangle him.

DOC: Still intact. I am, aren't I? Still intact.

Silence stacked inside silence, ensorcelled there, shroud.

KATE: What's wrong, Doc? What is it? Go on back to sleep. It's late. Already too late.

He is houghing up blood in ropes now. It rashes the pillows come morning. Snarls on his face, in his hair; he warps them away with the rye.

And so life unsutures, unsutures and sleaves, looses its stitches lung by lung unstrapping each strand of membrane, shred. Each ravel of ragged breath. Chews itself, clewing, shed.

DOC: But it hurts. Hurts like hell. The very devil. It hurts too much to breathe.

KATE: Well, course it does.

DOC: Ah, well, sorry, darlin'. You are right. Of course it does. Cannot imagine what I could have been thinking. But say, do tell, Kate, were I to weep for us now, would you wear my tears like diamonds? Medals and medallions? Would you braid them like bijoux? Their Braille? Katie, say it, would you lace them like lamps at your breast? To light my way? When I pass weightless as wind through that vale?

KATE: There there, Doc. It's OK. OK to scream. Go ahead and scream now, go ahead, when there's nothing left, no relief or remedy, no recourse but to scream against these throes. Go ahead. Just *mustn't let them hear you.*

One last tug then, a nightcap to unrattle, quiet down, try for sleep again. To scream perhaps. To scream. Or lie awake to pound your palms with stone until they bleed raw in your pampered, immaculate hands.

Listening nightly to the wet rustle of his lungs, their language, each deathcough his notion of the last bristling moment, *now,*

...ing his way out of hell only to work his way back in. Over
...d over again.

And wherever he looked
there was an absence of light
that he knew would not fit
in his fists;
he could not catch
half
of what he had cast or
crush what he could not contain.

It is coming. It is come. At last. The end of the world. *Ahead
of time.*

Last night I dreamed him alive buggered with lighted ta[.] slathered with sweet balms, anointing oils, lards, paraffins, tu[.] pentines, acetones, shellacs, lacquers, conductor gels, silicones, polyurethanes, dimethyls, liquid Lucites, a dozen aerosol acceler- ants, unctioned in extremis, doused with kerosenes and cooking oils, spermaceti, creosotes, greases, soaked with gasolines, butyl, butane, propane, JP4 & 5, black powder, white phosphor, dechlo- rided sodium, petrol bomb and Molotov, nitro and ampho, with napalm, strung dangling to dervish the highbough of a mesquite acetylened to human twisting torch maddened marionette bonfire varnished unfigured with flame, *fire puppet,* cut down extin- guished left to maunder the desert hairless skinless sexless now, charred brochette face burnt off, crisp mush melt crust roulade, smelted to the briquette hardness of black eschar shrunk carbon effigy the rest of his days. As if a page had been purged, say, voided of its Void upon the pyromantic pyre on whose thermals the body ascends. For as immolation consumes the corpus, so is the spirit cleansed, and what it leaves behind is immortality— those ashes in which legend incends.

When I awoke my long-nine still was smoldering in the sheets beside me, having failed to ignite their fabric, so sodden with the sweat flopped off my fever.

Flouting fate every inch of the way.

So decided, aw what the hell, why not go ahead—just last, an- other day. All day:

the drift of the light from her eyes
the lift of the scent from her skin
her hair
the lilt of its sift as it travels my cheek
I try but I cannot remember
I look upon the face in this photograph
study its features

tilt it this way and that
seek the apropos angle
some key to the code
the more that I try, the more that I fail
I cannot even conjure a sense of her absence
the heat of her blood on my flesh
the warmth seeped through of the press of her
my rising heart, its sunken sun
and sometimes I think I almost miss her, think I must at last
utter the words it occurs to me hourly to utter:
Help me, help me please, won't you?
Please?
Mother?

Nothing I think or leave unthought, say or leave unsaid, do or leave undone, nothing I write or leave unwritten, there is nothing I can make happen now to help you. My words cannot keep you alive, breathe you over this rift, billow your lungs with lanternlight, lend voice to the looming abyss. Down all the drafts of time, no sentence can stir such winds.

Your text, its tale, your story is emptiness.

No next time when the lungs stop,
like that last sentence on the tongue,
hangs in the air after the lungs have pressed
their last square inch of it out

—bp NICHOL

The final 57 days he was out of bed twice—once to pee, couldn't, once to shit, likewise.

The last two weeks he was delirious; nothing but fevertalk. Save the last 24 hours—silence.

When on Tuesday, November 8th, slightly after 10 a.m., he opened his eyes and asked for rye. And after Kate had fetched it for him, tilting the glass to his lips, he felt with his eyes around the room, each angle, down its length to the foot end of his bed, appeared to roll them deflexively and remark, half-grin acock through the grimace: Well I'll be goddamned. This is funny.

Which, to him, is doubtless exactly what it was. His own life had played him for the mark, as his death beat the longest of un-beatable odds. He had died—damn!—with his boots off. In bed.

And then his eyes looked at me, looked at my eyes and into them, into and through them—I swear I felt them on the back of my skull—and I could see them ebb and wane, drain off, flow out, stop seeing, just . . . turn off. That they were too tired now, too tired to see, tired of everything, tired of life, this life, his, how his lungs were too tired to recall how to breathe, all of it fallen away, no rage, no more kicking against the dying of his days, the way he'd been bleeding out for centuries, bleeding like the last snow shrugged off a March sky, and so, poor Doc, cut loose, uncoiled, uncorded, no more. He had expended his earthly measure, as that measure exhausted him. Space shattered, time spent, out of chips

.d cards, he'd dealt himself lost, the first time in his life, this
.oser with no hand but its past.

And so I reached over, the palm of my hands at his lids, and
one after the other I closed them, then kissed and sealed them
shut, still warm, thinking that unless I kissed them, couldn't no
ways in creation stay put. *Could* not.

Later I thought why I thought that, 'bout them kisses, why I
done it, such a thing as that, but like they say, ain't no reckoning
some things. Rational accounting. Thing like that. Of the moment. Moment like that. But like I say, that's what I done, and
damned if I know why to this day. But this I do, this I do know—
glad I done it, just the same.

Later, leaving what little was left of him to the ministrations of
the undertaker, she managed to find the stairwell still sleepwalk-
ing, dazed her way down to the hotel saloon—it was, it suddenly
occurred to her, the day after her 37th birthday—bought herself
several shots of rye and a brace of absinthes, set 'em up in echelons atop the bar, and having watched herself as if in a dream
pound them back one after the other too numb to taste a thing,
raised the last glass reciting to no one in particular—

I drink, my love, to your profound disease;
Its was the better suit.

I could not have provided you this ease,
Nor this peace, absolute.

John Henry Holliday, 35 or 36, an unfailingly generous tr̶ per, 11.8.87, 10:03 a.m., of consumptive misadventure.

A sport and a gentleman, lately a raving if penniless Methodist; not a decayed tooth in his head. Homeless the bulk of his life, yet he cut a dashing, buccaneerish, anything-but-buffoonish figure.

Died in bed, mangled. Died chewed up, chawed on, drubbed and sore dragooned, both lungs run to whey. Trounced and trammeled out, all traveled out, at last.

Departed this world a pauper save for the clothes on his back and the guns to their rig; with the latter it was once said he blazed slicker than silver, if faster than the lightning in limelight.

"The decedent, an only child, was himself childless. Possessed of no harem of lovers nor kingdom of common tribes, we are told he is survived by a cousin, a Sister Mary Melanie of the Sisters of Mercy, in his home state of Georgia, and by his longtime sometime companion, the woman, Kate Elder, who saw him safely 'o'er the other side.' "

> *and at my grave*
> *when I lay dead*
> *that earthen cave*
> *my earthly bed*
> *tell my mourners*
> *come the day*
> *to drape themselves*
> *in white brocade*

And the headline in the afternoon paper: "LAST CALL: Death takes a Holliday." Laughs, to the last.

CREDITS, NOTES, ACKNOWLEDGMENTS

The poet John Berryman once wrote: "Originality [consists] less in the invention of materials, than the subsuming of materials into a . . . fresh unity. The [writer] invents some of his materials, and others he takes where he finds them. What he gives them is order, rhythm, significance, and he does this by means of style and the inscrutable operation of personality."

Here Berryman coincidentally describes, far better than I ever could, much of the aesthetic within which *Bucking the Tiger* was contoured and composed. It is, to be sure, a sort of scavenger/smuggler approach—this theft of bones—but then all writers, that they might ultimately give back, are users first—pillagers, plunderers, freebooters, graverobbers—and last. The author as magpie, and cobbler.

In the end, the object is always the same—to reconnoiter the poetry that lies at the heart of any history, to make the marrow sing.

The section beginning on page 12, with a tip of the hat to the concrete poet, bp Nichol.

The lyric on page 37 is from the Bo Diddley (Ellis McDaniel) song "Who Do You Love."

The line on page 55 is Thomas Nashe's.

The last sentence on page 66 contains two lines, combined and much altered, from Michael Ondaatje's *Coming Through Slaughter.*

The phrase in italics at the bottom of page 80 is John Fowles's, from *The Magus.*

The line in italics on page 108 is from George Ivan Morrison's song "Hard Nose the Highway."

The line in italics on page 129 is from Jorie Graham's poem "The Phase After History." I have altered its punctuation and typography.

The section "DOC AND BILLY: A True Story" arose from my research into both Holliday and Bonney arcana as it suggested its enjambment upon my reading of certain portions of Mr. Ondaatje's *The Collected Works of Billy the Kid,* bp Nichol's *The True Eventual Story of Billy the Kid* and N. Scott Momaday's *The Ancient Child.*

The poem on page 208–9 uses as its model that of a small portion of Louis Zukofsky's "Songs of Degrees."

The second full paragraph on page 259 is an adulteration and reconstitution of those lines from the W. H. Auden poem "Witnesses."

The line in italics on page 265 is Stephane Mallarmé's.

The lines in italics on page 335 are from "The Long Weekend of Louis Riel," by bp Nichol.

The line in boldface italics on page 350 is from Mallarmé's poem of the same name.

The verse on page 364 is N. Scott Momaday's, from his poem "Concession."

The character Zack Clamm was inspired—shirttail/third-cousin-like—by that of Jack Crabb as he first appeared in Thomas Berger's *Little Big Man,* and in his *The Return of Little Big Man.*

Of citable benefit to the author in the composition of this work were *Doc Holliday: A Family Portrait,* by Karen Holliday Tanner; *In Search of the Hollidays,* by Albert S. Pendleton, Jr., and Susan McKey Thomas; and *The Illustrated Life and Times Doc Holliday*, by Bob Boze Bell. While often at odds, each intimated certain orbits and glidepaths around material that over 150 years had grown distinctly nonflightworthy. To pursue Doc is to pilot largely in the dark; my thanks to these authors for the starlight.

And yet the real mystery persists: how one person arrives at another, stranger at stranger, the living at the dead. It needn't be much. A phrase in a court transcript: "One Holliday, commonly known as Doc." The name alone may suffice, the way it figures to the eye or scans on the ear. Perhaps the release of some long-locked-up image of childhood, the key in a fragment of dream. Something chance in the coupling trips in the brain, the register of a vibration, a click of recognition, the chemistry of an attraction, a whisper of resonance or invisible beckoning, this moment of silver that brings you up short, spark on a summoning wind.

The spark tantalizes, provokes; out of reach, it arrests. The wind calls. You must follow.

It is the sense of an opening, that there may be an entré here, a beginning to be made or foothold granted, some connection to be completed, its circuit circled, a compass squared. You are playing a hunch: that what you are willing to invest may coax a return in kind. This mutual visitation. And so, though nothing is promised—for nothing, ever, is promised—the pursuit begins, the quarrying. His excavation. To take years.

Luckily, it doesn't happen often. There is a cost to descending the decline of what one has the temerity to exhume. Because it always is personal, and over time becomes only more personal. And mysterious. This commingling of one's life with another's. The assumption of the mask until its fit feels so right you forget you are wearing it, until it conflates as one with your own. While nderneath you grow older, ever older, contemplating the bones of the dead. Trying to make them glisten. To burnish his bones.

This doubtless is no way for one person to behave towards another, but there is no other way. This is the only way. The seeking. Step by step, wayless, through the mirror.

Thanks to: Sarah Chalfant, heroine; Gentleman John Glusman; Nance Davidson; and to my mother and father, who provided for the genesis and completion of this work in more ways than they know.

And to Paul Metcalf, whose selfless advice, unfaltering faith and steadying hand were sources of such sustenance in the midst of so much devastation; that you might, my friend, have approved.